ONLY YOU

"Francis Ray's graceful writing style and realistically complex characters give her latest contemporary romance its extraordinary emotional richness and depth."

—*Chicago Tribune*

"It's a joy to read this always fresh and exciting saga."

—*Romantic Times BOOKreviews* (4 Stars)

"The powerful descriptive powers of Francis Ray allow the reader to step into the story and become an active part of the surrender . . . If you love a great love story, *Only You* should be on your list." —*Fallen Angel Reviews*

"Riveting emotion and charismatic scenes that make this book captivating . . . a beautiful story of love and romance." —*Night Owl Romance*

"A beautiful love story as only Francis Ray can tell it."

—*Singletitles.com*

"Readers will find a warm and wonderful contemporary romance with plenty of humor and drama. Adding a fun warmth and reality to these characters and a plot that moves quickly add all the needed incentive to read this fun book." —*Multicultural Romance Writers*

MORE...

IRRESISTIBLE YOU

"A pleasurable story . . . a well-developed story and continuous plot." —*Romantic Times BOOKreviews*

"Like the previous titles in this series, *Irresistible You* is another winner . . . Witty and charming . . . Author Francis Ray has a true gift for drawing the readers in and never letting them go." —*Multicultural Romance Writers*

YOU AND NO OTHER

"The warmth and sincerity of the Graysons bring another book to life . . . delightfully realistic." —*Romantic Times*

"Astonishing sequel . . . the best romance of the new year . . . the Graysons are sure to leave a smile on your face and a longing in your heart for their next story."
—*ARomanceReview.com*

"There are three more [Grayson] children with great love stories in the future." —*Booklist*

SOMEONE TO LOVE ME

"Another great romance novel." —*Booklist*

"The plot moves quickly, and the characters are interesting." —*Romantic Times*

"The characters give as good as they get, and their romance is very believable." —*All About Romance*

UNTIL THERE WAS
YOU

FRANCIS RAY

St. Martin's Paperbacks

UNTIL THERE WAS YOU

Copyright © 1999 by Francis Ray.
"Christmas and You" copyright © 2008 by Francis Ray.
Excerpt from *Nobody But You* copyright © 2008 by Francis Ray.

Cover photograph © Shirley Green.

All rights reserved.

For information address St. Martin's Press, 175 Fifth Avenue, New York, NY 10010.

ISBN: 0-312-94418-7
EAN: 978-0-312-94418-6

Printed in the United States of America

BET Books edition / August 1999
St. Martin's Paperbacks edition / November 2008

St. Martin's Paperbacks are published by St. Martin's Press, 175 Fifth Avenue, New York, NY 10010.

10 9 8 7 6 5 4 3 2

With love to my family.

THE GRAYSONS OF NEW MEXICO—THE FALCONS OF TEXAS

Cousins by marriage—friends by choice
Bold men and women who risk it all for love

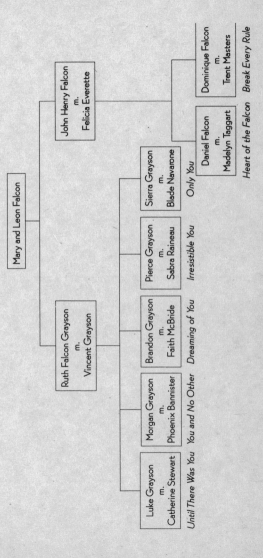

PROLOGUE

THE WEDDING OF TRENT MASTERS AND DOMINIQUE Falcon was without a doubt *the* most spectacular event of the Dallas social season. Their reception at the luxurious Mansion on Turtle Creek in the Pavilion Suite was to be the crowning event of the joyously happy occasion. No expense was spared, no detail was too small to ensure that the bride and groom and two hundred and fifty of their closest relatives and friends went home jubilant and immensely happy.

For four guests they had failed miserably.

In a private alcove of the beautifully decorated room replete with lush pink roses, breathtaking swan ice sculptures, a scrumptious buffet, and an endless supply of Krug Clos du Mesnil champagne, these stern-faced four stood apart and stared in stunned disbelief at the smiling groom twirling his bride around the polished oak floor.

"The resemblance is uncanny."

"The first time I saw him I almost dropped my teeth."

"Same here."

"But I can't believe he'd keep a secret like this."

"Me either."

"I think we all agree on that."

"Then there is only one answer. He didn't know."

The four stared at each other as the certainty grew. One

nodded. "If what we're thinking is right. But we could be all wrong."

"What if we're not?"

The answer wasn't long in coming. "We have to find out for sure. I don't think any of us could sleep at night knowing the possibility was there and we did nothing about it."

"I guess that settles it then. We contact the one person who can find the answers for us discreetly."

"It could take a long time."

"Then the quicker we get started the quicker we can know for sure."

"If we're right, this could create a lot of problems for everyone."

"I know," came the worried voice. "And may God help us all."

SEVERAL FEET AWAY, LUKE GRAYSON WATCHED THE small group of people hurriedly leave the ballroom. Something was up. He'd noticed them first because their expressions had been so serious when everyone else in the room had been happy celebrating the wedding of Dominique and Trent. Luke's scowl deepened as another thought struck. Offer free drinks and food and people would celebrate anything.

"Smile, it's not your wedding."

Luke flickered an annoyed glance around at the smiling face of his younger brother Brandon. "Very funny."

The grin on Brandon's handsome face widened. "I thought so."

Since Brandon was perpetually happy, Luke ignored the comment and nodded toward the alcove. "Did you happen to see the four people standing over there deep in conversation a moment ago?"

Brandon's sharp black gaze swept the empty area before refocusing on Luke. "Work or pleasure?"

"Neither. I just wondered who they were."

"Relatives or in-laws most likely," Brandon lamented with a sigh that lifted his broad shoulders and had several watchful women in the room heaving their own sighs.

Luke's dark brows bunched. "Why do you say that?"

Dimples winked in Brandon's golden bronzed face. "You're not going to like the answer."

"And you can't wait to tell me?" Certainty rang in Luke's deep voice.

Brandon's answering laughter was rich with enjoyment. "The last three women I've approached have told me they're related before I could get my name out." Black eyes twinkled. "They apparently had made inquiries."

"I wonder if Mama knows the real reason you opened The Red Cactus?" Luke asked.

Brandon's eyes twinkled with devilish merriment. "I hope not."

Luke slowly shook his dark head, causing his shoulder-length black hair to move sensuously across his broad shoulders. Without a hint of malice he said, "One day that pretty face of yours is going to get you in trouble."

Brandon gleefully slapped Luke on the back. "If it does and I can't handle it, I'll just shout for my big brother."

Both men laughed at the idiocy of such an idea. They wouldn't hesitate to come help the other out, but there wasn't much the wildly independent and self-assured Graysons couldn't handle on their own.

"Glad to see you finally decided to enjoy yourself."

Still smiling, Luke watched his other brother, Morgan, eighteen months younger, join them. The two of them had lovingly grown up taking great pride in alternately trying to best or irritate the other. Depending on whatever felt right at the time. He doubted it would change. Morgan definitely had bested him tonight.

Unlike his rented black tux, Morgan's white tuxedo was hand-tailored and fit perfectly. He wore the suit with his usual casual elegance and panache. "You actually enjoy dressing like a penguin, don't you?"

"Some of us enjoy the finer things in life," Morgan said, swirling the fluted glass of sparkling cider between his long, elegant fingers.

"Don't forget the softer things," Brandon said, his words ending in a chuckle.

Morgan snorted. "As if you'd let us."

"It's not me you have to worry about forgetting. It's Mama."

Luke tensed. "What are you talking about, Brandon?"

His younger brother took his time, smiling to a trio of women who had passed them for the second time in as many minutes, then brought his attention back to his almost snarling brothers. "I overheard Mama telling Aunt Felicia that by this time next year, she'd have one of her children married and her own grandchild on the way."

Luke clenched his teeth to hold back an expletive. It was worse than he thought. He loved his mother, they all did, but she was as stubborn as they came when she went after what she thought was best for her children.

It wouldn't matter to her that none of the five in the Grayson brood, as he and his brothers and sister had been referred to growing up in Santa Fe, were remotely interested in getting married. Or that they weren't even in steady relationships. Those necessary preludes to marriage wouldn't deter their mother, who'd walk through slivers of glass with a smile on her face if she thought marriage would benefit them in some way. "I think we're in trouble," he finally said.

"You can say that again." Morgan's furrowed brow gave his strong, intelligent face a brooding look women adored and wished without exception that they might be the one to make him smile.

Luke's troubled gaze went to Morgan's. Then, in the way they sometimes silently communicated, they smiled.

Brandon recognized the look and sobered. "Oh, no you don't. You two are up to something and it had better not involve me getting measured for another one of these things," he said, frowning down at his black tuxedo.

"Calm down," Luke said. "A restaurant owner's schedule is too irregular for a wife. Not to mention this is your first year, and although The Red Cactus is doing well, you never know in today's economy."

"Besides, we can't have the poor woman worried about all the women you work with and the bills," Morgan continued, his gaze going to the tall, slender man easily moving toward them through the crowd of people. "Now, an investment banker is a different matter altogether."

Brandon grinned. As long as he wasn't the one they were plotting against, he wasn't going to bring up the fact that Luke owned Manhunters, Inc., a lucrative private investigative firm or that Morgan had a thriving private law practice.

Pierce Grayson, the youngest and fourth brother, stopped and folded his arms over his chest. He was also the shortest at six foot three, which had irritated him to no end growing up. "If either of you think I'm going to sacrifice myself on the altar of marriage to save you, I suggest you think again. I've just begun to live."

"You'd live better with a wife," Luke said, still holding on to his plan. Next to Morgan, Pierce had that suave elegance women went for. "You wouldn't want to disappoint Mama, would you?"

Pierce's arms came to his sides. "You always reminded us that you were the oldest and to follow your lead, and if you didn't do it, we shouldn't. When you walk down the aisle, I'll give the matter the consideration I think it deserves."

Three pairs of eyes centered on Luke's unhappy expression. "Bankers are just as sneaky and slippery as lawyers."

Morgan and Pierce slapped their hands together in a high five.

Ignoring the woman trying to get his attention, Luke rubbed his chin with blunt-tipped fingers, which, unlike Morgan's and Pierce's, were calloused and without a manicure. "Looks like there's only one answer."

The brothers exchanged looks for all of five seconds and then said, "Run." As if in formation, they made a smart turn in unison and started toward the entrance. Less than six feet away they stopped abruptly.

Arms folded, her right foot tapping on the polished hardwood floor, Sierra Grayson shook her head at her older brothers. She had learned early that being female and considered the runt in a house full of six-foot-plus brothers had more advantages than disadvantages. She'd been handling men all her life and considered herself somewhat of a minor expert on the matter. "You weren't thinking of leaving before the bride and groom, were you?" she asked sweetly.

Luke wasn't fooled. Sierra might be small in size, reaching only to the middle of his chest, but that had nothing to do with her considerable brain power. People who thought differently lived to regret their mistake. "We thought we might go outside for some fresh air."

Sierra glanced beyond them to the wide expanse of open French doors on the other side of the room leading to the garden terrace where candlelit white-linen-draped tables, eager wait staff, and champagne had been set up for just such a purpose. "Coming from one of the best trackers in the southwest, I find your poor sense of direction rather difficult to believe."

The glint in the mirror image of her black eyes gave her away. "You know," Luke said.

The corners of her mouth lifted. "I think you'll make a handsome groom."

Luke's mouth tightened into a thin line. "I'm not getting married."

"Me either," grumbled his brothers.

Sierra laughed. "You should see the horrified expressions on your faces. You'd think Mama planned to tie you up and hurl you down a mine shaft."

"You wouldn't be so happy if you thought Mama was planning your wedding," Luke said and watched the truth of his words take the amusement from her exquisite, heart-shaped face.

"Watch it, big brother." Sierra punctuated each word with a pink manicured nail the exact color of her tea-length maid-of-honor gown and matching pumps. "After living with the four of you, then in a college dormitory instead of the apartment by myself I wanted, I'm not giving up my own place and freedom to cook and clean for some dolt who can't remember to put the seat down on the toilet or pick up his own clothes."

"If I remember correctly, you were the one always leaving your things all over the house," Morgan told her.

Sierra made a face, her temper cooling as fast as it had blown. "You only noticed because you're such a neat nut."

"I guess each of us has our own reasons for not wanting to fall in with Mama's scheme." Luke watched each of his siblings nod, then continued, "Then all we have to do is stick together and keep our heads. We don't want to end up like Daniel and Dominique."

"I don't want to get married, but I've never seen either of them this happy before," Brandon pointed out. "Daniel is so proud of Little Daniel. He acts like he's the first baby ever born."

"Little Daniel is the firstborn of any of the cousins," Sierra reminded him, her expression softening. "But you have to admit he's beautiful and smiling already. With all that curly black hair he looks like a precious little doll."

Morgan nodded his agreement. "And well-behaved. Didn't make a peep during the wedding ceremony."

"Daniel said he sleeps all through the night," Pierce added.

"He's got Falcon blood in him, what do you expect?" Luke said, a mixture of exasperation and pride in his voice. "But which of you is ready to become a parent?"

Stunned horror on their faces was his answer. "We're all happy for Daniel and Dominique if that's what they want, but our lives are headed down a different path. Each of us has to help the other out and watch each other's back because if one of us slips and falls, we all go down. Mama wouldn't be satisfied until all of us were married."

Sierra shuddered.

Brandon tugged the collar of his shirt.

Pierce swallowed.

Morgan gulped his sparkling cider.

Luke nodded emphatically, then held out his hand palm down. A succession of golden bronzed hands followed until they were stacked one atop the other. "One for all and all for one."

"One for all and all for one," they repeated as they had since the first time in a sacred ceremony under a full moon when they had stood and asked God and the Master of Breath to honor their request to keep them together always without the blood sacrifice.

Eight-year-old Luke hadn't thought he'd mind cutting his finger, but the others were too young to be given the task. He hadn't known until months later when his maternal grandfather praised him for his wisdom, then upbraided him for his stupidity, and said that cutting your finger and joining the bloody cut with another was something the people of Hollywood, not Native Americans, had conceived.

At the time, it had felt good to embrace the god of their Muskogee mother and African-American father under the full moon in unity. It felt good now. Grinning at each other, they released hands.

ACROSS THE LAVISHLY DECORATED ROOM, RUTH Grayson smiled. She knew her children well. Bless their stubborn hearts. Made another pact to stand together, had they? She'd see about that. She wanted grandchildren. More, she wanted them all happily wed. It wasn't jealousy of her brother John Henry's children, Daniel and Dominique, that had set her on this path, but love.

Since they were dragging their feet, it was up to her. It seemed a mother's job was never done.

"I think they're on to you," Felicia Falcon said, looking stunning as the mother of the bride in a Dior blush rose satin suit and crown hat. "I shudder to think of what might have happened if Dominique and Daniel had been around each other while he was falling in love."

"Don't worry," Ruth advised her sister-in-law, her confidence undiminished. "The day I can't unthink my children hasn't dawned."

Felicia smiled with remembered pleasure. "You're right, of course. Daniel actually thought he could keep me from finding out what was going on between him and Madelyn."

The women shared a laugh only mothers could understand and appreciate.

"Felicia, I believe they've finally slowed the music down enough for the old folks to dance," John Henry Falcon joked as he joined his wife and sister. The five-piece string band was doing a stirring rendition of Tina Turner's

"Break Every Rule." "Want to try and keep your feet out from under mine?"

Felicia looked out from beneath her lush lashes provocatively. "If you hold me close and move extremely slow, that shouldn't be a problem."

"I think I can handle that." Taking her arm he led her to the dance floor, then he sent her into an intricate spin, caught her, then dipped her backward. "How's that?"

Dancers stopped and applauded. Felicia couldn't stop the laughter that bubbled from her. How she loved this man. "Show-off."

Pulling Felicia into his arms, John Henry whispered in her ear, "You haven't seen anything yet. Just wait until I get you alone in our suite."

Felicia's body quivered in delicious anticipation. She pressed closer to her husband's strong body. Happiness and contentment flowed through her. Life was extraordinarily good.

They always did look good together, Ruth thought, and didn't they have a marvelous reason to be happy and pleased with themselves tonight. Come this time next year, she would also.

Her loving but determined gaze searched the room for her children and she saw them leave through the terrace doors. Luke led the way. As the eldest, he had always taken care of the younger children and set a good example for them to follow. It was fitting that in this he would take the lead as well.

Luke would be the first.

CHAPTER ONE

LUKE GRAYSON WAS RUNNING AWAY.

The thought brought a grimace to his handsome features as he tossed his worn duffel bag into the passenger seat of his oversize Dodge Ram truck. He'd never run away from anything in his life, and the idea that he had to now didn't go down easy. But what else could he do? he asked himself as he backed out of his driveway in the quiet residential area outside of Santa Fe. He'd pit his skills of survival against anyone or anything. Heck, he had before and won.

But this new opponent was tougher, craftier than anyone he had ever come up against. Every move he made was countered and matched. It made things worse, not better, that this newest adversary was his mother.

Ruth Grayson was proving to be sneakier than Luke thought. You'd think after thirty-four years a man would know his own mother. Heck, you'd think she'd know him. But no, she wasn't taking no for an answer. She wanted him married, and married was what he was going to be.

Every time he looked up, there was a woman in his face. It hadn't meant squat to his mother that Santa Fe had only a small population of men and women of color and even less of Muskogee Creek. She had gained the aid of her relatives and friends in her wide academic and civic circle, and suddenly women were coming from all over the country to visit. Of course, she had volunteered him to show them around.

Only his love and respect for her kept him silent. But that was exactly what his crafty mother had counted on. She knew none of her children would disrespect her. But enough was enough. He'd just come back from taking Shirley Hinton, number twenty-seven, to the Albuquerque International Airport. She was pleasant enough, but she had the most annoying habit of giggling. Unfortunately she tended to giggle over the smallest things. Her fifth-grade students in Oklahoma probably enjoyed her jubilance, but after two days it began to grate on his nerves. Knowing his mother, she had already lined up number twenty-eight.

His mother's family, the Falcons, were known for their stubbornness. To some it was called bullheaded. The results were the same. Once they started on something, they saw it through to the end. No excuses. No time-outs. For centuries that singlemindedness had helped his Native American ancestors overcome obstacles that would have overwhelmed a lesser people.

Now his mother had singled him out, and he was in trouble.

Luke didn't breathe easier until the lights of Santa Fe were reflected in his rearview mirror, then winked out completely. Safe. Leaning back against the smooth leather seat, he almost relaxed. In less than fifteen minutes he'd be at his cabin. Alone. The thought eased his grip on the steering wheel.

Since it was Friday and nearing midnight, he could look forward to two whole days of just being by himself. He wouldn't have to worry about who might call or drop by unexpectedly as he had for the months since Dominique and Trent's wedding. Shaking his dark head, he slowed to turn onto the two-lane blacktop. As soon as the

Dodge Ram straightened, he increased his speed, his need for the peacefulness of the cabin growing.

The narrow road twisted like a mad serpent as it climbed higher into the Sangre de Cristo Mountains. Inky blackness surrounded him. The only illumination was his headlights that sliced though the night. Previous trips let Luke know that only a few feet from his wheels was a sheer drop of a hundred feet, and that drop increased with each rotation of his wheels. The road was not one you traveled at night unless you knew it. Those who had tried and failed weren't given second chances.

Five and a half miles after leaving the main road, Luke turned into a paved driveway. The truck bounced over gravel and came to a halt in front of a six-foot-high steel gate. Fishing the key out of the glove compartment, he quickly opened the gate, drove through, then swung it shut without bothering to lock it. The lock was to keep people out. He couldn't see the log cabin through the trees, but the calming of his soul told him it was there.

Waiting.

Aided by the glowing full moon, his keen eyesight picked out the towering peaked roof of the log cabin above the pine and spruce trees less than a minute later. Proud and sturdy, the log structure, properly cared for, would stand for generations to come. He and Daniel had made sure of that. Neither of them saw the sense of building something that would last only their lifetime. True seers thought not just of themselves, but of the future.

He had taken great pride in helping design the contemporary western theme of the house with its exposed log posts, expansive walls of glass, and unusual radiant-rock floor that heated in the winter, but in the summer allowed the heat to dissipate into a cool mass. He never forgot to give thanks to the Master of Breath for the gift of the trees and the healing link to Mother Earth. In the early days, a log house would have been impossible in Santa Fe due to the shortage of big trees.

Switching off the motor, Luke grabbed his bag and bounded up the wooden steps. In his mind's eye he could already visualize the home's light and warm interior, anticipate the series of four huge logs in the entry that rose to the loft with its shapely, curvilinear staircase, the great room filled with the natural, sun-washed colors. At last, he'd have some peace and quiet. Enormously pleased that he had outmaneuvered his mother and wouldn't be bothered by a woman for two whole days, he unlocked the door, hit the light switch on the wall, and entered the cabin.

The click of a gun stopped Luke two steps inside the open living area. He tensed. His dark head came up sharply. More rage than fear filled his eyes as he stared down the black hole of the gun barrel leveled at him, then beyond to the person holding the deadly weapon. His rage increased on seeing the gender of the person.

A slender black woman stood in the room he loved so well, holding a .380 steadily in both hands, her arms outstretched and straight, her legs braced in a wide stance. Neither his tension nor anger lessened because a woman held the gun that could blow a sizable hole in him. In his experience, a woman could be just as deadly as a man. More so because most people didn't expect them to be that vicious or cold-blooded. Again, Luke's experience had taught him otherwise.

"Who are—"

"I'll ask the questions," she said, cutting him off. "Who are you and what are you doing here?"

The accent was East Coast, cultured and cool. At another time, Luke might have been more amicable to answering her questions, but something about a gun being pointed at him in his own house pissed him off. "A man doesn't like staring down the barrel of a gun."

"Then I suggest you answer my questions. Neither one of us would like it very much if my finger happened to slip while I'm waiting."

Black eyes blazed. Luke tried to figure out if she were a real threat or simply a smart-mouth. He might not be able to tell the color of her dark eyes, but he could see no fear or hesitation in them. She'd pull the trigger if she had to. "You better make sure the first one counts."

A sleek eyebrow arched as a smile played around her lips. The semiautomatic lowered to roughly six inches below his navel. "Feel like talking now?"

"What I feel like is breaking your neck."

"Wouldn't be the first time I've heard that, and I doubt it will be the last," she told him matter-of-factly.

For the first time he really looked at her, looked beyond the weapon that could spit out six deadly bullets before he took two steps, beyond his initial surprise and anger to the woman easily holding the gun.

Tall and beautifully shaped, she had endless legs, which were shown to perfection by the side slits of the tautly pulled long gray silk nightgown. Her stunning face was feminine and delicately sculptured with a small nose, high cheekbones, and lush, sensual lips. On her slender feet were gray velvet slippers with a velvet bow.

There was no makeup on her rich mahogany skin. Her shoulder-length curly black hair was mussed. Apparently she had been in bed. Alone if he didn't miss his guess. He didn't think a woman who could so calmly hold a gun on a man would have much use for a man who hid while she faced an unknown adversary.

If she were alone, there was another point to consider.

The cabin was high in the mountains and since the lock on the gate and front door hadn't been broken, it stood to reason that she had a key. He hadn't checked the windows to see if they had been broken, but he didn't need to. They were impenetrable. He'd seen to that.

A key meant she had permission to be there and that could only come from one person, Daniel Falcon, who shared ownership of the cabin. But try as he might, Luke couldn't think of one of Daniel's female acquaintances who would appear so comfortable holding a gun on a man. Or his male acquaintances for that matter.

"Luke Grayson," he finally said.

Up went her brow again. "Prove it."

"My wallet is in my hip pocket."

"Get it. Two fingers."

Trying not to let his anger overrule common sense, he did as she requested. He didn't like someone holding a gun on him, but he would like even less ending up with a bullet hole in him again. Time enough to think of a suitable retribution. "Here."

"Toss it." The level of the gun lifted to his abdomen. Her gaze didn't waver. "Very carefully."

The hand-tooled, brown leather billfold landed midway between them on a colorful Navajo rug. She never took her eyes from him. Luke cursed the woman and whomever had taught her to keep her eyes on the target no matter what.

"Seems we have a problem," she said mildly. "I'd ask you to kick it over, but I have a feeling the results would be about the same."

Luke folded his arms.

"You're just stubborn enough to be who you say you are. Unfortunately, I can't take a chance." Shifting the gun to her left hand, she crossed the room to the phone on the end table, hit the speaker, then the redial button.

An impatient male voice answered on the second ring. "Make it quick."

"Sorry, but this is Catherine and I have a situation at the cabin that is not as empty as you thought."

A razor sharpness entered the man's voice. "Who?"

"I'm calling you because I'm not sure. There's a mountain of a man who looks like he could rip my head off standing ten feet in front of me. Says his name is Luke Grayson, but not much else."

"Describe him."

"Tall, six feet four, brawny with go-to-hell looks that match his attitude. Long, thick straight black hair tied at the back with a rawhide thong, black eyes as sharp as a wolf's fangs. The broken nose indicates I'm not the first person he had a disagreement with. Western style of dress, blue chambray shirt, obscene fitting jeans, and scuffed skin boots. Some silly women might find all that pent-up intensity and bulging muscles attractive." She shrugged a dismissive shoulder. "Too caveman for me. Guess the gun in my hand ticked him off."

"Catherine, tell me you're kidding?"

"About the gun or him being ticked?"

"Both."

"Afraid I can't do that."

Laughter boomed over the line. "I can't believe you got the drop on him. I'll never let him live it down."

The frown eased from her forehead. "Then he is your cousin?"

"Sounds like it. Luke, stop scaring Catherine," the male voice commanded.

Luke didn't bother pointing out that she was the one holding the gun. "Tell her to put the gun away, Daniel, before I forget she's a woman."

"He's legit, Catherine. Luke, meet Catherine."

"But—"

"Sorry, gotta go. Time for my son's midnight feeding and he's not known for his patience. Night." The line went dead.

Catherine looked at the angry man, snapped on the safety, and lowered the gun. He still looked ready to blow. His problem. He had scared ten years off her life. But at least this time it wasn't her imagination. "I'm already in the bedroom on the right. You'll have to take one of the others."

"Aren't you forgetting something?" he asked tightly.

"Not unless you want to take my order for breakfast," she ventured mildly.

The scowl on his handsome face deepened.

She shrugged. The thin strap of her nightgown slid over her shoulder. She didn't bother pulling it back up. "I didn't think so. Good night."

Entering her bedroom, Catherine closed the door behind her and leaned against it, her body trembling. She'd been almost asleep when she'd heard the noise outside. At home she had thought she'd heard someone several times outside her house, but the police had never been able to find anything. For a moment, she'd thought she was imagining things again. Then, she had heard the slam of a door.

The peacefulness of the woods and the isolation no longer seemed quite so beautiful and safe. She hadn't gotten the gun until she heard someone come up on the porch. By the time she'd retrieved the weapon out of her suitcase and opened her bedroom door, Luke was inside.

The size of him, and his easy entrance into the cabin had her automatically lifting the weapon. Some people could be trusted only when they could be controlled. Although she didn't like guns, didn't like what they could do to human flesh, experience had taught her she needed an edge.

Before she began her weapon training, her instructor had taken her to a busy hospital emergency room. That night she saw more than she wanted to of the damage a bullet could do to a person. Derrick Rodgers had wanted her to respect the weapon and its power. The police didn't call it deadly force for nothing.

Pushing away from the door, she looked at the gleaming automatic in her hand.

"Wonder if the tall man would be as ticked if he knew there wasn't a bullet in the chamber or a clip in the gun?"

Probably not, she thought. And Derrick wouldn't be any happier. He had taught her to be certain she needed a gun before she pulled it, but once she made the decision, she had better be ready for action. Unfortunately, the streets of Los Angeles at night, like those of many metropolitan cities in the 1990s, were sometimes just as dangerous as in the 1790s. That, too, was a lesson she had learned.

Sighing, she walked over to her suitcase. At least it wouldn't take her long to repack. She had come to the cabin for rest and relaxation, to get away from everything and enjoy some badly needed downtime. That was impossible with Luke Grayson around. Even if they hadn't gotten off to a bad start, he didn't look to be the restful type. Too intense. Too dangerous looking.

Los Angeles was full of big, powerfully built men who prided themselves on their well-toned bronzed bodies. Somehow she knew Luke's wasn't manufactured in a gym or fitness center or the result of steroids. He didn't have that beefy, bulging appearance that totally turned her off.

Yet, it wasn't just his size that unsettled her, it was also the intense way he had looked at her. She'd taken that dig at him for her own benefit. A woman could get into a lot of trouble with a man like that. And if there was one thing she prided herself on, it was staying clear of men who couldn't be easily forgotten.

She shrugged the thought and the nightgown off, then reached for her bra. She was leaving. She had enough on her mind without adding an angry man to the list. Driving down the narrow mountain road at night wasn't something she was particularly looking forward to, but she had faced worse things and survived.

LUKE WAS STEAMED. HE DIDN'T LIKE GUNS BEING pointed at him. Liked it even less that he had let a probable amateur get the drop on him again. The incident was too much of a reminder of the one that had occurred during his six-year tenure as an FBI field agent in Lincoln, Nebraska. One minute he and his partner had been interviewing a bank embezzlement suspect, the next thing he knew, the man had a gun and was shouting he wasn't going to jail.

Luke would never forget the look of surprise and horror on the man's pasty face when the gun he was holding in his shaking hand went off. In those seconds afterward, shocked disbelief had held the man immobile. By the time he had recovered, he had been advised of his rights and handcuffed, all the time babbling he was sorry. With the searing pain in his left shoulder, the gunman hadn't received any sympathy from Luke. The wound had left a three-inch scar on Luke's forearm and a lasting impression.

You could be just as dead by accident as you could be on purpose. Save him from amateurs. But at least Catherine had been cooler than the embezzler.

The natural curiosity that had helped him build one of the most respected and profitable investigative agencies in the state kicked in, momentarily sidetracking his anger. How had she learned that much courage and control, and why did she need it?

Luke gazed at the closed bedroom door, then picked up the phone and hit redial.

It took four rings before Daniel answered. "Feeding time. Bye."

Luke's grip on the phone tightened. He happened to know Daniel's wife, Madelyn, was breast-feeding. What the hell use was Daniel?

Luke lifted his hand to hit the redial button again, then hung up instead. All the questions he wanted to ask about Catherine, at least the most important ones, were already answered.

To Luke's knowledge, Daniel had never let anyone except family members use the cabin. The call she placed had gone to Daniel's private line at his home in Houston, Texas. So whomever the gun-toting Catherine was, Daniel trusted and liked her. And his cousin wasn't a man easily fooled, if at all, no matter how shapely or how appealingly the package was wrapped.

Besides, Daniel was ga-ga over his wife, and, since Daniel Jr.'s arrival, acted as if he had been gifted with the world, and was a walking, talking encyclopedia on infant care and child development. Only close family members caught a glimpse of Daniel Jr. at his first outing, his Aunt Dominique's wedding; fewer still were able to hold him because Daniel had been concerned with "germs." His dark gaze narrowed. Whatever Catherine was to Daniel, it wasn't romantic. But did she have to pull a gun on him?

Feeling his anger escalating, Luke decided to go outside before he pounded on Catherine's door for the answers. Unless she opened it, all he would get was a sore fist beating against the solid oak door. Threatening a man with a gun was bad enough, but she had added insult to injury when she threatened his private parts.

She'd stepped over the line, way over. Leave it to a woman to be that sadistic. And since she was Daniel's guest, he'd have to let her get away with it. At least Luke had had the satisfaction of arresting the guy who'd shot him.

Outside, Luke crossed the wooden porch, then went down the three steps to stand beneath the full moon and listen to the night sounds. The chirp of the crickets, the hoot of the pigmy owl, the howl of a coyote came to him.

The end of spring was a tempestuous time in and around Santa Fe. You could easily go through high winds, heavy snow, blinding sunshine, or drenching rain in a twenty-four-hour period. Tonight the air was crisp and clean, the winds calm, the temperature hovering in the low sixties. Perfect. He drew in a deep breath, then slowly pushed it out and let nature calm him.

The immensity of the natural surroundings never ceased to touch him. He never tired of the changing landscape, of seeing the vastness of the Southwestern desert gradually give way to the forested peaks of Jemez Mountains on the west and Sangre de Cristo Mountains to the east. If one were still, one could hear the wind whispering through piñon pines, or even stiller, hear the drums and chanting of the ancient ones. The Pueblo Indians' legendary name for the city, "the dancing grounds of the sun," was an apt description for the vastness of the land that soothed the soul and left one in awe of the Creator.

He enjoyed his home and working in Santa Fe, but for the revival of his spirit he found it necessary to get away. Just himself, the Master of Breath, and God to enjoy all they had created for the earth's inhabitants to enjoy . . . if they'd simply take the time long enough to be still, to look and listen. Most people, like his sister and brothers, didn't.

Of all his siblings, he was the only one who could stay at the cabin for an extended period of time and be perfectly happy. A week was the absolute limit for his three brothers. Less for his sister.

Morgan always had a case in court or a client to see. Pierce would be worried about the stock market and his own growing list of clients. Brandon missed his business and the many women in his life. Sierra claimed it was too isolated since the nearest store was seven miles away down a winding two-lane mountain road that had a sheer drop most of the way. What if she ran out of milk or bread? Give her the convenience of a city and its shops.

Luke almost smiled. More likely Sierra's reasons were more due to there being only five houses in a radius of fifteen miles. And none were for sale. That certainly put a cramp in the style of the top residential realtor in Santa Fe. His little sister could sell a lean-to hanging off a cliff and would thoroughly enjoy herself while doing it.

Opening his eyes, an unpleasant thought struck him. What if Sierra had been spending the night alone and a stranger had walked in? Knowing his feisty sister, she would have drop-kicked the guy first and asked questions later. She'd better. Surprise was sometimes the only advantage you had against your opponent.

Luke struggled with the irrefutable knowledge. He didn't want to forgive Catherine or at least see she was justified. The reason he was being so stiff-necked didn't elude him. She was a woman and at the moment, he was pissed at all women.

The cabin door opened and he whirled around. Catherine, one hand holding a large suitcase, the other on the door knob. Seeing him, she stopped. For a long time they just stared at each other, then she closed the door, and continued across the wide porch and down the steps to stand in front of him.

"I decided I'm not the roommate type."

CHAPTER TWO

LUKE'S COOLING TEMPER FLARED. WHOEVER SHE WAS, she sure knew how to insult a man. He didn't even try to keep the sharpness out of his voice. "I don't force myself on women."

Her smooth brow arched. "Calm down, Tall Man. I wasn't questioning your honor. I just decided the rustic life isn't for me."

Ignoring the irritating name she called him, Luke's gaze ran over the red jacket, white linen blouse and black slacks, ridiculously high black heels, and designer luggage, and thought she was probably right. She smelled and looked expensive and exotic. Her don't-touch-me attitude reminded him of the frilly, startling golden blossom of the prickly pear cactus flowers that bloomed only once a year.

The flower was tempting to pick, but the base had sharp spines that kept them from being plucked. But if one knew how, anything was possible and the rewards were all the sweeter.

Unexpectedly he felt a tug of something totally male and primitive to her female and ruthlessly squashed it. "You expect me to take you down the mountain tonight?"

"My rental is around back in the garage. Goodbye." She switched the suitcase to her other hand, then went around the house.

Luke went after her, his booted steps, unlike the sharp clatter of her heels on the paved walkway, were soundless. He needed to have one question answered. "Is this your first trip here?"

"Yes," she said, continuing to the garage that was a hundred feet back from the cabin. Fifteen feet away the motion light over the logged structure kicked on, illuminating them.

"You have any experience driving mountain roads?"

Setting her luggage aside, she pulled one of the lightweight oak finished aluminum double doors to one side. "After tonight I will." When she turned to get her suitcase Luke stood in her way. Up went her brow again. "Yes?"

If she wanted it spelled out for her, he'd be more than happy to accommodate her. "I can't imagine Daniel putting up with a snob, so there must be another reason why you'd rather leave than apologize."

"Me?" Her eyes rounded as she stared up at him. "Why should I apologize for defending myself?"

For some reason he wished again he could tell the color of her very annoyed eyes. "I wasn't going to hurt you," he defended hotly, his hands on his hips.

"And how was I to know that?" she asked just as hotly. "Daniel said you haven't used the cabin in a couple of months because your business keeps you so busy. He assured me I'd be alone."

"I needed a break," he admitted reluctantly, but not from his business. His matchmaking mother was about to drive him over the deep end.

She didn't lower her chin or her steady gaze. "So did I."

Heavy black eyebrows lifted. His innate curiosity kicked in again. "From what?"

Her chin went up a notch. "That's my business." She

stepped around him. "Nice chatting with you, but I must be going."

"You aren't going anywhere," he told her flatly.

Picking up her case, she whirled. He could almost see the steam coming out of her ears. "I beg your pardon?"

"Fat chance of that happening," he told her and watched her eyes narrow. Fire and spirit. Intriguing eyes, fascinating face—if he were looking. He wasn't. "Driving down these mountains at night can be tricky. If you won't think about yourself, think about the other person who happened to have the bad luck of being on the road with you."

Catherine's grip on the handle tightened. She glanced at her rental she had picked up at the Albuquerque International Airport, a nice, nondescript beige Ford Taurus. She had needed that anonymity. Unfortunately, at the moment, she needed the power and maneuverability of her Porsche.

Luke seemed to realize her hesitation. "Stay until morning, and then if you still want to go, you can."

There was no hesitation in her reply. "I'll want to go."

"Fine." He grabbed the garage door. "Move out of the way."

"I can do it."

"I didn't say you couldn't." His large hand remained on the door.

She stepped out of the way and watched him close the garage door, his movements smooth and easy. He moved extremely well for such a big man. Like a wild animal, all grace and power and strength. She shivered and glanced away.

Silently, they walked back to the cabin. "Good night," she said, the moment they were inside. Somehow he made her feel awkward and off-balance. She wasn't sure she had ever felt that way around a man before. She was sure she didn't like it one bit.

"Good night and I meant what I said about you being safe," he said, his deep voice as steady and direct as his gaze.

Catherine simply stared at him. Fifteen minutes ago he had wanted to separate her head from her shoulders, now he was trying to reassure her. Oddly it wasn't necessary. She trusted him because she trusted Daniel Falcon, a man whose integrity was impeccable, and he hadn't been able to praise his cousin, Luke Grayson, enough.

To Daniel's way of thinking, Luke was an honorable man. Tonight he had proved Daniel to be right. Although she didn't like to think about it, Luke had seen her in her nightgown and could not have cared less. Even after the danger she presented was over, his black eyes had held anger, not lust.

A lifetime ago, she might have idly wondered why he wasn't interested. Now she was thankful he wasn't. "I'm sorry about the gun," she finally said.

He gave a curt nod. "I guess you had cause."

Stiff-necked and stubborn, but then, so was she at times. "I guess I did."

Dark brows bunched. "Who taught you to handle a gun?"

She guessed she owed him that. "A private instructor," she answered and turned to leave.

"Maybe I should know your entire name since we're going to be sleeping under the same roof."

She swung back around and stared into the depths of his piercing black eyes. An unexpected ball of heat rolled through her. Her hand flexed. "Catherine Stewart."

"You have much use for a gun in your line of work, Catherine?"

Once, she could have laughed at such a question. Unfortunately she had begun to think differently six months ago, but that was her own business. "I'm a child psychologist and teach at UCLA."

His eyebrows bunched. He well remembered his psychology instructors. None looked like the sensual woman standing before him. If they had, he definitely would have sat in the front row. "You don't look old enough."

"Same thing my first-time students whisper behind my back. By midterm they're singing a different tune," she said with quiet pride.

"Make them sweat, do you?"

"I make them learn," she corrected emphatically.

"I just bet you do," he said, the corner of his mouth slightly tilted.

Catherine caught herself watching his mouth, waiting for the smile to break free. When it didn't happen, she almost sighed in regret, then realized what she had been doing. "Good night." She turned and went quickly to her bedroom.

Moistening her dry lips, she closed her eyes and leaned against the door. Maybe she should have gone. Something told her that if she wasn't careful, Luke Grayson could be just as dangerous to her peace of mind as driving down the mountain.

CATHERINE AWOKE SHORTLY AFTER DAWN SATURDAY morning and watched through the two double windows in her room as the sun pushed away the night shadows. She hadn't expected to sleep that long. Too many things were on her mind these days.

Sitting up in bed, she scooted back against the carved headboard. The chair of psychology at her university had indicated her name was among those being considered to head the Department of Developmental Psychology. Which, while a coup for her, meant even longer hours and more responsibility. Meanwhile, the publisher of her children's stories was making noises that they wanted to send her on another grueling and demanding tour. Children's advocacy groups were pressuring her to become a national spokesperson. Everyone wanted something from her.

She couldn't think about any of that until she straightened out her own life. And as her no-nonsense mother had told her, no one could do that but her. Easier said than done, and it was becoming more difficult by the day.

Delicate fingers rubbed her temple. Maybe, as she hoped and everyone had said, all she needed was some downtime. This was the first vacation she had taken in three years.

Daniel had told her the woods were peaceful and serene. After spending the past three days aimlessly wandering them, she had come to believe him. Too bad he wasn't right about having the cabin to herself as well.

To be fair, that wasn't Daniel's fault or Luke's. She was the outsider. It was just that she needed time to sort through her life and she felt she could do it here. There was something about the woods that called to her, soothed her. There was nothing that said she had to be happy about leaving. Throwing back the covers, she bounded out of bed.

LUKE HEARD CATHERINE'S FEET HIT THE FLOOR. HE'D been awake for the past two hours, unconsciously listening for the sound. He had thought it would come closer to noon than eight. Despite her being at the cabin, he had figured her to be the type of woman who required pampering. Everything about her screamed wealth and privilege. Including her attitude. She was a woman used to being answered to rather than answering to someone.

A scowl deepened the lines around his eyes as he remembered the gun she'd held on him. In her nightgown no less, and she hadn't batted an eyelash. He had devoted too much time last night to wondering if her action was out of brave necessity or if she thought nothing of it since she was used to spending a lot of time with men in her nightgown. With a body and face like hers, she wouldn't have the gown on for long.

With a grunt of self-disgust he climbed out of bed and headed for the walk-in shower. Like a rookie, he had let Catherine take him by surprise a second time. This time in his dreams. He hadn't thought he'd paid that much attention to what she was wearing, but apparently he had.

In his dream he could recall every sensual detail of the high, proud thrust of her breasts against the lace bodice, the smooth slope of her shoulders, the slender curves of her body, and long, shapely legs. The mussed hair added to the sensual image and gave her the look of a woman who had been thoroughly satisfied in bed.

A muttered curse hissed through clenched teeth. What he needed was a good run. Unfortunately, the reason he needed the exercise was the reason he couldn't go. He usually went in little more than briefs. Too revealing in his present state.

His irritation increasing, Luke turned his attention to trying to figure out the answer to his original questions. What had made Catherine so handy with a gun, and why had Daniel sent her to the cabin? He was all for self-protection, but the stopping power of the automatic signified more than that.

His cousin wasn't a whimsical man. He valued, as Luke did, the close bond of family and friendship. To them, the words held meaning. You didn't turn your back on either.

Luke didn't like to think that he had let his cousin down in some way. The ties that held them were strong and unbreakable. If Catherine had problems, and Daniel wanted her here, she was staying. Even if Luke had to tie her down.

Shutting off the shower, he reached for a large fluffy blue bath towel. He was pulling on his jeans when he smelled coffee. His morning brightened. Maybe she was cooking breakfast with real bacon and eggs. Despite the cholesterol, both were personal weaknesses of his.

He grabbed his shirt and quickly stuffed his arms into the sleeves. Maybe it wouldn't be such a hardship having her around. He wasn't the greatest cook, and his last satisfying meal was three days ago. It was difficult to enjoy eating when you knew the woman sitting across from you was sizing you up for a wedding ring through your nose.

Slipping his feet into a pair of handmade moccasins that he wore while in the house, he headed for the kitchen. The closer he came, the headier the aroma. His mouth was actually watering when he stepped into the kitchen.

Catherine wasn't there. He frowned and chalked up his sense of disappointment to not finding her cooking.

The sound of the front door closing had his frown deepening. He walked into the entryway and opened the front door. If she hadn't been wearing the red jacket again, he might have missed seeing her heading for the woods. Lines radiated across his forehead. Where was she going? She'd probably never been in the woods in her life before now. It would be his bad luck that she'd end up falling and getting hurt.

The thought of her being in pain brought an unexpected sharp wrench in his gut. Must be hunger pains, he thought, rubbing his stomach as he started back toward his room, grumbling all the way. Sitting on the bed, he removed his moccasins and pulled on his boots. He might as well go after her. Whether he liked it or not, she was on his property and therefore, technically his responsibility. To think he had come up here to get away from women—and now he had to go chase one down.

Women.

Nothing had gone right since he had walked into the cabin last night, and probably wouldn't for the time Catherine was here.

Women had a way of complicating and messing up a man's life the way nothing else could. Why any man would even consider getting married was beyond Luke's comprehension. He enjoyed a woman (on his terms) as well as the next man, but he always, always wanted the door open so he could move on when he was ready.

The phone was ringing when he came out of his room. He veered in that direction. No one knew he was up here except Daniel. For the first time he might be glad he had relented and installed a phone as Daniel and his brothers and sister wanted.

"Hello."

"Who's is this? Where's Catherine?"

Luke knew fear when he heard it. It was there in the thin, almost shrill, East Coast accent of the female voice. New York he guessed. Dismissing his irritation at being interrogated on his own phone in his own house, he answered the first question. "Luke Grayson."

The answer didn't appease her. "Who are you? What are you doing there? Where's Catherine?" The questions came as rapidly as automatic gunfire.

"I own this cabin with Dan—"

"I want to speak with Catherine immediately." The demand that cut him off was brisk and authoritarian.

Patience, he reminded himself. "She just left for a walk in the woods."

"Catherine's not the outdoors type."

"On that we agree," he said with a note of sarcasm.

"You put her on the phone or I'm calling the police. You have two minutes."

Lord, deliver him from high-strung women. "Look, lady. I told you Catherine went for a walk. I may not be able to find her and bring her back in two minutes."

"That's your problem." Click.

Luke stared at the dead phone. Just his luck that one of Catherine's friends was as unstable as she was. But his curiosity and his protective instincts were aroused again.

Catherine and her friend weren't the trusting type. Trust was a learned response, which meant that somewhere along the way, theirs had been violated. Hanging up the phone, he headed for the door. This time he was getting some answers.

HE DIDN'T HAVE ANY TROUBLE FOLLOWING THE IMPRESsion of her tennis shoes in the dew-kissed grass. From the time he could walk and talk, his grandfather and uncles had taught him the old ways of the People. For his ancestors to survive, game had to be hunted. Those days might be gone, but the traditions of his People were preserved and passed on lest they be lost.

He heard her before he saw her. Her voice, soft and persuasive.

"It's all right, I won't hurt you. Come on, that's it. There's more where that came from."

Coming into the small clearing of spruce trees, he saw her and couldn't believe his eyes. Catherine, on her knees, was two feet away from a half-grown wolf hybrid. The dirty animal was gulping down the slices of wheat bread as fast as she threw them. What worried Luke was what the animal would do once the food was gone. Hybrids were unpredictable and high-strung. He could fade back into the woods or . . .

Luke began slowly moving toward them. He was ten feet away when the animal's head came up. Luke could tell almost to the second when the wind shifted, carrying his scent. A growl rumbled from the animal's thin chest as he turned toward Luke, then with one sharp bark he was gone.

Catherine turned to see what had caused the animal to run and stared up into Luke's angry face. She opened her mouth to give him a stern reprimand for scaring her animal away, but somehow the words got lost when her gaze drifted downward. The first five buttons of his white shirt were undone, revealing rope-hard muscles that made her mouth water, then dry. Her reaction annoyed her to no end. She had seen a man's chest before, but, honesty made her admit, never one so sculptured and bronzed.

"I realize you're from the city, but don't you have better sense than to feed a strange animal?"

His censure effectively brought her back to her senses. Clutching the bread sack in her hand, she pushed to her feet. "He wasn't going to harm me. Why did you have to scare him away?"

Wide-legged, hands on narrow hips, he continued to glare at her. "That was a hybrid you were feeding."

She stopped dusting off the knee of her black linen slacks. "Hybrid?"

"Half-wolf/half-dog or descendants of," he explained impatiently. "They were popular pets at one time until people learned that wolves, no matter how much you dilute the genes, aren't meant to be shut up or tamed unless they choose."

"That explains the worn collar on his neck." Her lips tightened. "And the scars on his back."

A curse hissed through Luke's teeth.

"Exactly." She could almost forgive him. "After three days of trying to get him to trust another human, you come along and ruin it."

"Well, excuse me." He looked like a warrior about to go into battle, and he was taking no prisoners. "I was trying to save your pretty neck."

The way he said it, it wasn't a compliment. Her chin lifted. "Thanks, but I'm used to protecting my neck from wolves."

His eyes narrowed. "I just bet you are, but you might have gotten more than a hickey."

"Just let a man try to put one of those disgusting things on my neck."

"What are you going to do, shoot him like you tried to do to me last night?"

Her chin went up. "I apologized for that."

"Yeah, you did." He looked her over. "If you were planning to feed the hybrid, why didn't you bring your gun?"

Horror washed across her face. "I wouldn't have shot the poor animal."

Somehow her admission escalated his anger. "But you wouldn't hesitate to blow a hole in me."

She waved her slim hand in dismissal. "The gun wasn't loaded."

His hands came to his sides. "What?"

She and her big mouth. She hadn't thought he would like hearing that. "I didn't have time," she said, hoping the lie would placate him. It didn't.

"Women."

He spat out the word as if it left a bad taste in his mouth. A very sensual mouth at that. "You have a problem with women?" she asked, wondering why she was standing there arguing with him instead of going back to the cabin and leaving.

"They're illogical and scattered," he told her with an emphatic nod of his Stetson-covered head.

Bread sack clutched in her hand, Catherine glared up

at him. "On what do you base such an idiotic assumption?"

His black eyes narrowed, but he answered, "Some woman with a heavy East Coast accent called while I was leaving the cabin. She demanded that she speak to you, gave me two minutes to find you, then hung up before I could get her name. If that isn't illogical and scattered, I don't know what is."

Making a face, Catherine started back for the cabin. "When Helena gets excited or nervous, her accent becomes more pronounced."

Luke matched his steps to hers. "How do you know who it was?"

"Only three women know I'm here. My mother wouldn't have warned you, Dianne would have charmed you, and neither have East Coast accents," Catherine explained.

Without thinking, Luke caught her elbow and helped her over a log. He was surprised how fragile she felt, and even more surprised that he was reluctant to release her. "Why did she sound so upset?"

"Literary agents tend to be very protective of their clients," she answered.

"Client?"

"Yes, I write children's stories."

He frowned, his gaze running over her again. Would this woman always surprise him? The red jacket's collar was turned up, framing her beautiful mahogany face with its sensual lower lips and eyes the color of . . . melted dark chocolate, he finally determined. A face too exotic and too tempting for anything as tame and harmless as children's stories. "I thought you taught psychology?"

"I do. Most of the professors publish books or research papers. It's almost a prerequisite if you hope to obtain tenure." She shrugged slim shoulders. "I've been writing children's stories since I was a child myself."

"You publish anything yet?"

A small smile of satisfaction played around her mouth. "Yes."

"Is that how you know Daniel? He bought one of your books for Daniel junior?"

"He's purchased all of them, but I've known Daniel and his family since I was a baby. I was at Daniel's wedding reception and Dominique's wedding."

"I don't remember seeing you." Of that he was certain.

She lifted a brow at the slightly accusatory tone. "I was on a tight schedule and only stayed a short time at both occasions."

Pausing, she bent over to pluck a wild daisy. Her black slacks gently cupped her rounded hips. Luke shoved his hands into his pockets before they did something ungentlemanly, foolish, and possibly dangerous. He didn't doubt he'd soon find himself looking down the barrel of her gun again, and this time it would be loaded. "You're from Boston then?"

"Yes, Daniel and my brother, Alex, went through prep school together."

Rich and pampered, just like he'd imagined. A year's tuition to Daniel's private school cost more than some people made in a year. "You don't look like you write children's stories to me."

Used to the remark, but no less annoyed by it, she pushed to her feet. "How many children's authors have you met?"

Although he knew the trap waiting for him, he could see no way around it. "You're the first."

"And you call women illogical and scattered, yet you make an inane statement like that. Men," she said and started walking again.

Luke tugged the brim of his black Stetson and followed. Women. Daniel was going to owe him big time for
this.

BY THE TIME THEY EMERGED FROM THE WOODS, A
black and white state police patrol car was pulling up in
front of the cabin. A faint trail of red dust followed, then
settled as the car stopped.

"Guess your two minutes were up," Catherine said
blithely.

Luke gritted his teeth, caught her elbow, and continued
toward the cabin. Daniel's bill was escalating more by the
minute.

A young patrolman emerged from the car, then put on
his black regulation hat. "Hello, Luke, Miss."

"Hello, Johnny," Luke greeted. "I guess I don't have to
ask why you're here?"

The young man momentarily looked embarrassed.
"We got a call to check on a Dr. Catherine Stewart. The
order came from way up. Since I was patrolling Interstate
25, the sergeant sent me."

"Dr. Catherine Stewart, Patrolman Johnny Wesley,"
Luke introduced. "As you can see, she's all right."

Surprise swept across the officer's face. "You're a
doctor?"

"I have a doctorate in psychology," she told him.

The admiration in his appreciative male gaze increased. "Nice to meet you, Dr. Stewart," he said tipping
his hat. "It certainly wouldn't be difficult to tell you my
troubles."

"Brother," Luke muttered and barely kept from rolling
his eyes.

Ignoring Luke, Catherine stepped forward, glad to be
able to free herself from the surprising heat emanating from
his fingers on her arm, and extended her hand. "Patrolman

Wesley, I'm sorry for any inconvenience I've caused. I planned on being up here alone, and my friend in New York must have become alarmed when Luke answered the phone."

A wide grin on his face, the young man accepted her hand in his and held on. "Don't worry about it, Dr. Stewart, part of my job."

"That's nice of you to be so understanding," she said, sliding her hand free.

The officer flushed. Catherine's smile widened to put him at ease. "If you'll excuse me, I better call Helena and let her know I'm all right."

Luke couldn't help but notice the rapt expression in the officer's face. He never took his eyes off her as she went into the house. At twenty-one, Johnny was the impressionable type, but turning into an outstanding patrolman from all reports, according to Sergeant Owens.

The state police for New Mexico covered a great deal of isolated territory and often had to go into dangerous situations by themselves with no backup. No matter what, they always had to be alert, never let their guard down. Luke knew if the by-the-book officer could see the top graduate of the academy thinking about a woman instead of getting back to his patrol, he'd go ballistic.

"Hadn't you better radio in and let the sergeant know everything is all right?"

"I did that the moment I saw it was really you." Leaning against the hood of the car, he crossed his legs and continued to stare at the door. "How is she related to you and Daniel?"

"She's not."

Abruptly straightening, Johnny brought his attention back to Luke, his expression wary as his gaze traveled over Luke's partially buttoned shirt. "She's not?"

Luke didn't need to be a rocket scientist to figure out

where Johnny's mind had incorrectly traveled. "She's a friend of Daniel's. I didn't know she was up here."

Johnny brightened and settled back against the dusty black and white. "How long is she staying?"

"She's leaving today," Luke said.

Thin shoulders slumped beneath the starched charcoal-gray shirt. "Just my luck."

The front door of the cabin opened and Catherine hurried down the steps. She carried the bread sack in her hand.

"Where are you going?" Luke asked, afraid he already knew the answer.

Smiling, she leaned toward him. Her red lips slowly parting, she said, "Guess?"

The word came out in a throaty, provocative purr. Unexpectedly, something inside Luke tightened. He had a crazy impulse to drag her into his arms, put his lips on hers, and really give her something to purr about. His eyes darkened.

The teasing smile slipped from her face. Catherine felt as if she were in a vacuum alone with Luke and someone was sucking out all the air. And the only way to get it back was to . . .

He stepped back. "A hybrid is nothing to play with."

"I'm not playing," she said, unsure of what had just happened to her, and if she were talking about the animal or him. One thing she was sure of, she had to leave or she was going to do something totally foolish and out of character for her.

"What hybrid?" the patrolman asked.

"The wolf hybrid Catherine found in the woods," Luke answered.

The young man frowned. "He's right, Dr. Stewart. You should be careful."

"I can take care of myself, but thanks for your concern. Goodbye, Officer Wesley," she told him.

The young man tipped his hat. "Goodbye, Ma'am."

Catherine headed for the woods. Maybe it was a good thing she was leaving. Luke affected her in the most unusual ways. After feeding the hybrid she'd named Hero, she was leaving.

"Stubborn woman," Luke muttered.

"And beautiful," Officer Wesley added with a heavy sigh.

Luke didn't take his gaze from Catherine going deeper into the woods. "A bad combination."

"You're going after her?"

Luke hadn't realized he was doing exactly that. He didn't slow. "Daniel would never forgive me if anything happened to her."

"I could go in for you," Johnny offered hopefully.

"Thanks, but I'll take care of it." Luke's pace increased to keep her in his sight. When he caught up with her, she was going to listen to reason. Of all the women for Daniel to send to the cabin, why did it have to be someone so stubborn, and so damn beautiful and compelling? Just his bad luck that he never liked anything easy or predictable.

TRY AS SHE MIGHT, CATHERINE COULDN'T KEEP HER mind totally on the hybrid. She was still too conscious of Luke. Of all the times for her to be attracted to a man, why now, and why to someone as opinionated as Luke? Didn't she have enough on her mind without this? So what if he had a body that would make most women's mouths salivate, she had never gone in for the superficial.

But that conviction left her with her present predicament, because Luke was more than rippling muscles and incredible abs, he could be gentle and thoughtful. She had never met anyone like him before. He had the most piercing black eyes she had ever seen, his mouth, even when scowling, looked unbelievably tempting and kissable. Despite her best efforts, there was something about the man that pulled her. Life certainly hadn't been playing fair with her lately.

Pushing a low limb of a pine tree aside, she went deeper into the woods, her feet soundless on the budding grass. She was so caught up in her musings, she never heard the gunshot until it was too late.

CHAPTER THREE

A SCREAM TORE THROUGH CATHERINE'S THROAT AS two powerful arms grabbed her from behind and hurled her to the ground. She opened her mouth to scream again, but the impact of landing knocked the air from her as she came down on the hard body of her attacker. Before she could draw in another breath, she was twisted. This time she was on her back, her body completely covered.

Fear turned to something totally different as she stared up into the hard, piercing eyes of Luke Grayson. Her jacket had opened and only the thin layers of their clothes separated them. His muscular legs bracketed hers, his manhood pressed against her stomach. She fought the slow flickering heat of desire building in her and found it overpowering. There was only one way. She came out fighting. "Must you always scare me half to death?"

"Excuse me, I thought you might be in danger," he said tightly.

"It's your fault," she told him. "You might have warned me if you were going to let someone hunt on your property."

"There's no hunting on this land. Ever."

Her eyes widened. "You mean to tell me you don't know who is out there shooting?"

"Give the lady a cigar."

Her body tensed beneath his. Her frightened gaze went

to the left, then right, before centering wildly on his again. Instantly he regretted his curtness. "You're safe, Catherine. Probably some kid trying out his new gun."

"Y-you're sure?"

"I'm sure," he reassured. "It's not the first time it's happened."

Her body shuddered beneath his. "This is the last time I'll ever go to a supposedly isolated cabin for a few days of rest and relaxation." Her eyes closed, then slowly reopened. "How long do you think we have to stay here until it's safe?"

Interesting question with her soft body beneath his, her sexy perfume doing crazy things to his body and imagination. "Not long. If whoever it was was going to fire again, the shot would have come already."

She tensed again. "Do you think whoever it is is still out there?"

His face hardened. "I hope so. No trespassing signs are clearly posted. Stay here, I'm going to find out who fired that shot."

She clutched his shoulders, her eyes frightened. "You can't go out there. It's too dangerous."

Not as dangerous as remaining where he was. "I've done this before."

"I don't care. You're not doing it now," she told him fiercely. "Daniel would never forgive me if I let you go and something happened to you."

Somehow her answer annoyed him. He rolled and stood. "Stay here."

"If you're going, I'm go—"

Catherine found herself yanked to her feet and pushed behind him. "Quiet," he ordered, his tone flat and hard. Her heart beating wildly in her chest, she obeyed. Seconds later Patrolman Wesley came running through the woods toward them.

"I heard the shot. You two all right?"

"Yeah. I was just about to check it out." Luke nodded to the east. "Came from that direction."

Catherine breathed easier on seeing the patrolman. "Now that he's here, I'm sure he'll want to handle things."

"This is my property and if someone is hunting on it, I want to know," Luke told her flatly. "Go back to the cabin and wait."

Her chin lifted. He certainly liked giving orders. He'd soon learn she wasn't used to taking them. "If some gun-happy person is out there, don't you think I'm safer with you?"

Luke gave her a look that would have made most men run. Unfortunately, the besotted young man was looking at Catherine and completely missed it.

"Whoever fired that shot is probably gone by now, Dr. Stewart, but if you'd feel safer with us, then you should come with us," Officer Wesley offered.

Too smart to gloat, Catherine smiled. "Thank you, I would."

Luke glared at the both of them. "I'll lead. Catherine, you stay behind me."

"Why are you leading?" she asked.

"Because he's the best tracker in the Southwest," the officer told her.

Luke had already started off in the direction he had indicated. Having little hope of stopping him, Catherine followed.

Five minutes later, Luke saw what he had been dreading. *Blood.* An expletive sizzled free. He turned to block her way. "Johnny, take Catherine back to the cabin."

"Why? What is it?" she questioned, trying to step around him.

Unrelenting hands grabbed her firmly by the shoulders, stopping her. "This time you're going to do as you're told."

She didn't understand the black rage in his eyes, but she instinctively knew she wasn't in any danger from him. She opened her mouth to tell him she wasn't leaving, but the low growl stopped her.

She stared toward the ominous sound and barely kept from crying out. Hero, his left front paw raised, oozed blood from a wound on his shoulder. She started toward him, and again found herself thrust behind Luke.

His teeth bared, the animal took a halting step toward them.

"I got him, Luke."

Catherine looked back at the officer. Her eyes widened in horror as she saw the gun in his hand. "You can't. It's not his fault." She clutched Luke's arm. "Please, you can't let him be shot."

"Catherine, I want you to slowly back up until you're behind Johnny. And for once, don't argue."

She had no intention of doing as Luke said until the hybrid took another menacing step toward them. She didn't want the animal killed, but neither did she want Luke to be injured. He'd stand between her and the animal until she was safe. She didn't question that irrefutable knowledge. Slowly she did as he requested, expecting him to follow as soon as she was safe.

"I got her, Luke." Johnny pulled Catherine behind him, his gun still drawn.

"Luke, come on," she told him, wishing there was something she could do to help the hybrid.

"Don't do anything unless it's to keep Catherine safe," Luke said.

"What is he talking about?"

"Understood," the patrolman answered Luke, and ignored Catherine.

Her annoyance at both men turned to fear for Luke as she watched him slowly crouch down until he was eye level with the wounded animal. A chill ran through her. Instinctively she took a step to stop whatever it was he was doing.

Johnny blocked her path. His young face was worried, but determined. "The best way to help both of them is to stay still and quiet."

Feeling helpless and more frightened than she ever remembered, Catherine circled her arms around her and waited. For a long time there was silence. It was almost as if the earth and all its inhabitants were holding their breath, waiting.

Then the sound came in a flowing murmur of words from Luke to the animal in a language she had never heard before. Although she didn't understand what he said, she understood the reassuring tone that poured over her.

Inch by incredible inch Luke worked his way to the animal. Catherine didn't know how much time had passed, how many times words had been interspersed with silence. Her breath caught, held as Luke lifted his hand out to the animal's head. Instead of sharp teeth, a tongue licked his fingers. Removing his shirt, Luke wrapped it around the animal's shoulder, then picked him up in his arms.

"We better get him to the vet."

Luke caught Catherine's puzzled gaze on him as he passed her carrying the animal back to the cabin. He didn't blame her. It was totally out of her realm of understanding, but not to his people. Everything was possible if the belief and connection were strong enough.

"Open the back of the truck," he ordered Johnny. Then he laid the animal down on the bed of the truck and climbed in himself. "Call Youngblood and tell him to meet us at his clinic, then get back out there and try to find out who did this."

"Sure thing, Luke," Johnny said and ran to his patrol car.

Luke turned to Catherine. "I sure hope you can drive a standard shift."

"Since I was twelve," she answered, glad to be able to help in some way.

"Grab my keys and wallet off the dresser. Richard Youngblood's veterinary clinic is just inside the Santa Fe city limits."

Catherine raced inside the cabin, grabbed the things he requested and was almost out the door before she ran back to get him a shirt. Inside her room, she snatched her purse off the top of her suitcase, then rushed back outside. "Here."

"Thanks." He stuck his arms through the arms of the chambray shirt without bothering to button it. "If this wasn't an emergency, I wouldn't let you drive my truck."

"Somehow, I figured as much."

HER HANDS GRIPPING THE STEERING WHEEL, CATHERINE made herself not look back as she drove down the mountain. However, once she stopped at the main highway she couldn't help one quick glance. Sitting cross-legged, Luke's hand steadily stroked the head of the animal, his voice low and soothing.

Facing forward, she shifted the truck into gear and hit the highway with a burst of speed. She didn't slow down until Luke knocked on the rear window.

He pointed to a cluster of one-story adobe buildings. She pulled up to the one that had a sign reading YOUNG-BLOOD ANIMAL CLINIC over the door. The glass front door banged open, and a slender, copper-toned man of average height wearing a white lab coat came hustling out. He had a syringe in his hand.

He whistled on seeing the animal. "You do believe in living dangerously."

"Makes life more interesting that way," Luke said, watching the hybrid carefully. He was too weak to put up much of a fight, but with his sharp teeth that didn't matter. "You better let me do that."

"I've received a few nips in the past," the doctor said, sliding the syringe in his pocket and letting down the tailgate to climb in. "You just watch his head."

"Is there anything I can do to help?" Catherine asked.

"Stay back," both men said in unison without even looking in her direction.

She was becoming tired of being treated as if she were brainless and needed protection, but decided to argue the point later.

Dr. Youngblood took the syringe out of his pocket and took the cap off. "This takes about four seconds to start working."

Luke moved closer to animal and started stroking his head. Once again he began talking to the animal. The hybrid blinked when the needle went in, then in a matter of seconds slowly closed his eyes.

"I wish you could teach me how to do that," the doctor said when the animal was asleep.

"Grandfather tried," Luke said. Picking up the animal, Luke got out of the truck and headed for the clinic.

"That he did," the doctor said, opening the door and leading Luke into a small examining room in the back. "Put him on the table." Clicking on an overhead light, he drew on a pair of plastic gloves and began to probe the wound. He glanced up. "I'm going to need some help. My assistant ran off with a truck driver last week."

Before Catherine could say a word, Luke took her arm

and led her outside the room. "Wait in the front room until we're finished."

"I'm not helpless or squeamish, you know."

"Never said you were. We'll call if we need you." Stepping back, he closed the door.

CATHERINE PACED THE FLOOR, THEN TOSSED ASIDE one magazine after the other. Her nerves frayed, she went back to the examining room and listened at the door to try and find out how Hero was doing. All she heard was low murmuring. She was actually glad to hear the phone ring to give her something to do. She hadn't needed Luke to stick his head out and yell for her to take a message.

Sitting behind the cluttered desk, she soon discovered the veterinarian had a thriving practice. In less than thirty minutes, he had two drop-ins and three calls for appointments. Locating the appointment book on his desk in his surprisingly neat office, if she didn't count the stacks of unfiled records on top, she checked his schedule.

She asked the drop-ins to come back in the afternoon, and scheduled the other appointments for the next day, careful to tell everyone she would call if their appointment needed to be changed. Since he was taking care of Hero, it was the least she could do.

Patrolman Wesley stopped by fifteen minutes after they arrived and headed straight for the examining room. A ringing phone kept Catherine from following. He came back out while she was still trying to explain to the elderly caller that she knew nothing about the procedure for spaying her cat. Tipping his hat, Johnny left as quickly and as quietly as he had come.

When the door to the examining room finally opened almost forty-five minutes after their arrival, she was out of her chair and down the hall in a flash. "How is he?"

"Fine. He'll be even better once he rests for a couple of days and gets some food inside him," the doctor told her.

Relief coursed through her. "Did Patrolman Wesley find out who fired the shot?"

"No. He followed two sets of tracks to the road," Luke told her, anger creeping into his voice. "From the indentation and size, they were either small men or kids. More likely kids out testing the gun some irresponsible parent blithely gave them."

"And shot Hero." Catherine bit her lower lip. "Maybe if I hadn't tried to feed him, he would have been more leery of them."

"Now who is being idiotic?" Luke asked her. He didn't wait for her to answer. "It took you three days to get him to come near you. Yet, he still growled at me, even tried to protect you after he was shot. Just because he had begun to trust you doesn't mean he trusted anyone else."

Hope shone in her chocolate brown eyes. "You think so?"

"Trust me on this," he said, surprising himself by tenderly pushing a strand of black hair behind her ear.

She smiled. "Thank you."

Luke felt the all-too-familiar clutch in his gut, the growing need to pull her into his arms and taste her lips. The way she was looking at him, he wouldn't get any resistance. But something told him one taste would lead to another, and that would lead to something he wasn't sure he wanted to deal with.

"Don't I get a thanks?" Dr. Youngblood asked with amusement. "After all, I'm the one who actually did all the work."

Catherine blushed and stepped away from Luke. "Of course, Dr. Youngblood. I can't thank you enough."

"I'm glad I was able to help out, Miss . . ."

"Stewart, Catherine Stewart." She held out her hand. "Please call me Catherine."

"I'd like to, and often."

Catherine blinked.

"Cut it out, Youngblood. You're getting worse than Brandon." Taking Catherine's arm, he led her back down the hallway toward the door.

"Wait," she cried when she saw he wasn't going to stop. "I forgot to tell him about the appointments I made, and I need to get my purse to pay him."

"He can read and I'll take care of the bill later." Luke kept walking.

"No, I still feel responsible," she said, digging in her heels.

"Don't worry about the bill, Catherine." Dr. Youngblood stuck his hands in his pockets and grinned at the proprietary way Luke was acting. Interesting. "Unlike some of my clients, I know he's good for it."

"No, I want to take care of it." Pulling away from Luke, she crossed the small room and picked up the appointment book to show him her notations. "I scheduled you two appointments for this afternoon. The first is at one, the other is at three."

"Any chance you want a job permanently?" he asked mildly.

"She has a job. She teaches at UCLA and is a writer," Luke said, unaware of the pride in his voice.

Dr. Youngblood stared at her. "What field?"

"Psychology and I write children's stories."

"Any chance of moonlighting?"

She laughed at the hopefulness in his strong face. "Sorry, after the workshop and conference I'm leaving."

"What workshop and conference?" Luke wanted to know.

She turned startled eyes up to him, surprised he was

standing so close. "The ones I'm scheduled to do next week in Santa Fe."

"About your books?"

"Somewhat. I specialize in child development and nurturing. My last book dealt heavily with the subject and has gotten a lot of media attention," she said. "I'm conducting a parenting seminar on Tuesday and Wednesday, using my latest book, *Listening*, as a guide, then I'm lecturing at the American Psychological Association conference on Friday."

"I'm impressed," Dr. Youngblood said.

Catherine barely heard him. She had been watching Luke, and from his unhappy expression, he wasn't taking the news very well.

"I thought you were leaving," his words were almost accusatory.

"The cabin, not Santa Fe." Somehow the thought that he wanted her gone bothered her more than she wanted to admit. Turning before he could see how his words hurt her, she picked up the purse to get her wallet. "Dr. Youngblood, if there's a conflict in the scheduled appointments, I'd be happy to call and reschedule."

"Please call me Richard, and they're fine."

She nodded, her actions becoming more agitated as she shoved things to one side and then the other without finding her clutch in the red drawstring bag. *Please. Don't let this happen. Not again.* Upending her purse, she dumped the contents on the receptionist's desk. "It's got to be here. It's got to be."

Frowning, Luke's fingers gently closed around her wrists to stop her frantic search. "It's all right, I'll pay the bill. Don't get upset over it."

She looked at her things scattered on the desk, then back up to him. "But I had it. I know I did. I know it was there."

Her gaze was almost wild. Everything was finally catching up with her, he thought. "The way you were running around getting everything, it could have fallen out and you never would have noticed."

"I want to go back to the cabin," she said, her voice panicky, her hand trembling as she repacked her bag.

"We'll go now," Luke said and helped put her everything back into her purse. "Thanks again, Richard. We better be going."

His attention on Catherine, Dr. Youngblood frowned. "You'll find your wallet, and don't worry about the hybrid."

Nodding again, she bit her lower lip.

His hand on her elbow, Luke led her outside, his concern growing when he felt her trembling. He wouldn't have thought the woman who confronted him with a gun and befriended a half-wild hybrid wolf would react so strongly to misplacing her wallet. "Don't worry. It's at the cabin."

She didn't answer him or say another word on the way back to the cabin. Her stillness made Luke uncomfortable. He had known her for less than twenty-four hours, but he had learned in that short time that she was a woman who was seldom motionless or shy about expressing her opinion.

As soon as he pulled up in front of the cabin, she opened her door and ran inside. Puzzled, his worry increasing, he followed.

He found her standing by the bed clutching a red leather wallet. The tension in him eased. He remembered how frantic Sierra had been when she had lost hers while they were on vacation. The loss of the money hadn't been as frightening as the thought of someone getting their hands on her credit cards. Sierra, as she was fond of saying, was "born to shop" and she had the credit cards to prove it. "See, I told you it probably fell out of your purse."

She turned to him, her eyes no less wild. Tension whipped back through him. "Catherine, what is it?"

"N-nothing. I guess everything is finally catching up with me." She bit her lower lip before continuing, "If you don't mind, I-I think I'll rest for a while before I leave."

He walked farther into the room. "You don't have to leave at all."

Her head downcast, she sat on the bed. "Thank you, but it's best that I find someplace else to stay."

Her voice sounded thin, stretched to its endurance. The sight of her troubled bothered him in ways he hadn't expected. He wanted to go to her, make everything right for her again. At that moment, he would have given anything to have her arguing with him again. "Daniel wanted you to stay here."

Her head lifted, her eyes troubled. "That was before he knew you were coming."

"We'll talk about it once you've rested." He studied her drawn features. "Can I get you anything?"

Clutching the wallet in her hand she shook her head and turned away.

"If you need anything, anything at all, just call. I'll be outside." Closing the door, he knew without a shadow of doubt that she wouldn't call, but that she needed something and it tore at his gut that he didn't know what it was or how to give it to her.

CHAPTER FOUR

SHE WASN'T GOING CRAZY! SHE WASN'T!

Catherine repeated the words over and over in her mind, but somehow the more she repeated them, the less sure of herself she became. Because the undeniable proof that she just might be was becoming increasingly difficult to dismiss. Until now she had been able to find a reasonable explanation to her periods of "forgetfulness." No longer did she have that luxury.

She was sitting on a bed that she had no memory of making, a bed she could have sworn was rumpled from a restless night when she had left it that morning to go for a walk in the woods, that she could have sworn was in the same rumpled state when she had hurriedly returned to get her purse and drive Luke to the veterinary clinic with Hero. Just as she would have sworn that in the days she had been at the cabin, there had been no reason to remove her wallet from her purse. Yet, she had returned and found her bed made, the wallet lying on top of the cream-colored down comforter.

Inanimate objects couldn't move on their own. She had learned that irrefutable fact as a small child faced with the responsibility of putting her menagerie of dolls and stuffed animals back in their proper places once she finished playing with them. That was one lesson her third-grade teacher hadn't had to teach her.

Catherine's gaze went from the red wallet in her hand to the bed. "So are you reaching a breaking point or is your brain trying to tell you something?"

As a psychologist she knew the immense capabilities of the brain, including shutting itself down before reaching overload when the person refused to do so. Her lapses, if that's what they were, could be no more than her brain telling her to slow down. Unfortunately, she wasn't sure she had that option. Her career was both her happiness and her pain, but she wouldn't have it any other way.

Lying back on the bed, she stared up at the beamed ceiling. The worst thing about her "lapses" was that she was unable to confide in anyone. Her family had worried and seen her through enough, they didn't need another crisis. Her agent, Helena, would care, but hover, and the last thing she needed was hovering over.

Her department chair might not be so willing to recommend her for the head of developmental psychology if he thought she was having emotional problems. Lee Perkins would win hands down. Although he was a noted psychologist, in her opinion he saw the position as a stepping stone to being chair of the department, and not for the good it could do.

The university was very proud of her research projects, her fame as an author, her growing reputation as a child advocate. But that would quickly change if word leaked out about her forgetfulness. An absent-minded professor was cute only in the movies. She had friends and associates, but she wasn't sure she was ready to discuss her situation with them. So who?

Unconsciously her gaze went to the door. *Luke.* She dismissed the idea almost before it formed completely. He'd undoubtedly tell Daniel, and Daniel wouldn't stop until he had called her brother, Alex. She'd just have to work it out on her own.

She had healed others. Why couldn't she heal herself?

She drew her knees up to her chest. She was trying. Lord knew, she was trying.

IN THE IMMENSE OPEN AREA OF THE CABIN, LUKE HAD kept watch on Catherine's closed door as morning gave way to the afternoon. He had taken a shower and changed clothes since he returned, but he was reasonably sure Catherine hadn't come out during that time. Nor had he heard her make a sound. Something more than a missing wallet was going on, an idiot could see that. He just couldn't figure out what.

Obviously Daniel didn't have the entire story either. Thinking back on their brief conversation of the night before, he had initially been concerned, then amused. Did his concern have a deeper reason than the obvious?

Luke picked up the phone and dialed. He had to go through the maid, then the nanny, who had to have the easiest job in the world since there weren't more than a couple of hours out of a day that Daniel Jr. wasn't in his parents' sight and in their care, and finally Higgins before he spoke to Daniel.

"You have more security than the president," Luke said, a hint of frustration in his voice.

Amused laughter came through the line. "Be glad you got through. Since Madelyn has gone back to work, Saturday is our day to spend with just the three of us."

Shaking his head, Luke sat on the edge of the tufted corner of the circular sofa. It was difficult at times to believe that a man who was once so immersed in business as Daniel had been, had made a complete turnabout for his family. "So what's on the agenda today?"

"I finally talked Madelyn into letting me teach little Daniel how to swim."

Luke chuckled as a picture of the five-month-old cherubic Daniel Jr., who kept a toothless smile on his happy face, flashed into his mind. "Daniel, you never cease to amaze me."

"Sometimes I surprise myself. Fatherhood is as scary as hell, but I wouldn't have missed it for the world." His voice took on a serious note. "How are things coming with the case you're handling for me?"

"We've narrowed it down to three prospects. My agents are in the three cities now. We should have things finalized within two weeks, three at the latest."

"Good. I don't have to tell you how much this means to me and to them."

"No. That's why my best people are working on this."

"I've always known I could count on you. By the way, how are things at the cabin with you and Catherine?"

Luke debated how to answer the question. He wanted answers, but he didn't want to invade her privacy. "Fine, but we had some problems. Someone decided to go hunting and shot a wolf hybrid Catherine had befriended. Although Richard said the animal will be fine, she's pretty upset."

"Damn," Daniel hissed, then hurriedly said, "Sorry, Madelyn. I didn't mean to say that. It just slipped out. Little Daniel is too smart and too well-mannered to repeat what I said. Aren't you, son? You wouldn't get your father in trouble by saying such a bad word, would you? See, he's grinning. That means no."

Luke chuckled. "You better hope and pray he doesn't."

"Amen," Daniel said, then asked, "I don't suppose you caught whoever did it?"

"No. Johnny Wesley was here when it happened and tracked them to where a four-wheeler was parked on the road."

"Why was he there?"

"I answered the phone and Catherine's agent became

worried about her. The sergeant sent Johnny out in less than three minutes," Luke told him. "I still haven't decided if it was because of your clout or her agent's that got things moving so fast."

"Don't cut yourself short. The officials at the state police department respect you a great deal since you've helped them track down criminals who thought that they would get lost in the mountains," Daniel reminded him.

"I guess. I just hate that Catherine was there when we found the animal."

"That must have been tough. She's always had a soft spot for animals and children," Daniel commented. "I never thought anything like this would happen when I sent her up to the cabin to take a break. She certainly didn't need this after all the things she has had to go through."

"What things?" Luke asked, knowing his voice was sharp and unable to do anything about it.

"I don't guess she'd mind me telling you. Some woman she had given testimony against in a case of neglect blamed Catherine instead of her own behavior for the judge removing her children from the home. She's an alcoholic. She got drunk again and attacked Catherine with her kid's baseball bat as she was coming home one night."

An expletive sizzled from his lips as Luke surged to his feet. "What happened?"

"Fortunately, Catherine can take care of herself. It helped that her next-door neighbor was out walking his dog and helped subdue the woman."

"Where is the woman now?"

"In a rehab center. Beside the night of her arrest, she never spent another day in jail."

Luke's grip on the phone tightened. "How the hell did that happen?"

"The woman came from a background of money and

hired herself a high-priced lawyer who was able to get the charges reduced by saying that taking her children had made her act irrationally; she had joined AA and was under treatment and wasn't a threat to anyone since she was now under care."

"That's one of the reasons I left the FBI. Too many loopholes once you bring the criminals in. Innocent people have to lock themselves behind bars while the criminals run free."

"I hear you. Do me a favor and watch out for Catherine. She's good people."

"Consider it done. I'll let you get back to swimming lessons. Bye."

"Bye."

Luke slowly hung up the phone, his troubled gaze once again going to Catherine's closed bedroom door. He had been right on both counts. Something more than the wallet was bothering Catherine and Daniel didn't have a clue. The bad thing was, neither did Luke.

CATHERINE WOKE TO THE SOFT, BUT PERSISTENT sound of tapping on the door of her bedroom. By the lengthening of shadows in her room, she realized it was late afternoon. Her eyes widened. Abruptly she sat up in the bed. How could she have gone to sleep with her life in turmoil? The answer came instantly. Easy. You've been sleeping badly for weeks. Your brain decided it was time to rest.

"Catherine? Catherine, are you all right?"

She frowned at the concern she heard in Luke's deep voice. She thought he would be ready to throw her out long before now. "Yes, just a moment." Throwing her legs over the side of the bed, she answered the door.

She'd forgotten how tall he was, how wide his shoulders were. She caught herself before lifting her hand to touch him, to draw strength from him. A woman could take comfort in the arms of such a powerful man and never have to be afraid again.

"You sure you're all right?"

She turned toward her suitcase. She really had to get a grip. In the past, she had never needed a man to fight her battles and she didn't need one now. "Yes. I must have dozed off. I'll be out of your way in no time." When she turned he was standing in her path. She jumped and stepped back abruptly, her fingers clutching the case.

Black eyes studied her intently. "Sorry, I didn't mean to startle you."

She moistened her lips. "You move quietly for a big man."

"Are you afraid to stay here with me?"

Her indignant gaze lifted to meet his. "Of course not."

"Then why are you in such a hurry to leave?" he asked reasonably.

"You didn't expect anyone here and neither did I," she answered.

"That's a fact, but the cabin has over thirty-five hundred square feet, we should be able to stay out of each other's way until tomorrow."

"Tomorrow?" she repeated with a frown.

"I have to get back to Santa Fe."

"You don't look too happy about it," she commented.

"I'm not." His mother probably had number twenty-eight already lined up.

"You want to talk about it?"

"Not especially. At least not on a empty stomach. How about we go into town and get something to eat?"

It was tempting. Unbelievably so. The sooner she left Luke, the better. "No, thank you."

His gaze narrowed. "I knew you didn't trust me."

"I do trust you. I just think I should leave."

"You're running from something, Catherine. If not from me, then what is it?"

She barely managed to stifle her gasp. "I'm not running from anything," she blurted, but her heart was pounding, her palms were sweaty.

"Glad to hear it." Taking her suitcase from her hand, he tossed it on the bed. "Now that that's settled, let's go get something to eat."

She looked from her suitcase back to Luke. "Did anyone ever tell you, you're pushy and overbearing?"

"Too many times to count." He reached for her hand.

Used to his take-charge manner by now, she edged back. "The only place I'm going is to find a hotel."

"With the beginning of tourist season upon us, you must be kidding," he said with a note of disbelief in his voice. "Hotels are booked months in advance around here."

"I'm sure I can find something," she said, holding on to her plan to leave.

"What if you don't?"

"I'll cross that bridge when I come to it."

Hands on his narrow hips, he stared down at her. "I won't even say the word, but you know what you're being."

Her chin lifted. "I am not being idiotic."

"Could have fooled me. I wonder what Daniel would have to say about your leaving?"

"What?" She was beginning to sound like a parrot and she didn't like it one bit.

"Since he asked me to look after you, I'd have to let him know you'd left without knowing where you were going to sleep tonight."

Uneasiness swept through her. "When did you talk to Daniel?"

"While you were asleep."

She swallowed. "Why would he ask you to take care of me?" she asked, fear mixed with desperation in her voice.

Without thought his hands gently settled on her shoulders. He stared down into her wide eyes. "I told him about the shooting and that you were upset that your wolf hybrid was wounded. What else was there for me to say?"

She looked away. "N-nothing."

His hands flexed on her shoulders, then fell. He had interrogated enough people to know when one was lying. "So if you don't want Daniel upset with me, you'll stay in the cabin. At least have dinner with me and think about it. I may not be the best company, but it's better than sitting alone in a hotel room . . . that is, if you're lucky enough to find one."

Time on her hands was exactly what she didn't want. But Luke was too perceptive. "If hotel rooms are difficult to obtain, I should be looking for one instead of wasting time eating."

"What do you plan to do, drive to every hotel and ask if they have a vacancy?"

"There must be a centralized booking agency," she said.

"Not that I know of, but it still comes back to why you're in such a hurry to leave." He glanced around. "You don't like your room?"

"It's beautiful."

"It's too remote here?"

"That's the reason I came here."

"Then I ask you again, why are you leaving?"

She shoved her hand through her hair. She bet he'd passed the interrogation classes with straight A's. "After this morning, it's not so remote any longer."

A muscle leaped in his bronzed jaw. "Whoever it was is not coming back. But if you're afraid to be alone after I'm gone, I'm sure, Mary, the housekeeper, would be willing to stay up here with you."

"I'm not afraid. I can take care of myself," she said,

incensed that he thought she needed someone to watch over her. Worse, that her erratic behavior had given him cause.

"You don't have to convince me. Not many women or men could have handled themselves as well as you did last night."

Catherine stared up at him in surprise and delight at the unexpected compliment. She had thought he'd never forgive her for what happened. If she didn't know better, she'd think he was trying to bolster her courage. She took a deep breath. Perhaps he was. It all came down to how much more of her self-respect she was willing to sacrifice.

"If we're going out to eat, I'm taking a bath and changing clothes first."

Although his expression remained unchanged, relief rushed through him. "We'll check on your hybrid on the way. I'll wait outside."

Catherine stared at the closed door and hoped she was making the right decision. She didn't want to be alone, but her mind was developing the annoying habit of creating little fantasies where Luke was concerned. There could never be anything between them.

She had to remember that. Forgetting would be disastrous.

After showering, Catherine dressed in caramel-colored gabardine pants and an ecru-colored blouse, then slipped on low-heeled shoes. She tried to tell herself that she didn't care what Luke thought of her, but she watched his face carefully as she came out of the bedroom.

"Glad you didn't take all day. I'm starved."

She wanted to clobber him, but she was the one who needed the bash over the head for letting herself be concerned over Luke's opinion of her. Men generally occupied very little of her time or thoughts. "I'm not promising anything about staying."

"Good enough." He clasped her elbow and headed out the door.

THE HYBRID WAS DOING AS WELL AS COULD BE expected, Dr. Youngblood reported. The animal didn't like his cage and made sure anyone who came within hearing distance knew it. Once again Luke worked his magic and had the animal literally eating out of his hand. He frowned when Catherine bent down beside him and stroked the animal's head.

They were outside before he said, "One day you're going to try and tame the wrong animal."

She glanced at him and again thought of the easy way he moved, like a wild healthy animal, and was glad he didn't know how close to the truth he really was. Forcing herself not to stare at the revealing way his well-worn jeans fit his long, muscular legs and hips, she climbed inside the truck and fastened her seat belt. She definitely was not spending the night with Luke.

LUKE PULLED INTO THE CROWDED PARKING LOT OF THE Red Cactus near the Plaza in downtown Santa Fe. The casually elegant cafe was housed in a territorial-style adobe house built in 1867. Indian corn and chile ristras dangled in the windows. The two-story structure with its traditional flat roof already had a line forming outside.

Getting out of the truck, Luke went around and opened Catherine's door. "Come on."

Grabbing her red jacket, she got out of the truck, frowning at the fast-growing line that curved around to the small garden patio on the north side of the restaurant where customers were outside laughing and dining. "Maybe we should have called for reservations."

Luke closed the door and reached for her elbow. "There's always a table for us."

"Us?"

"My brother owns the Red Cactus," he said, holding her arm to steer her across the busy parking lot.

Even with her long legs she had difficulty keeping up with him. "Does your family eat here that often?"

"Depends. Mostly I get mine to go." He waited until a Jeep passed, then assisted her onto the sidewalk.

"He's losing a lot of money that way," Catherine said.

Luke led her around the line forming out the double wooden doors. "So his accountant tried to tell him."

"What did your brother say?" She smiled at the customers who glared at them as they passed through the open brick courtyard. Luke didn't seem to notice.

"Threatened to fire him."

As soon as the hostess saw them, she smiled and picked up two menus in the shape of red cacti. The menu cactus had a black Stetson tilted to one side and a black bandanna around its spiny neck.

"Good evening, Mr. Grayson, welcome back to the Red Cactus. Your table is ready." She turned to a slim, attractive woman with straight black hair. "Nacona will show you to your table."

"This way," she said pleasantly.

Catherine glanced appreciatively around the restaurant as she followed the young woman. The floor was richly tiled, the decor distinctive Southwestern with large potted and hanging plants. The tables were solid wood and the benches and chairs upholstered in a beautiful red and black weave. The napkins were cloth. Thick white adobe walls were decorated with museum quality Indian art. On the way to their table they passed two kiva fireplaces.

Nacona stopped beside an oversized booth in the back of the restaurant. Catherine slid into one of the seats, but made no motion to move over farther for Luke. He took the hint and sat across from her. Removing the RESERVED sign, Nacona handed them their menus. "Your waitress will be with you in a moment. Can I get you anything to drink in the meantime?"

"They have some excellent house wine and mixed drinks," Luke said.

She debated only a moment. If Luke or his family had a problem with alcohol, they wouldn't serve the beverage. "Margarita."

"Make mine the usual," Luke told the woman.

"I'll be back with those in a minute."

Catherine leaned against the high back of the large wooden booth that almost dwarfed her. "That was done rather smoothly."

"Morgan's idea. He didn't want anyone getting upset because we were seated ahead of them."

Catherine thought for a minute. "The lawyer."

"Right." Luke leaned forward, placing his folded arms on the scarred wooden surface of the table. "You seem to know a lot about me, and I know very little about you."

Usually she didn't like talking about herself, but somehow talking to Luke, when he wasn't being arrogant, was easy. "Thanks," she said, accepting her drink. She took a sip, her tongue licking the salt from around her mouth. *Fantastic.* "If you want to be bored."

"I'm willing to chance it," he said, hoping she didn't flick her tongue out like that again. Made him think he'd like to lean across the table and taste her mouth, taste everything on her. He gulped his iced tea.

CHAPTER FIVE

THE WAITRESS ARRIVED BEFORE CATHERINE COULD SAY anything. Dressed in an off-the-shoulder white blouse and slim, short black skirt, the young woman was as friendly as the other women had been and just as slender and shapely. Idly, Catherine wondered if having a good figure was a requirement for employment. She hoped Luke's brother wasn't that superficial.

"Hello, Luke, Miss. Are you ready to order or do you need more time?"

"Hi, Paula," Luke greeted, then asked Catherine, "You ever been to New Mexico before or had any Southwestern foods?"

"No, but I like some Tex-Mex and Cal-Mex dishes . . . if they aren't too spicy," she clarified.

"New Mexican cuisine is similar, but not the same. It's a result of the Southwestern history. The native Indians taught the Spanish about corn and the Spanish reciprocated with their chiles. So an integral ingredient of the food here is the red or green chile. Although the food can get hot, you probably won't find a dish as spicy as the Mexican jalapeño."

Catherine lifted a delicate brow. "Are we talking blow-torch versus furnace?"

Luke almost smiled. "Cautious, huh?"

"I don't think those chiles ristras dangling from the

walls are just for decoration," she said mildly, glancing at her menu before looking across the table at Luke. "What's good without being spicy?"

"Everything."

Her head came up at the sound of the intriguingly sexy male voice. The face didn't disappoint. High cheekbones stretched over golden bronzed skin. His eyes were as black as the thick hair on his well-shaped head. He had lips that could probably talk a woman into giving him just about anything. From his six-foot-plus height, he gazed warmly down at her.

He was dressed in creased blue jeans and a melon-colored Polo shirt that stretched over a muscular chest. Polished red eel-skin boots were on his feet. She didn't need but one guess to know he was Luke's brother. A younger, more care-free version, who obviously knew the effect his smile had on women.

Making women's knees weak must be a family trait.

"Aren't you going to introduce us, Luke?" Brandon asked, not taking his eyes from Catherine.

"Don't you have some paperwork to do or something?" Luke didn't know why, but he didn't like the way Catherine was staring at Brandon.

"It can wait." Brandon's smile broadened as he extended his hand. "Since my brother seems to have forgotten his manners, I'm Brandon Grayson."

Catherine lifted her hand and found it clasped in Brandon's larger one, but unlike when she had shaken Luke's, there was no spark. At least she was selective in her idiocy. "Catherine Stewart, and you have a fantastic place here."

"Thanks." Still holding her hand, Brandon sat down beside her. She had no choice but to scoot over. "I'd be honored to give you a tour."

"She's not interested in a tour, Brandon," Luke said tightly.

Surprised by the irritation in Luke's voice, she simply stared at him.

"Don't mind him," Brandon told her. "I guess he forgot to eat his prunes this morning."

"Brandon," Luke growled.

Catherine burst out laughing.

The bubbling sound increased Luke's annoyance. Ten seconds and Brandon had her laughing. He'd had to practically drag her here.

"Save the jokes until after we eat," Luke said with a disgusted grunt.

"If a woman as beautiful as Catherine was with me, the last thing I would think about was food."

Catherine blinked, not sure how to respond.

"So what are you doing later on tonight when you dump the old man?"

She laughed again. She had learned the hard way how to distinguish the difference between a man who was really interested, a man out for a quickie, or one playfully flirtatious. Brandon was definitely the latter. "You and Dr. Youngblood must keep the women very happy in Santa Fe."

Brandon grinned brashly back at her. "We do try."

"Cut it out, Brandon," Luke warned. He'd forgotten Brandon was supposed to "tempt" any woman Luke brought into the restaurant. "You're making Catherine uncomfortable. She's not number twenty-eight."

Her curious gaze went from Brandon to Luke. "Number twenty-eight?"

Brandon's went from Catherine's to Luke. "You mean this is a real date?"

"Of course not."

"No."

Catherine and Luke's denial came almost at the same time, then they stared at each other. She was the first to look away. "I think I'm what's considered as a charity case."

"That's a crock and you know it," Luke bit out.

Catherine faced the argument head on. "We wouldn't be here if you weren't trying to watch over me and make me stay at the cabin, and you know it."

"We spent last night together. I can't see why you're in such a hurry to leave when you don't even know where you're going."

She sucked in her breath sharply. Her cheeks heated. "It's not the way it sounded," she told an amused Brandon. "We only met last night at the cabin. I didn't know Luke was coming and he didn't know I was there."

Now Luke was the one who shifted uncomfortably in his seat. "Daniel sent her."

A grin spread across Brandon's boyishly handsome face. "Curiouser and curiouser. That must have been an interesting surprise for both of you."

Luke grunted again.

Catherine bit her lower lip.

"Do I draw my own conclusions or is someone going to tell me what happened?" Brandon asked, folding his arms.

"She pulled a gun on me."

Catherine felt her face heating again. "I didn't know who you were."

"Sounds like a perfectly normal reaction to me. You should be happy Catherine isn't the trigger-happy type," Brandon said mildly. "I'm pleased that you have no new bullet holes in you."

"New?" Catherine asked, her voice strained, her body beginning to shake.

Luke frowned at his brother. "Long ago and forgotten."

Distressed eyes stared at him. "I'm so sorry I pointed the gun at you. It must have brought back horrible memories."

Luke leaned over the table, his hand reaching for hers. Nothing was as terrible as seeing her upset again. He didn't think until later how easily and naturally she placed hers in his. "You were justified in what you did. Only next time, put a clip in the chamber."

"I've seen what bullets can do to the flesh." She bit her lower lip. "I thought I could bluff my way through."

"Did your instructor tell you to bluff?" Luke asked, his voice terse.

"No. He cautioned me not to pull the gun unless I was sure I needed it, but if I did, be ready to use it," she admitted.

"Damn right," Luke said with conviction. "Bluffing works better if you have something to back you up. Next time put the clip in."

Her gaze fell, her hands trembled in his. "I hope there won't be a next time."

"You sound as if you think there might be."

Her eyes widened. She snatched her hand back. "Oh, no," she quickly assured him. "I was just speaking in general." Hurriedly she picked up the menu and turned to Brandon. "I haven't eaten all day, what do you suggest?"

"Why didn't you say something earlier?" Brandon came out of the booth; gone was the playfulness and in its place the efficient, caring restaurateur. He rattled off several dishes and ended by saying, "It's all freshly prepared on a mesquite-wood grill."

Catherine opted for a traditional meal while Luke went for Southwestern. Brandon left the table only to return shortly with a basket of tortilla chips, salsa, a sampler of three salad specials—shrimp and shredded-crab salad, egg noodle salad, and artichoke heart/calamari salad— homemade rolls and cinnamon-honey butter.

"Nibble on this until I can get your food prepared," Brandon said, then he was gone again.

Catherine stared at all the food, then at Brandon in amazement. "He's going to cook our food?"

"Yeah. He often does when it's as busy as it is tonight," Luke said scooping up a generous amount of salsa on a chip. "Claims it keeps him from getting rusty. The family figured it's because he doesn't like putting our orders ahead of his other customers' or for us to wait."

Catherine dipped a forkful of the egg noodle salad into the sesame-seed sauce. *Fabulous.* "He's funny, conscientious, a fantastic cook, and good looking. He's going to make some woman a very good husband."

Luke went still. "You looking to fill the position?"

Catherine blinked, then stared at him across the table. "Of course not. I just met your brother."

"If you knew him longer?" He didn't know why he couldn't let the subject rest.

She placed her fork on her salad plate. "Set your mind at ease. I have no intention of marrying your brother or anyone else."

Luke saw the hurt and something else in her brown eyes and sought to make amends. "Sorry. Guess I'm touchy on the subject of marriage."

"You want to talk about it?"

He could easily see why she was a psychologist, and it wasn't just because she was easy to look at. Her warm brown sincere eyes and caring manner would lure almost anyone to spill their guts. He wasn't the talkative type, but he owed her an explanation. "Ever since Dominique's wedding my mother has been parading women in front of me trying to marry me off."

"So that's what the number twenty-eight meant?"

He nodded. "I got the impression from some of them that I could be a clone to Bigfoot and they'd still happily say 'I do.'"

"Have you told your mother how you feel?"

"In every way I know how, but she has it in her head that I'd be happier married, and married is what I'm going to be." He sighed. "She loves me."

"What does your father say?"

"I lost my father when I was eight."

Sadness showed in her deep brown eyes and spilled over in her voice. "Luke, I'm sorry. I didn't know."

Luke folded his arms on the table. "The memories are good ones so I don't mind remembering. My father was one of the first black commercial pilots with a major airline. On his third trip to Brazil his plane went down. I'll never forget the look on my mother's face when she got off the phone or the feeling of helplessness. Since I was the eldest of my three brothers and sister, Dad had always left me in charge and somehow I had failed."

"You were just a child," she told him.

"As an adult I realize that, but then, all I wanted to do was make it better for my mother and my brothers and sister." His hand atop the table flexed. "We prayed to my mother's god and to my father's that he'd survive the crash and come home to us. An airline representative came the next morning. They'd located the wreckage in the mountains. Three people survived out of one hundred and seventy-four. My father wasn't one of them."

Without thinking, she reached across the table to grasp his hand. "Oh, Luke."

His hand closed over hers. "I was angry at the world, the gods I prayed to. My father was a good man, he shouldn't have had to die on a mountain half a world away." His thumb stroked across the top of her hand. "I'd hear Mama weeping late at night so we wouldn't hear her cry. That was the hardest, knowing she was hurting and I couldn't help her because she didn't want to upset us. But because of her shielding us, we couldn't help each other."

Catherine thought of her shielding her family from her own secrets. "She only did what she thought was best."

"I know, but that didn't make it any better. So the next time I heard her, I woke up my brothers and sister and took them into her bedroom. Before she could wipe the tears away we were all in bed with her crying ourselves, but in the midst of the tears, we started remembering the good times with Dad, remembering how he loved us and how he would have wanted us to be happy.

"Morgan went to get the picture album and the tears turned to laughter. There would always be sorrow, a certain emptiness for his sudden passage, but we'd always be thankful that God and the Master of Breath had allowed him to be with us for as long as he was. You remember and go on. Family helped."

"Children need close relationships and assurance."

"So do adults," he told her, his gaze direct. "Any friend of Daniel's is a friend of mine. If you need help with anything, you only have to ask."

She came upright in her seat, dragging her hand back with her. "I can take care of myself."

This time he wasn't going to be sidetracked. "In most things you probably can, but sometimes we run into situations we aren't equipped to handle."

"I can take care of myself," she repeated for her own benefit as much as for his.

"All I'm saying is that I'm here." He glanced around to see Brandon coming toward them. "Our food is ready."

Aware that Luke suspected she was hiding something and watched her, Catherine thought she would be too uneasy to eat any of the steak she had ordered. But after one delicious bite of the tender beef, she realized how hungry she was. As she ate, she began to relax. Luke not asking any more probing questions helped. So did the soft muted music. She even let Luke coax her into sampling a tiny bite of his grilled cactus dipped in ramesco sauce. His lips twitched at the distasteful expression on her face.

"It's an acquired taste." He was about to take another bite of his filet when the hairs on the back of his neck stood up. He looked around. Three women were heading straight for him. His mother was one of them.

Although he knew there was only a thick adobe wall behind him, he found himself looking for an avenue of escape anyway.

"Luke, what is it? What's the matter?"

"Trouble" was all he was able to say before the women arrived. Slowly he came to his feet and nodded in greeting.

"Luke," a woman in her early sixties wearing a herringbone tweed jacket atop a gray cashmere turtleneck and ankle-length black pleated skirt greeted him absently. Her main attention was on Catherine. "Dr. Stewart, it really is you," she gushed effusively. "I'm Amanda Poole, Women's League president. I hope you will forgive the intrusion, but when one of the committee members called to tell me that she saw you enter the restaurant with Luke, I simply had to rush right over."

Smiling, Catherine stood. She truly enjoyed meeting her reading public. "I'm glad you did, Mrs. Poole."

"Please call me Amanda," she said, pressing a hand to her breasts. "The lecture series you're doing on parenting has been one of the most well-received we've ever had. The auditorium at St. John's College is completely sold out."

"I'm always pleased to hear the attendance is up. It's all about the children."

"You're so right," Amanda agreed.

"Good evening, Dr. Stewart," greeted a tall elegant woman. "Luke."

"Hello, Mama," Luke said, wondering why she didn't seemed pleased to be there. He thought she'd be doing back-flips to find him with a woman.

"Oh, forgive me," Amanda said, flushing to the roots of her red dyed hair. "Dr. Stewart, I'd like to introduce two of the key people of our organization, Ruth Grayson, past president of the Women's League, and Gloria Harris, the program chairman."

Catherine's gaze immediately went to Luke's mother. Tall, imposing, reserved. As with Brandon, the family resemblance was strong. She remained a striking woman despite having a son in his early thirties. Coal black hair hung down her back in a thick braid. Her trim figure was well-dressed in a textured brown jacket, denim shirt, and brown trousers.

And she acted as if the last place she wanted to be was standing there. Catherine's disappointment was immense. "I'm pleased to meet you, Mrs. Grayson. Mrs. Harris."

Pretty, petite, in her mid-twenties, and stylish in a pale lavender pantsuit, Gloria Harris laughed, her ringless left hand combing back her short, auburn hair. "It's Miss. I'm waiting for the right man to ask me."

Catherine thought she saw Luke grimace out of the corner of her eyes; she knew she saw his mother's lips press together tightly in disapproval. At least she wasn't the only woman his mother deemed unsuitable. "I'm sure it's only a matter of time."

"I'm hoping," Gloria said, her gaze going back to Luke.

"It's been nice meeting you, but we don't want to keep you from your dinner," Ruth Grayson said, grabbing hold of Amanda's arm. "Goodbye, Luke. Dr. Stewart."

"Wait, Ruth," Amanda said, pulling free with a frown that quickly disappeared as she faced Catherine. "I'm sure Dr. Stewart doesn't mind us taking a little more of her time."

"Not at all," Catherine said, trying not to let it bother her that for some reason Luke's mother didn't want to be around her. "Would you like to sit down?"

"Yes, thank you," Gloria said, going to Luke's seat. He had no choice but to sit back down. She quickly scooted over beside him. Across from them, Amanda was doing the same with Catherine. Ruth gradually sank down in the seat beside the other woman.

"It's such an honor and a privilege meeting you," Amanda said. "I can hardly believe you're actually here."

"Thank you for saying so, I'm looking forward to presenting the workshop."

"My grandchildren have all of your books," Amanda continued. "The youngest, Michelle, is four and won't go to bed without Mr. Rabbit."

Gloria had her own testimony. "I've bought your books as gifts for my nieces and nephews. I plan to have you autograph a set for the children I hope to have one day. Every child should have the privilege of reading or having your books read to them." She turned to Luke. "Don't you think so?"

"I haven't read her books, but I agree with you that children should read and be read to."

"I'll be too old to see them, let alone read to them, by the time you give me any grandchildren," his mother, arms folded, grumbled.

Luke's mouth flattened into a thin, straight line.

"I'm sure Luke is just waiting for the right woman, Mrs. Grayson," Gloria said, seemingly unaware that his body was stiff beside hers. "Luke is going to make a wonderful father, don't you think, Dr. Stewart?"

Something cold clutched in Catherine's heart. "I'm sure he will."

Amanda took a small white card out of her purse and handed it to Catherine. "My number if you need anything. What hotel are you staying in?"

"At a friend's house," Luke quickly told them, noting Catherine's panicked look at him.

"Anyone I know?" asked Gloria, her smile fading as she gazed from Luke to Catherine.

"You might, but Dr. Stewart prefers keeping a low profile," Luke said.

His mother's eyes narrowed as she studied her son, then a nervous Dr. Stewart. She stood. "Of course she does. It was nice meeting you. Good night."

Sending an annoyed glance at Ruth, Amanda nevertheless stood. "Do you need someone to pick you up?"

"No, I have a car," Catherine said.

"Well then, we'll see you Tuesday morning at nine thirty in the auditorium of St. John's College."

"Good night, Luke." Gloria clearly hated to leave.

"Did you come together?" Luke asked.

"No, we came in separate cars," Amanda answered.

"It's getting dark. I'll better see you to your cars." He stood. The parking lot was well-lit, but it never hurt to be cautious.

"You don't have to, Luke," his mother said in a rush.

He frowned at her strange behavior. "Mama, you know one of us always walks out with you." He turned to Catherine. "I'll be back. Make sure you don't eat the rest of my grilled cactus."

Up went her eyebrow. "I'll try to restrain myself."

IT WAS A GOOD THING GLORIA COULDN'T READ MINDS, Luke thought as he escorted the ladies to their cars. Her senseless chatter was giving him a headache. He was more than happy to open the door to her Lexus and see her on her way. Mrs. Poole's Infiniti was only a few cars away. "Good night, Mrs. Poole."

"Good night, Amanda," Ruth said. "Luke, you better get back inside."

"Ruth, for someone who worked so hard to get Dr. Stewart here, you're certainly in a hurry to leave," Amanda said.

"If I didn't know you better, I'd think you were either sorry you invited her here or wanted to keep her all to your family and yourself."

Luke tensed. "Mama invited her here?"

"We'll talk about it later, Amanda," Ruth said.

Obviously Amanda wanted to talk about it now. "Indirectly," Mrs. Poole told Luke. "When your mother put Dr. Stewart's name into submission as the speaker for our annual conference, we didn't think we had a chance of getting her here. She has credentials a mile long and commands high dollars on the lecture circuit, which she routinely signs over to charities for children. But less than a week after Gloria contacted her, her agent called to accept the invitation." Amanda's smile returned.

"Other women's leagues around the country were green with envy. Ruth was as elated as the rest of us. That's why I don't understand this sudden change." She turned to Ruth. "I wouldn't have called and told you Gloria and I were going to meet her if I had known you'd act this way."

Luke stared down at his mother. She refused to meet his gaze.

"I just thought it impolite to disturb her while she was eating," Ruth defended.

"She didn't seem to mind," Amanda said.

"What else could she do? What would you have said in such a situation?" Ruth asked.

"Oh, dear," Amanda said, obviously distressed. "Luke, do you think we offended her?"

Now his mother was looking at him. He ought to ignore the plea for help in her eyes and let her sink. The thought was gone as quickly as it had come. "In the short time I've known Dr. Stewart she's been gracious and caring, but tonight was the first time she's eaten all day."

"Oh, dear," the older woman repeated. "She probably thinks we're gauche."

"She'll think the truth," Luke said with one of his rare smiles because Amanda looked so startled. "That you admire her work so much, you couldn't wait to meet her."

"You really think so?"

"I'm positive," he reassured. He genuinely liked the effusive woman, who, despite her husband's millions, remained down-to-earth and unassuming. "Cath—Dr. Stewart isn't shy about expressing her opinion. If she hadn't wanted to talk with you, she wouldn't have invited you to sit down. But I think Mama was right in rushing you along."

Amanda looked apologetically at Ruth. "I'm sorry, Ruth. I should have known better."

"Don't worry about it, Amanda. Your enthusiasm was genuine and warm," Ruth said. "Everyone wants to be appreciated for their work. I'm sure Dr. Stewart was pleased."

Amanda stopped clutching the link chain shoulder strap of her black quilted bag. "I do admire her."

"That came through beautifully," Ruth told her. "Now, you better get home. Good night."

"Good night," Amanda said and got into her car.

The silver car had barely straightened before Luke's mother said, "Good night" and hurried away. He let her get to her 4×4, then placed himself in front of the door. "Luke, hadn't you better get back to Dr. Stewart?"

"Not until I find out how you did it."

She lifted puzzled eyes to his. "Did what?"

"Worked it so that Catherine would be number twenty-eight."

CHAPTER SIX

"LUKE, I'VE ASKED YOU NOT TO REFER TO OUR GUESTS in such a demeaning and impersonal manner," his mother chastised.

"They're not my guests, they're yours, and you're stalling."

She unnecessarily straightened the collar of his blue oxford shirt. "I have no reason to stall."

"Then tell me how you did it."

She let out a weary sigh. "You have such a suspicious mind. I should have never let you read all those mystery novels when you were growing up."

"Catherine is in the restaurant waiting, and I'm not leaving until I have an answer."

"You're also stubborn."

"I learned from the master."

Her shoulders slumped in defeat. "The committee needed a speaker. I had seen Dr. Stewart during an interview on an early morning talk show and I thought she'd be perfect."

"It helped that she was young and single," Luke said tersely.

"It helped that she was intelligent, a noted child psychologist, and a distinguished author."

Luke stuck to his argument. "How did you find out the connection to Daniel?"

"She mentioned on the show that she was from Boston and had grown up in an affluent neighborhood. I just took a chance that Felicia might know her."

"I might have known Aunt Felicia was in on this, too." He snorted. "Number fifteen was from Boston. Her nose was so high up, if it had rained she would have drowned like a turkey."

"Luke, that's enough. Karolyn was a wonderful young lady."

"I don't care how wonderful any of them are. This has got to stop, and it stops now." He leaned closer. "If I get one inkling that there will be a number twenty-nine, I'm moving my office to Phoenix."

Her black eyes widened in fear and distress. "You'd leave your poor old mother alone?"

"If one of us called you old, you'd brain us. You're sixty-two and in better shape and healthier than some women half your age. Besides, Morgan and the others would be here if you needed anything."

"But I've always depended on you."

Luke couldn't deny that. Since his father had died, Luke had been the man of the house, the leader. She'd discussed everything with him. He'd known about her plans to leave her close-knit family in Oklahoma and teach at St. John's College in Santa Fe before anyone else knew. The college, as a drawing point to the young music teacher, offered tuition remission for her five children. She hadn't hesitated. Education was valued. She'd always put her children first.

"I'd come if you called."

Her palm rested on his chest. "But it wouldn't be the same."

He hugged her to him. He couldn't think of anything else to do. "I'd miss you, too. Why don't you start on Morgan? He wouldn't suspect a thing."

Lifting her head, she smiled. "That's an idea. But you've always been the leader."

"So you figured if you married me off, the rest would fall in line."

"Let's say it wouldn't be as difficult."

He groaned. "Mama, it's not dignified for a grown man to beg, but I'm begging you. Please stop this."

She brushed his hair back from his face as if he were a little boy. "Don't I always do what's best for my children?"

"That's what I'm afraid of."

LUKE ALWAYS THOUGHT THE BEST WAY TO SAY SOME-thing was straight out and up front. As soon as he slid into the booth seat he said, "You're number twenty-eight!"

"What!" Catherine's eyes widened. Abruptly she set her drink down. "That's impossible. Your mother doesn't even like me. She couldn't wait to leave."

"All an act to throw me off. You're number twenty-eight, all right." He continued when the disbelief on her face didn't disappear. "She got Aunt Felicia to help get you here."

The swift rise of elation that his mother liked her was quickly drowned out by damning reality. If Luke's mother really knew about her, Catherine would be the last person she'd choose for her son. The reality made the fantasy that much more painful. Catherine did what she always did when she was cornered. "Well, she can just go out and get number twenty-nine."

"Number twenty-nine won't show up until the coast is clear," Luke said with an irritated twist of his mouth. "One thing about my mother, she always gives the women a clear playing field. Yesterday afternoon I put number twenty-seven on the plane. She probably didn't expect you until Monday evening."

Catherine shook her head. "But I don't understand. How did she expect to get us together?"

Luke shoved his plate aside. "She would have found a way. She's probably rubbing her hands together in triumph that we're already together."

"We aren't together," Catherine felt compelled to point out. "We're having dinner."

"It's a good thing she doesn't know we spent the night together," he said. "Ouch. You kicked me."

"I will again if you don't stop saying that." Digging in her purse, she pulled out her wallet and laid a twenty and a ten on the table.

Rubbing his shin, he glared across the table at her. "Put your money up. I'll take care of the bill."

She stood and pulled on her red jacket. "I'd rather pay for my own."

Studying her intently, he unhurriedly came to his feet. "Why are you so upset? I'm the one she's trying to marry off."

"You figure it out," she said. "Please take me back to the cabin. I need to find a room."

"So you're still set on leaving?"

"Yes." The word came out without hesitation. Luke was a temptation she couldn't afford.

He pulled out his wallet and laid some bills on top of hers. "You won't change your mind?"

"No."

"In that case, why don't we start looking now?"

Surprise widened her eyes, then she remembered she was number twenty-eight. He probably couldn't wait to get rid of her. Wasn't that what she wanted? "Thanks, but I can do it myself."

"I insist," he said, leading her to the back of the restaurant. "We'll say goodbye to Brandon, then I'll drive you around. I've lived in Santa Fe since I was a little boy. With my help, you won't miss one place to rent a room."

SANTA FE HAD OVER FOUR THOUSAND ROOMS IN hotels, motels, and bed and breakfast inns. Catherine knew because she had read it in a brochure she had picked up in one of the many lobbies she had gone into inquiring about vacancies. There were none. After being told the same thing, numerous times and dreading going back to see Luke's face, she had found a phone booth, taken out her calling card, and started through the yellow pages.

The answer was always the same. No vacancy.

She had traveled enough to know that there *were* rooms available, but she didn't rank high enough to get them to release one. Her mother wouldn't have any such difficulty. Her clout was what had prompted the New Mexico State Police to move so quickly. Helena had no shame in throwing United States Senator Elizabeth Stewart's name around when she wanted people to move.

If Catherine called her mother, she'd have a room in five minutes. But her mother would want an explanation as to why she had left the cabin. Telling her that she was wildly attracted to a man who was too perceptive about the troubles she was having, her trouble being her periods of forgetfulness, would only worry her and have her and the entire family on the next plane.

Sighing, Catherine left the hotel. Darkness had fallen. The night was cool. She found Luke, arms folded, Stetson tipped down over his face, in the truck. As soon as she opened the door, he kicked up the brim of his hat with his thumb and flicked on the motor in one smooth motion.

"There's another one a block over."

"It's full."

"The—"

"It's full, too."

He switched off the motor. "What do you want to do?"

Her gaze straight ahead, her hands clutching her purse, she said, "Since you don't want me at the cabin, I'm not sure."

"When did I say I didn't want you at the cabin?"

"You didn't say it exactly. But you didn't even let me go back to the cabin before you start looking for a room for me." She tried to keep the unexpected hurt from her voice, but it slipped through.

"Women." He started the motor and pulled away from the curb. "I've been trying all afternoon to get you to stay at the cabin. You were determined not to listen. I figured the only way to let you get it out of your system was to let you see there were no rooms available. I wasn't about to let you hunt on your own. As stubborn as you are, you probably would have slept in your car rather than call me to come get you."

"Come get me?"

"You have no business driving that road at night," he barked, slowing to let some jaywalking pedestrians cross the narrow streets. "Going up, the driver is on the cliff side."

He had taken her by surprise. Again. He was a man who took his responsibilities seriously. "Luke?"

"Yeah?"

"Thank you."

He did a double take. He had expected her to come out swinging. _Women._

THE NEXT MORNING CATHERINE WOKE WITH A PLAN. Showering and dressing in a loose knit white top and navy slacks, she headed for the kitchen. She was going to cook breakfast for Luke. It was the least she could do after all he had done for her.

She paused briefly in the large living area, marveling

again at how beautiful the room was. The contemporary cabin was nothing like what she had expected. The hip roof with its concentric circle of logs, the track lighting, the almond-colored walls, and overstuffed furniture was inviting and homey. But she was learning to expect the unexpected from Luke. Last night was no exception.

After they returned, she thought there would be some awkwardness about going to bed, but after making sure she didn't need anything, he had said good night and gone to his room. Since it was only a little after eight, his early retirement had been for her benefit. Feeling somewhat bereft, she had gone to her room and instead of reading or working on her next children's book, had prepared for bed.

When she climbed beneath the covers, instead of tossing and worrying, she had another surprise. She had gone to sleep. Humming, she started for the kitchen again.

Sometime during the night she had heard a guitar playing the tune on the radio. The melody was hauntingly beautiful and lonely. A lover looking for the other half of his lost soul. It was almost as if the music was playing just to her, for her. As if she were the other person being sought. Assured and strangely comforted, she had slept more peacefully than she had in months.

Shaking her head at the impracticality of her thought, she opened one of the enameled overhead cabinets with its sleek, rounded corners, her hand already reaching for the package of freshly ground coffee she had brought with her. Her heart rate accelerated when she didn't see the red package.

She knew it was there. It had to be. Only yesterday morning she had made coffee. Opening cabinet after cabinet the results was always the same. No coffee. . . .

"What are you looking for?"

Whirling around, she stared into Luke's puzzled

features. Realizing she probably looked as frantic as she felt, she turned and opened another cabinet. "The coffee."

"You're looking in the wrong place."

The silver knob of the cabinet in her hand, she turned back to him. "Where is it?"

Going to the pantry at the end of the L-shaped kitchen, he picked up a can of coffee and held it out to her. "Here you go. Mary always makes sure we're well-stocked."

She stared at the round blue and white can in growing fear. Her free hand flexed as she tried to keep her voice even. "Mine's another brand. Maybe you moved it?"

He set the can on the granite countertop, his gaze wary. "Sorry, I haven't seen it."

Somehow she knew what his answer would be. She couldn't go on like this. She had to know if she was going crazy. Slowly she closed the door. "I think I'll go into town and buy some more."

"What wrong with this coffee?"

"I like mine freshly ground," she told him, already moving out of the kitchen to her bedroom. As she suspected, he followed.

"I'll drive you then."

She had expected that also. No one could ever accuse Luke of shirking his duties. Picking up her purse, she grabbed the car keys from the dresser. "No. It won't take that long and I'll be back before you know it."

"You're going to a lot of trouble for a cup of coffee." He followed her to the garage and opened the door for her.

"Just call me eccentric." She forced a smile and got into the car. She reached for the door. Luke stood in the way. "I really have to go."

For a long moment, he stared down at her. "Be careful driving down the mountain."

"I will." The door closed. Putting the car into gear, she drove off.

CATHERINE STOPPED AT THE FIRST STORE SHE CAME TO. Hurriedly she got out of the car and went to the pay phone at the end of the graveled parking lot. For once she had change. In a matter of moments her call had gone through. Her spirits plummeted lower at the sound of Helena's recorded voice on her answering machine. Her grip on the phone tightening, Catherine began speaking as soon as the beep ended.

"Helena, it's Catherine. Everything is all right, but I need to ask you to do me a favor. It's for a friend. I need for you to check around and get me the number of a security expert. He must be discreet and able to devote his—"

"Why do you need a security expert?"

Catherine whirled. Luke stood two feet in front of her. "Why do you need a security expert?" he repeated.

Incensed, she hung up the phone. "How dare you listen to a private conversation! After all that talk about my being able to trust you, you have the audacity to follow me."

"Why do you need a private investigator?" he repeated calmly.

"None of your business."

Stepping around her, he picked up the receiver. Sliding his hand into the pocket of his jeans, he drew out some coins and laid them on the metal shelf. He deposited thirty-five cents and began dialing.

"Who are you calling?" she asked.

"Maybe your brother can give me the answer?"

"You don't know my brother's number."

"Daniel does."

She gasped, then reached around him to disconnect the phone. "Will you stay out of something that doesn't concern you?"

Removing her hand, he positioned his body in front of the phone, deposited the returned thirty-five cents, and began redialing.

"Please, don't call Daniel."

Pausing, he glanced over his shoulder. "Then tell me what's going on."

"I can't," she wailed.

He dialed another number.

"Please, Luke, don't call."

He looked over his shoulder again. His grip on the phone tightened on seeing the misery in her beautiful face. "Whatever it is, I give you my word, I'll help you, but you have to tell me."

Her hand tunneled through her hair. "I'm not sure anyone can help me."

"If you thought that, you wouldn't have wanted a private investigator."

"Desperate people do desperate things," she said.

He slammed down the phone, the noise deafening. "The woman who held a gun on me and befriended a wolf hybrid wouldn't wallow in self-pity. If there was a problem, she'd try her best to find a way out of it."

As expected, her head snapped up, her brown eyes flashed. "I should have shot you when I had the chance."

"Be thankful you didn't or you wouldn't have me to help you out of whatever mess you've gotten yourself into. Now talk or this time I'm making the call."

She didn't doubt him for a minute. However, she still couldn't make herself say the words. "Can we go back to the cabin first?"

His narrowed eyes studied her. "Call Helena back and tell her you won't be needing a security expert after all."

"But you haven't heard what I have to say. I may need one."

"If you do, you're looking at him." He stepped aside. "Now make the call."

CATHERINE ALTERNATED BETWEEN BEING ANGRY WITH Luke and annoyed with herself as she drove back to the cabin. She had let Luke intimidate her, had caved in and let him tell her what to do. Under his watchful eye she had made the phone call back to Helena. To make matters worse, a small part of her was glad he had followed her, glad he had forced the issue. She wanted to lay her head on his broad shoulders and tell him her fears as much as she wanted to tell him to take a flying leap. Luke confused, irritated, and drew her in equal portions.

She stopped the car in front of the cabin. By the time she had reached the first step, Luke was there to take her arm. "Afraid I'll lock myself in my room?"

"The thought had crossed my mind."

The thought had crossed her mind, also. She had briefly visualized a scenario of going through the window in her bedroom and escaping. Two things had changed her mind. She had run away from enough in her life, and Luke would undoubtedly come after her. She glanced at the hard line of his jaw. He wouldn't be too happy when he found her.

In the conversation area of the great room, he released her. "Talk."

She shot him an irritated look. Impatience radiated from him. "This isn't easy for me."

"It isn't easy for me either to see you happy and playful one moment, then frantic and afraid the next."

She slowly realized something. Luke wasn't angry at her, but for her. He was a leader, a healer, he'd want to help anyone in pain or trouble. She certainly qualified on all counts. "I don't know where to start."

"The beginning usually works."

She let out a deep sigh. "It's so simple to you. Things used to be just as simple for me."

"What happened to change things?"

"Six months ago I couldn't find my wallet." Folding her arms around her she walked to the wide expanse of windows and looked out to the forest and mountains beyond. "It was in my purse that morning. I remember putting it back after paying for my gas and recording it in my date book as I do everything. But when I went to get it to pay for the lunch I'd ordered, I couldn't find it. There were several people in and out of my office at the university that morning, people I trusted. My assistant insisted on calling the campus police. They had interviewed four students who had been in my office when the teacher who uses the classroom after me came in with my wallet." She turned to him. "Everything was inside. The money, credit cards, everything."

"It could have fallen out."

"That's just it. I never take my purse to class. I have a briefcase and leave it in my office."

"Locked?"

She sighed before answering. "Yes."

"Was it locked that time?"

"Yes."

"Go on."

"Three days later I received my favorite flowers that I hadn't ordered. The next day I couldn't find my house keys. They later turned up in the door. Four days later a sterling silver bracelet I had admired in a jewelry store window, but didn't order, arrived. I thought I was having blackouts and went to see a neurologist. Everything checked out fine." She looked at him.

"I remember being so happy with the good results. I told myself I was just overworked, that I needed some time off. Unfortunately, I didn't have the time. It was in the middle of midterms. I had exams to prepare, then grade, grad students to deal with, an assistant who was often more trouble than she was worth." Her arms came to her sides.

"And as soon as that was over, I was scheduled for a series of talk shows and book signings to promote my latest book." Her voice became strained. "A week later I began hearing noises outside my house. I called the police twice and they never found anything. Afterward, I didn't call anymore."

"Is that why you learned to use a gun?"

"Yes."

"Go on."

She took heart that he was still listening. "A month ago Daniel called to ask me if it was all right to send a complete set of my books to autograph as a gift for a child's birthday party Daniel Jr. had been invited to. He must have heard the weariness in my voice. He suggested I come early and stay at the cabin. I jumped at the chance. I called my agent and told her to let the Women's League cancel my hotel reservation and that I would make my own arrangements. I came up here expecting peace and quiet."

"Only things weren't quiet."

She went to her purse and took out her red wallet. "I don't remember leaving this on the bed. I don't even remember making the bed."

Pushing up from his seat, he went to her. "Take it easy, Catherine."

"How can you tell me to take it easy when I may be going crazy?"

"You're not going crazy."

"How do you know?" she asked, her voice unsteady.

His answer was simple. "Because I've been around neurotic, schizophrenic people before and you're not one of them."

"I thought so too until six months ago."

Taking her arm, he guided her to the sofa and sat beside her. "Keep thinking it. Whoever is behind this wants you to start doubting yourself."

"Luke, you don't know how much I want to place the blame anywhere but on me." She clutched the wallet in her hands. "I had the crazy idea of installing surveillance cameras in my home. So I can see if I'm really doing all these things."

"So that's why you wanted the security expert."

"Yes."

"Then I was right to follow you."

"What do you mean?"

"You're looking at your security expert for the time you're in Santa Fe."

"What exactly is it that you do?"

"I run an investigative service called Manhunters in Santa Fe. We do everything from missing persons to forensic accounting."

She frowned. "What's that?"

"Catching the bad guy in white-collar crime. Most of the Fortune 500 companies have their own people to investigate sophisticated kickbacks and money-laundering schemes, but sometimes they run up against a dead end and call me. Either I'll go or send one of my people in," he explained, then continued by saying, "You can't wait until you go home. Whoever is doing this followed you to Santa Fe."

Eyes huge, Catherine fought to keep the fear at bay. "They were in my bedroom."

His face became stony. "While we were gone to the clinic probably. Neither one of us thought about locking the door or the gate."

"I'm sorry," she said, genuinely distressed. "I know how much this place means to you and Daniel, and to have someone invade your privacy because of me is unforgivable."

"You have nothing to be sorry for," he said flatly. "But I can guarantee the person who is behind this will."

Catherine shivered at the deadly fury in his voice. "Maybe I should move out."

"You're staying. I'm going to be watching you."

Heat lanced through her. "I thought you were leaving."

"Not anymore."

"What about your business? Your mother?"

"Security work is my business. As for my mother, this will work to my advantage. As long as she thinks we're involved, she won't try to line me up with anyone else."

"I see." Somehow she didn't like being used as a front.

He came to his feet. "I need to check your bedroom. Do you mind?"

"No. I need to take the sheets off and wash them." There was no way she could sleep on them now.

Pausing, he stared down into her drawn face. "You want to move into another bedroom?"

Standing, she glanced up to the second floor. "The other bedrooms are upstairs."

Without thought, his hand rested on her arm. "He won't find it so easy to get back in or to you. I promise."

She believed him. "I've run enough."

His hand gently squeezed. "Come on, after I finish I'll show you where the fresh linen is and help you make up your bed."

CHAPTER SEVEN

LUKE HAD DELIBERATELY GIVEN CATHERINE SOMETHING else to think about besides the person who had stolen into her room, but he had also started his own active imagination. When she went to bed that night he wanted her to think of him handling her sheets, him in her bedroom, him staring across the bed at her instead of a nameless adversary.

From her nervousness he'd succeeded. From his own heightened awareness of her, he had succeeded too well. Now, they were back in the great room. With her sitting across from him, the clear, bright sunlight behind her pouring over her, he was having a difficult time trying not to imagine how she would look with nothing but sunshine on her beautiful mahogany skin.

"Tell me about yourself and don't leave anything out," he asked, glad his voice sounded calm and normal.

She twisted uncomfortably in her seat. "Is this necessary?"

"It is if you want to find out who's doing this. Whoever is behind this has no plans to stop." He leaned forward in his seat. "Following you to Santa Fe and up here shows it. Wish I would have caught the bastard when he was in the cabin."

"It could have been a woman."

His gaze sharpened. "Why do you say that?"

She told him about Rena Bailey, the baseball bat–

wielding woman. "She's supposedly in rehab for her alcoholism. By now she should be able to go home on weekend passes. I seriously doubt that she'll stick to the end of the program. She's yet to admit she has a problem. She thinks of her two children as possessions, not the precious gifts they are."

"I'll check it out." He scribbled something on paper. "What about the men in your life?"

Her smooth brow lifted. Icicles hung from each slowly enunciated word. "I beg your pardon?"

He should have phrased the question better. He hadn't because he was too interested in the answer. A bad sign he was getting in over his head. "Are you involved with anyone at the present?"

"No."

Despite his best efforts, he couldn't deny that her answer mattered. "Your last serious relationship then?"

"That would be when I was a senior in college and engaged."

Luke's pen poised over his paper. His mouth didn't gape, but just barely. "You've got to be kidding."

"Why is it so hard to believe I was engaged?"

"That's the easy part."

"Before you ask me a lot of unnecessary questions, I haven't seen Roderick in years, he's now happily married and has three children."

There was something in her voice. Regret. Bitterness. "You still care for the guy?"

"No. Next question?"

He wanted to probe, but not for the case. He wanted to know about any guy who had ever meant anything to her. Too much. Too wrong. "How about the last guy you dated?"

"I guess that would be Lee Perkins. He's also an associate professor at my university. We dated for about a month and then decided to go our separate ways."

Black eyebrows bunched. "Who decided to call a halt to things?"

"I did."

"Why?" he probed.

"Is this necessary?"

"I wouldn't ask if it weren't necessary."

"His attitude. He's an excellent instructor, but he's always looking for a way to climb and he doesn't care at whose expense."

"He try to climb over you?" he asked, his voice biting.

"No, but he did to another professor at the university last year," she told him.

"You still dated him knowing that?"

"Give me some credit," she said, her voice sharpening with annoyance. "We went out before then."

"Are you trying to tell me that the last time you had a meaningful date with a guy was over a year ago?"

"I told you that earlier," she said, her irritation growing. "Going out with Lee was more socializing, so I'd say the last meaningful date was more like three years?"

He stared at her sitting on the sofa. She looked fragile and beautiful and desirable. Any man who saw her would want her. "Why?"

She shifted in her chair. "I've led a very busy life with teaching, writing, and unfortunately I'm often called upon by Child Protective Services or the district attorney's office as an expert witness to assess a child's needs and mental status, which makes my schedule even tighter."

"You don't like being called, do you?"

"I hate turning my back on a needy child more," she said with conviction.

Sitting back in his chair, he stared at her. Something still didn't add up. "Other women have busy schedules and still have time to date."

She picked nonexistent lint from her blue pants before lifting her head. "They must be better organized than I am. If I didn't have my date book, I'd be lost."

His interest peaked. "Where is your date book?"

"In my room."

"I'd like to see it."

"You won't be able to read it. It's in shorthand."

"I'd like to see it please."

Without bothering to slip her shoes back on, she went to her room, obtained the leather-bound burgundy book from her suitcase, and handed it to Luke, then waited for him to ask her to decipher her notes. Instead he began flipping pages.

Puzzled, she positioned herself behind him so she could read the pages over his shoulder, almost afraid of what she might see. But no, the notations were just as she had written. More pages were turned.

"You read shorthand." It was a statement.

"You learn a lot as an FBI agent." He flipped a few more pages, then looked up at her. "Will Dr. Perkins and your assistant be attending the Psychology Association Conference in Santa Fe?"

Frowning at the question, she nodded. "Yes, but why do you ask?"

"Seems you left out a few things."

She propped her hands on her hips. "I told you everything."

His gaze sharpened. "What about you being up against Perkins for department head, what about the disciplinary actions you're going to bring against your assistant for falsifying research data if she doesn't resign before the fall semester, what about this Tolliver person always in your face saying if it wasn't for your parents you wouldn't have advanced so fast and who you knocked out of the speaker's position for the psychology conference this week, what about the neighbor who helped you and now wants a more intimate form of thanks?"

She jerked the book from his hand. "Those are personal notations. You shouldn't have read them."

He surged to his feet. "How the hell else was I supposed to find out? You didn't tell me anything more than what you had to."

"I know those people. They may not be perfect, but they wouldn't do this," she said, but her voice lacked conviction.

The trembling voice got to him. "Don't." He pulled the book out of her hand, tossed it aside, then brought her into his arms in one easy motion. Clutching his shirt front, she pressed her cheek against his chest.

"They wouldn't do this."

He hated adding to her troubles, but there was no other way. "You know better than most that with the right motivation and the right circumstances, a person will do anything."

Unconsciously she snuggled closer to his hard length, seeking and finding the comfort she'd somehow always known she'd find in his strong embrace. Her eyes drifted shut in growing disillusionment. "I wanted to find out what was going on, but it's almost worse knowing someone hates me this much."

Her slim, elegant body fit perfectly against his. It seemed natural and right for his lips to brush across her hair, her cheek. Her head lifted, her lips were parted and beckoning.

Luke stared at temptation. An inch closer and he'd taste her tender lips and find out how she looked wearing nothing but sunshine. But he'd lose something he wasn't sure he could get back. He waited until her eyes opened and cleared.

Dropping his hands, he stepped back. "Their loss, not yours."

"No, mine," she mumbled and turned away.

"What?"

"Nothing." Luke wasn't for her. But somehow her body kept forgetting. Crossing to the couch, she picked up her datebook. "I thought I was being so clever. That's how they were able to find out things about me, isn't it?"

"Most likely," he said, not liking the defeated look in her face. "If not that, they would have found another way."

"Somehow that doesn't make me feel better." She held the book out to him. "I guess you'll need this."

He kept his gaze on her, noting the tiredness, the growing disillusionment. He couldn't give her much, but he could give her this. "Why don't you read it and let me know if you find anything else?" Her privacy had been invaded enough. "Start at least six months before your billfold came up missing."

Her expression cleared at the suggestion. "Thanks, Luke."

"I'll be in the office off the kitchen." He walked away feeling both the pull of her gaze and the pull of her body, and wondering how long he'd be able to resist both.

Catherine's gaze tracked Luke's well-muscled body until he disappeared around a corner. He was strength and grace and power. He was tough when he had to be, but there was also a tenderness for those not as strong. Whatever forces, whether his mother or fate, had brought them together, she'd always be thankful.

Settling down with her notebook in what was becoming her favorite spot, an oversize tan leather chair in the great room, Catherine began reading as Luke had instructed. Luke might not have wanted to invade any more of her privacy, but he expected a full report.

She started at the beginning of June of the year before. Most of it was boring. She had to wonder a few times, on reading how filled her days were, how she got everything done. Yet, as Luke had said, other women had comparable schedules and still found time to date. She would have, too, if she had thought it would lead to anything.

Hers wouldn't have. No man wanted a sterile wife.

Her eyes shut tight against the misery that found no ease. She had asked herself "why me?" too many times to count. There was never an answer. Her gynecologist was sorry she had prescribed birth control pills to regulate Catherine's menstrual cycle, sorry that instead of doing what they were intended to do, they had created numerous tumors in her fallopian tubes. They weren't discovered until her annual pap smear came up abnormal.

Opening her eyes, she leaned her head against the back of the seat. She had been so frightened when she had gone into surgery to have the tumors removed. During the operation her doctor discovered small tumors on her uterine wall as well. She had come through the surgery without complications, but her recovery had been slow and painful.

Six weeks later when she had gone in for her checkup, her gynecologist had been apologetic again. Catherine was given less than a 5 percent chance of conceiving, and if that miracle did happen, due to the scarring of her uterus, the possibility of carrying to term was almost nil. After six months, all bets were off . . . unless she had the surgery again.

She had always wanted children and was devastated by the report. Tearfully she had told her fiancé, Roderick, the heartbreaking news, expecting him to be as disappointed as she was, but never expecting him to send his mother to call off the engagement . . . or his mother's painful words. "Roderick has a commitment to the family to carry on the legacy of the generations before him. That means children and grandchildren. You couldn't possibly think he or any other sensible man would marry a woman who is barren."

Catherine had returned his ring by special delivery. Her family was hurt for her and angry at Roderick for not telling her in person. She couldn't blame him. He wanted something she had been unable to give him.

In the fall she had started on her master's program, then progressed to earn her doctorate. She kept her dates, if she had them, light and simple. Working with children became her greatest joy and greatest heartache. She had to witness the abuse, neglect, and abandonment of children whom she would have made any sacrifice to have, to hold, to love.

She wasn't given that choice. Only once, a few months after she received her doctorate, had she mentioned her sterility to a man she was dating. He was a friend of the family, successful, intelligent—or so she had thought. He was delighted by the news and proceeded to try to take her into the bedroom instead of out to dinner as planned. They could have sex all they wanted and he didn't have to wear a tiresome condom. She had sent the selfish, egotistical bastard home and never told another man.

She had filled her life and tried not to regret too much what she would never have—a husband and family. In her career, she had counseled with and seen too many women who had traded their bodies for empty words of love and companionship. She had vowed that wouldn't happen to her. If she made love to any man, it would mean something to both of them. So far, she had yet to meet such a man.

"You didn't go to sleep, did you?"

Startled, she looked over her shoulder to see Luke standing there, hands on hips, staring at her. Her heart thudded in her chest. She had kept her vow because she had never met Luke Grayson.

Luke made her body hum and vibrate with sensual longing. But he'd want a whole woman. Never before had she felt regret so keenly as she did now.

Frowning, he came closer. "You found something else in your notebook."

She tucked her head. "No."

"You're sure."

"Positive." She stood. "I think I'll take a walk. I haven't explored the woods behind the house yet."

His frown deepened. "You want me to go with you?"

"No." She laid the book on the end table as she passed.

"Don't go far."

She kept walking. "I won't."

LUKE DIDN'T FEEL AS IF HE WERE IMPOSING OR violating a trust in the least as he followed Catherine. He wanted to make sure no one was in the woods with her. Once he had determined that he'd leave her to find what peace she could. The deeper she went, the slower her steps, the farther her shoulders drooped.

Circling around in front of the spruce and pine trees, he saw her face. His breath caught. Gone was the smart-mouthed woman who held a gun on him and tossed out one-liners, and in her place was a woman in abject misery. When she stopped to sit in the midst of wildflowers, then lifted her head to the sky, Luke saw moisture glistening on her bronzed mahogany skin. Tears.

She was hurting. Her head lowered, and it was all he could do not to go to her. But somehow he knew she wouldn't want that, knew she wouldn't want anyone to see her vulnerability. Tough. He'd give her thirty minutes and then he was coming back for her.

Silently he slipped away and returned to the cabin. With each step he discovered walking away was one of the hardest things he had ever done.

WIPING AWAY THE USELESS TEARS, CATHERINE POSI-tioned her hands beside her. She hadn't cried in years. It wasn't lost on her that it had been over a man then, also. Maybe because her life was in turmoil, she was looking for a man to fix it because one had failed her in the past.

Closing her eyes she visualized Luke staring down at her lips and shivered, then dismissed her theory completely. Her attraction to a virile specimen of manhood and some person's vengeance against her just happened to be occurring at the same time. She just had to decide if she wanted the attraction to lead to anything deeper. Luke wouldn't, couldn't be hers forever. When her morning flight left next Sunday for Los Angeles, she'd be on it.

LUKE WAS UNLOCKING THE GLASS DOOR OFF THE LOG-post back deck when the phone rang. Expecting reports from his agents on Catherine's associates, he quickly crossed to the phone and picked it up. "Hello."

"Who is this?"

Not again! But this time he heard the authority behind the question. "Luke Grayson."

There was a long pause before the woman said, "May I please speak with Catherine?"

"She went for a walk. I can go find her if you'd like."

"I was under the impression that she would be alone in the cabin."

One thing about Catherine, her friends really looked out for her. "I own the cabin with Daniel. Neither Catherine nor I knew the other would be here."

"And how long have you been there?"

"Late Friday night," he said. After another extended pause he felt compelled to add, "Catherine tried to find a room last night in Santa Fe, but they were all booked."

"Was there a reason she wanted to leave?" The voice had taken on a distinctive edge. Whoever the woman was, she was tough.

"She didn't want to impose."

"How long will you be there?"

He didn't mind setting her mind at ease, but enough was enough. "Who's asking?"

"Her mother, Elizabeth Stewart."

Uh-oh. "She's fine, Mrs. Stewart. If you need to check on me, ask Daniel."

"My secretary is doing that now."

"Yes, ma'am." Add thorough and smart to the toughness.

"Mr. Grayson, please have my daughter call me at my office in Washington when she comes in."

"Washington?" He was also waiting for Catherine's background information to come in.

"I'm a U.S. Senator for California. I make a wonderful friend or a bad enemy. Goodbye."

Luke hung up the phone and left the cabin in search of Catherine. Her mother would happily rip his tonsils out if he caused her daughter any harm. He didn't want to cause her harm, he wanted to lay her down and make love to her like there was no tomorrow. He also never wanted to see her unhappy again. It surprised him how much he wanted both in equal portions.

He discovered her picking Santa Fe phlox and Jacob's ladder. The bunches of pink and narrow clusters of yellow wild flowers dangled from her hand. For a long time, he simply stood and admired how beautiful she was, how gracefully she moved. Whatever she had been bothered about before, she seemed to have worked it through. Glancing up, she caught him staring at her and smiled.

"Luke."

The husky timbre of her voice caressed him. "You had another phone call. Your mother."

Her eyes widened. She clutched the stems of the large

pink flowers in her hands. The sight angered him. "I didn't tell her anything."

Quickly she came to him. "I'm sorry, I should have known."

"Yes, you should."

Tilting her head, she stared up at him, her smile curving her lips. "You aren't very gracious if someone questions your integrity, are you?"

"Nope." He reached out and caught the hand that was free of flowers. "Your mother is waiting."

Her heart rate kicked up at the contact. Taking a calming breath, she tried to collect her thoughts. However, the one that kept reoccurring was that of being in Luke's arms again, only this time kissing him, loving him. "S-she interrogated you?"

He gazed down at her. "How did you know?"

"She was a lawyer before she decided to go into politics," she explained.

"She must have been good."

"She was."

"Talent must run in your family." Together they walked up on the wooden deck. "Make your call. I'll wait here."

"All right," she said.

"Well?" he prompted when she didn't leave.

She swallowed. "You're still holding my hand."

Luke looked down at their connecting hands as if he had never seen either of them before, then back up to her. He quickly released her hand and stepped back. "Sorry."

"Are you really?"

"Go make the call, Catherine."

"I'll still expect an answer when I come out."

He stared down into her face, his gaze going to her soft lips. "Your mother is waiting."

"I won't forget," she said and went into the house.

Luke watched her go. That was his problem. He remembered too much.

"DOES HE LOOK LIKE HE SOUNDS?" ELIZABETH STEWART asked when she was sure her daughter was fine.

"Better." Catherine and her mother had always been good friends and talked openly with each other.

"Everything all right?"

Catherine sat on the edge of the sofa. "I'm a big girl."

"That's why I'm asking."

"Luke's an honorable man."

"He's a man."

"There's no denying that."

"Daniel says he's all right. But you remember, you're only going to be there until next Sunday."

"I remember." Sadness touched her words.

"Baby, you're sure you aren't getting in over your head?"

"No," she admitted honestly.

"In that case, tell Luke I meant what I said."

"About what?"

"He'll know."

AFTER HANGING UP THE PHONE, CATHERINE WENT outside. Luke was sitting in one of the wicker chairs, a guitar in his lap. His dark head was bent, his long fingers coaxing a tune from the instrument. So it had been him playing and not the radio. Somehow, seeing him now, a small part of her realized she had known all along.

Luke held the instrument with infinite gentleness. He'd hold and caress a woman the same way, coaxing and demanding in equal parts until she gave and gave.

With his head still bent, he glanced up at her. Her breath caught. Despite what she kept telling herself, more and more she thought of being that woman. She remembered the plaintive song from last night and shivered.

"I didn't know you played."

"Family requirement. Mama's a music teacher and thought it taught us discipline. The baby grand in the great room is hers." He stroked a couple of the guitar notes. "Everything all right?"

"I should ask you that." Walking to him she leaned back on the wooden rail and placed her hands beside her. "Mother told me to tell you she meant what she said."

His fingers danced lightly across the strings. "Never doubted the lady for a second."

"You're going to tell me what she said?"

He leaned back and stared up at her. "That she could be a good friend or a bad enemy." Maybe they both needed to hear it.

"Did it make an impression on you?"

He strummed the strings, then placed his hands on them. "Yep."

"You're going to listen to her?"

"I'm going to try."

"Because she told you to?"

"Because it's best all the way around."

"You and my mother seem to have put the horse before the cart. There is nothing between us, not one hint of indiscretion. Not one kiss."

His gaze pierced her. "You don't want to go there, Catherine."

"Why not?" She folded her arms so he wouldn't notice her hands were trembling. She had made up her mind. She wanted Luke and she had always gone after what she wanted no matter how difficult it might seem. Luke was a man she could trust and depend on, but he wouldn't want anything permanent. "A kiss would be a prelude to something. You might be a lousy kisser."

His eyes darkened with emotion. "You really don't want to push this."

"How would you know what I want? You're going to listen to my mother. I thought you had more courage than that." She started past him and gasped as she found herself yanked into his lap.

He stared down into her wide eyes. "Some animals aren't meant to be teased or petted."

"I wasn't doing either."

"Yes you were."

"Aren't you the least curious?"

Lord help him, but he was. He thought of all the reasons why he shouldn't, then fastened his lips to hers. The instant his touched the softness, his tongue swept into her mouth. Sweetness and fire. Greed stampeded through him. He eagerly sought more of the taste, the maddening duel of tongues. His hand just as eagerly sought the softness of her warm, scented flesh. Buttons and hooks yielded to the expertise of his fingers.

Catherine felt herself caught up in the kiss, the mindlessness she had read about, but never experienced. She became all need and want. Sensations spiraled through her. She pressed closer, giving, wanting to give more. Her hands dove into his thick hair as she hung on.

Breathing hard, Luke lifted his head and stared down into her eyes; eyes that were dazed with passion, with desire.

"Luke." His name was a plea that he could not answer.

"I guess we have our answer." Standing, he brought her with him, then set her firmly away.

Unsteadily she swayed on her feet, then forced her trembling legs to obey. "I think we have more questions than answers."

"Catherine, this is not going to happen again." He

shoved his hand through his hair. "I'm not going to fall into my mother's trap or become involved with a client."

"So you're going to deny what's between us?"

"There's nothing between us. Neither one of us can afford to forget you're number twenty-eight."

Her head jerked backward. Hurt and embarrassment swept across her expressive features. "I won't bother you again." With trembling fingers she buttoned her blouse. "You can continue to develop your technique on number twenty-nine."

He watched her go. Shoulders straight, her steps unsteady. The sight tore through him, and made him confess, "Cath, I never kissed any of the other women. Shouldn't have kissed you."

She turned back to him, her face softening, the rigidity leaving her body. She took one step toward him.

He took two steps back. "That doesn't change anything. I only told you because you have enough to deal with already. But it won't change things. It's not going to happen again."

Her smile was slow and knowing. "If you say so, Luke."

A curse slipped past his lips as he watched the provocative sway of her hips. She was doing that on purpose. Just his worsening bad luck to be attracted to one of the most stubborn and the most sensual women he'd ever had the misfortune to meet.

CHAPTER EIGHT

AN HOUR LATER, LUKE DECIDED HIS EMOTIONS WERE under control enough to go inside. Passing the great room he saw Catherine in his favorite spot, a tan leather over-stuffed chair in front of the towering, twenty-six-foot arched window. Over the tree tops was a commanding view of the mountains. Against her sharply bent legs was a laptop.

She had such a look of dismay on her face that he asked, "Is everything okay?"

The deep sadness in her eyes made him forget to be cautious and he quickly crossed to her. "Did something else happen?"

"No." She glanced down at the computer screen. "I was doing research for my next book and found some information I didn't like."

Hunkering down beside her, he saw a gray wolf on the screen. "They've been hunted almost into extinction. Only the red wolf and the gray remain. Once there were thousands. My mother's people believe they are our guardians and watch over us—our overseers."

She twisted toward him. Only inches separated their faces. "They do? What an interesting concept."

"Yes." Luke pushed to his feet. Away from the seductive pull of her perfume and her tempting mouth. "Native

Americans are matriarchal. My mother's family is of the wolf clan."

"Is that why you were able to communicate with the wolf?"

"Partly."

"Well?"

The corners of his mouth tilted. She certainly didn't like her questions not being answered. "Some things are not for outsiders to learn."

Setting the laptop aside, she pulled her feet beneath her and stared up at him. "Are you serious?"

"There are many aspects of our culture that are to be passed down, but only to the People. That is why outsiders aren't allowed to witness or photograph certain ceremonies even today." His voice roughened. "The dream-catcher is a widely known example of one aspect of the Native American culture that wasn't supposed to be shown to the outside world."

"But why? It would seem to me that the more people knew about it the better."

"You are speaking from your need to preserve your African-American history. Native Americans have different beliefs."

"But you're a part of both."

"And I respect both for their sameness and their differences. Both came through incredibly difficult times, both survived."

Her face saddened. "I have a few biracial patients who are having a difficult time adjusting. They don't know to which world they belong."

"It's not easy sometimes. You have to learn that skin color doesn't make the person, but what's on the inside."

She angled her head up to his strong profile. Luke was

a man. First and foremost. "I bet neither you nor Daniel had problems with your dual heritage."

He shook his dark head. "No. We were taught to be proud of and embrace both our heritages. My mother and father made sure we learned what the text books continuously leave out about the many contributions and inventions of African-Americans. My mother and maternal grandparents and her other relatives made sure of the same thing about my Native American heritage."

Her gaze warmed. "I'd say they should be very proud of the results."

He felt the blessing of her smile all the way to his soul. "I better let you get back to your research."

"Luke, what do you think I should do about Hero once he's well enough to leave the clinic?"

"Naming him wasn't smart, Catherine."

"Tell me something I don't know." She shoved her hand through her hair. "On the Internet I located a lady in California who has a sort of preserve for wolf hybrids. Maybe I could send him there."

"Wolf hybrids have an even more difficult time surviving than wolves," he told her. "Some people might think it's best to keep them contained, that they can't survive on their own, but would you like to live your life in a cage, no matter how gilded?"

"No."

"Neither would I. People fear what they don't understand and can't control," Luke said, his voice harsh.

"Not all the time," she said softly.

"If you want what's best for him, set him free." He walked from the room without a backward glance.

Catherine slumped back in her seat, wondering if Luke were talking about Hero or himself, and afraid he meant both.

* * *

LUKE AND CATHERINE APPARENTLY FELT IT BETTER TO stay out of each other's way that evening and most of the next day. After sharing the breakfast they had cooked together, she went to work on her story in the great room, and he went to his office off the kitchen. Every hour or so he'd go in to check on her. Always she'd have her head in front of the computer screen either inputting information or reading.

When night approached, he cut on the lights. She had looked up absently, smiled, said thanks, and gone back to her laptop. He had to admire her ability to concentrate for such long periods of time. In his inquiry about her, he found there was a great deal more to admire.

Catherine Elizabeth Stewart was a certified genius, had published a research paper every year of the six she had been a professor at her university, and was a well-established author with fifty-nine children's stories to her credit. She had every right to be snooty, and wasn't. No wonder all the members of the Women's League admired her so much, his mother included.

Getting up, he went to the kitchen to prepare dinner. It wouldn't be as elaborate as Brandon's, but it would be filling. He decided on ham sandwiches and took them out with a cola.

"Eat."

"In a minute," she said, her fingers rapidly racing across the keys.

The minute turned into five, then ten. "Catherine."

"Yes?" She kept on typing.

"If you're going to do the workshop tomorrow, you need to eat and get a good night's sleep."

"You always make sure I sleep well now."

"What are you talking about?"

"You and your music. They're my salvation," she said simply, never lifting her head.

He couldn't have said anything at that moment if his life had depended on it. His throat and heart were too full. Clearing his throat, he managed, "Eat." He'd work on his heart later.

Glancing up, she gave him a quick smile and picked up her sandwich. "Yes, boss."

SEVERAL MEMBERS OF THE WOMEN'S LEAGUE WERE waiting for Catherine and Luke, his mother included, when they arrived at the auditorium the next morning. Although Gloria Harris didn't appear too pleased to see them together, none of the other women seemed to think anything about it. His mother couldn't stop smiling. And as Amanda Poole had said, every seat in the amphitheater was taken.

"I'll be waiting for you to finish," Luke said.

"The workshop won't be over until two, you sure you don't want to pick me up then?"

"I'm staying."

"Thanks."

Amanda Poole rushed up to them. "Everyone is seated."

Catherine tuned to Luke, her uneasiness returning.

"I'll be here if you need me." Unobtrusively his hand stroked hers.

Relaxing, she walked on the stage. Amanda followed.

CATHERINE WAS A GREAT SPEAKER. SHE WAS FUNNY, IN-formative, direct. She didn't sugar-coat the "crisis," as she called it, of the state of parenting, but she gave hope without being preachy or judgmental. Her love of children and her strong belief and support of their welfare came through in every word.

When they broke for lunch, several people from the

audience came on stage and followed her to where they were being served. If not for Amanda and Luke's mother, she might have missed lunch completely. As it was, he didn't see how she managed to eat and answer all the questions people asked her.

"Is talking back ever acceptable?"

"What about potty training?"

"How do I get him to keep his room clean?"

"Should I ignore the bad words?"

Luke had to lean closer on that one. Daniel might need some help.

The afternoon session went just as well as the morning one. By the time the last person had piled out of the auditorium it was three-thirty. When Amanda suggested they go for drinks and wind down, everyone agreed. Shrugging her shoulders, Catherine waved and allowed herself to be carried along with the group of laughing, chattering women. This time his mother was all smiles.

DURING THE NEXT TWO HOURS, CATHERINE BECAME very well acquainted with the expression, "If looks could kill." Gloria Harris said very little through drinks, which turned into dinner, or during a slow stroll through the plaza, the bustling heart of Santa Fe tourist attraction. The reason for Gloria's changed attitude, all six foot four of gorgeous toned muscles, wasn't difficult to figure out. She wanted Luke. Catherine couldn't fault her. It so happened she wanted him, too.

"Catherine, don't you think this Navajo turquoise and silver necklace is lovely?" Luke's mother asked, admiring the piece through the store window.

"It's stunning," Catherine agreed. The large center stone hung from a heavy silver chain linked to smaller turquoise stones. "But so is everything. I've never seen a better collection of galleries and shops with such a wide variety of merchandise." She laughed. "I have a few friends who would max out their credit cards here."

Ruth looked at her warmly. "I'm glad you're enjoying yourself."

"I am, thanks. But I better be getting back."

"Luke won't worry as long as you're with me."

Catherine glanced around sharply, but the other three women who were with them were across the street admiring Native American sandpaintings. "You're doomed to disappointment. Nothing is going to happen between us."

Ruth didn't act surprised by her announcement, and Catherine liked her better for not denying what she had done. The older woman took Catherine's arm and started walking down the narrow street. "Young people are so impatient. When you get older, you learn things take time."

Catherine stopped. "I'm leaving Sunday after the Psychology Association Conference."

"Sunday is a long way off. A lot could happen," Ruth said, then continued before Catherine could comment. "I better go pull Amanda away or we'll never finish the tour. She can put my daughter, Sierra, to shame when it comes to shopping. And that's saying a lot."

Shaking her head at Ruth's singlemindedness, Catherine turned back around to look at the necklace. Her mother's birthday was coming up. A thin black woman and little girl slowly walking toward her caught her attention instead. Their unsmiling, almost grim faces and slightly disheveled appearances stood out markedly in the sea of well-dressed, happy shoppers and vacationers. The woman noticed Catherine watching her, and immediately ducked her head and sped up.

"Mama, can we stop and eat? I'm hungry."

The little girl in jeans and a blouse, sporting two fat pony tails on the side of her head, looked to be about four, and like most children her age, spoke in loud tones when tired or upset.

Biting her lower lip, the woman in a faded dress bent down to whisper something to the child, causing her to laugh. Straightening abruptly, the woman swayed, then steadied herself by bracing her hand against the wall of the boutique next to her.

Catherine rushed to them. "Are you all right?"

The woman's sunken eyes widened. Catherine had seen fear before. "I only want to help."

"I'm fine." Pulling the little girl closer to her, she clutched the canvas bag in her hand and walked away. She had gone only a few halting steps when she swayed again. She reached out her hand toward the wall. It wavered without making contact, then the woman's slim body went limp.

Catherine caught her and eased the unconscious woman to the sidewalk. Ruth and the three women from the League rushed over. Others followed. In seconds they were surrounded by a crowd of curious onlookers.

The little girl started crying, her wails loud and piercing over her mother's unresponsiveness. "Mamaaa. Mamaaa!"

"Catherine, what happened?" Ruth asked, kneeling by the child and trying unsuccessfully to soothe her.

"Her mother fainted," Catherine said, glad to see the woman's eyelids fluttering. Her pulse was steady. "Take it easy."

The young woman's eyes opened. They were dark brown and terrified. Frantic, she glanced around, discovered her child in the arms of a stranger, then reached for the crying child and pulled her to her chest.

"Do I need to call an ambulance?" asked a policeman.

The woman became even more frightened. "I-I'm fine."

The officer observed the woman's untidy appearance,

her evasive eye contact, her agitation. "What's your name?"

"I-I—"

"Can't you see she isn't well enough to talk?"

His attention switched to Catherine. "Who are you?"

"Dr. Catherine Stewart, I'm lecturing at St. John's College."

"Do you know this woman?" he asked.

Catherine didn't like to lie, but neither did she like the sheer panic on the face of the woman. "Yes."

"So you tell me her name."

Caught, Catherine could only stare at the officer.

"I'll vouch for both women if my word is good enough, Officer Byrd?" Luke said, crouching down beside a relieved-looking Catherine.

"You know it is, Grayson. You need any help?"

"No, thank you. We can manage from here," Luke told him. "It would help if you could give us some breathing room."

"You got it." The policeman turned to the crowd. "Everything is under control. Let's move back and give the woman some air. We don't want to frighten the little girl."

"Why am I not surprised?" Luke whispered to Catherine.

"Thank you, Luke. I don't know what I would have done," Catherine told him.

"You would have thought of something," Luke said, then turned to the woman. "Do you think you can stand?"

The eye contact was brief. Without answering, the woman tried to stand and keep the child in her arms at the same time. A task that proved impossible. She would have never made it without Luke's holding her arm and helping her. He frowned on feeling how slight her weight, how thin her arm. "My truck is just a short distance from here. Is there someplace I can take you?"

"No."

"But, Mama, I'm tired of walking."

Panic and something close to defeat revealed itself in the woman's eyes. She bent unsteadily to the little girl. "It's not much farther."

"But I'm hungry," the little girl wailed, tears filling her eyes.

Dropping to her knees, the frail woman pulled the child into her arms. "Shhhh. Mama knows."

Catherine leaned down to the little girl. "How about a glass of milk and a hamburger?"

The woman's reaction was swift. "We don't need your help."

Catherine ignored the anger. She had seen the love and helplessness in the mother's face. "I was asking your little girl. You wouldn't deny her, would you?"

The child's eyes were huge. "Mama, could I? You could have some too if the lady doesn't mind?"

Catherine felt her throat tighten. "I don't mind."

The woman's head lowered, her chin almost touching her chest. Her body trembled.

"Mama?" the little girl said. "May I?"

The woman's head came up, misery stared back at Catherine, then her gaze dropped. "Could we get it to go?"

"There's a restaurant just around the corner," Luke said. If he didn't miss his guess, it had been a long time since either of them had had regular meals.

The woman stared into the hopeful face of her child, then back at Catherine, and stood. "She likes mustard."

Catherine held out her hand. "My name's Catherine Stewart."

Hesitantly the woman's lifted. "Naomi." She moistened her dry lips. "Naomi Jones."

"Mama, that's no—"

"Kayla," Naomi interrupted, her gaze skittering to Catherine. "You mustn't interrupt when adults are talking."

Kayla's head fell. "I'm sorry. I forgot."

Naomi's hand rested on her daughter's shoulder. "I know, sweetheart."

If her last name was Jones, he was Superman, Luke thought, but didn't say anything while Catherine introduced him. He and the woman nodded. Catherine might be fooled, but he wasn't. The woman was hiding more than her name, and until he knew why, he wasn't leaving Catherine alone with her.

LUKE HAD A DIFFICULT TIME, BUT HE FINALLY convinced his mother and her friends that all of them would make the woman even more nervous than she was if they all followed her to the restaurant. The best possible person to handle the situation, whatever it was, was Catherine. He gave them the task of going ahead to the Red Cactus to put in an order for food.

Luckily on weekdays the restaurant wasn't as crowded as on weekends. The woman hesitated on seeing where they were going, but Catherine, who had been telling the little girl the story of a fuzzy caterpillar who turned into a beautiful butterfly, reached for the child's hand and kept walking. The mother had no choice but to follow.

After only a cursory glance, Nacona showed them to the family booth, then handed them menus, and Kayla crayons and a small coloring book. "What would you like to drink?"

Kayla gripped the brown color in her hand, looked at her mother, then at Catherine. "Is it all right if I have a orange soda instead of milk with my hamburger?"

"It certainly is," Catherine said, charmed by the well-mannered child. "In fact, I think I'll have one with you."

"Make mine the same," Luke said. "Mrs. Jones?"

Naomi put her hands in her lap. "Water."

"Four orange sodas, chicken fingers, salsa and chips," Luke said. "Brandon already has the food orders."

"Be right back." Gathering up the menus, the waitress left.

"What brought you to Santa Fe, Mrs. Jones?" Luke asked, feeling she wasn't from around there.

"I'm just passing through." She picked up a crayon, and began to color the leaves of the tree while her daughter did the trunk.

"Where are you heading?" Luke continued.

"Albuquerque." She didn't look up.

"Here you go." The waitress set up the collapsible stand, then placed the large serving tray on top. Efficiently, she served their drinks, set the appetizers and chips within arm's reach of everyone, then gave each one a small white plate. "Brandon said to tell you the food will be out in minutes. Enjoy."

By the time she left, Kayla already had a chip in her mouth and was crunching loudly. She reached for another before she had finished the first.

"Slow down, sweetheart."

Nodding, she reached for her drink.

NAOMI BRUSHED HER DAUGHTER'S HAIR BACK AND tried to relax. It was difficult with the powerfully built man watching her. He didn't trust her. That was fine. She didn't trust him either. Staying Kayla's hand when she reached for a fifth chip, Naomi tried not to think that she had eaten only an apple today, a bite of Kayla's sandwich the day before that, and the day before that, nothing.

She brushed her hand across her daughter's head again. Kayla was eating and that was the important thing.

Catherine picked up a chip and munched. "Try one, Naomi. Kayla and I can testify they're very good."

"They sure are, Mama." To demonstrate, she picked up one. A chicken tender was already in the other hand.

"I'm not hungry," Naomi lied.

Luke braced his arm on the table. "Brandon is sure going to hate hearing that."

"Brandon?"

"That's me. Welcome to the Red Cactus." He set the serving tray down and began placing food in front of Kayla and Naomi, who was sitting on the other side of the booth. "Here's your salad. The vegetable soup is homemade. If you want seconds, yell, but I recommend you try the Cornish game hen first. I brought everything out so you could eat at your leisure. Here's your hamburger, young lady, with mustard on the side and plenty of french fries."

Kayla took her first bite without mustard.

Naomi didn't notice, she was staring at the amount of food in front of them. "I didn't order anything."

"Luke did."

Her startled gaze went to Luke.

"Now Kayla won't have to share." Luke slid out of the booth and stood next to his brother. "Excuse me, I need to speak to Brandon about something."

"Me too." Catherine scooted out behind him. "Kayla, finish all of your food and when I get back I can tell you about the adventures of the butterfly when he was free."

"Yes, ma'am," she said around a mouth full of food.

Her mother released an audible sigh of relief as they left. Catherine wanted to help, but Naomi could tell Luke didn't believe her. Although she hated lying, hated deception of any kind, she had to become better at both if she expected to keep them safe.

One slip and he'd be able to find them.

Nervously, she glanced around the restaurant. No one was paying any attention to her. They were all enjoying their meals. Her anxiety didn't lessen. She had relaxed the other time and had lived to regret her mistake.

Staring down at Kayla, Naomi watched her daughter swirl a french fry around in ketchup. She wished she could hurry her along, but the first pangs of hunger had been satisfied and now she was eating more slowly. It had torn Naomi's heart to see her daughter grabbing for a simple chip.

Her hands trembling, she put mustard on the bun, then cut it in half. How had she let their lives come to this?

"You want some of mine, Mama?"

"No thanks, sweetheart."

"Aren't you going to eat?" Kayla paused, waiting for an answer.

Luke had been right in that also. Kayla had taken to watching to make sure her mother ate. Leaning over, she kissed her daughter's forehead, and said a silent prayer that she would be able to protect her.

"Yes, sweetheart. Mama is going to eat." Naomi picked up her soup spoon, not knowing when she'd have the chance to eat again. She had exactly four dollars and thirty-three cents in her pockets and no hope for getting more.

CHAPTER NINE

CATHERINE FOLLOWED LUKE AND BRANDON AS THEY wove their way to the other side of the restaurant, then down a narrow hallway lit by heavy cast bronze sconces. On the stark walls were black and white photographs of famous people who had eaten at the restaurant. Catherine only had a brief glance at the smiling faces before Luke ushered her into a room behind Brandon.

The small office was a comfortable contrast of new and old. The computer was state of the art, but the desk it sat upon was an antique oak table. On the wall to the far left was a hand-painted mural depicting images of the Native American culture in vibrant reds, yellows, blues, and greens. Leaning against it was an antique, cottonwood pueblo ladder. From the ladder hung a vintage Pendleton blanket, and a tooled Muskogee medicine man's pouch. On the shelves beneath were Indian pottery. Scattered on the sandstone floor were Navajo rugs.

"Have a seat," Brandon said, indicating the red leather chairs in front of his desk. Behind the desk were certificates and awards from noted cooking schools and culinary magazines.

"No, thank you," Catherine said and turned to Luke. "I appreciate everything that you've done, but you're frightening her with all your questions."

"She's hiding something," he said.

"Yes, she is, and she's not going to tell us after knowing us for only a few minutes, and certainly not if you're badgering her with your suspicions," she told him. "They're both hungry and tired. Let's help them first, and if Naomi wants to tell us, fine, if not, we still help."

He stared down into her worried face. "Picking up more strays?"

She placed her hand on his chest. "Some are not as strong or as fortunate as others."

His hand caught hers, his thumb absently stroking the back of her hand. "You can't save the world."

"I'd settle for a few."

"I thought that would be your answer." Lightly he touched her cheek with their joined hands. "Go on back out there before they skip out on you."

Her brown eyes grew large and liquid. "I'm not sure they have any place to go."

"I'm not giving up my bed."

Catherine felt heat spiral all the way to her toes. "I wouldn't ask you to do that."

"Good." He led her to the door. "I'll be out there in a minute."

Brandon had watched the exchange with curious interest. "Almost the entire time you two were together, one of you was touching the other. I've never known you to be the demonstrative type."

"You must be mistaken." Luke crossed the office.

"I'm not, but I'll let it slide for the moment," Brandon said. "Now that Catherine is gone, do you mind telling me who that woman is and what is going on?"

Luke picked up the phone on the large hand-carved table and punched out a number. "I don't know, but I will shortly, I promise you."

*   *   *

CATHERINE ARRIVED TO HEAR NAOMI COAXING KAYLA to hurry up. Luke had been right. "I'm back. Sorry that took so long." She slid into the booth.

Naomi's nervous gaze swept to her, then back to Kayla. "That's all right."

Catherine noted with pleasure Kayla and her mother had eaten a good portion of their meal. "Would you like anything else?"

"No, thank you." Picking up a napkin, she cleansed Kayla's face and hands. "We've taken enough of your time."

"Not at all," Catherine said. "I'm actually in the city on business for a conference. So you're actually doing me a favor."

"I'm all finished, you're gonna tell me the story of the caterpillar," Kayla asked excitedly.

Naomi was already scooting out of the booth, taking her daughter with her. "Maybe another time. Honey, we have to leave."

"Mama, I wanted to hear the story," Kayla wailed.

"Another time, Kayla."

"When?" the little girl asked in a loud, carrying voice.

Naomi glanced around nervously. People were turning to see what was going on. More than fear of embarrassment was fear of discovery. "Honey, please just come on."

"Naomi, you don't have to leave. I want to help you," Catherine told her. "If not for yourself, then for Kayla."

Her words had the desired effect. Naomi stopped trying to leave, but her eyes were wide. She looked as if she would bolt at the least provocation.

Catherine leaned over and spoke softly. "I'm not here to judge or preach. I just want to help."

"I really appreciate all you've done, but—"

"Naomi, you have nothing to fear from me."

"What about him?" She nodded in the direction Luke had taken.

Catherine smiled. "He takes a while to get to know, but he's a good man."

"Your man?" Naomi asked, her tone worried.

Catherine flushed. "I'm not sure."

Naomi's face tightened. "Be sure. Be very sure."

Now Catherine was positive a man was the reason behind Naomi's fear. "I will be. But now we need to talk about you and what's best for Kayla. If you want to tell me what's going on, fine. If not, fine. I'll still help in any way I can."

Some of the wariness left Naomi's face. "You really mean that, don't you?"

"Yes." Catherine placed her arms on the table. "How can I help to make things better?"

Naomi glanced down into the attentive eyes of her daughter. "Honey, why don't you finish coloring while I talk with Catherine?"

"Can I have another soda while I'm doing it?" Kayla asked, her red crayon poised.

"You've had enough, Kayla."

"Yes, ma'am." Kayla began coloring her cactus.

"She's very well-mannered." Catherine had counseled with too many permissive parents who thought the easy way out was to let their children have their way. They soon learned, without rules and guidelines, children made themselves and everyone else's lives miserable.

"Sometimes," Naomi said, but she hugged the little girl to her, then rocked her shoulder into Kayla's. Apparently it was an old game because they repeated the motion a couple of times before Kayla went back to coloring.

"I'm going to sit by Catherine a few minutes, you finish coloring." Getting up, Naomi went to sit by Catherine. "I know you said you were here for a conference, but you seem to know the man who owns this restaurant. Do you think he'd give me a job cleaning up the place after it closes?"

"So you and Kayla wouldn't have to be separated?" Catherine guessed.

"I don't like leaving her," Naomi admitted. "Could you just ask him?"

"I'll ask, but I can't guarantee anything."

"Thank you." Naomi went back to her seat.

Catherine left to find Brandon. Offering Naomi money would have only hurt her pride. She wanted work, not a handout. Catherine just wasn't sure she was going to be able to give her what she needed, a chance to hold up her head and take care of her child. Seeing Brandon leaving his office, she realized she was about to find out.

His dark brow furrowed on seeing her. "She skip out on you?"

"No. She didn't. Brandon, she needs a job and—"

He held up both hands. "I have a full staff and people on the waiting list?"

Catherine didn't doubt his word. "If you hire her, I'd pay her salary."

His eyebrow rose. "You really are a soft touch."

"She and her little girl need help," Catherine defended.

"So Luke says, but how do you think the staff will react to me hiring her when they have friends and relatives on the waiting list? I expect them to be honest and they have the right to expect the same thing from me."

Catherine's sigh was long and deep.

"Besides, she doesn't have two qualities I look for." He chuckled at the affronted expression on her face. "If you knew my mother and sister, you'd know I'd have to leave town if a woman's figure had anything to do with hiring staff. I look for a calm demeanor and friendliness. Your friend has neither."

Catherine brightened. "She wanted to clean up after the restaurant closed."

He shook his dark head. "Some of my mother's music students already have the job."

"So there's nothing she can do?"

"I'm afraid not."

He curved his arm around her dejected shoulder. "Sorry."

The door opened behind them. Catherine glanced around and saw Luke, his face hard.

Worried, she immediately went to him, placing her hand lightly on his chest. "Is something the matter?"

Brandon said nothing, just stared at his brother.

Luke didn't know what to say. He'd trust Brandon with his life, but that hadn't stopped the quick spurt of jealousy when he saw Catherine standing easily in his arms. "Sorry," Luke finally said, chagrined.

Brandon shook his head. "I hope it isn't catching?"

Catherine's concern increased. "Are you sick?" The hand that had been resting on his chest palmed his forehead.

Her hand closed over his and brought it down to his side. "I'm not one of your strays."

"I never thought you were," she said softly.

For a long time they simply stared at each other.

"Luke, remember we're supposed to watch the other's back. You aren't forgetting, are you?" Brandon warned.

Luke dropped Catherine's hand, then rammed both of his into his pockets. "Why are you here instead of with Naomi?"

"She wanted me to ask Brandon for a job." Catherine sighed for more reasons than one. She now understood Brandon's cryptic message only too well. "He didn't have one."

So that's what had been going on. "If she's passing through, why does she need a job?"

"I don't know."

"Why don't we go find out?"

NAOMI HUGGED KAYLA WHEN SHE SAW LUKE AND Catherine approaching. She read Brandon's answer on Catherine's face ten feet away. She thought she had prepared herself for the disappointment. She hadn't. "Thanks for asking."

Catherine sat down and scooted over for Luke. "This is a tourist town, so there must be plenty of job openings."

"Yes, you're right," Naomi said. "It was just a thought. Thank you again for the dinner." She turned to Kayla. "Come on, sweetheart. We have to go."

"I don't wanna."

"Kayla, please."

"Mama, it gets cold and I"—her head drooped—"I get scared."

"Oh, Kayla," Naomi cried, gathering the child against her. "I'd never let anything happen to you. Never." But she had made other promises, promises she had not been able to keep. She had promised her the world the night she was born and she didn't even have a bed to sleep in. Naomi could have wept out of shame, out of inadequacy. Luke and Catherine probably thought she was the worst mother in the world. At times she agreed with them.

"If you're finished, we can leave," Luke said quietly.

Naomi gathered Kayla in her arms, and started from the room, blinking back tears. The cooling evening temperature invaded her thin dress. Sitting Kayla down, she pulled her windbreaker out of her canvas tote. "Put this on."

Out of the corner of his eye, Luke saw Catherine digging in her purse. He closed his hand over hers. "Here is my truck."

"Of course. We didn't mean to take up so much of your time. Thank you both." Naomi stared down at the top of her daughter's bowed head. "Say thank you, Kayla."

Kayla kept staring at her feet. "Thank you."

"Where are you staying?" Luke asked.

Naomi's head came up sharply. "Why would you want to know that?"

"To make sure you get there safely," he answered. "It will be dark soon."

Fear shot through Naomi. She'd never make it back in time. "I can manage."

Catherine approached the younger woman. "Naomi, are you sure? The decisions you make affect both you and Kayla. Don't let misplaced pride or fear guide you."

Naomi wanted to trust again, but was afraid to. Somehow it was easier than being disappointed again. "Why should either of you care?"

"Why shouldn't we is probably a better question," Catherine said. "Could you walk away from a child in need?"

Naomi swallowed and glanced away, feeling Kayla's hand tremble in hers.

Luke walked over to the truck and opened the door. "There's enough room for all of us."

"Trust him," Catherine said. "Trust us."

Picking up Kayla, Naomi got into the truck.

THE ROADRUNNER INN, TWO MILES SOUTH OF THE plaza, was exactly what it looked to be, a thirty-year-old roadside motel that offered a cheap room and little else. The fake adobe wall was faded and chipped. The roadrunner's upper lights were out, making it appear headless.

It took Luke all of one minute checking under the hood of the thirteen-year-old Honda Civic to determine it wasn't salvageable. He slammed down the hood. "The engine is shot. Cost more to repair it than the car is worth."

"I know," Naomi said, her voice trembling.

"How did you get into town?" Catherine asked.

"We've been able to catch a ride with a couple going to the Plaza," Naomi explained.

"Do they also bring you back?" Catherine's brow knitted.

The silence stretched until Naomi said, "No. It's not so far once you get started."

"Mama carried me because I get tired," Kayla admitted, leaning against her mother.

Two miles was two miles, and with a tired child it had to seem like ten, Catherine thought.

Luke glanced around at the look-alike units. "Which one is yours?"

Pride meant nothing if her daughter wasn't cared for. "I don't have a room here anymore. The manager let me keep my car here because I had no place else to go."

"Mama, I don't want to sleep in the car tonight. It gets cold."

Naomi turned to Catherine, her face desperate. "If you could possibly loan . . ." Her trembling voice trailed off, she bit her lower lip.

"Luke?" Catherine caught his hand.

A woman's voice shouldn't reach down to your soul and tug, her touch shouldn't make him crave more. Luke had no intention of letting Naomi and her daughter sleep in her car again, but Catherine's pleading expectation and trust in him to right the world got to him. Too much so. His mouth tightened. "Get what you need and let's get out of here."

Naomi unlocked the car door, grabbed a paper sack and quickly stuffed clothes into the bag. She wasn't foolish enough to think people gave something for nothing, but she'd worry about the consequences later. For one night at least, Kayla wouldn't be cold or afraid. "We're ready."

"WHY ARE WE STOPPING HERE?" NAOMI ASKED WHEN Luke stopped in front of an imposing white stucco two-story hotel shaded by large elm and spruce trees. A stone fountain spewed water five feet into the air.

Catherine wanted to ask the same question. Luke knew the hotel was full.

"I'll be back in a minute," he said and got out.

In a short time, he came back and opened the passenger door. "We can reach your room through the open court-yard."

Naomi's mouth gaped. She stared at the immaculate grounds and imposing facade. "I can't afford to stay here."

Luke picked up a dozing Kayla. "We'll discuss it later."

Naomi's apprehension increased as she passed the grassy courtyard and saw the luxury swimming pool and hot tub. Her nervousness turned to surprised delight inside the spacious room, tastefully decorated with cornflower-blue carpet and a navy blue bedspread on the brass bed. On the pristine walls were Native American prints. Two easy chairs flanked a tiled table. The TV was inside the top half of the hand-carved armoire: the mini-refrigerator and honor bar occupied the bottom half.

After placing the little girl on the bed, Luke handed her the key. "Complimentary continental buffet breakfast is served from six-thirty to ten in the dining room."

"Mr. Grayson, I— Thank you."

"Do you want a job?"

"Yes."

"I'll check around. Good night."

"Good night, Naomi," Catherine said, taking the other

woman's trembling hands in hers. "I'll be busy most of tomorrow, but I'm sure I'll see you in the afternoon."

"You don't have to bother."

"I want to," Catherine said. "I haven't finished telling Kayla what happened to the butterfly when it was free."

"No, you haven't," Naomi said, tears of gratitude glistening in her eyes. "Good night and thank you."

"Good night."

CATHERINE'S STEPS WERE CONSIDERABLY LIGHTER ON the way back to the truck. "That was nice of you, Luke, but if you could get her a room, why didn't you get me one?"

He opened the truck door for Catherine to get in. "Would you believe they just had a cancellation?"

She folded her arms and refused to budge. "No."

"Would you believe I was worried you'd get into more trouble?"

Her arms came to her sides, her smile was huge. "That I'd believe."

LUKE SLOWED DOWN AND PULLED INTO DR. YOUNG-blood's clinic. "Might as well check on your other stray."

Smiling, Catherine got out of the truck. She was on to Luke now. He might try to play hard, but he was a marshmallow. Opening the door to the clinic, he ushered her inside.

"I'll be there in a minute," a voice yelled from the back of the clinic. A few minutes later Dr. Youngblood came out. "I might have known it was you two. Hero is cutting up royally."

"That means he's feeling better," Catherine said, already heading to the back where the animals were caged.

Luke caught her hand. "Not without me."

"Come on, then," she said, tugging him to the kennel. She heard Hero before she saw him. His bark was distinctive and high pitched. "Hi, it's good to see you, too. Soon you'll be out of here."

"Then what?" Dr. Youngblood asked, leaning against the wall.

"I'm not sure." She glanced up at the doctor. "How long before he's well enough to leave?"

"Five, six days at the most."

"Sunday. I have until Sunday." Unconsciously her hand tightened on Luke's.

His gaze caught hers and both realized the other was thinking time was running out for them.

The phone rang and Dr. Youngblood groaned. "If I ever see Cheryl again, I may do something drastic to her."

Catherine pushed to her feet. She needed some time to herself. "I'll get it."

Richard hunkered down beside Luke, noting with admiration the way he had quieted Hero.

"Still haven't found anyone to help?" Luke asked, absently stroking the animal's head.

"No," Richard lamented. "Guess I couldn't blame Cheryl for running out on me. The pay isn't that good and sick animals can be pretty unpredictable."

"I think I may have someone for you."

Dr. Youngblood's strong face became pleaful. "Luke, you wouldn't joke at a time like this, would you?"

"No, but you should know something first." Quickly Luke told what he knew about Naomi and her daughter, and finished by saying, "For reasons I can't tell you, I need to be able to keep tabs on Naomi."

Lines radiated across Richard's forehead. "Is she a suspect in some crime?"

"I don't know how deep the lies go. I do know she's running from something and afraid of her own shadow."

Luke pushed to his feet. Hero and Richard followed. "Her daughter, Kayla, is the exact opposite. Lively and open. She'll have to come to work with her mother."

"Is she pretty?"

"She'll be a heartbreaker in fifteen years or so."

Richard shook his head. "The mother."

Luke shrugged. "She's looks all right."

"Tall, thin, short, wide? Is she as beautiful as Catherine?"

"No one could be that beautiful," Luke said with feelings.

"My, my," Richard said, grinning.

Luke scowled. "She looks all right, I guess. I don't know anything about her except she's afraid of something or someone and down on her luck. Not exactly the kind of woman you would want to get involved with."

"Who said anything about becoming involved?" Richard asked, his smile growing. "I was simply trying to figure out how much you were going to owe me for the great sacrifice I'm going to be making."

"You would, wouldn't you?"

"You better believe it."

Luke was still trying to figure how much it was going to cost him when they arrived back at the receptionist's desk. "Catherine, Richard is going to hire Naomi as his receptionist and Kayla can come with her."

She surged up from the desk. "That's wonder—oh, no!"

Luke crossed to her in three long strides, his eyes searching her face. "What's the matter?"

"She won't have anything to wear."

Luke tried to slow his heartbeat and not yell at Catherine for scaring him at the same time. "Women."

The look she sent him told him she knew exactly what he thought of her outburst.

"I'm not particular." Richard folded his arms. "Jeans are fine."

Catherine's anxiety deepened. "I don't think she has any. Kayla's and her clothes were in a sack."

"A sack!" Richard jerked to his full height, his gaze going to Luke. "You didn't mention that."

"I said she didn't have much," Luke reminded him.

"I'd buy her some clothes, but I don't want to offend her." Catherine's expression became thoughtful. "But I don't want her embarrassed or to put you in a bad position with your patients either."

"I have some things, if they fit." Richard went to his office closet and came back with an animal-print smock on a bright pink background and pink pants. "Cheryl always said they clashed with her red hair."

Catherine rushed over to the clothes. "They're perfect."

"So she's a small woman?" Richard asked.

"Very, she looks like a china doll with huge black eyes."

"You can see for yourself first thing in the morning when you pick her up from the Executive Inn. Room 105," Luke said.

CHAPTER TEN

IF NAOMI HADN'T BEEN AFRAID THE PHONE WOULD wake Kayla, she never would have picked up the receiver. As it was, she tried to disguise her voice, "Hello."

"Naomi, is that you?"

Relief and a small amount of shame swept through Naomi. When was she going to stop being such a coward? "Yes, Catherine, it's me."

"Good. I've great news. Luke has found you a job."

"A job?" Naomi repeated, then plopped down on the bed.

"Isn't that wonderful? You'll be able to bring Kayla with you. Dr. Youngblood said she could nap on the couch in his office or watch the TV he never has time to watch anymore."

Things were going too fast. "Dr. Youngblood?"

Catherine laughed. "Sorry, I guess I got excited. Dr. Youngblood has a veterinary clinic in Santa Fe. He wants you to be his receptionist. He even supplies uniforms, meals, and cleaning."

Naomi couldn't take it all in. She stood, then immediately sat back down. Her shaking legs wouldn't support her. "A-are you sure?"

"I'll let you talk to him."

"No, I—"

"Hello, Mrs. Jones," greeted a smooth male voice. "I'm Dr. Youngblood."

Naomi's grip on the phone tightened on thinking of the forms she'd have to fill out. Forms that required certain information she didn't want anyone to know.

"Mrs. Jones?"

"Y-Yes?" Her voice was shaky.

"Is everything all right?"

"Yes. I'm just tired."

"I understand. Why don't we take it easy, and tomorrow I'll pick you and your daughter up around ten?"

"We'll be ready." Naomi hung up the phone unable to keep the growing fear at bay.

He knew all the ways of finding a person, and he had strong reasons for trying. One slip and she'd be lost, and he'd win, and she might never see Kayla again.

RICHARD SLOWLY HUNG UP THE PHONE. "SHE SOUNDED frightened to death."

Catherine's rising spirits plummeted. "I was hoping talking to you would do the exact opposite."

"Sorry."

"It's not your fault." She picked up her purse and pulled out her wallet.

"I told you I'd take care of the hybrid's bill," Luke said, annoyed.

"It's not for Hero." She handed Richard two fifties. "I included dry cleaning and meals without your permission."

"Dry cleaning and meals are included in the salary," Richard said, straight-faced.

"I don't believe you for a minute." Catherine returned the money to her wallet. "If I can ever return the favor, just ask."

Richard grinned. "Your smile is thanks enough."

"Good night, Youngblood," Luke growled, taking Catherine's arm and leading her to the truck. It was a good thing he didn't see Richard wink or Catherine smother a laugh, or he might have really lost it.

Luke slammed her door and went around, got in, and slammed his door. Flicking on the motor, he put the truck in gear and pulled out. "Youngblood should spend more time practicing medicine than flirting."

"Luke."

"Yeah?"

"You ever flirted with a woman?"

His startled gaze switched to her. "What?"

"Flirted with a woman."

He shifted the gears as he passed a semi. "What kind of question is that?"

"One I would like an answer to," she said, twisting in her seat, hating the restraint of the seat belt.

"You can't always have your way."

She laughed. "Luke, you have no idea of the trouble you'd be in if I had my way."

He swung his gaze to her. The blast of an angry motorist had him jerking the wheel. He had veered over in the other lane. "Not another word until we're home, and I mean it."

Catherine sat back in her seat, a little smile on her face. Luke had said home, not cabin.

LUKE HAD NEVER HAD ANY DIFFICULTY WITH KEEPING women pigeonholed. He wasn't the playboy type like his brothers. He didn't believe in a lot of women cluttering up his life. One was sometimes too much. You went into a relationship with the rules laid out. Apparently no one had told Catherine.

Stopping in front of the cabin, he got out. Catherine was already around the hood of the truck and heading for the front door. No doubt, she couldn't wait to tie him up in knots again.

He stopped her just as she went to unlock the front door. After checking to make sure his device had not been disturbed, he opened the door and stepped aside for her to enter. Brushing past him, she hit the track light that illuminated the great room and kept walking. Tossing her purse on the couch, she sat down, spread her arms on the back of the cushion, and crossed her legs.

"Why are you so uptight?"

He jammed his hands in his pockets. "I am not uptight."

"Luke, please, let's be honest here."

His dark head came up. "No one questions my honesty."

She rose from the couch so fast, he stepped back. She kept walking until their bodies touched. "Now, say that again."

"Why are you pushing this? You're not the kind of woman to have affairs."

"I've never felt this way before."

His black eyes widened, then closed. "Go to bed, Catherine."

"Which one?"

His eyes blinked open. She stared up at him, her desire for him open and unguarded. Heat like molten lava spread to him, clouding reason.

He pulled her into his arms, kissing her lips, tasting her. On the couch, his greedy hand sought her silken flesh, desperately eager for more. Her clothes easily yielded to his determined assault. His mouth closed over her nipple, causing her to arch up.

Need and want spiraled through him.

"Luke." Her hands went to the button of his pants.

"No." His breathing rough and ragged, he pulled her to him, stopping her. "Enough."

"Lu—"

"No."

"Just tell me, why?"

Lifting his head he stared down into her eyes dazed with passion. "Because you have enough to deal with. This wouldn't last."

The truth of his words didn't make the pain any less. "That's exactly the reason you don't have to stop. I don't expect anything from you, but what you're willing to give here and now."

His face became fierce. "What kind of talk is that? You're not that type of woman."

"I've never wanted like this before."

His body got harder. He surged to his feet. "Catherine, don't keep doing this."

She sat up not bothering to button her jacket or hook her bra. Luke's gaze dipped to her taut breast. His hands clenched.

Spirals of heat and need coursed through her. She drew in a deep, steadying breath, then another and another. Luke wouldn't be the man she cared about if he couldn't control his desire or thought only of his own need. She stood, somehow making her quivering legs support her. "Good night, Luke."

"Good night, Catherine."

LUKE COULDN'T PLAY, COULDN'T SLEEP. DEEP INSIDE him was an odd ache that left him restless and edgy. After two hours of prowling his room, he suddenly realized the reason.

Pulling on his jeans, he started for the kitchen. He hadn't eaten since lunch and mesquite grilled chicken breasts had never been one of his favorite foods. Passing Catherine's room, he stopped on noticing the open door.

"Catherine?"

"Yes?"

He jerked around. The sound had come from the great room. Going closer, his gaze searched the room until he found her in his chair, her feet tucked under her. He snapped the table light on. "Why are you up?"

"You weren't playing and I couldn't sleep."

"Cath—"

"I didn't mean to disturb you. I would have gone outside, but I didn't think you'd want me to do that."

"Cath—"

"Even at night it's beautiful here. I'll miss your woods and your mountains very much when I go home."

"Catherine, it wouldn't work and it would hurt more than it would heal." She looked so alone and defenseless. Why wouldn't she look at him?

"I don't need healing, Luke. My feelings for you have nothing to do with the other."

"Doesn't it?" he challenged.

She turned her head to look at him. "I admit to having behaved irrationally at times these last few months, but that doesn't mean I'd offer my body to any man who helped me. Robert can attest to that."

"The neighbor," Luke gritted out.

Gracefully she came to her feet. "I think I'll go back to my room."

He caught her arm as she passed. Her skin was soft and warm beneath the silk. His fingers flexed. "I took some psychology classes."

A delicate brow lifted. "A degree is a prerequisite for acceptance into the FBI so that doesn't come as a surprise."

"You're very calm all of a sudden."

"I'm trying."

"I guess your feelings for me didn't matter as much as you thought?" The question surprised him as much as it seemed to surprise her.

"And you've jumped to the illogical conclusion that because I'm not falling apart, you don't matter?"

"I didn't say that."

She sighed. "Luke, you may have taken classes, but I taught the course."

His mouth tightened.

Her hand lifted to rest lightly against his chest. "You're the reason I'm not falling apart. You make me stronger, not weaker. I hurt, but even if I could, I wouldn't change how I feel about you."

"I would," he told her, but a small part of him wasn't so sure.

Her face saddened. "I know you aren't happy about wanting me, but I'd be lying if I didn't admit to being pleased that you care just a little." A smile touched her face. "I don't think you have counted many women in that number."

"How do you know?" he asked almost defensively.

"You're fighting this too hard." She stepped closer until their bodies touched. "Which one of us are you trying to protect, Luke?"

The heat of her body, the tantalizing scent of her perfume struck his senses like a sledgehammer. Hunger gnawed at him. He wanted. He needed. Releasing her, he stepped back. "You might not be so blasé next week when you return home."

"I might not be alive next week."

Fear and panic swept through him. His hands clamped around her arms. His eyes were wild, desperate, his voice frantic. "Did something else happen you didn't tell me about?"

Startled eyes stared up at him. "No. I only meant no one can predict the future."

He heard her words, but he couldn't quite control the shudder that racked his body, the cold that invaded his soul. So he did the only thing he could to right his world, he crushed her to him.

Her hands held him almost as fiercely as he held her. "I'm fine," she repeated. "Marvelous actually, since you're holding me."

"Nothing is going to happen to you." The words were fierce. "Whoever is out there is trying to rattle you, not hurt you."

"Like I said, there are different kinds of hurt."

"Cath." His hand swept up and down the elegant curve of her back. "You don't give up, do you?"

"Not when something is important." Her cheek nuzzled the hard wall of his muscled chest, then she lifted her head. "Besides, I only have until Sunday to work on you."

He didn't know if her words pleased or scared him. "And I thought Mama was stubborn."

She lowered her head back to his chest. "She probably already has my replacement lined up."

Strong fingers lifted her chin. "Replacing you is impossible."

"Oh, Luke."

Luke considered himself a strong man, but not when looking into the eyes of a woman he wanted, a woman who wanted him just as much. His lips were a gentle brush against hers. "Good night. Again."

"Will you play for me?"

"Yes."

"Then I guess I better turn in. The sooner I go to sleep, the quicker I can see you again."

Luke returned to his room and picked up his guitar. He was in trouble, but he couldn't quite recapture his anger. Instead he visualized Catherine pulling off her robe and sliding beneath the sheets he had smoothed with his hands. And God help him, he imagined himself sliding beneath them with her and then into her.

His fingers touched the strings without him being aware of it. The sounds started soft, slow, mournful. The melody was hauntingly beautiful, yet soulful and sad, blues at its most elemental and basic. A lover yearning for that which was lost to him. The sound reached down into the depth of your heart, going deep where even you were afraid to admit to yourself you hurt and needed that badly.

On the other side of the wall, Catherine, who had been waiting for the sound, scooted up against the heavily carved, antique headboard. She didn't bother turning on the light, enough illumination was provided by the moonlight streaming through the slightly open shutters on the two windows. Besides, it seemed fitting the music be heard in half-shadows. Lying in bed, she listened as Luke played.

One song blended into the other, each more mournful than the last, each one tugging at the heart and going deep for the emotions. There was no escape from the music. None. Nor did she wish there to be. Luke was touching her in the only way that he thought he could. He was wrong and before Sunday arrived, she was going to prove it to him.

When the last note came, she slid beneath the covers, unconsciously running her hands over the cool cotton sheet where Luke had touched. A smile curved her lips as sleep claimed her. Number twenty-eight was going to be Luke's lucky number.

CATHERINE WOKE IN AN OPTIMISTIC MOOD. AS THE morning before, she and Luke prepared breakfast together. After eating and cleaning up the kitchen, she went to get dressed. Humming, she pulled on a short, fitted red skirt, then a matching jacket with a portrait collar. She had planned wearing it when she spoke at the Psychological

Association Conference, but she needed something that would keep Luke's mind on her all day.

From the admiring glint in his black eyes when she emerged from the bedroom, she had been right. His eyes roamed over her like silent, caressing fingers. She shivered, her gaze was no less admiring on him. He looked maddeningly handsome in the single-breasted oatmeal-colored sports coat and chocolate-colored slacks. He'd look even better in nothing at all.

She flushed, then smiled at the naughty, but oh so delicious thought.

Crossing to her, he took her arm and started from the house. "You're awful happy this morning."

"Yes, I am," she admitted. "I've got a feeling something wonderful is going to happen today."

RICHARD DIDN'T KNOW WHAT TO EXPECT WHEN HE knocked on number 105. It certainly wasn't the tiny woman who peered cautiously at him with huge, weary black eyes through the tiny slit in the hotel door. He smiled to put her at ease. "Good morning, Mrs. Jones. I'm Dr. Youngblood."

The opening didn't widen. Clearly she wasn't ready to trust him completely. "Good morning. If you'd wait, we'll be out in a minute."

He handed her the uniform. "You'll need this."

The door opened wider. He had a chance to see her face. Soft, pretty, but wearing lines of strain. A slim hand with short unvarnished nails took the plastic-covered hanger. "Thank you. I won't be long."

The door closed. Richard's brow bunched. Luke was definitely right. She was scared.

In less than five minutes, the door opened. Naomi walked out holding the hand of her little girl. Her eyes were no less afraid. Like a mistreated animal, hurt by man, afraid to trust. He had lost count of the number he had patiently taught to trust again.

"Thank you for giving me the job. I'll work hard."

Like a dutiful child, she repeated the words as if she had rehearsed them all night, as if afraid the job would be taken from her. "The job is yours for as long as you want. I'm the one who should be thanking you." He glanced at the little girl by her side. "You must be Kayla."

Delighted, she grinned, showing small white teeth. "You know my name."

Richard squatted down. "Catherine and Luke told me. I happen to know you like hamburgers with mustard and that's exactly what we're having for lunch."

"Wow," she said, then looked up at her mother. "Did you hear?"

"Yes." Naomi smiled.

Richard happened to be looking up at her when she did. The smile transformed her face, taking away the shadows, the lines of strain, to reveal a lovely young woman with delicate features and a soft, kissable mouth.

He stood. Wrong thought. Wrong woman. "I'm ready if you are."

"Yes." She bit her lip, her hand going around her daughter's shoulder. "We're ready."

NAOMI WAS NERVOUS. SOMEHOW SHE HADN'T expected Dr. Youngblood to be so young or so gentle and patient with Kayla. Especially the patience. From the time Kayla had been buckled into her seat, she had started asking questions about the animals he cared for. Naomi hadn't tried to curb her daughter's inquisitiveness. The more she kept Dr. Youngblood occupied answering questions, the less time he had to ask her questions.

Now, touring the clinic, Kayla was still asking questions. "Can I play with the animals sometimes?"

"No, Kayla." Dr. Youngblood led them back out to the front. "Just like you shouldn't play with strangers, you shouldn't play with strange animals."

"But if I played with them they'd become my friend and they wouldn't be like a stranger," she reasoned.

Naomi had to smile.

"But until they became your friend, they'd still be strangers and the answer is still no." He turned to Naomi. "You have a very sharp daughter."

"Especially when she wants her way."

Richard's gaze strayed to her lips. This time she caught him. She stiffened and took a step back.

He could ignore his blunder or face the situation head on. "I apologize for that. It won't happen again."

She eased toward the door, taking Kayla with her.

"Mama, what's the matter?"

Richard felt as if he had destroyed something precious. "You have nothing to fear from me, but until you learn that, we'll leave the doors open. As you can see from the desk, I need your help. If you want, we'll take one day at a time and you get paid at the end of every day."

Naomi paused.

Richard pulled out his wallet and laid sixty dollars on the desk. "It's all I have on me. I'll get the rest before you get off."

Naomi glanced at the money that would buy Kayla food, a place to sleep where she wouldn't be scared. Picking it up, she shoved it deep in the pocket of her pants. "We'll take one day at a time."

The front door opened. The phone rang. Richard was thankful to both. "Let's get started."

RICHARD WAS CAREFUL TO MAINTAIN DISTANCE BE-tween himself and Naomi while he took her through her on-the-job training. Thankfully, she was smart and picked up on things quickly. An added plus was that she spoke Spanish. He had started to ask how she learned the language, but one glance at her closed expression had him discarding the idea.

By the time lunch arrived he was actually considering paying Luke for suggesting her. People loved their pets just as much as parents loved their children and were just as devoted to them. Naomi seemed instinctively to understand this and reassure them. More importantly, she seemed genuinely concerned regarding each animal's health. He'd heard more than one elderly person telling her the life story of a beloved companion.

During lunch, Kayla may have lingered over her burger while watching the cartoon channel, but Naomi finished quickly and went back to her desk. His previous receptionist went out to lunch each day and was invariably late getting back. But in Cheryl's defense, he hadn't paid her the salary he was paying Naomi or bought her lunch.

"Dr. Youngblood. Your one o'clock is here," Naomi said from the door. "I put them in room A."

"Thank you." By the time he had finished speaking, she was gone. Her distrust bothered him and he had no one to blame but himself. Slowly, he got up from his desk and went to room A. This wasn't the first time he had struck out with a woman, but it was the first time he had struck out without even picking up the bat.

OUT OF THE CORNER OF HER EYE, NAOMI WATCHED Dr. Youngblood enter the exam room as she had off and on for most of the afternoon. Her breath fluttered over her lips as she alphabetized the patients' charts on her desk. She hadn't been able to catch him, didn't know if she wanted to, but occasionally she could feel him watching her. The only reason she hadn't taken Kayla and run was that she no longer felt threatened. Oddly, she couldn't explain why.

Perhaps it was the careful way he made sure he kept his distance or the way he gave the same respect and care to paying as well as nonpaying clients or the way he held Kayla's hand and helped her measure the animals' food. His hands were strong and gentle as they cared for his patients, his voice self-assured as he calmed worried pet owners. Nothing she had seen today indicated he would force himself on a woman. She had to stop judging all men because of the actions of one.

Excusing herself to the people in the waiting room, she went to his office to file the charts. Kayla was on the couch asleep. Unable to resist, she bent and kissed her soft cheek. "He won't find us, I promise."

Straightening, she turned and saw Dr. Youngblood. Her face paled. Her fingernails dug into the manila folders.

"I need your help," he said, then he was gone.

Her hands trembling, Naomi laid the charts on the desk and followed, wondering if he had heard, and how far sixty-four dollars and thirty-three cents would take her and Kayla if they had to run again.

CHAPTER ELEVEN

A WOMAN WHO LOOKED SEXY AND SMELLED ALLURING the way Catherine did could make a man forget himself. Luke hoped he was up to the challenge. From childhood he had been taught respect, patience, and self-control. Catherine was certainly testing him this morning.

The neckline of her jacket bared a hint of shoulders, then plunged dramatically down to her softly rounded breasts. Everything was demurely covered, but each time she moved, the red material seemed to shift, offering a peek that never quite kept its promise. That didn't keep him from looking. By the time the evening session was winding down, he could have ripped the jacket off with his teeth.

She knew it, too. He still couldn't believe that was her foot rubbing against his leg during lunch. When he got her home, he was going to . . . Run like hell.

He checked his watch, then saw what he hoped was the last person to ask a question make his way to the back mike, one of three, positioned in the aisle of the auditorium.

"Neither your introduction nor your bio on the back of the program mentioned you were married. Are you?"

Holding up her hand, Catherine quieted the annoyed murmurs in the audience. "No."

"You got any children?"

Her hands on the wooden podium clenched. "No."

"Then how can you try to tell me how to raise my kids?" the short, balding man asked belligerently.

Catherine had no difficulty answering his question. "Because I have no biased opinions, no reason to justify my actions of what I did or did not do or could not do. I simply deal in the facts."

"Facts you've gotten in a research lab and not trying to deal with a child who won't study or breaks curfew," he continued angrily.

Catherine had dealt with outraged parents before who lashed out due to frustration. "I've worked with problem children almost daily for the past ten years until a few months ago. I've seen them frightened, belligerent, apathetic. Children can go without a lot of things, but love is not one of them, and while blood ties are important, they are not essential to giving that love and support."

"But the fact remains you don't have any children."

"No, I don't have that blessing, and that's a big reason why I work so hard to help those who do," she said with absolute conviction.

The auditorium erupted in applause. By the time the sound died, a middle-aged woman with gray hair was speaking into the middle mike. "I'd just like to say I agree with Dr. Stewart. My husband and I have three adopted children and if someone tried to tell me they weren't mine just because I didn't carry them nine months, they'd have a fight on their hands."

Catherine made herself relax. "Parenting is one of the most underappreciated, the most thankless jobs anyone could ever have if it isn't done out of love. Establishing rules and guidelines is never easy. Make no mistake, children will test them again and again, they'll push you to your limits it seems sometimes, but if you're consistent and discipline with love and understanding, and a little recollection of what it was like to be young, being a parent can be the greatest, most rewarding privilege in the world. Thank you."

The audience came to their feet and continued applauding as Catherine took her seat. Luke was among them, unaware that he was grinning. Seems the daughter was just as tough as her mother.

A delighted Amanda Poole came to the podium. "If everyone will adjourn to the room next door, Dr. Stewart's books will be on sale and she'll be available for autographing."

People began filing out of the auditorium. Luke went to Catherine. "Very well done. I saw him scuttle out when the audience began to applaud."

"He wasn't angry at me," Catherine said, the knots gradually loosening in her stomach.

Luke grunted. "I might have known you'd forgive the guy."

"Excuse me, Dr. Stewart, we need to get to the next room," Amanda said.

"There's no need to hurry," Gloria said, joining them on stage. "I just checked again. The books didn't arrive."

"What?" Amanda said. "How could you let this happen?"

"Dr. Stewart called and said she'd take care of the books."

Catherine was already shaking her head. "I never order my own books."

Gloria was unrelenting. "I wouldn't know anything about that. But you specifically called. The bookstore here in town was disappointed."

"What will we do?" Amanda asked, watching the people file out. "We led people to believe they would be able to buy books and get your autograph when they signed up."

"I'm sure they'll understand," Ruth said. "Apparently there was a mix-up in communication somewhere."

"I just want everyone to know I didn't make it," Gloria said, glaring at a silent Catherine.

"May I make a suggestion, Mrs. Poole?" Luke asked.

"Please do."

"Tell the people the shipment was delayed and will be here Saturday. There will be a special signing with wine and cheese at the Red Cactus, and for their trouble, each book will have a ten percent discount. Or they can pay full price and the ten percent will go to the Women's League."

"Luke, that's a wonderful idea," Ruth said.

"But can Brandon's restaurant hold five hundred people?" asked a worried Amanda.

"It will be a crush, but so much the better," Luke told her.

"You're right." Amanda beamed.

"I'll go tell them," Ruth offered.

"Tell them to save their program, Mama," Luke said. "It will be their invitation."

"It will be just like a literary event," one of the other women said with growing enthusiasm.

"This will be better than the signing here," Ruth agreed, relief in her voice.

"Who is going to pay for the wine and cheese?" Gloria asked, arms crossed, glaring at Catherine.

"I'll take care of everything," Luke said, noting how quiet Catherine was. "You ready?"

She turned to Ruth. "I think I should go with you. Everyone may not be able to attend Saturday. I could sign their programs and talk with them."

"Catherine, I knew I was right to invite you." Ruth hooked her arm through Catherine's. "Let's go."

Luke found himself staring after Catherine again as

the group of women left the auditorium. He followed. This time they weren't leaving him behind.

LUKE MAY HAVE FOLLOWED, BUT HE NEVER GOT A chance to speak with Catherine privately. People were understanding about the "delayed" shipment of books and excited about the signing at the Red Cactus. As he had suspected, some of the people attending the conference already had books for her to sign or had left without buying books. His mother suggested they mark the programs of those remaining or people would show up just for the wine and cheese. The exclusivity of the signing appealed to people even more.

An hour later when the last person filed out of the room, the participants and the members of the Women's League were eagerly anticipating the book signing Saturday morning.

Luke waited until they were inside his truck before he asked. "You're all right?"

"They slipped up this time," she said.

"What?"

Her beautiful face shone. "They slipped up. There is a notation in my notebook that says 'order books' before speaking engagements like this one where a bookstore is not directly involved." Her smile grew. "But I don't order them. It's a reminder for me to remind Helena to make sure everything is in place. I was so upset when I left, I forgot to call."

He'd never seen anything more beautiful. "If they made one mistake, there will be others."

Her smile disappeared. "I can't wait to find out who is behind this and why."

"You let me take care of that." The thought of her confronting whoever it was knotted his stomach. "You can never predict how a person will act when cornered."

The certainty in his voice told her he was speaking from experience. Not too far behind was the thought of him being wounded. Fear for him coursed through her. "If I can't confront whoever it is, neither can you. You just find out who it is and tell the police."

Switching on the motor, he backed out of his parking space. "I don't work that way."

"You do this time or you're fired."

"Did I try to tell you how to run your workshop?"

"Luke—"

"Trust me, Catherine, to know what I'm doing and to do it right."

Maybe because he had tried reasoning instead of dictating to her, she heard herself say, "If you get one scratch, I'll never forgive you."

His hand closed over her trembling one. "Deal."

LUKE'S FIRST STOP WAS THE RED CACTUS, EXPLAINING to Brandon only that there had been a mix-up in ordering Catherine's books and he had volunteered his restaurant for the signing. Since the first reservation wasn't until 12 P.M., no problem. They'd had private parties there before. As Luke had expected, Brandon could take care of the wine and cheese trays. Catherine barely finished thanking Brandon before Luke was telling her they had another stop to make.

The next stop was the bookstore. The owner, who had felt slighted, was only too pleased to order her most recent books. Especially when Catherine offered to do a signing for him Saturday afternoon, and Luke told him about the ten percent, then assured him he'd reimburse him every penny. The owner cheerfully gave Catherine a discount when she purchased a pop-up children's book and a stuffed teddy bear. He couldn't thank them enough as they left the store.

"You will not pay the ten percent." Catherine buckled her seat belt. "I will."

"We'll talk about it later."

Catherine sent him a look of annoyance. "I seemed to remember you telling Naomi the same thing. I won't be put off so easily."

"Somehow I didn't think you would."

Their next stop was the clinic. Naomi was on the phone so Catherine waved and went to the back to find Kayla. The little girl was coloring, her tongue stuck in her cheek.

"Ready to hear about the butterfly?"

"Miss Catherine." Bounding up, the little girl ran to Catherine and hugged her.

Gracefully, Catherine sat down on the carpeted floor and placed the sack between them. "I have a couple of surprises for you."

"What? What?" Kayla danced from one tennis shoe–clad foot to the other.

Laughing, Catherine began drawing out her purchases for the little girl. First the pop-up book, then Kayla's excited cries rang higher when Catherine pulled out an eighteen-inch brown teddy bear dressed in a blue and white cable knit sweater with a scarf tied around his neck.

"Thank you," Kayla said, hugging the toy tightly to her chest. "I'll take good care of him."

Naomi, having heard the laughter, came to the door. Kayla ran to her with her teddy bear. "Look, Mama. Look."

Naomi's hand trembled as she touched her daughter's glowing face. "I see, sweetheart."

Luke folded his arms and said nothing. But if Naomi gave Catherine a hard time about the gifts, they were going to have a private talk.

"I hope you don't mind." Catherine folded her legs beside her. "I was in the bookstore and I couldn't resist.

Neither my brother nor I have any children, so my relatives' and friends' children get the full benefits."

"I— Thank you," Naomi said, touched. "Did you thank her?"

"Yes, ma'am. Now, I'm going to show Dr. Richard."

"Kayla—" But Kayla was already past her. The two had quickly established a rapport. She was usually shy around men—with good reason. Last night she hadn't said two words to Luke. With Dr. Youngblood, she couldn't stop talking. He'd bought her an animal coloring book and colors when he'd gone out for their lunch. Together they had flipped through each page, deciding what she should color first. A puppy.

Running down to the kennel, Kayla opened the door and went inside and straight to Richard. "See what Miss Catherine brought me? I'm going to call him Teddy, and if he gets sick, you can cure him."

"I'll consider it a privilege to treat such a fine gentleman." Richard took the stuffed animal and looked the bear over. "Maybe we should give him an examination to make sure he's healthy."

"Could we?" Awe and excitement were in her voice and face.

Standing, he reached for her hand. Naomi stood in the doorway, weary, watchful. If only the mother was as easy to give her trust. "Would you like to join us during the exam?"

"You have a patient coming."

"I'll explain to them if we run over," he said. "They'll understand."

Confusion caused fine lines to radiate across her forehead. "Why would you do that?"

"Because I promised and I never break a promise." He stepped past her and saw Luke and Catherine. His brows furrowed, he glanced back at Hero, who hadn't barked.

Richard closed the door to the kennel. "Hello, Luke, Catherine."

"Hi, Richard."

"Hello, Richard. How's Hero?" Catherine asked.

"Coming along as well as I expected." Richard remained in front of the door. "If you don't mind, I'd like for you not to go in. He has a difficult time adjusting when you leave."

"Oh," Catherine said, clearly disappointed.

Luke regarded the doctor with probing eyes, then said, "We should be going and let them get back to work."

"Goodbye, Kayla, Naomi. I'll see you tomorrow." She leaned down to the little girl. "We have some unfinished business about a butterfly."

"Dr. Richard and me will take good care of Teddy." Kayla hugged the bear to her.

"I'm sure you will." She looked up at Luke. "What's the next stop?"

"Home."

The single word never ceased to make Catherine's heart flutter. Then she glanced at Naomi, who had no home. "When is closing time?"

"The last patient is due in ten minutes," Naomi said.

"Great. Then afterward we can all go out to dinner. My treat. I had a great day and I feel like celebrating," Catherine said, careful not to look at Luke. "How about it, Richard? Naomi?"

"Naomi and I already have a dinner engagement," Richard said.

Startled, Naomi glanced around at him. "I don't know what you're talking about."

Richard explained. "The twelve-thirty appointment, El Cid with Mr. Carillo. His family has owned The Carillo House, a family restaurant, for generations. He and I have an agreement, he pays me with dinner for me and my staff, and since his place has the best real Mexican food in the city, it's a fair trade."

Naomi was already shaking her dark head.

"He had a nice doggy," Kayla said.

"Yes, he has," Richard said. "You'll upset the entire family if you don't show up. You don't even have to change clothes. We can go straight from here, and then I'll take you and Kayla back to the hotel."

Naomi glanced down at her uniform, then ran her hand over the front.

"You look fine." By the time she brought her head up, he was talking to Kayla. "So do you." The little girl grinned up at him. Shamelessly, he pressed his point. "The portions are very generous, and he had to tell you about his five grand-daughters whose parents work in the restaurant. Kayla can meet some children her own age."

"Can we, Mama? I'd like to play with them and I can show them Teddy."

"I suppose it would be all right," Naomi finally said.

"Great. Kayla, you and I better examine Teddy to en-sure he's up to his first outing." Holding the little girl's hand in his, he went into the exam room.

Naomi regarded their leaving as if she wasn't sure what had happened. Her hand went to the V neck of her printed top.

"You made the right decision," Catherine told her.

"I hope so." The opening of the door had her moving down the hall to the receptionist area. In came a willowy brunette holding a small brown and white dog, his nose stuck snugly in the crook of her arm. "Good evening."

Neither the greeting nor the smile was returned. "I'm Mrs. Floyd. I have an appointment to see Richard."

Naomi's smile wavered. "He'll be out shortly. Would you like to take a seat?"

Her strawberry-colored lips pursed, the woman started

to sit down, then saw Luke. The pout on her pretty face
quickly turned to a smile. With her free hand, she swept
back her hair from the collar of her sky blue velvet jacket.
Diamonds and sapphires sparkled on her fingers. "Luke,
what a wonderful surprise."

"Hello, Sybil." Luke regarded the animal. "Shakespeare worn out from chasing cars?"

She laughed, then hit him playfully on the chest. "That
was only once, but I'm concerned that he doesn't seem as
active as usual. He won't play with any of his toys."

"Richard will fix him up." He pulled Catherine to his
side. "I'd like you to meet a friend of the family. Dr.
Catherine Stewart. Sybil Floyd."

The wattage of the woman's smile dimmed considerably. "Dr. Stewart."

"Hello, Ms. Floyd," Catherine greeted, automatically
extending her hand. After a brief, telling hesitation Sybil
lifted hers. The contact was brief.

"My sister mentioned you." Her hand stroked the head
of the little dog.

"I'm afraid I'm at a disadvantage."

"Gloria Harris."

Now Catherine understood the coldness. "You should
be very proud of her. She did a wonderful job of getting
the parenting workshop together."

Surprise glinted in Sybil's eyes. "Why, thank you."

Behind them, the door opened and Richard and Kayla
came out. "Hi, Sybil."

"Hello, Richard," Sybil's voice mellowed to spun
sugar, then she looked behind him. "Where's the patient?"

"Here he is." Kayla held up Teddy to her. "We checked
Teddy out and Dr. Richard let me listen to his heart and
everything."

Sybil barely glanced at Teddy or the child. "Richard,
could we please see Shakespeare now?"

"Go on into the room I came out of," he said, his voice stiff.

"You won't be long, will you?"

"No."

"Goodbye, Luke." Holding the animal closer, she went into the room he had indicated.

"She didn't like Teddy," Kayla said, her head down.

Catherine started to comfort the child, but Richard was already bending. "As long as you love Teddy, that's all he cares about," he said. "I bet he thinks he's the luckiest bear in the world to have a pretty little girl like you to love and care for him. Catherine knew that, and that's why she bought him for you."

Her head came up, and, her smile blossoming, she hugged the animal. "I love Teddy and I'll take good care of him no matter what."

Richard's hand brushed her hair. "I know you will." He stood and regarded Naomi, who had her hands gripped. Anger emitted from her in waves. "I'll be out shortly and we can go eat." He turned to Luke and Catherine. "See you tomorrow."

"Goodbye, Richard," Catherine said. "Thanks." They both knew for what.

"Bye, Richard," Luke said, then, "Watch yourself."

"Always." After one final look at Naomi, he went into the exam room.

Naomi started for Kayla. Catherine shook her head. The child was smiling and talking to her new friend.

Luke crouched down. "Dr. Youngblood is right, Catherine knew Teddy belonged to you. I think I see him smiling. He won't be lonely anymore in the store by himself because now he has you."

"He won't, will he?" Kayla gazed up at Catherine. "Thank you, Miss Catherine."

Looking at Luke and Kayla together, Catherine felt her

heart catch. He would make a devoted, understanding father. Squatting, she hugged Kayla. "You're welcome. Don't feed Teddy too much dinner or he'll have a tummy ache and won't be able to sleep."

She nodded solemnly. "I won't."

Catching Catherine's elbow, Luke stood. "Don't let Sybil ruin your dinner. Richard will take care of her."

"I . . . thank you," Naomi said, her trembling hand on Kayla's shoulders.

Catherine smiled. "That's what friends are for. See you tomorrow."

His hand sliding from her elbow to her hand, Luke walked with Catherine to the truck. "Like I said, Richard will take care of it and Sybil will feel it a lot more from him."

"Because he's a man?" Catherine got into the truck, still angry at the coldness of the woman toward a child.

Luke slid in beside her and backed out of the small parking lot before answering, "Because he knows that she has him picked for husband number three."

Catherine tsked. "Richard has more sense."

"How can you be so sure?"

She shot him a quick glance. "Richard doesn't strike me as the superficial type. He'd want substance in a woman."

Luke grunted. "She has that."

"Not *that*. A good plastic surgeon can give a woman a double D," she snapped, and turned a stiff shoulder toward him. "Men."

He didn't like the sound of that. Remembering what had happened last time, he slowed down and let the plodding truck get two car lengths in front of him. "What's wrong with you? If anyone should be upset, it's me."

"And why is that?"

"You're quick to say that Richard wouldn't be taken in, but you obviously think I would."

"You're the one who seems to think so highly of her *substance*," Catherine said, sarcasm dripping from her voice.

"I do not. I only said . . . why the hell are we arguing over a woman who we both know is as shallow as water in a teaspoon?" he grated.

"I'm not sure," Catherine said, knowing she wasn't being honest. She was jealous. "Maybe I'm hungry."

"You want to stop and get something or wait until we get home?"

"Let's go home."

"Home it is."

HER FACE TIGHT WITH ANGER, SYBIL CAME OUT OF THE exam room and slammed out of the office. The adobe walls were too thick to shudder, but the windows weren't.

Richard didn't even glance in their direction. "The three of you ready to go eat?"

"We are," cried Kayla.

"Go pick up your things, Kayla," Naomi said, her attention on Richard.

"Yes, ma'am." She ran out of the room. For once Naomi didn't tell her to slow down.

"She's not coming back, is she?" Naomi said.

Richard pulled off his lab coat. "I hope not."

"I pulled Shakespeare's record. She brings the dog in often and she always pays." Naomi frowned, for once her gaze direct as she searched his face. "You barely know Kayla."

"Money isn't the issue here. There is never a reason for rudeness, especially to a defenseless child." Draping the coat over his arm, he started for his office.

"Dr. Youngblood?"

He turned. "Yes?"

"Thank you for caring." Her voice trembled.

The rigidity left his shoulders. "You're welcome, Naomi, and don't you think you should call me Richard? Everyone else does."

A stillness invaded her body. "I'd prefer not to."

"As you wish." He continued into his office.

Returning to her chair, Naomi straightened her desk. Nothing was as she wished for a very, very long time.

THE CARILLO WAS JUST OFF THE PLAZA. NO SOONER had Richard walked into the restaurant than Mr. Carillo and several of his family members converged on him. As he had expected, Naomi and Kayla were greeted just as warmly. By the time they had reached their table, Mr. Carillo's four-year-old granddaughter, Linda, was getting acquainted with Kayla and Teddy.

While Naomi's attention was on her daughter, Richard spoke hurriedly to Mr. Carillo. His olive face saddened, then he took their orders personally. Service was impeccable, the food delicious.

Seeing Naomi relax and eat was worth the small lie, Richard thought. He still couldn't get the picture of her eating only half her hamburger, then carefully wrapping the other half and putting it in her canvas bag when she thought he wasn't looking.

Leaving the restaurant, he drove them back to their hotel and walked them to their door despite Naomi's insistence that he didn't have to. "I just want to make sure you and Kayla get inside safely."

Opening the door, Naomi ushered Kayla into the room, then turned and stood in the opening of the doorway that dwarfed her petite body. "Thank you."

Richard was acutely conscious that she still didn't trust him. It bothered him, especially since he may have given her cause. "I'll go by an ATM machine and get the rest of your money," he said. "Should I bring it back here or leave it at the desk?"

Naomi's shy gaze fastened on him for a split second, then dropped to his chest. "Tomorrow will be fine. You must be tired."

"A little," he confessed, breathing a little easier now that he hadn't scared her away. "It's been tough at times doing both jobs. I'm glad I have you."

Her gaze zipped back up, then down again. "Good night." The door closed.

Richard glanced skyward and wondered what the hell was wrong with him. He was scaring Naomi to death when all he wanted to do was help her. *Is that all?* a little voice asked. The scowl on Richard's face was the only answer.

DUSK WAS SETTLING AS LUKE AND CATHERINE LEFT THE cabin and made their way through the woods after dinner that night. The piñon and aspen trees were thick with leaves, the grass lush beneath their feet. The summer before had been mild, the runoff water from the mountains plentiful, and all the inhabitants had benefited.

"Where are all the animals I usually see?" she asked.

"All except the night hunters are getting settled for the night," Luke told her. "It's not much farther. You said you wanted to celebrate, and I have something to show you that does exactly that. Can you make it?"

"Easy. I may have grown up in the city, but I'm no wimp."

"I know that better than most." His hand closed around her arm as they stepped into a clearing. "There."

"Oh my, Luke, it's beautiful," she whispered softly and took a step closer to the edge of the placid pool of water.

The beauty of the small, hidden lake never ceased to touch him, the rush of the water spilling down from the mountains and over rocks to soothe him, the timelessness of the place to help him remember his own mortality. "It's been my favorite place since I first saw it."

On bended knees, Catherine scooped up a palm of water, then laughed, shaking the moisture away. "It's like ice."

A shiver went through Luke at the crystal sound. He caught himself tilting his head to catch the slight echo the surrounding trees and rocks created, wanting her to laugh again when the sound faded into nothingness.

"Is it safe to drink?"

He worked his shoulders as if that would rid him of the disappointment. It didn't. "If you don't mind your teeth aching. The water comes from high in the snowcapped mountains. Because of the angle of the sun, it keeps the water from heating up until late summer."

She sat back on her heels and stared up at him. "What do you call heating up?"

"Sixty or a little below." He barely jumped back in time to miss being splattered with the water she splashed at him. "It's not that bad once you've been in it for a while."

Using one hand to support herself, she sat down, then crossed her pants-covered legs beneath her. "It might be worth getting frostbite." She turned to him as he sat down beside her. "Thanks for sharing."

He wanted to reach out to touch, to claim. The growing need to do so surprised and aggravated him.

"How did you find this place?"

"Chasing an executive who was involved in a kickback scheme with his brother-in-law," Luke recalled with a chuckle. "He rabbited the moment he saw me and the CEO of the company drive up. But he soon discovered that running on a treadmill and through a forest are worlds apart."

"I knew it was natural," she blurted, sounding pleased with herself.

"What?"

She flushed and glanced out across the water. Thinking about Luke's well-toned body was going to get her into trouble. "Nothing. How long ago was that?"

"Six years ago," he responded. "I couldn't swing it, so I asked Daniel to come in with me."

"From the way Daniel talked, you can name your own price now."

"I get by." But nothing compared to the money her family had. He stood. "We better get back."

"All right." She held her hand out to him.

He was slow in extending his. When she was upright, he released her because he didn't want to. He couldn't decide if Sunday was too far away or too close.

CATHERINE BARELY KEPT FROM SIGHING WHEN THEY walked back to the cabin. Unlike the trek there, Luke hadn't held her hand and there was no leisurely stroll. She got the distinct impression he wanted to run.

As was his practice, Luke checked to make sure no one had entered the cabin, then unlocked the door and let her in. "I'll be in the office working."

Her trembling hand rested on one of the huge log posts in the entryway to unobtrusively block his path. "You mind if I bring my laptop and join you?"

She almost smiled at the frantic look on his face. He hadn't expected that. "The office is kind of cramped."

"I don't mind." She started toward her room. "I'll be back in a minute."

"I work better alone." The words sounded weak to his own ears.

Slowly she turned around to face him. "Of course. Have you found out anything?"

He shook his head. "As far as we can tell, neither Perkins, your assistant, nor Tolliver have been out of the city for the past week, nor have they had any large with-drawals from their accounts."

Her arms circled her waist. "You mean they might be paying someone."

"Sounds reasonable. They'd want an alibi and hiding out undetected takes skill and patience," he told her.

"So now, I have to worry about two people."

He hated the fear that flared in her eyes. "I'm going to find out who is behind this, but chances are it's someone from the university. Rena Bailey is still in rehab and hasn't been out on a pass or seen anyone since she went in, and your neighbor is in Europe on vacation."

Catherine leaned against one of the log posts. "I still find it difficult to believe one of my colleagues would do something like this."

"From what I read and what you've told me, no one else has a reason to try and discredit you," he told her. "If they were trying to get to your parents or your brother by using you, they'd come at you a lot heavier."

Her gaze held his. "So, I'm the target."

There was no easy way. "Yes."

Nodding, she straightened. "At least my family is safe."

"You are, too."

"Thanks to you."

Her smile was all that he could have wished for and something he could never have. "I better get to work."

"Good night, Luke."

"Good night." Before he allowed himself to even think of something foolish, he turned and went to his office.

HER PLAN OF SEDUCTION CERTAINLY WASN'T WORKING out, Catherine thought as she paced her bedroom. Here she was all perfumed and wearing the sexiest nightgown she had brought and hadn't the foggiest notion of how to get Luke into her bedroom or herself into his.

Screaming was out. She didn't want to scare him. She didn't like the idea of faking an illness. Luke would have her to a hospital before you could say thermometer. There had to be a way. Time certainly wasn't on her side.

She had finally found a man she respected, admired, and cared enough about to want to be intimate with. What's more, he wouldn't want anything long term. Luke couldn't have been more perfect if she had ordered him. He was caring, gentle, and had a body that made her insides shiver just thinking about it.

And he was determined they not become lovers because he admired and respected her.

Sighing, she admitted defeat. She might as well go to bed. Glancing at the closed plantation shutters, she sighed again.

Waking up and being able to see the woods each morning had been one of the pleasurable things she liked about the cabin. From her bedroom window in her condo in Los Angeles, she saw another building. The first morning here she had seen a deer, the next a flight of birds. Just the peacefulness of the woods themselves had been soothing.

Once finding out someone had been in her room, she had keep the shutters nearly closed. The room was beautifully decorated, but she wasn't going to be able to stare at the four walls tonight. She was too tense and on edge.

She took a step closer. Maybe she would crack them just a little more so the moonlight could filter through. With her mind made up, she crossed the room and opened the shutters . . . and stared into two glowing eyes.

Her scream was loud and piercing. She staggered back, then turned to run. With three running steps she barreled into something warm and solid. Luke.

"What is it?"

Trying to pull away, she pointed behind her.

Luke was shoving her behind him when he recognized the sight and the sound. "It's all right, Cath, it's a pigmy owl."

Only then did she stop struggling and peered behind her. The two eyes winked back at her. "Oh."

Luke stared down at her. His face fierce. "Is that all you can say after scaring ten years off my life again? By the time this case is solved I'll probably have more gray hair on my head than Daniel."

She swallowed. "I didn't mean to scream, it just happened. When you came in I was going to get my gun—"

"What?"

"My gu—"

Suddenly she was eye level with a very angry Luke. "Don't you ever even think of something so idiotic. Don't you even put yourself in danger."

"Luke, I've been tr—"

"Never!" he shouted. "Understood?"

"Yes," she told him but he still looked ready to destroy something. Catherine wasn't worried. Luke would protect her with his life. He was hopping mad because she might have put herself in danger.

"If you want I'll go outside and scare him off."

Despite the situation, Catherine began to see the possibilities. Now that her heart wasn't trying to beat its way out of her chest. "Are you always this grouchy when you're awakened from a sound sleep?"

"I wasn't asleep."

She allowed herself the luxury of just staring at his magnificent body clad in tiny black briefs which in no way disguised his masculinity. His chest was broad, the muscles hard and roped. The legs sturdy and strong. The feet long. "Aren't you dressed for bed?"

"I wear even less to bed."

Her heart started pounding again. "Don't bother on my account."

He laughed, his hand cupping her cheek. "Cath, will you always surprise me?"

"I certainly hope so," she whispered, loving the way he endearingly shortened her name.

He slowly pushed the silk robe over her arms. The gray material pooled at her feet. "The night I arrived at the cabin I dreamed about you standing before me again wearing this." His lips brushed across her bare shoulders. "Without the gun, of course."

She shivered. "Luke, I'm not sure how much longer my legs will hold me."

He picked her up, then stared down into her face, his gaze intent. "The first time should be in a bed."

Heat licked through her veins. "You aren't the type of man to break his word, are you?"

Placing her on top of the cool cotton sheet, his lips brushed against hers. "Never, and never about something this important to me."

"Luke."

His lips kissed her cheek, her eyelids. "You say my name as if it's everything to you."

"It is." Trembling hands palmed his strong, handsome face. "I don't want to disappoint you. I want this to be right for you."

Tender lips brushed her palms. "Disappointing me would be impossible. Just being here with you gives me more satisfaction than you can imagine." He brushed his lips across hers again. "Any way between us will be the right way."

She relaxed, and pushed the doubts from her mind. Luke was what she wanted and she'd trust him to guide her. "Are there a lot of ways?"

He grinned. "More than you can imagine."

"Hadn't we better get started?"

"Need something first." He started to pull away. Her hands around his neck stopped him.

She pressed her cheek against his chest. Looking at him was impossible when she said, "I won't get pregnant." Saying *can't* was even more impossible.

Strong fingers lifted her chin. He studied her a long time. "Neither one of us can afford to be wrong about this."

"I'm aware of that." Uncomfortable, she lowered her gaze. "I—if you want to wear something because you have health conc—"

"Catherine," he interrupted gently. "My concern is for you. I can tell this is difficult for you, but I have to be sure."

"The pill makes me sure," she said softly, mixing a truth with a lie, mixing the past with the present.

"Honey," he hugged her to him, his lips brushing her hair. "I knew I was off base in asking about your past relationships, and I'm still not sure if I did it for me or for the investigation, but I know there was probably very little need for the pill in the past." Lifting his head, he kissed her closed eyelids and watched them slowly rise. "You're smart enough not to depend on a man to protect you. We don't have to talk about it again."

"Maybe there is one thing you should know."

She looked so vulnerable, so fragile, so serious. Gently, his hand swept her hair back from her face. "I'm listening."

"You're my test case."

His eyes widened. He stared down at her. The enormity of what she was saying slowing sinking into him, his heart, and touching his soul, his spirit. "You humble me."

"That doesn't mean you're going to be noble and go back to your room, does it?" she asked, a bit worried.

Instead of answering, he brushed his lips against hers, a tender, slow glide that comforted and inflamed. He kept the maddening, slow pace up until she squirmed beneath him, her lips trying to find his. Finally, she nipped his lower lip.

"Stop teasing me," she ordered.

"I might have known you'd be bossy."

"I—"

Whatever she had been about to say was cut off by his mouth on hers. This time there was nothing fleeting in the fusing of his lips to hers, nor was there in the bold thrust of his tongue in her mouth. A man claiming his woman.

Catherine caught her breath at the bold attack on her senses, then caught Luke by his loose hair and met him. A woman claiming her man.

One kiss turned into another and another, each one leaving her a little more breathless, a little needier.

"Does the light bother you?" he asked between kisses.

"Not having you touch me bothers me," she answered, drawing his head back.

His strong, callused hands were everywhere on her body, and everywhere, they inflamed. Teeth and tongue tugged and lapped the hard point of her nipple. Exquisite sensations swept through her. But somehow it wasn't enough.

She jumped as his hand swept down the inside of her thigh. Always coming closer, but never quite close enough to the heat burning her. The silk became unbearable. When Catherine would have ripped it from her body, Luke did it for her.

The sound of rending silk matched her moans as his mouth closed over her bare nipple and suckled. Then his finger dipped, seeking the source of her heat and need. The twin assaults were too much. Arching her back, his name a moan on her lips, she came undone.

Opening her eyes, she saw him poised over her. "You are all that I desire."

His words melted her heart and inflamed her body. She felt herself stretch to accommodate him, felt the fleeting discomfort, then knew a moment of perfect bliss and satisfaction when they were joined completely. She was unaware of the wonder on her face, the tears gliding down her cheeks.

Luke kissed away each one. Her tears washing away his fear that he might hurt her.

Her hand shook as she reached up to brush the thick, straight black hair from his face. "Until there was you, I didn't know what desire was."

Luke's breath caught. Only this woman could touch the deepest, most vital part of him. "I'm finding out neither did I."

He began to move, slowly in and out of her hot, sleek body. The tightness of her, the feel of her nearly sent him over the edge. More than that was seeing the flush of arousal, the pleasure sweeping across her face again. He wanted to linger there forever, make it perfect, unforgettable for her. He couldn't.

Her slick velvet sheath called to him too strongly. Need had never trampled through him this strongly. The driving of his hips increased. Her legs wrapped around his hips, she eagerly met him. Then it happened. They both jerked and went still, suspended. Fulfillment . . .

Luke collapsed and rolled over on his side, bringing Catherine with him. His breath rushed out as if he had run ten miles, his heart pounded. He could conquer the world with Catherine's light weight pressed against him. He felt unbelievably fantastic.

From a deep inner source, he found the strength to run his hand down her back, to kiss her damp forehead. "You all right?"

Too full to speak, she nodded.

Luke lifted her chin and stared into her teary eyes. He kissed them. "You're sure?"

"I never knew it could be so beautiful." Trembling hands touched his lips. "Thank you."

"I know a way to thank each other."

Catherine yelped when he came off the bed, taking her with him. Her arms tightened around his neck as he walked from the room. "I thought we were going to make love again."

"We are." Luke headed for the stairs. "First, you take a soak."

"What if I wanted to make love?" she asked, looking up at him through a sweep of her lashes.

He grinned down at her. "I plan for us to do both."

CHAPTER TWELVE

CATHERINE SUPPOSED SHE SHOULD HAVE BEEN EMBARrassed about her nakedness as she sat on the bath towel on the edge of the monster garden tub upstairs in one of the bathrooms. She wasn't. She wanted to see Luke's body and couldn't see her acting prudish when she watched him with her tongue practically hanging out.

Picking her up, Luke stepped into the warm soapy water. "You'll be feeling better in no time."

"Are you an expert on the subject?" She had meant the question to come out teasing. It had come out accusatory. Immediately she was contrite. "I'm sorry, Luke, please don't answer that. Why don't you leave me up here and I'll be back down in a little bit?"

His hand slid from beneath her legs, settling her in his lap. "Tired of me already?"

She sent him a quick glance. "Of course not."

His knuckles brushed over her nipple, felt her shiver. "Good."

She leaned against him, her head downcast. "All right, I'm jealous. My behavior is immature and unsophisticated and I apologize."

Catching her around the waist, he twisted her so she faced him, straddling him, his gaze direct. "You're the first woman I've ever made love to in this cabin. Since we may go by my house before you leave, I've never made love to a woman there either."

She felt miserable. "Luke, I'm sorry."

He lifted her chin. "Don't be. I wanted to rip the head off the guy you were engaged to. I'm still not sure how I'll react when I see Perkins. If I ever see your neighbor, he better hope it is on one of my good days. Any more questions?"

She reached down between them, felt his erection stir in her hand. "I think it's already been answered."

CATHERINE WOKE WITH A SMILE ON HER FACE, HER BACK pressed against Luke, his arm curved around her. Sunlight shone through the window of his bedroom. She stirred.

"About time you woke up." Tender lips brushed across her shoulder, belying the gruff words.

Her smile growing, she turned around to face him. "Why didn't you wake me up?" She nipped his chin.

"Because I'm the reason you're so sleepy."

"Yes, you are." She grinned and scooted closer, her hand roaming freely. She loved the touch, the feel, the smell of him.

"Your first meeting is at ten. It's almost eight. You're going to be late if you keep this up," Luke said, but his heart wasn't in it. He was hard and getting harder.

Her tongue circled his nipple. He groaned. She teased him with her tongue all the way to the other nipple. Kissed, laved, then blew. "We could skip breakfast."

Her nail stroked the inside of his thigh. He shuddered.

She started kissing her way down his broad chest, then abruptly lifted her head on reaching his navel. Mischief gleamed in her eyes. "But if you insist." She started to roll from the bed.

With a fierce growl, he pulled her down under him. Her

bubbling laughter stopped when he joined them with a thrust of his hips. If they were going to be late, they might as well enjoy themselves.

CATHERINE FELT WONDERFUL, ABSOLUTELY MAR-velous. Her feet barely touched the tiled floor of the hotel's lobby where registration tables had been set up. She saw a lot of old acquaintances and colleagues as she moved through the line. Finished, she went to where Luke waited. She might feel marvelous, but he looked marvelous in the charcoal tweed jacket. Better, she knew what he looked like without the jacket.

"If you don't stop looking at me that way, we're going to be the talk of the hotel."

She grinned impishly. "I'll try, but it won't be easy."

"Where to next?" he asked, catching her hand and starting down the crowded hallway.

"Finding my department chair, Dr. Watts, and the rest of the people from my university."

His hand tightened. "Perkins included."

She stopped and stepped in front of him. "He never even got a peck on the cheek."

"In that case, I'll let him live."

Catherine started to laugh, then noticed the hard glint in Luke's eyes.

"I told you I'm possessive."

Suddenly the light affair she wanted was becoming much more serious. She should have realized that before. When she had been plotting to seduce Luke, she hadn't taken into consideration his feelings. One of the many reasons she cared about Luke was that he had values and morals. "I'd never do anything to hurt you, but when my plane leaves Sunday, I'll be on it."

"I haven't asked you to do anything different, have I?"

His easy acceptance brought a mixture of relief and a sharp pain of regret. "No."

"This place is becoming more crowded by the minute. Why don't we go eat lunch, then come back and try again?" he suggested.

"That's fine . . ." They had missed breakfast and coffee.

Luke's hand, which had been holding Catherine's, lifted to her back, his thoughts in a swirl. With any other woman, he would have been happy that she wanted no strings, no ties—with Catherine he wanted to tie her to him and never let her out of his sight. Maybe because she was refreshingly different from all the other women he had dated or made love to. Whatever, the time until Sunday wasn't going to be nearly long enough to be with her.

Leaving the registration area they strolled down the hand-painted corridors, then past the shopping court. Over their heads, wooden balconies and beam ends protruded over the tops of windows and the lobby.

Silently they joined the line for lunch. Through the huge potted plants, Catherine could see a tiled indoor-garden patio lit by a skylight. "I hope the food here is as good as at Brandon's place," Catherine said, uncomfortable with the silence that had grown between them.

"Probably not, since Brandon recently hired away the head chef from this restaurant."

Catherine chuckled. "I bet those two in the kitchen is something to see."

"It's not for the fainthearted," Luke agreed, then reached for his pager on his belt and read the message. "It's from the clinic."

"Hero or Naomi and Kayla?" Catherine questioned worriedly.

"I don't know, but I intend to find out."

"I'm going, too."

"I never expected anything different." His hand in the small of her back, they hurried through the lobby.

"HERO WON'T EAT," DR. YOUNGBLOOD SAID, SQUATTING in front of the wolf hybrid's cage.

"Since when?" Catherine asked from beside the doctor.

"Tuesday."

Startled eyes turned to him. "But today is Thursday."

"I know." Frustration was in the doctor's voice. "Sometimes animals get that way, but soon snap out of it, and I thought Hero would do the same."

Catherine stroked his nose through the wires. "What's the matter with him?"

"He hates being caged in," Luke answered, his voice tight.

"But he has to stay here until he's well," Catherine said, glancing between the two men.

"That's just it, Catherine, he's not going to get well if he doesn't eat, and as long as he's in here, he won't eat." Dr. Youngblood's fingers clamped through the wire. "It's your decision."

"What decision?"

"Set him free or keep him here and watch him grieve himself to death." Luke pushed to his feet, away from the shock in Catherine's eyes.

Her trembling finger stroked the hybrid's black nose. "Where would I send him? I haven't contacted the woman in California."

"He can come back to the cabin," Luke heard himself saying.

"But you aren't up there all the time," Catherine pointed out. "Who will take care of him?"

"He'll take care of himself. You're leaving Sunday, remember?"

Her hand clenched. "Yes, I remember."

Richard looked between the two and decided to stay out of it. "I can sedate him so he'll be easier to handle."

"That won't be necessary." Luke squatted down, his gaze on the animal's. "Just bring the truck around to the back."

"I won't let you do it again," Catherine said.

"What?"

"You're not going to put yourself in danger. Saturday we had no choice. We'll take him sedated or we won't take him at all."

"I know what I'm doing!" he snapped.

"And we both know why. You're angry for Hero, angry at the situation that brought him here, and you're punishing me, too, and I won't have it. I won't," she told him, her voice almost as loud.

Hero lifted his head.

Richard decided it was a good time to leave. "I'll be in my office."

Luke came to his feet. He stared down into her face. The sparkle of tears in her huge brown eyes got to him. "Ah, hell."

She leaned into him, her arms circling his waist. "Don't you dare make me regret last night." She sniffed. "And this morning."

Nothing she could have said would have disturbed him more. She had been all that he could want in a woman, a lover. He pulled her flush against him. "I miss you already." The words just slipped out, but he had no wish to call them back.

Troubled, she lifted her head and gazed into his eyes. "Then we shouldn't waste our time being angry. Let's just enjoy the time we have together."

"Is that your professional or personal opinion?" he asked, smiling.

She breathed easier, then cocked a brow. "Both will cost you."

"Sassy woman."

Laughter spilled from her as he picked her up and swung her around, his lips fastening on hers. They were both breathing heavily when he sat her on her feet and lifted his head.

Hero stood barking at them.

"We're going to take you home, Hero. Aren't we, Luke?"

"Yes," Luke said, but he knew in that instant that he would never view the cabin the same once Catherine left. Being alone didn't sound so appealing anymore.

"EAVESDROPPING."

Naomi whirled around from the door leading to the kennel. Dr. Youngblood stood in front of her. She had seen him leave, then became concerned on hearing the raised voices. She didn't even try to lie. "He was yelling at her."

"Yes, and she was yelling right back."

She couldn't stop trembling. "She shouldn't have done that."

"Luke has shown you that he's a good man."

"People pretend sometimes to get what they want." The words were said with absolute surety and biting bitterness.

It was all he could do not to reach out and touch her. Knowing he couldn't, he tried to reassure her another way. "I don't, and neither does Luke."

Naomi looked at the door. "He doesn't smile a lot and he can look tough."

Richard took a small amount of pleasure because she hadn't included him in her on-target analysis of Luke, but he was then left with the uncomfortable speculation of what her thoughts were of him. "Luke would happily slice off his arm before he harmed a hair on her head."

Her troubled gaze came back to him. "You're just taking his side because you're his friend."

He didn't have to think about her opinion of him any longer. "If Luke was the type of man you're insinuating he is, he wouldn't be my friend."

Naomi seemed just as startled by Richard's terse announcement as she was by the laughter coming from the kennel.

His voice gentled. "Catherine can hold her own."

"I guess." Naomi started back to her desk. Richard didn't move. "Is there something you wanted?"

Coming from another woman Richard might have laughed at the question and then proceeded to leave little doubt as to exactly what he wanted. With Naomi, he stepped aside. "No."

Naomi hated being a coward, but she edged by Richard and hurried back to check on Kayla, who was happily building a house with the block set Richard had given her that morning. Teddy sat beside her. She wouldn't have let her daughter accept the blocks except she had been so happy. Money had been too tight for toys. Leaving the office, her gaze was drawn to the long hallway. Richard was still there, watching, waiting.

She didn't know why the look frightened and confused her in equal parts. Swallowing, she hurried to her desk.

Behind her, the door to the kennel opened. Luke came out holding Catherine's hand. "We'd appreciate if you'd sedate him."

Richard's gaze slid from Catherine to Luke. There were few times, if any, that he could remember Luke changing his mind on anything. And he'd never seen Luke keep a woman so close to him. "I'll get it ready."

"While you're doing that, I'll go visit with Naomi." Catherine went to the front.

"I'll stay here," Luke told her.

For the first time in their long friendship, Richard dreaded talking to Luke. The reason why flickered a worried glance at Catherine, then beyond to him. *Naomi.*

LUKE FOLLOWED THE DOCTOR INTO ONE OF THE small exam rooms and watched him tear the paper from a disposable syringe. "You learn anything more about Naomi?"

Lifting the vial, Richard plunged the needle through the rubber stopper and drew out the sedative. "She's a caring mother and a very good receptionist."

"Don't get funny with me, Richard. You know what I mean."

Capping the syringe, Richard returned the medicine to the locked cabinet. "Exactly why do you want to know so much about Naomi?"

"It has something to do with a case I'm working on."

"What kind of case?" Richard paused at the door.

"It's confidential," Luke said. "You learn anything about her I need to know?"

"Nothing I haven't already told you." Richard started back to the kennel. Naomi wasn't a threat to anyone. Whatever the case Luke was working on, she wasn't a part of it. Of that he was certain. He wasn't going to do anything that would cause her to get that frightened, haunted look in her eyes again.

"SO, HOW WAS DINNER LAST NIGHT?" CATHERINE ASKED.

"Fine," Naomi said. Her gaze wandered over Catherine's stylish cranberry-colored fitted jacket and long, slim skirt. "You look very nice. What kind of conference and workshop are you attending?"

"I finished the parenting workshop yesterday and tomorrow I'm speaking at the American Psychological Association." Catherine kept her gaze steady. "I'm a child psychologist and teach at UCLA."

Fear and shock in equal parts raced across the younger woman's face. Her hands braced against the edge of the desk as if preparing to bolt.

Catherine casually edged a hip on the corner of the desk. "My profession hasn't changed since we met. Have I given you any indication that I'd do anything that might harm or upset you or Kayla?"

The answer wasn't long in coming. "No."

"And I won't." Feeling that the crisis had passed, Catherine opened her purse, took out a card, and handed it to Naomi. "You're a good mother who happens to have hit upon some rough times. It's not my place to judge you. I'm leaving Sunday. Call collect if you want to talk or if I can help you in any way."

Naomi clutched the white card with simple black lettering. "I've never met anyone like you."

Catherine laughed. "I'll take that as a compliment. But I'm also learning sometimes we all need a little help."

Both women turned at the sound of the exam room door opening. Both women stared at the men who stared back before going into the kennel. Naomi spoke first. "Luke teach you that?"

"Yes," Catherine admitted, unaware of her face and voice softening.

"Be careful, Catherine," Naomi warned. "Men change sometimes, and not for the better."

"Occasionally, but my parents have been married for thirty-nine years and my father is just as devoted to my mother as when they were first married." She braced one hand on the desk top. "Sure, I have friends and relatives who are not so happy, but marriage, like life, is what you make of it. Both sides have to be willing to work at making it work. It won't just happen."

Biting her lip, Naomi gazed out the window as if she

could view her past through it. "What if nothing makes it work?"

"You consider your options and decide upon a course of action, to stay or go. But no one can make that decision for you," Catherine told her.

"What . . . what if you decide to go and the other person doesn't want to let you?" Naomi asked, her voice unsteady.

Catherine had answered the same question many times in the past, and she always took it seriously. "There are certain steps a person can take to ensure that they do."

Naomi brought her attention back to Catherine, her eyes without hope. "Maybe for some, but not for all."

Catherine wanted to deny the words, but her own personal experience had taught her that justice was indeed blind at times. "Helena Allen's name is on the back of the card. She is a business associate and close friend who will always know where to find me if you can't reach me, if there is ever a reason you might want to leave Santa Fe. I hope not. It seems like a wonderful place to stay. Children need stability."

Naomi's gaze hardened. "They also need to be safe."

Catherine took no comfort in knowing she had been right. "If something happens, trust Luke, trust Richard."

"He doesn't like me."

There was no reason for clarification. Naomi had been wary of Luke from the first. "Luke is looking into a matter for me and is suspicious of anything that doesn't seem right."

Fear leaped into Naomi's eyes, but this time it was for someone other than herself or her daughter. "Someone's after you, too?" The words had barely left her mouth before she realized what she had said. "I . . . I meant . . ." her voice trailed off.

"It seems that way," Catherine admitted, wanting to

put Naomi back at ease and to get her to realize she wasn't by herself. Briefly she gave her a very light scenario of why Luke was helping her, and ended by saying, "It was difficult to admit there was a situation in my life I couldn't handle. I'm extremely close to my parents and brother, but I didn't go to them. I'm not sure I would have told anyone if Luke hadn't pushed the issue. I'll always be grateful he did. I can sleep now."

Naomi looked at her thoughtfully. "My parents are dead, and I don't have any close relatives. It's just me and Kayla."

"Blood relatives are wonderful, but there are other people who could be just as close if you'll let them," Catherine told her. "It's like every good thing you want out of life, you have to be willing to try, and keep trying."

"I'll try."

"Good enough."

CATHERINE WAS READY FOR HERO'S AWAKENING. THREE packages of dog food were waiting for him in one of the two stainless steel bowls she found in the kitchen. In the other was fresh water. She had promised to replace both.

Hero didn't even sniff at the food after he came groggily to his feet. For a long time he stared at them. In a single gliding motion Luke stepped in front of Catherine. "You're free."

The wolf hybrid looked to the left, then to the right as if testing the truth of Luke's words, then looked back at Luke. "Show some sense and stay deep in the woods."

The animal turned and trotted off. He stopped at the edge of the forest, looked back, then faded into the shadows.

"He didn't even eat." Catherine stepped from around Luke.

"There is enough small game out there to keep him fat and happy."

Making a face, Catherine leaned into him. "I write children's books with some of those same small animals, and they have just as much right to survive."

Luke didn't even consider pointing out the food chain and reminding her of the beef and bacon she had eaten. Catherine was too soft-hearted. "You want to leave this out here?"

The sadness in her face vanished. "Could I?"

"Sure." The squirrels and birds would have it carried away or eaten by morning, but Catherine didn't need to know that. She worried enough as it was. His arm around her, they started up the front steps of the cabin. As they did, it occurred to him that in the past he had never felt so protective toward another woman. His arm tightened.

Inside the house, she turned in his arms and began unbuttoning his shirt. "I have to attend the reception tonight at seven. What do you think we should do to help pass the time?"

His hands went to the buttons on her jacket. "I'm sure we'll think of something."

HOLDING KAYLA'S HAND, NAOMI WAITED FOR RICHARD to lock the clinic door. Although it was past six and the clinic was scheduled to close at five, Richard had two emergencies. Both were the results of the same fight between a dog and a cat. Both pet owners had wanted Richard to treat their animal first, and not treat the other at all. Richard handled the situation calmly.

He had told both owners that after he examined both patients he'd determine who should be treated first, and if neither one of them liked it they could leave now. It was his clinic. Both grumbled. Both stayed.

"Sorry again," he told her, turning from the locked door. "The good thing is you get overtime."

It was on the tip of her tongue to tell him he didn't have to, then she remembered she needed every penny. "Thank you."

Opening the back door of his Jeep, he lifted Kayla into the seat. As usual, she sat Teddy beside her. Richard strapped both in. "You two comfortable?"

"Uh-huh," Kayla said, glancing over at the bear seated beside her.

Richard had to smile at the pretty child and at the careful way she took care of her new friend. Closing the door, he went around to the driver's side and slid in. Naomi had watched his every move. Neither mother nor daughter took chances with things that were important to them.

Starting the motor, he checked his rear view mirror to back out. "Kayla must have learned her mothering skills from you."

Naomi's swift intake of breath had his head turning abruptly toward her. She stared back at him with tormented eyes, her lower lip trembling, the sack containing Kayla's books crushed to her chest.

He touched her on the arm before he thought not to. She jerked away, but not before he felt her shiver. "Naomi, what is it?"

"Nothing."

Even if he hadn't heard the anguish in the single strained word, he would have known she wasn't telling the truth. But unsure of how to proceed or of how hard to push her, he straightened and put the car into gear. "Yes, there is, but I'll let it pass for now."

Pulling onto the street, he headed for her hotel.

"I'm a good mother." The blurted words came out raspy, choked, full of anger and a tiny bit of fear.

Something moved in his chest. Something hard and

dangerous. Flicking on the signal, he took the next available opening of the busy traffic to pull into the parking lot of a grocery store. The vehicle barely rolled to a stop before he shoved the gear into park and turned to her rigid profile. "I owe you another apology. When I said Kayla learned her mothering skills from you, I thought you'd know without it being said that it was a compliment. She watches over Teddy, talks to him. She had to learn from someone. I've seen children come into the clinic and all they know how to do is scold and spank their dolls or stuffed animals. That too was learned. You give Kayla what money can't buy, unconditional love and affection."

Naomi continued to hold the sack and refused to face him. "I don't know who's been telling you such nonsense, but if you ever doubt you're a good mother, just look into the happy, contented face of your daughter." Shifting the car into gear, he pulled off, then stopped. "But remember, just like she learned to be open and loving, she can learn to live in fear. I don't think you want that for her." This time he took off and didn't stop until he was at her hotel.

They both got out. Naomi reached Kayla first and drew her into her arms, her body trembling. Quietly she walked to her hotel room door.

Some of his anger rolled out of him. "I'll pick you up in the morning at nine."

"I . . ." She moistened her lips.

"You're not quitting," he told her, trying to keep his voice soft for her sake and the watchful Kayla.

Naomi stared at him. "I wasn't going to quit."

Slightly embarrassed, Richard found himself again at a loss for words.

Reaching deep down inside herself, Naomi sought the courage to reach out. Catherine and Richard were both right. Kayla needed stability, and they both needed friends. "I'd like to find another place to live that isn't so expensive.

Maybe a room in a house where I could cook or clean to help pay for the room. Could you help me?"

With a concerted effort, Richard resisted grinning like a fool because she asked for his help. "Luke's sister is a realtor, I'll check with her."

"Thanks, and"—she took a deep breath—"I'm sorry I misjudged you. I should have known better."

"Apology accepted, if you'll do one thing for me."

"All right," she answered without hesitation or fear.

Her reward was a smile she found much too appealing. "Let's all go out to dinner again."

The lightness Naomi had been feeling seconds earlier vanished. Dinner meant dressing up in something besides the few unsuitable clothes she owned. Last night she had washed the one dress she possessed in the bathtub. Secondhand when purchased, the blue material had faded from countless washings. The little yellow and white flowers were no longer distinguishable. A picture of the well-dressed Sybil flashed into her mind. "No, thank you."

"Teddy and I want to go with Dr. Richard," Kayla cried.

"We'll get something later," she told her daughter, then faced Richard. "Good night, and thank you."

"Good night, Naomi. Good night, Kayla."

Richard started back to the truck, a plan forming. As his grandfather used to say, there was more than one way to skin a cat.

NAOMI JUMPED WHEN THE KNOCK SOUNDED ON THE door. Moistening her lips, she set the iron on its base and cautiously went to the door. "Yes?"

"It's Richard."

She glanced down at the faded T-shirt and frayed blue jeans that had nothing to do with fashion, and bit her lips.

Kayla came off the couch where she had been watching TV. "Open up, Mama, it's Dr. Richard."

Having little choice, Naomi unhooked the safety chain and opened the door. He was smiling again, and for some odd reason this time it made her want to cry. Her hand rubbed against the side of her leg and suddenly she knew the reason why. "Dr. Youngblood, I didn't expect you."

He handed her a large pizza box. "They had a two for one special."

"Pizza," Kayla shouted. "My favorite."

Naomi noted the two large drinks and salad on top. "And I suppose those were on special, also."

"You can't eat pizza without salad and a drink," Richard said, his face serious, but his eyes twinkling. "Well, good night."

"Wait," she said, then stepped out on faith. "Would you like to join us?"

His hand went into his pocket. "I'd like nothing better if I didn't have another appointment."

She wasn't disappointed, she told herself, but she couldn't quite make herself believe. "Of course. Thanks again and good night."

"Good night."

Naomi closed the door and set the pizza box on the coffee table. "Go wash your hands, Kayla, so you can eat."

"I wish Dr. Richard could have stayed," she said and went into the bathroom with dragging feet.

"So do I, Kayla. So do I."

"I'M READY."

Luke looked up from where he was sitting on the couch and for a moment his mind went blank. His mouth dried, his body hardened. All he could do was stare. She was breathtaking.

The red dress clung like it had been poured over a hot, bare body. Long-sleeved and stopping just above the knees, it shouldn't have made his breath catch, his palms sweat.

But it did.

Slowly he came to his feet. "That's some dress."

She crossed to him on another pair of killer red heels with a little strap over her toes and one around her ankle. Sexy and bare.

"I wondered if you'd notice."

His hand settled on her trim waist, felt the heat of her body, smelled the scent that was uniquely hers. "If we wouldn't be late for the reception, I'd show you."

"We don't have to stay long," she said, her hands sliding up the front of his white shirt. Her red nail played with a button.

"I'm counting on it."

THE PUEBLO BALLROOM WAS FILLED TO CAPACITY WITH chattering, laughing attendees, spouses, and guests of the American Psychological Association annual conference. Business at the three cash bars was brisk. The crowd around the several buffet tables was four deep.

This was definitely not Luke's idea of having a good time. But that was the last thing on his mind. There was a strong possibility that a person in the room wanted to harm Catherine.

His intense gaze scanned the room. "See them yet?"

She shook her head, then stepped aside for a couple to pass. "There are a lot of people here."

"I thought people in your profession were supposed to be somber."

"Occasionally, so at conferences and out-of-town meetings, we tend to let go."

"I'll say."

"Come on, let's try over by the buffet line." His hand in hers, she moved through the throng of people. "Dr. Perkins always makes it a point to hit the buffet table early."

"He likes to eat?"

"He likes to be first," Catherine told him, then through a small break in the crowd, she saw them. "There's Dr. Perkins, and my assistant, Dr. Jackie Sims, is with him."

"Which ones?" Luke asked.

"She's wearing the green beaded dress. He's in the Valentino suit."

Luke studied the two in the buffet line. Jackie was tall and curveless. In her mid-thirties, she had a short cap of hair. Lee Perkins was of average height and build. Clean-shaven, he had short wavy hair.

Jackie, a wine glass in her hand, saw Catherine and stiffened. The adoring gaze on her face froze, then hardened into solid ice. Lee Perkins's reaction was the exact opposite. His brown eyes lit. A grin spread across his handsome features. He took Jackie's hand in his, and they left the line.

"Good evening, Jackie. Lee," Catherine greeted without a shred of the uneasiness she felt when they neared.

"Catherine," Lee said, his hot gaze moving over her, stopping a moment at her breasts before lifting to her face. "I wondered when I'd see you. You're looking lovely as usual."

"Thank you." Catherine flexed her fingers to let Luke know he was squeezing her fingers. His grip relaxed. His thumb slid over her knuckles in apology. Apparently he had seen where Lee's gaze had wandered. "I'd like to introduce a friend of mine, Luke Grayson. Dr. Jackie Sims, and Dr. Lee Perkins."

Lee, who had barely glanced at Luke, did so now. His gaze became curious. "Grayson, you're not in academia, are you?"

"No." Luke had been prepared to dislike the man on contact. That Perkins hadn't yet given him a valid reason annoyed him.

Dr. Perkins frowned. "What is your expertise?"

"Deviant human behavior."

Catherine's lips quivered to keep from smiling. "He's very good at it, too. Jackie, I didn't expect you to be here."

The other woman's mouth narrowed. "I'm a member of the association and I have just as much right to be here as anyone."

"I think you know that's not what I meant."

Lee glanced between the two women and smiled like a well-fed cat. "Now, ladies."

Catherine frowned at him.

"You're staying in the hotel?" Dr. Perkins asked.

"No, with friends," Catherine said easily. "I came up early to do a workshop."

"Always our busy little worker, aren't you, Catherine?"

As a group they turned to see a short, bearded man approach. His hair was as gray as his close-cropped beard and sports coat. He looked every one of his sixty-two years.

"Dr. Tolliver, good evening," Catherine said, staring down at him from her greater height.

Calculating blue eyes fastened on Catherine. "You won't find it always so easy, Dr. Stewart. Some of us have to pay our dues."

"I'll put my record up against yours any day," Catherine told him calmly.

"I've had thirty-two distinguished years at the university," he reminded her. "I've forgotten more than you've ever learned."

"I seriously doubt that," Luke said.

"Who are you?" Dr. Tolliver snapped.

"A friend."

The older man's lips curled. "Is that what they're calling it these days?"

Luke reached for the man. Catherine was faster. Five inches taller, she stared down into Tolliver's startled face.

"I've had it with you. I've tried every way I know how to be professional. You won't let me be. I can't help it if the program committee chose me over you."

He flushed. "How dare you bring that up!"

"You started this, and unless you want me to finish it with a meeting with Dr. Watts, I suggest you drop it here and now."

"One day you'll get yours," he announced, then disappeared back into the crowd.

"Don't mind him, Catherine," Lee said. "I think he's been in his lab too long. Come on and let's get something to eat." He leaned over, a persuasive smile on his face. "You can share mine."

Catherine heard a guttural sound and didn't know if the source was Luke or Jackie. "Thanks, but I want to see Dr. Watts first."

"Trying to make points for the department head?" Jackie asked snidely. "The position is as good as Lee's."

Lee managed to look confident and embarrassed at the same time. "As much as I hate to admit it, she's right, Catherine. Besides my outstanding record, I'm a heck of a fund-raiser."

Catherine was unimpressed. "I'm aware of that, Lee, and you'll be the first person I ask, after I'm department head, for fund-raising ideas."

Luke's laugh was rich and full. "Your mother would be proud."

"You know Senator Stewart?" Dr. Perkins asked, his brow furrowed.

"I can truthfully say I'm on her list."

Catherine laughed and leaned into Luke. His arm automatically came up around her.

"My goodness." Lee's eyes widened. "Tolliver was right."

"About time you noticed," muttered Jackie.

"What about your phone call?" Lee asked.

Tension wiped through Catherine. "What phone call?"

Lee cast a worried, sidelong glance at Jackie. "It doesn't matter. We'll be going."

Luke's hand on Lee's arm kept him in place. "Catherine asked you a question."

His head lifted. "If that's the way you want it. She called me last Monday and told me she wanted to pick up where we'd left off and we could start at the conference."

"I never called you," Catherine denied heatedly. "It must have been someone else."

"Catherine, don't you think I'd recognize the sound of your voice? It was you." His gaze grew cynical. He looked at Luke. "Obviously you were trying to better your chances of becoming department head."

"I didn't call you," she repeated, her voice shaky.

"If she said she didn't call you, she didn't," Luke told him.

"And how do you know?" Jackie asked. "You two joined at the hip or something?"

"Let's go, Catherine." Luke gently grasped her arm and started to leave.

"Poor Catherine. Maybe she forgot, like she forgot where she left her billfold and her house keys?" Jackie suggested snidely, sipping her drink. "Definitely not the actions of a rational person. Who can tell what someone like that might do or say to harm someone's career? I'm sure Dr. Watts would like to hear one of his candidates is showing signs of instability."

"I'm sure he would." Catching Jackie's arm, Lee walked off.

His arm sliding around her, Luke led a distressed Catherine out of the ballroom and to his truck. He opened the door for her to get in. Instead she gazed up at him with worried eyes. "I thought it would stop."

"I know." He pulled her into his arms. "I promise you I'll find out who is doing this and stop them."

Her hands clutched the lapels of his coat. "How?"

Tightening his hold on her, he answered, praying to be right, determined to be right. "By keeping an eye on you, and investigating everyone with an interest in discrediting you. He or she is going to make a mistake, and when they do, I'll be there waiting."

CHAPTER THIRTEEN

NAOMI WAS PREPARING TO GIVE KAYLA HER BATH WHEN a knock sounded on the door. Her heart rate sped up. Turning off the water, she went into the bedroom and glanced at the clock. 7:15 P.M. Kayla was in bed on her stomach, coloring.

She stepped closer, wishing there were a peep hole. "Who is it?"

"Ruth Grayson, Luke's mother, and Amanda Poole, a friend of mine. We were with Catherine when she met you," came the answer.

If Naomi hadn't been so puzzled by their visit, she might have thought her phrasing gracious at best. Slowly she opened the door. She recognized the taller of the two women as Luke's mother instantly. Not because she remembered her face, but because of the striking resemblance. The big difference was the woman's smile. She couldn't recall him ever smiling. Whereas Richard smiled as easily as a nightingale sang. She flushed at the thought.

"Yes?"

"Hello, Naomi," Ruth greeted with unmistakable warmth. "This is my friend and associate, Amanda Poole."

Amanda extended her hand and smiled in reassurance. "I'm glad to see you're feeling better."

"Thank you," Naomi said automatically, still unsure of the reason for their visit.

"I hope you don't mind that we dropped by without calling first," Ruth said, excitement ringing in her voice. "But we couldn't wait to show you."

The bewilderment in Naomi's face didn't clear.

The women lifted two bulging shopping bags. "A store in town always gives the Women's League first crack at its sales items before offering them to their preferred customers, then to the general public," Ruth explained.

"We made out like a bandit, and we can't wait to see if these things fit," Amanda added.

"I'm sorry," Naomi said, her brow furrowed. "I don't understand."

Ruth laughed at herself. "I'm sorry. I should have explained better. You and your daughter's names were submitted to the Women's League, a support network, as deserving of our services. And since Dr. Catherine Stewart had taken such a personal interest in you, and since she just completed one of the most successful workshops we've ever had, we came right over."

Although the need was there, so was pride. "Charity, you mean?"

"We prefer to think of what little we do as a bridge to help people over an uncertain period in their lives," Ruth said.

"We've all needed help at times," Amanda said.

Naomi gazed at the well-dressed women and couldn't imagine either of them ever being as desperate as she had been. Then she recalled stuffing Kayla's and her clothes in a sack. Shame hit her. "D-did Catherine send you?"

"Although all referrals are confidential, I can say Catherine didn't initiate the process," Ruth said patiently, then held up one of the white shopping bags again. "Don't you want to see what we brought for you and your daughter?"

Naomi hesitated as she fought a war between need and

pride. It hurt to know they looked so needy. Perhaps it was the motel manager who let her keep her car at the motel and use the bathroom facilities. She didn't think for a second it was Luke or, for that matter, Richard.

Naomi was thinking of a way to refuse, had the words forming politely in her head when Ruth pulled out a darling yellow appliquéd knit top with pants to match. Naomi didn't have to look around to visualize her daughter in clothes that were clean, but faded, and secondhand when purchased.

Ruth pressed her advantage. "Isn't this the most precious outfit you've ever seen? I bet it would fit your little girl perfectly."

Without looking at the size, Naomi knew it would.

Amanda was just as persuasive. The long-sleeved dress spilling from her hand was a soft peach knit with a flared skirt. She clucked her tongue. "I moaned when they didn't have this in my size."

Ruth chuckled. "You should have seen her going through the racks."

Amanda's laughter joined in. "I seem to remember you doing the same thing a couple of times."

"Nothing like the hunt to find that special something at a sale to get the juices flowing." Ruth turned to Naomi. "Come on and let's get started and see what fits."

Stepping back, Naomi opened the door wider. Pride was one thing, stupidity another. Her daughter deserved a nice outfit. "I'd appreciate a few things for Kayla, but you must have other women on your list."

"We do, and with the money Catherine helped raise from her lecture, Amanda and I are going to have our hands full for the next couple of days." Ruth upended the shopping bags on the couch. Clothes in different hues and textures spilled out. "Of course we have a clothes closet, but there's nothing like a new dress or new lingerie."

Naomi couldn't resist picking up a silky-looking nightgown in pale pink. Her "nightgown" was a man's XL
T-shirt she had purchased at a thrift store for twenty-five
cents. "If you're sure you have enough for the other
women."

"We have enough."

RUTH AND AMANDA LEFT AN HOUR LATER. RICHARD
waited for them at his Jeep. His grin broadened on seeing
only one shopping bag. "You succeeded, I see."

"The poor thing. She was so needy and still thought of
others," Ruth told him. "My heart went out to her."

"Makes me realize how blessed my family is," Amanda
said.

Richard opened the front door, then the back door.
"Like I said, I'll reimburse you for whatever you spent."

"Like we told you, the Women's League is sponsoring
Naomi and Kayla." Ruth climbed into the back seat.

Amanda took the front. "Assisting families like Naomi's
is what we're about."

"I realize that," he said, not wanting to offend the two
women who had helped him out. The sight of Naomi in
the tattered jeans had struck him to the core. Closing their
doors, he went around to the driver's side and slid in.

"Richard, the Women's League has to operate on certain principles. Buying a woman's clothes with money a
man provided would be unthinkable." Ruth shook her
head. "Everything we told Naomi is the truth. If you want
to help, make a general donation so the next Naomi and
Kayla can feel special with new clothes. We'll always be
grateful for clothing donations, but there is a certain look
in a person's face who has hit upon difficult times when
they slip on a coat or a dress that no one else has worn. Or
open a tube of new lipstick or remove a razor from the

package. It's almost like a reaffirmation that they're worthwhile."

Richard started the motor wishing he could have seen Naomi's face. "You'll have that donation, and any time I can be of service to the Women's League, just let me know."

The two women exchanged a meaningful look. "Well, we are still desperately in need of bachelors for the annual charity auction the Women's League has coming up in the fall," Amanda said, her smile charming.

His shoulders slumped, then straightened on thinking Naomi and Kayla would need more than a sack to carry their clothes in now. "Count me in."

"Brandon leaves the room every time I mention the auction." Ruth scooted forward. "Maybe you could casually work on him."

If he had to be paraded on stage before a crowd of screaming women, he might as well have his good friend with him. "It'll be my pleasure, Mrs. Grayson."

She patted him on the shoulder before sitting back. "You always were a nice young man, Richard. I wish Luke and my other children were so agreeable."

LUKE PULLED UP IN FRONT OF THE CABIN. THE headlights sliced across the front. He cut the motor. Usually Catherine got out with him. This time she remained, head bowed, her hands clamped together. He cursed whoever had caused her pain. Getting out, he opened her door and took her arm.

"Come on, Catherine. Let's get inside and get you to bed."

Silently she came out of the truck. His arm circled her waist. Together they started up the short walkway. Two steps later, Luke tensed. Whirling, he shoved Catherine behind him and looked into the inky blackness beyond the perimeter of the porch light.

"Luke?"

"Someone is out there. I want you to back up to the front door. I'll stay in front of you."

"But—"

"Now, Cath. Move."

Gripping the back of Luke's coat, she did as he asked. She knew it wouldn't do any good to argue. With each step she prayed they'd reach safety before whatever it was that Luke sensed came after them.

Halfway across the porch, she reached back, her fingertips touching the doorknob. Just a little bit closer. She took another step backward and . . .

"Aahhhhhh!" She went down, inadvertently jerking on Luke's coat as she did.

"Catherine!" Her name ripped from his lips in a cry of fury and fear as he tried to keep from falling on her and catch her before she fell. He landed solidly on the hard log porch. Catherine was half on, half off him. Pulling her into the protective circle of his arms, he rammed his key in the lock and hauled her inside and closed the door.

For the first time cursing all the windows, he picked her up and went to his office. Hitting the light switch, he set her from him, almost afraid of what he would see. His eyes ran over her the same time as his hands. "What happened? Are you hurt?"

"I-I slipped on something."

"Slipped?" Relief coursed through him until he recalled the cases of people being unaware of being injured due to shock. His hand continued their inspection, then he touched something moist on her back. Looking down at his fingers, he saw the red smears.

His hand clenched to still the trembling. "I need to take your dress off, honey."

She frowned. "Luke, don't you think we need to find out who is out there before we make love?"

"We will, as soon as I take care of this." His hands were already at the side zipper.

Catherine gazed up at him curiously, but allowed the dress to be pulled over her head. She stood before him in a red lacy demi-bra, high-cut panties and thigh-high flesh-toned sheers.

Luke's breath trembled out over his lips at what he had to do next. Although his voice shook, it was gentle. "I'm going to turn you around."

Her hand touched his cheek. "Luke, are you all right? You didn't bump your head when you fell, did you?"

"No, honey." Swallowing the fear and the lump in his throat, he slowly turned her and saw the smooth, un-blemished slope of her back, the unmarred curve of her shoulder. Relief rushed through him. "Not yours. Not yours."

Concerned, she turned to face him, and only had a moment to glimpse the strange look on his face, hear the hoarse whisper of her name on his lips before his mouth came down on hers.

She tasted desperation on his lips mixed with searing passion. Something was wrong, but she didn't hesitate to match the urgency of the kiss. Luke needed her, that was all that mattered.

She sank into the heat, the passion, her arms around his neck, her hand deep into his long hair, staking her own claim. *I'm here*, her mouth and body cried. *Take from me what you will.* The kiss deepened and for a space of time, the world ceased to exist around them as they lost themselves in each other.

Finally he lifted his head, picked her up in his arms, and sat in the oyster-colored love seat across from his desk. "Catherine."

Slim hands palmed his face. "I'm here, Luke. Please tell me what's the matter."

For a moment his eyes closed, his grip tightening before he could force the words out. "I thought you had been shot."

Her eyes widened in surprise. "What? But . . . but why? There wasn't a gunshot."

"Silencer," he said succinctly.

The confusion didn't clear from her face. "I know you thought someone was out there, but what made you think whoever it was had used a silencer?"

Curving his arm around her waist so she wouldn't fall, he leaned over and picked up her dress. "There was blood on the back of your dress."

"What?" Taking the dress, she turned it until she saw the darkened area on the back. Her hands began to tremble. "But how did it get there?"

"That's what I'm going to find out." Standing up with her in his arms, he set her to her feet, then pulled off his jacket and placed it around her shoulders. "Stay here until I can close all the shutters and draw the curtains."

She stared up at him with worried eyes. "I don't suppose it would do any good to ask you to wait until Officer Wesley or some other policeman can come out."

He adjusted the coat on her shoulders. "This part of the county is patrolled by the state police. There may be less than four men on duty to patrol thirty square miles of some of the most rugged terrain in the state. I have no idea how long it would take a patrolman to get here, and when he did, he'd come alone."

"And you wouldn't want to put someone else in danger," she said, sure of the answer.

"I'll be careful."

Her voice shook despite her smile. "One scratch and you answer to me, remember?"

"I remember." Going to his desk, he unlocked a drawer. The gun he pulled out was as lethal as it looked. He crossed to her and handed the weapon to her. "The safety is off."

Catherine swallowed. "What about you?"

"I have one in my bedroom." Black eyes blazed. "I'll let you know when I'm coming back. If anyone else shows their face, shoot."

"I . . ."

"Shoot," he interrupted, the sharpness of his voice leaving no room for argument. "The no-scratch rule also goes for you."

She nodded. "Be careful and hurry back."

Kissing her brief and hard, he walked from the room. His first stop was his bedroom to get his 9mm. After closing the shutters, he activated the outside shutters of the great room, then closed the others by hand. Finished, he went to Catherine's closet and got her robe and house shoes. He didn't think she had realized the reason she had slipped was that she had stepped in blood.

On the way back to his office he placed a call to the state police department. He wasn't waiting, but he didn't want Catherine alone if things went sour outside. The blood could be another attempt to rattle her, or it could mean whoever it was was upping the stakes.

"It's me," he said before entering his office. She was in his arms the moment he appeared in the doorway.

"I don't like this."

"It'll be over soon. Here, put this on." Removing his jacket, he helped her into her robe. "Sit down."

Reluctantly, she did. "You closed everything up."

"Yes." He put her gray slippers on her feet. "The house is impenetrable."

"Then we're safe. You don't have to go out."

"Catherine, if someone is out there, I can catch them and put an end to this."

"You can also get yourself shot," she cried.

"No one is getting shot." He took her trembling hands in his. "I'm going out the back door and I want you to lock it. I'll circle behind whoever it is."

"It's dark out there. How do you expect to find him?"

"The moon is full and I have excellent night vision." Releasing her hands, he began unbuttoning his white shirt, then pulled it out of his slacks and tossed it on the love seat behind her. "He won't know I'm there until it's too late."

Catherine watched the transformation from hunted to hunter. Lustrous black hair framed his chiseled features. The eyes that looked back at her were fierce. His heavily muscled chest gleamed in the light. Power and strength emanated from him. *Warrior.* The word leaped into her brain, her senses.

Suddenly she realized something: she loved him with a fierceness that shook her. "I plan on inspecting every inch of you when you get back."

A smile took the harshness from his face. "As long as I have the same privilege. Once I'm gone, come back in here and wait." Without another word, he left the room.

Luke had left a minimum of light on. Unlocking the back door, he opened it only wide enough to slip through sideways. Before she had time to touch him, the door closed soundlessly. He was gone.

HE VAULTED OFF THE PATIO AND LANDED SILENTLY, then he was running for the covering of the woods. Circling the house he found nothing. A couple of times he thought he heard something, but each time he stopped, there was only silence.

He was about to give up and go back into the house

when he saw the distinctive bar lights on top of the approaching vehicle. Shoving the gun into the waistband of his slacks, he left the woods and walked toward the car.

Opening the door, Patrolman Wesley got out. "Luke, I heard you had trouble."

"Ye—"

The low, ominous growl stopped his flow of words. "Johnny, get back in the car. *Now!*" shouted Luke, running toward him.

Eyes wide, the patrolman jumped back in the car, closing the door. A heavy weight hit the car a split second later. Through the window he saw the bared fangs of a wolf.

"Damn," the young man hissed.

"It's all right. He's a friend," Luke said, taking a step closer to the animal. Now he knew who had been watching. The source of the blood was another matter, but if he was right, Catherine's pet was in a lot of trouble.

"It's all right." Luke's hand touched the raised hair on the animal's neck. The hybrid looked around and the growling ceased. "That's it, just keep looking at me. Just keep looking at me."

Luke lost track of time, but finally the hybrid got down from the car. "Johnny, you better go."

The patrolman cracked the window. "Your report said something about blood on your porch."

"He probably brought his kill up here. We just brought him from Richard's clinic today," Luke informed him.

"Would the other part of that 'we' happen to be Dr. Stewart?" he asked.

"Yes."

"I'd heard that she was still in town. Thought about driving back up here to see if she was here." He glanced at the house. "I would have wasted my time, wouldn't I?"

"Yes," the answer was simple.

"Should have guessed."

"Sorry for the call," Luke said.

The patrolman switched his attention to the placid animal standing next to Luke, then to Luke without his shirt, a 9mm in the waistband of his pants. Luke wasn't the type of man to overreact. "You know, if he had bitten someone I'd have to take him in to be quarantined. There's no proof that the rabies vaccine is effective in wolf hybrids."

They both knew it wouldn't stop at being quarantined. The animal would have to be euthanized, his brain then shipped off to a laboratory for testing. Despite no positive results having ever been found in the animals killed, the barbaric and cruel practice continued. "There's also no proof they're carriers either."

"No, there isn't." The motor started. "I guess it's lucky for everyone concerned that the blood on your porch is from a kill."

"Yes, it is."

"Now that that's settled, is there anything else I can do for you?" He rubbed his hands across his eyes. "Sometimes these eyes get so tired, I can't tell a dog from a wolf."

Luke didn't hesitate. "You might want to put out a bulletin to surrounding emergency rooms to report any animal bites to the authorities."

"Sure thing. I patrol a lot of miles. Never can tell when a dog might catch a thief breaking and entering." He shoved the car into gear.

"Thanks, Johnny. I'll be at the La Fonda with Catherine at her psychology conference if you find out anything."

"Anytime. I would have never lived it down if he had gotten me in the rear. Good night."

"Good night," Luke said, then glanced down at the wolf hybrid. "Now, what am I going to do with you?" The animal stared up at him. "Come on."

On the porch he inspected the bloody smears. "I bet you surprised the hell out of whoever it was." Opening the door, he started to yell for Catherine, but she was already there. Hero barked.

"Hero." Laughing, Catherine kneeled and patted him on the head. "I should be upset at you for what you did."

Luke lifted a heavy brow. "That being?"

"You know what you said about the small animals." She gazed at the hybrid in slight disappointment. "I guess he didn't like the other food."

"I guess not." Luke opened the door again.

"You aren't going to put him outside, are you?"

"He needs a bath. I came in to tell you so you wouldn't worry."

"I'll get some shampoo and towels." She was up and running.

Luke gazed down at the animal. "For making Catherine laugh and protecting the house, you can stay the night. But in the morning, you're gone."

IN THE MORNING HERO GULPED DOWN THE OTHER half of the loaf of wheat bread, a pound of medium-well-done chuck, a can of cubed chicken, and five biscuits. Catherine couldn't have been happier that her pet was eating. Luke watched the antics of the two at the breakfast table and kept his opinions to himself.

Early that morning, he had slipped from beside a sleeping Catherine and gone to the porch. After scraping some of the blood-stained wood shavings into a glass tube, he had washed off the porch.

He had already followed the spots to the edge of the walk. Whoever it was had been brazen enough to drive up to the house. Since the gate had been locked when Luke arrived, he or she must have a duplicate key and probably one to the house as well. That wouldn't happen again.

Luke had already made arrangements for someone to

watch the house while they were gone. He didn't think whoever it was last night would come back, but he wasn't taking any chances.

He just wished he knew what they were planning next. Why had they been trying to get into the house?

"Luke, are you ready to go?"

He came out of his musing to see Catherine staring down at him, her hand on his shoulder. She was a beautiful woman, a generous lover, a caring friend. It tore him up inside that someone wanted to cause her harm and he couldn't stop them.

"Luke, what's the matter?"

Not wanting her to worry, he reached for her hand, then kissed her palm. "I was just thinking how beautiful you are and how beautiful you looked first thing this morning."

Catherine blushed. She had awakened on the couch with Luke sitting beside her. With his gaze locked on her, he had slowly pulled the comforter away from her naked body. The heat of his gaze, more than the heat of the sun coming through the wall of glass, seared her. Then his lips and hands had followed until she was a quivering mass of need and desire. She had been mad for him to make love to her, and she had delightfully driven him to the same frenzied need.

"Not half as beautiful as you," she finally said, her heart full of love that she could never tell him of.

One side of his mouth curved upward, he stood. "Your eyes need examining. Come on, Shelby should be here by now, and I want to introduce him to your pct."

Sadness crossed her expressive face. "I'm sorry I brought this to Daniel's and your home."

His arms circled her waist. Intently he stared down at her. "Are you sorry we met?"

"Never," she said without hesitation, her gaze steady.

"Neither am I. This is how it was meant to be. The fault is not yours, but belongs to whoever is doing this." His large hands lifted to palm her face. "Soon this will be over and we can get on with our lives."

Her sadness deepened. Getting on with her life no longer had any comfort, because eventually it would be without Luke.

"You believe me, don't you?"

Because she loved him, there was only one answer. "Yes."

CHAPTER FOURTEEN

NAOMI SAW NOTHING WRONG IN PUTTING ON THE peach-colored dress that morning. The uniform she had washed was dry, but she hadn't had time to ask room service for the iron and ironing board again. She and Kayla had leisurely eaten their breakfast without Naomi having to worry and feel guilty about sneaking food into her canvas bag.

Last night she had thrown out the food taken from her previous two mornings at the buffet, and placed the napkins she had hidden the food in on the sink where the maid could see them. Thanks to Richard paying her every day, she no longer felt so desperate.

After checking her lipstick and light makeup, she left the bathroom. With each step of her new taupe flats, she thanked her benefactors again and again. Their thoughtfulness had extended beyond the necessities to a few luxuries that caused her to feel as if her life was finally turning around for the better.

A knock sounded on the door.

"It's Dr. Richard. Can I get it?" Kayla asked, her eyes full of excitement. Naomi smiled and silently thanked the women again. She wasn't the only one who was excited about her clothes.

"Let me be sure," she said. "Dr. Youngblood?"

No answer.

Frowning, wishing again for a peephole, she took another step closer. "Dr. Youngblood, is that you?"

"Maybe it's the ladies again?" Kayla offered.

Unconsciously, Naomi's hand settled on her daughter's shoulders. Neither Richard nor the women had hesitated in announcing themselves. Then she saw the doorknob turn. She lunged to put the safety chain on, but never made it.

The door swung upon and in stepped the man she hated and feared, and prayed nightly never to see again. "Hi, honey. I'm home."

"Mama," Kayla whimpered, her small arms trying with all their might to encompass her mother.

Desperately Naomi wanted to pick her up and reassure her, but fear for her daughter held her immobile. Keep his attention on her, she told herself. Not on Kayla. "What-what do you want, Gordon?"

Pushing the door closed, he stepped closer, towering menacingly over her. "I give you one guess."

Naomi stared at him. In another foolish lifetime she had been proud of his good looks, and muscular build; proud of the way people looked at him with respect. That was before she discovered the true darkness lurking in his heart.

"I'm not coming back."

His grating laughter mocked her. "Oh, yes you are, and this time you're staying. You're not going to embarrass me in front of my friends and family again."

"You can't make me."

"Can't I?" He lunged for the child, snatching her up.

Naomi was on him in a flash. Her small fist pounded his back, screaming and sobbing for him to stop. He fought her off as easily as a horse would a pesky fly. Then he said the words that tore her heart from her chest. "Stop it or Kayla will be the one that suffers."

Tears streaming down her cheek, she shook her head. "Please, Gordon, I'll do anything. Just let me have her back."

Fury raced across his flushed face. "You've always loved her better than me. Haven't you?"

The argument was an old and painful one. "Please, Gordon, she's just a child."

"Me and Kayla are going home. If you want to see her again, you better be in the car two seconds after I get there." Wrenching open the door, he stalked out, carrying the frightened child with him.

Naomi didn't hesitate. Heart pounding, she ran after them, her heart breaking anew to see the look of fear on Kayla's face, her lower lip trembling. Kayla wouldn't cry. She had learned early that tears made things worse, not better.

RICHARD WAS RUNNING LATE. HE HAD STOPPED BY THE bakery and picked up some donuts and danishes. Naomi needed to eat more. She always saw to it that Kayla ate while she ate little or did without. The day before at lunch he had made sure she didn't try to save any of her food by ordering chicken salad.

Pulling up behind a blue Pontiac convertible with the top up, he got out of the Jeep and started down the walkway whistling. The tune stopped abruptly on seeing a man hurrying toward him carrying Kayla, a terrorized Naomi behind them.

Alarmed, Richard caught her arm when she would have kept going past him. "Naomi, what's going on?"

The man whirled around and stared at him with cold eyes. "Stay out of something that doesn't concern you." He glared at Naomi. "Come on here, we have a long ways to go."

Richard saw the tears mixed with fear in her eyes. His

stomach clenched. "You don't have to go if you don't want to."

The man's face distorted with fury. "The hell she don't. She's my wife."

Something cold clutched Richard's heart. "You don't have to go if you don't want to," he repeated, trying to keep his voice calm despite the emotions raging through him.

Cruel fingers snatched Naomi away from Richard. "If I weren't holding this kid, I'd kick your butt."

"Then why don't you put her down and try?" Richard asked tightly.

Gordon batted away Naomi's frantic hands reaching for Kayla. "Another time." Turning, he stalked away. Naomi started after them.

Again, Richard caught her arm. "Nao—"

"Let me go," she cried in mounting terror. "He'll leave and I'll never see her again."

"Do you want to go?"

"Please," she cried, her eyes locked on Kayla as Gordon opened the door on the driver's side. "Please." Tears ran down her cheek.

The instant Richard released her, she started running. No sooner had she opened the car door and gotten in than the Pontiac spun off.

NAOMI WAS THANKFUL GORDON COULDN'T DRIVE AND hold Kayla at the same time, and considered being the recipient of his hatred a small price to pay. "I see why you didn't want to come back. You turned into a slut just like my mother warned me you would."

He whipped around a car. Naomi closed her eyes, and held Kayla closer.

"Thought you were smart, leaving your car in the shopping mall and disappearing, didn't you? I knew you had run away. Thought you had covered your tracks, but you should have known I'd find you."

He stopped at the red light in a screech of tires. "The man you bought the used car from saw your picture in the paper and went to the police. When someone ran a check on the registration from Santa Fe, I contacted the police here and asked them to locate the car. They did in less than four hours. The manager of the motel where your heap broke down was too happy to tell your loving husband where you were after I explained you had left after a slight disagreement." Gordon sneered. "Thought it was nice of you to let him know you were all right and had a job. It was easy to get the key from the desk clerk at your hotel after I showed them my ID."

Stepping on the gas, the car shot off. Less than a block away, red lights flashed behind them. "Damn." Flicking on his signal, he pulled over to the side of the street. "This won't take but a minute."

Gordon reached into his hip pocket and pulled out a small, black case. By the time the police officer arrived at his window, Gordon was smiling broadly and showing his badge, which identified him as a San Antonio patrolman. "Good morning."

"Good morning." Through the lenses of his mirror shades, the policeman looked at the badge. "Always glad to see a fellow officer, but you were speeding a tad back there."

Knowing the routine, Gordon chuckled. "Guess I'm anxious to get back to San Antonio."

The policeman peered into the car. "Your wife and daughter?"

"Yes." Gordon shot Naomi a warning look. "Neither one is very happy with me this morning. They wanted to stay another day, but I'm on duty tomorrow night and it's going to be a hard drive as it is."

The officer nodded and straightened. "Then it's a good thing I stopped you. Your right front tire is going flat."

"Damn." Getting out of the car, Gordon walked to the front and stared down at the tire. "The tire is fine, what the hell are you talking about?"

"My mistake," the officer said mildly.

The passenger door opened and Gordon swung to tell Naomi to get back in the car. The sight of a police officer talking to her, then another patrol car pulling up, set him on another course. "What the hell is going on here?"

"Nothing, we hope, but we plan to find out," the officer said.

Naomi knew the routine. The police officers would question her and Gordon separately, then they'd leave. They were brothers. A strict code of silence prevailed. They'd listen politely, then turn a blind eye to his cruelty because she had no visible scars.

The scars that wounded Kayla's and her souls were just as deep and painful, more so. Physical wounds would heal in time. She had ceased to think theirs ever would. Hope just made it worse. Head down, she answered the questions automatically.

"Are you going with him of your own free will?"

"Yes."

"Do you fear for your life?"

"No."

"Has he threatened you or the child in any way?"

"No."

"If you could stay in Santa Fe, would you?"

Her head snapped up. "Richard," his name trembled across her lips.

"Dr. Richard," Kayla cried, launching herself into his arms.

Tears started flowing from Naomi's eyes, then flowed faster when Richard pulled her into his arms.

"Take your damn hands off my wife," Gordon yelled. Any progress he might have made was impeded by the police officer with him.

"I don't think you want to do anything that might detain you in Santa Fe."

Gordon whirled on the officer. "You threatening me?"

"Stating facts."

"She's my wife," he yelled.

Naomi's head came up. "No, I'm not. We were divorced over a year ago, but he just won't let me go. Two months ago I went to renew my restraining order against him, but some of his friends on the police force called him. Before I could go into the judge's chambers, he came. He told me if I obtained the restraining order again, he'd make me sorry."

"She belongs to me."

"I belong to myself," Naomi said, her voice growing stronger with each sentence. She turned to the officer beside her. "I'd like to retract my earlier statement. The reason is that I was afraid you'd be just like the other police officers who ignore my calls. My ex-husband is a cruel man who thinks of me as his possession, and has taken every opportunity to criticize and degrade me. I don't want to go with him. If you could arrange it, I never want to see him again."

"You bitch."

Naomi felt Richard tense beside her. There came a time when she had to stand up for herself. "No, I'm not, Gordon, and no matter how many times you call me that, I never was nor will be."

Richard's arms went around her shoulders. "We'll be at my clinic if you need us, officer."

"You come back here. Come back here," Gordon yelled. They kept walking.

The policeman opened Gordon's door. "Texas is a big state. You shouldn't have any trouble finding it."

"I can go where I want."

"Now that's where you're wrong. Seems like your day has been a long time coming, but it's finally here. I can almost guarantee it when your commanding officer receives my report. Better warn your buddies to watch for the fallout."

Getting in the car, Gordon slammed his car door, then pulled off in a defiant burst of speed. The officer smiled and walked to his car.

Red lights flashing, the officer pulled out in pursuit of Gordon. Some days he just loved his job.

RICHARD DROVE NAOMI AND KAYLA BACK TO THEIR hotel room. Naomi had elected to sit in the back with her daughter and he understood why. Parking the jeep, they went to her hotel room. The door was still open. Thankfully everything was safe.

"How did you know?" she asked, closing the door.

She looked frail and vulnerable. The fear wasn't completely gone from her eyes, but it wasn't as stark. "You didn't have your canvas bag and Kayla didn't have Teddy."

She swallowed. "Thank you."

"Why don't you take the day off with pay, and I'll pick you up in the morning?" he offered, sticking his hands in his pockets because he wanted to hold her again.

"No, you have a full schedule and I've already made you late." She picked up her canvas bag, and reached out for Kayla's hand. The child already had Teddy.

"You're sure?" he asked.

"I . . . I'd feel better if we were with you," she told him.

He gave in to temptation and the appeal in her eyes, and curved his arm around her shoulders. "So would I."

LUKE WAS ON EDGE. JOHNNY HAD COME BY TO tell him that his check had turned up nothing. He was back to where he started.

He couldn't shake the feeling that something was going down and he wasn't going to be able to stop it. It continued to worry him that someone had been bold enough and desperate enough to come to the house again. Why had they taken the risk to come back? And even though wounded, had taken time to lock the gate again.

"Boring you?" Catherine asked walking beside him down the wide hallway of the hotel.

"Nope. I kind of liked the last session." He winked at her. "Didn't know so much was out there on sexual repression."

She smiled. "You won't ever be on anyone's couch, and thanks to you, I won't either." Then, "Here it is."

On a large easel was her name in bold black letters on white poster board, the time and topic, "Raising an Emotionally Stable Child into a Responsible Adult in a Permissive Society: The Rules You Should Break and Those You Can't."

"I better take notes or get a tape for Daniel," Luke commented, opening the door for her.

"Daniel and Madelyn will be fine." She worked her way through the lingering crowd from the last lecture. "They are aware that with love, a child also needs consistent discipline, structure, and reinforcement of rules and regulations."

"I'm glad it's them and not me."

Catherine's hand trembled on her purse. "You don't want children?"

"Marriage and children go together, and since I'm opposed to the first, the second is never going to happen," he told her.

His statement brought misery to Catherine. She loved him, and with that love was a desire for his happiness above her own. She had seen how caring he was with Kayla. He was like many people, who, until confronted by a situation, said one thing, but deep down meant another. He'd make a supportive, loving father. He deserved children. "You might change your mind."

"Not likely," he told her, shaking his dark head.

"Dr. Stewart, I'm Kenneth Boman," a thin, sandy-haired young man said. "I'm supposed to do your slides."

"Thank you, Kenneth." Taking the round carousel case from Luke, she handed it to the young man. "They're already in order. I was told I could control the slide progression from the podium."

"That's right. This session should start in about five minutes." He glanced around the people still milling down the aisle. "I better start working my way to the projector. Hopefully, they'll clear out and we can start on time."

"Thank you." Catherine turned to Luke. "I suppose you're going to stay with me."

"Where you go, I go."

She smiled. "Go get a seat before you distract me."

"Yes, ma'am," he teased and took a seat on the front row. The room could hold three hundred people, and half that amount were standing and talking. Luke had serious doubts the session would start on time. However, five minutes later the final stragglers were taking their seats and a woman was walking to the podium.

Her introduction of Catherine was glowing, filled with praise of her work and her numerous accomplishments. Luke found himself again applauding wildly for her, a wide grin on his face. Coming to the stationary microphone, she glanced over the crowd until the applause died down.

"Good morning, I'd like to thank my esteemed colleague, Dr. Brent, for that wonderful introduction. For a moment, I must admit to looking around and wondering if I was being replaced by another speaker."

Laughter sounded throughout the audience.

"I wanted to hear laughter, for you to remember the sound, to remember how easily it rolled from your mouth, because the topic I'm going to talk about at times may hold little joy or laughter. What should be one of, if not *the* greatest joys in our lives has become a task that many grow to hate and few go into knowing what to expect. I'm speaking of parenthood. If not done responsibly, it can lead to heartbreak, as this first slide will show."

Catherine pushed the control button in her hand for the first slide.

Gasps sounded from the crowd. Many stood to their feet. Some palmed their faces. The picture of homeless children had elicited different responses, but never ones so strongly. Then she saw Luke running down the aisle toward the projector. Her heart thudding in her chest, she turned toward the screen.

Disgust, shame, and horror swept through her.

On the screen was a nude picture of her and two equally nude men committing the vilest sexual act she had ever seen.

CHAPTER FIFTEEN

SAVAGE FURY RODE LUKE LIKE A WILD THING. HE wanted to smash the projector and the projectionist, his mouth open, staring at the pornographic image on the screen. Instead he slammed down the switch to turn off the light control and flung the carousel back in the case. The entire process took less than three seconds, but that was three more additional seconds that had kept him from getting to Catherine.

Then, he saw her. His fury doubled. One small hand clutched the podium, the other curved around the waist of her bent body as if she had been dealt a mortal wound. He had never wanted to kill before: he wanted to do so now.

What took only seconds seemed like an eternity for him to reach her. His only thought was to get her away. His arm going around her waist, he whisked her out of the room. "I'm here, Cath. Hold on."

The murmuring audience watched their every step. A few followed them out into the hallway. Luke kept walking until they were by his truck. Unlocking the door, he shoved the case across the seat, then got in with Catherine.

"I promise I'll find out who did this."

She flinched and huddled her shivering body into his, hiding her face in the crook of his arm.

"Catherine, look at me." Shaking her head, she moved away from him.

Her pulling away from him sent him over the edge. He grabbed her shoulders and stared at her bent head. "Don't you dare fold, don't you dare give that bastard that satisfaction. You hear me? You're stronger than this."

Gradually her head came up. Torment and tears shone on her face. "I-I thought you might think . . ."

"Never." Tenderly, he brushed the tears aside, then followed with his lips. "Never."

Holding her, his hand ran the length of her back, then up again. With each sweep, her trembling lessened. "I'm going to take you to Brandon's place, then I'm going to the photographic lab of a friend of mine. Maybe he can give me some leads."

Her head lifted. Shame shimmered in her eyes. "I don't want anyone to see it again."

He understood her feeling of violation, hurt for her. "Your picture was superimposed on that negative. That needs to be verified by an unquestionable authority to help clear your reputation. Peter can do that for us."

Down went her head again. "I'll never be able to face any of them again."

Strong fingers lifted her chin. "The woman I know might bend, but she wouldn't break."

"They'll look at me and see that picture," she said, torment in her trembling voice.

"A few might, but if any group can separate myth from reality, it's people in your profession." His voice seethed with rage. "Before I'm through, they'll know that wasn't you, and the person behind this will wish he never started this."

"I hope you're right."

"Trust me." Kissing her on the forehead, he sat her in her seat and started the engine.

Dropping Catherine off at the Red Cactus, Luke stayed long enough to explain to Brandon what had happened. Not wanting her to dwell on the incident, Luke asked Brandon to let her help him with the inventory he took each Friday before ordering supplies. When Luke left they were working their way through the store room.

Peter Nolan's photographic studio was only a couple of blocks over from the Red Cactus. Tall and wiry with a red beard he'd cultivated since his mid-twenties, he was a renowned photographer of nature. People, he was often heard to say, disappointed, nature never did.

Handling the slide with tweezers to preserve any fingerprints, Peter placed it on top of the light box. "Just like you figured. Dr. Stewart's head was superimposed."

"Can you tell me anything about the original print?"

"Sorry. It's a stock print that could have been lifted from any number of porno magazines. Anyone with a scanner could have superimposed her face and taken the picture with transparency film." Clicking off the light, he replaced the slide. "A professional photographic lab wouldn't think anything of producing this slide."

Luke put the slide back into the carousel. "It's what I figured, but it was worth a shot."

"What are you going to do now?"

"What else? Put whoever did this on the hot seat."

THE SIGN OUTSIDE THE PUEBLO ROOM SAID LUNCHEON. Perfect, Luke thought. Opening the door, he headed straight for the podium. The speaker paused as Luke walked up on the raised platform, his gaze questioning.

"Sorry, I need to make an announcement." Whether in agreement or not, the man stepped back. "My name is Luke Grayson and I've just come from the studio of a photographic expert who is willing to give a written deposition that Dr. Stewart's picture was superimposed onto the slide in her presentation. As a friend of the family I'm offering a $15,000 reward for information leading to the arrest and conviction of the person or persons who staged such a cruel hoax." Murmurs went up from the crowd.

"Since the slides may have been tampered with before she left California and crossed state lines, the FBI has been called in. As a former agent, I assure you that the case will be thoroughly investigated and the guilty person or persons persecuted to the fullest extent of the law. I'll be at the Red Cactus restaurant waiting." He turned to the speaker. "I apologize again."

The man nodded.

The room was buzzing as Luke walked from the podium out the huge wooden double doors. The threat of the FBI combined with the monetary reward should loosen a tongue or two, he thought. Fear and greed were good incentives. He had a hunch that whoever was behind this was either here or had someone watching. They'd want every sick detail of Catherine's humiliation.

Taking up a position across from the Pueblo Room behind a giant yucca plant, he waited to see who left. He hoped one of them might be the projectionist. The switch could have been made before Catherine arrived, but Luke didn't think so. There was always the possibility of her checking the slides before her presentation. To be absolutely sure of going undetected, the switch had to be made at the last possible moment.

The reason behind the attempted break-in at the cabin last night became clear. Since the person hadn't gotten caught the first time, he or she had probably felt smug in returning. The hybrid had quickly changed their mind and plans. The switch now had to be done later, after the slides left her possession, after the carousel was removed from the case.

Luke watched people going in and out of the room, but none of their behavior was suspicious. He had called Brandon on his cell phone and asked him to call back if anyone came by with information. So far, the phone had remained silent.

From the increased noise level inside the ballroom, the luncheon speaker had finished and they were being served. He'd give it another ten minutes and then he was going back on the stage and find out how to contact the projectionist.

The door swung open. He spotted Kenneth Boman, the projectionist, coming out. Luke crossed to the young man and pulled him aside. He didn't waste time. "Did you notice anyone tampering with Dr. Stewart's slides?"

The young man's eyes glanced around him. "Did you mean it about the fifteen grand?"

"Yes."

A smile spread across his narrow face. "I know who switched the slides."

Excitement whipped through Luke. "Talk—and this better be the truth."

"He came up to me while I was preparing the projector. He went on and on about how much he admired Dr. Stewart's work."

"Did you see him switch the slides?" Luke questioned.

Kenneth's smile dissolved. "No, but it had to be him."

"Did he have a badge on?"

"Yes, but I didn't pay that much attention to it." His expression fell, then he brightened. "But I'd know him if I saw him again."

"You'll get your chance." Luke led him back across the lobby, called the hotel, then asked to be connected to the front desk. "This is the answering service for Drs. Lee Perkins and George Tolliver. Both have important calls they need to take immediately. They should be in the Pueblo Room. Could you please ask the person presiding over the luncheon to make an announcement? Yes, I'll hold."

Shortly, a man wearing the regulation maroon-colored sports jacket with the hotel crest on it came from the direction of the front desk and went inside the ballroom. "That's probably the conference manager going to deliver my message. Get ready. It shouldn't be long before they come out."

Lee Perkins came out with Jackie Sims. George Tolliver was a few feet behind.

"That's him. The tall one," proclaimed Kenneth in an excited rush.

Luke's eyes narrowed into black slits. It was all he could do not to cross the room and smash his fist into Perkins's face. Letting them get a little farther away, Luke prepared to follow.

The door opened again and a short, balding man came out the same time two women were rushing back inside. The women tried to go around him and take advantage of the open door. One did so smoothly. The taller and heavier of the two collided into his left side.

Grimacing, he cursed and grabbed his left arm.

"I'm sorry," the woman said, her face full of concern. "Are you all right?"

"You should watch where you're going," he hissed, his round face furious. "You clumsy fool."

The woman's face drained of color.

Grumbling, the man walked off with his right hand cupping and supporting his left elbow and arm. Something clicked in Luke's brain. He remembered the nasty attitude and the pudgy face of the balding man. He'd been just as abrupt and sneering when he questioned Catherine's credibility in her workshop. His black and white badge said PRESS.

"Do you remember him?" Luke asked.

"No."

Luke's gaze switched to Perkins moving easily down the hallway, his right hand holding Jackie's elbow, his left arm relaxed by his side, then went back to the man he had first seen at Catherine's workshop, holding his arm and wearing a press badge.

The easiest way to gain entrance into any large gathering was to say you were with the press. Most organizations were chomping at the bit for publicity and seldom if ever verified information. Slipping out from behind the plant, Luke followed.

As the man passed a combination stone trash receptacle/ash tray, he removed something from his pocket and tossed it into the bottom half, never slowing his pace.

Reaching the receptacle, Luke bent and peered inside. Dark as midnight and he didn't have a flashlight, but he had a strong hunch what was inside. He pushed to his feet. "Stay here and don't let anyone else use this."

"Does this mean I don't get my money?" Kenneth questioned, his expression worried.

"We'll talk about that later," Luke told him, keeping his eyes on the man favoring his left arm.

Passing a bank of phones, Luke heard Perkins shouting at the operator for disconnecting his call. Luke kept his gaze locked on the short, balding man holding his arm. After a brief stop at the front desk, he went to the elevator located across the lobby and stepped on with several other people.

After the elevator door closed, Luke went to the same desk clerk the man had spoken to. "Excuse me, I thought I recognized the gentleman who was just here, but he got on the elevator before I could stop him. Do you think he'll be back down soon?"

"Yes, sir. He's checking out."

"Thank you." Turning away from the desk clerk, Luke activated his cell phone on the way back to the receptacle.

"This is Luke Grayson, I need to speak to Sergeant Rodriquez immediately."

"Hi, Luke," came the jovial greeting moments later.

"Dakota, I need an officer to come to the La Fonda immediately," Luke said. "I'll be waiting by the La Plazuela. Tell him to come expecting to collect evidence and make an arrest."

"That hotel is always crowded. Do you think there will be any trouble?" Officer Rodriquez asked, concern in his voice.

"No, but I can't be sure," Luke answered truthfully.

"We're short-handed this shift and the crime-scene tech is out on another call. I'll take this one myself. See you in three."

The line went dead.

DAKOTA RODRIQUEZ, A SERGEANT FOR SIX OF HIS TEN years with the Santa Fe Police Department, arrived thirty seconds early. Another policeman was with him. Luke had expected as much. Dakota was a man who looked for the best and prepared for the worst. He carried his two hundred pounds on his six-foot frame as easily as he smiled and tipped his hat to the three women he passed.

He was also a man who didn't waste time when a crime might have been committed or the citizens might be in jeopardy. "What's up?"

Luke quickly explained. "I'm betting there's a slide in there that will clear Dr. Stewart's reputation."

"He hasn't come back down yet?" Sergeant Rodriquez glanced toward the front desk.

"If he has, he hasn't come this way," Luke told him.

The sergeant turned to the officer with him. "Till, you know what he looks like from Luke's description. I don't want him to leave the hotel until I've had a chance to talk with him. Position yourself at the entrance. If this goes down, I want it done nice and easy. Let's keep the citizens safe and happy."

"Yes, sir," Officer Till said, then went to the front of the hotel.

Dakota faced Luke. "All right, let's move this sucker over a bit and see if your instincts are as good as they used to be."

Less than ten seconds later Sergeant Rodriquez lifted a slide in his gloved hand from the top of the trash. Holding it up to the light, he and Luke saw an image of five teenagers, their faces as bleak as the deteriorating building behind them, huddling around a blazing fire in a fifty-gallon drum.

"You called it right, Luke." Dakota dropped the slide into a plastic bag.

"I'm going to break his neck," Luke announced, his face as hard as his voice.

The police officer's calm expression didn't change. "You do, and I'll have to arrest you."

"It might be worth it."

"Might, but your mother would never forgive me, not to mention your brothers and sister." He shook his head. "I could handle your brothers, but Sierra could slice a man's heart out without saying a word."

"Don't you forget it either," Luke told him without heat. "Come on, let's go find that scum."

THEY WERE WAITING FOR HIM WHEN HE STEPPED OFF the elevator. His eyes widened on seeing the uniformed officer step from a short hallway. Before he could do more than turn, Luke and Sergeant Rodriquez were on either side of him.

"I'm Sergeant Rodriquez with the Santa Fe Police Department, and I'd like a word with you please."

"What's this about?" The man asked, licking his thin lips.

"I'll explain everything if you'll just come with me," Sergeant Rodriquez told him.

"I have a plane to catch." He took a step toward the front desk. Luke, his face hard, blocked his path. The man shrank back.

"This won't take long," Sergeant Rodriquez said mildly from beside him. "I understand from your registration that your name is Sam Morris and you're from Los Angeles, California. Is that right?"

The man glanced at Luke and swallowed. "Yeah, but like I told you, I have to be going."

"Mr. Morris, I'm going to have to insist. We can make it official and do this in my office or we can step over here out of the way."

The man rolled his neck. "Sure. Sure. Just make it quick."

They moved to the short hallway where Luke and the policeman had emerged. "What's this all about?" Mr. Morris questioned.

Officer Rodriquez held up the slide. "Have you ever seen this before?"

"No." Morris's right eyelid twitched.

"You're lying, I saw you toss it in the trash," Luke said, no longer able to keep quiet.

"Now I understand what this is about." Morris spoke to the policeman. "He just offered a fifteen-thousand dollar reward for information and when he couldn't get any, he made some up. He's probably mad because he got left out of the threesome."

With a growl Luke reached for Morris. The policeman placed his body in his path. "Mr. Grayson is not the only one who saw you toss this away."

Morris's eyes widened. "Then he paid someone to lie."

"I don't lie. I saw you," Kenneth said from behind him.

Morris jerked his head around to glare at the newcomer.

Kenneth folded his lanky arms, glared back, then repeated, "I saw you."

"You're not going to lie your way out of this," Luke told him.

Morris moistened his lips. "Even if you could prove something, which you can't, there wasn't a crime committed. Sounds more like a practical joke."

"That's where you're wrong, Mr. Morris," the sergeant informed him. "Showing pornography is against the law, and if your fingerprints are on this slide, you're also guilty of theft."

The man laughed. "A misdemeanor at best."

"Not when you add breaking and entering, harassment, stalking, and wire tapping," Luke said, his voice tight and hard with restraint.

"You're reaching." Morris tried to sneer the words, but the slight tremble in his voice gave him away.

"You've been following Dr. Stewart for months. Her notebook helped, but you had to have more. You had to know about her plans to come to Santa Fe, and only a few close friends were told. The only way you could have known was to tap her phone line. You then used the recording for someone to learn to impersonate her voice." Luke's voice harshened. "Your blood stains I collected from my porch will confirm what I've said. You're looking at five years."

"Five years?" Mouth gaping, Morris stared at Officer Rodriquez.

"Minimum," the officer answered.

Morris's right eyelid began to twitch again. "Five years! No, I'm not going down alone. She said this would be so easy. She promised to take care of me."

"Who?" Luke asked sharply.

The man swallowed, then said. "Rena Bailey."

"Before you say anything further, Mr. Morris, I should advise you of your rights." Officer Rodriquez Mirandized him. "Do you understand these rights?"

Sweat beaded on Morris's balding pate. "Yeah. Yeah. I ain't taking this rap alone."

"Rena Bailey, the woman who attacked Dr. Stewart, is behind this?" Luke questioned.

He nodded. "She blames the doctor for her kids being taken away, being in jeopardy of losing her job, and her family turning against her. They won't return or accept her phone calls."

"So what's your connection?" Luke pressed.

"Purely business. My cousin is a nurse and works at the center. They have a thing going on. He hooked us up." He swept his hand over his balding pate. "Rena figured if Dr. Stewart was discredited, she could get back in her family's good graces and her job would be secure."

"What about her children?"

He worked his shoulders. "She don't care much for them, says they tie her down, but her parents are loaded and they're crazy about them, and Rena is counting on them inheriting big one day. In the meantime, she thought if she pulled this off right, her parents would pay her to let them keep the little boy and girl once she got out of rehab."

"She was wrong on all counts, and this time, she's going to go down hard," Luke said tersely. "And she's taking you and your cousin with her."

RICHARD KEPT WATCHING NAOMI, EXPECTING HER TO break down. She didn't. In fact as the morning progressed, she actually appeared more at ease with each passing hour. Seeing the final patient of the morning to the door, he locked it for lunch and went to her desk.

She watched him approach and spoke before he did. "I owe you an explanation."

"You don't owe me anything." He stuck his hands in his pockets. "The important thing is that you and Kayla are safe."

Her hand clenched the pen in her hand, then relaxed. "Once I feared that would never happen."

He had promised himself, but somehow he was kneeling by her chair, taking her hands in his. "You don't have to be afraid again. There are people who want to be your friends here."

Although her hands trembled, she didn't draw them back as he had feared. "I think I'm beginning to realize that. I could use a friend. Kayla and I both could."

"You got one."

"I'd like to tell you." She drew her hands back.

Richard knew she wasn't rejecting him, but drawing on her own strength. He pulled over a chair and sat down. "I'm listening."

"Gordon was always possessive while we were dating, but I was foolish enough to be flattered. I had never dated much, and Gordon was very popular and athletic. I was flattered he kept asking me out. I was in seventh heaven when he asked me to marry him six weeks later. But after we were married, his possessiveness became less and less flattering. He wanted to control my every movement." She bit her lips.

"I taught kindergarten in the public schools. He actually timed my going to work or the store. My few friends dwindled to none. Then I got pregnant with Kayla." Her hand nervously raked through her hair.

"He wanted me to have an abortion. Just him saying it sickened me. I told him I was leaving. He apologized and said he was just frightened that something would go wrong with the pregnancy. Stupid me, I believed him. But after Kayla was born, he became worse. He was jealous of his own child." She shook her head.

"He had grown up with just his mother, who had little time for him. She liked to socialize, play bingo, go clubbing. He told me he didn't matter to her. As a child he promised himself that he'd be the center of someone's life. In a rage, he told me that's why he had picked me . . . because I was quiet and he thought I'd be grateful. After Kayla was born, he couldn't understand that she needed my time and attention, too. It became a case of 'You love her more than me.' Then the verbal abuse began. He'd yell at her for the smallest thing.

"I left. He begged me to come back, said that he just loved us. I went back, but it was the same. I got a divorce and full custody six months ago after we had been separated for two years. He didn't fight it. It might have ended there, but his mother started talking to him about what people thought. He didn't want us, he was trying to please her. When I wouldn't go back, he threatened to take Kayla away from me. My lawyer assured me that wouldn't happen. The day after I told Gordon, my apartment was broken into and stripped while I was at work.

"I moved and it happened again three weeks later. All the new furniture, Kayla's clothes and toys, gone. I had used my one credit card to purchase them, and only had a little money stashed away for an emergency. I wasn't sure what to do next, but I knew I wasn't going back to Gordon. The day after my apartment was broken into, I went to pick Kayla up from preschool and met Gordon signing her out. Although the school had strict orders not to release her to anyone, they were letting him take her." Her hands started to tremble.

"If I had been a few minutes later, he might have taken her. I realized I had to run. I had already planned ahead and took the money hidden beneath a piece of carpet. I drove to the shopping mall, caught a bus to a used car lot and used almost all of the money I had to buy the car. We stayed in Dallas for six weeks, living in a motel. I was afraid to use my real name and I couldn't find a job. The car broke down, and I had to have it repaired. I thought if I could get to California he wouldn't come after me and I could use my real name and get a job. We never made it."

"Santa Fe is a good place to live," Richard said carefully. "I'd hate to lose you, but I'm sure you could get a job teaching here."

"I've been thinking the same thing." She drew a deep breath and stuck out her hand. "My name is Naomi June Reese."

Richard gently took her hand. "Pleased to meet you, Naomi June Reese."

A shy smile on her face, she pulled her hand free, then moistened her lips. "I'd like to ask another favor of you."

"Name it," Richard said softly.

"Could you take me to the court house? I'd like to file for a restraining order against Gordon."

Richard's hand closed over hers again. "All you ever have to do is ask."

CHAPTER SIXTEEN

"WHERE IS SHE?" LUKE ASKED BRANDON AS SOON AS HE entered the Red Cactus and saw his brother by the bar.

"In my office, but—" Brandon was left talking to Luke's broad back.

Hurrying down the hallway, Luke opened the door. Catherine stood a few feet away, her arms wrapped around her, her beautiful face a mixture of hope and anxiety. "Is it really over?"

"It's over." He'd called her after Dakota led Sam Morris off in handcuffs.

"Oh, Luke. Thank God. Thank you."

They moved at the same time. He caught her in his arms, his lips coming down on hers, reveling in the kiss and in her. After the briefest of hesitation, she met him the same way. It was a long, satisfying time before he lifted his head, glad to see shadows no longer lingered in her deep brown eyes. "I left a message at the hotel for your department chair so he can start spreading the word."

"I told you Luke would take care of everything."

Glancing up sharply, Luke saw his mother, felt Catherine go rigid in his arms. So *that* was the reason for her hesitation in returning his kiss. Of all the people to catch them, his mother was the worst. It didn't help that her close friend, Amanda Poole, was there also.

Both smiled indulgently at them. The best way to get

out of this sticky situation was to release Catherine and step away from her. Somehow he couldn't make himself do either. "What are you doing here?"

"Supporting Catherine, of course," his mother answered. "We came by for lunch and we knew something was wrong when we saw her. Although she wouldn't tell us until after you called."

Luke lifted a heavy brow. "Then how could you support her?"

"By being with her, of course," his mother stated as if that was obvious.

"We were horrified when she finally told us," Amanda added. "But we assured Dr. Stew . . . Catherine that her reputation would remain unblemished."

"They were wonderful," Catherine said, trying and failing to move away from Luke. His hold was inflexible.

"I'm proud of you, but then, I always have been," his mother said, her voice warm with approval.

"Thanks for staying with her," Luke said, appreciative they had helped Catherine, but definitely not liking the ecstatic grin on his mother's face.

"I tried to tell you she wasn't alone, but you were in too big of a hurry," Brandon said from behind him, then looked at Catherine and added, "Can't say that I blame you though."

Flushing, Catherine finally managed to step away from Luke. He very much wanted to pull her back into his arms, better yet, take her to the cabin, where they could be alone.

"Was it Dr. Tolliver or Dr. Perkins?" she asked, her voice not quite steady.

Despite his mother looking, his knuckles brushed across her cheek. "Neither. You were right about them. Rena Bailey was behind the whole sordid plot to discredit you."

Catherine shut her eyes briefly, then opened them. "I'm glad it wasn't either of them."

A betrayal by her associates would have cut deeply. "I know."

Her hand lifted to touch the strong line of his jaw, then paused. Snatching her hand down, she clenched it into a fist instead, then glanced sideways at his mother.

Ruth Grayson beamed happily back at her.

Luke had enough. "Would you mind giving us some privacy so I can discuss the case with my client?"

"Certainly," Ruth said. "Amanda and I have to be going anyway. See you in the morning."

Brandon closed the door behind them, leaving Luke and Catherine alone.

"Your mother saw us kissing," Catherine said, a note of worry in her voice.

Luke pulled her into his arms. "She's lucky that's all she saw me doing."

She stared up into his strong face. "Such as?"

The invitation in her eyes was unmistakable and undeniable. They both needed this. Hungrily his mouth closed over hers again, his tongue greedily seeking the hot, dark sweetness of her mouth. Incredibly sure hands swept down the gentle slope of her back to her soft hips, cupping them, holding them against the growing heaviness of his arousal. Her arms curved around his neck, her hands tangled in his hair. Instinctively she moved against him in a rhythm as old as the land around them.

Feeling the point of no return quickly approaching, Luke called upon all his willpower to release her sweet mouth and slide his hands up to her waist. But he wasn't strong enough to move away completely. He kissed her jaw, nibbled on her ear lobe.

Her breath caught, tangled. Restlessly she moved against him.

"I was crazy to start this," he said.

She kissed his chin, then laid her head on his chest, was comforted by the erratic beating of his heart that matched her own. "I'm glad you did. It was good to forget for a little while."

He pulled her closer with a fierce protectiveness he was unaware of. "The man she hired confessed to everything. Sergeant Rodriquez has probably already called the police in Los Angeles. Rena Bailey will be in jail by nightfall, and this time the federal government is involved because of the wiretapping. She won't find it so easy to go free."

"How much more will her children have to endure?"

One of the reasons he cared about Catherine was that despite her own problems, she always thought of others. "It will be tough for them, but they're better off with their grandparents. If her scheme to discredit you had worked, she had planned on working it so her parents paid her for keeping them," he said harshly. "Some women don't deserve children."

Catherine flinched.

Luke's expression and voice gentled. "Don't worry about the children, they're safe now."

"By saving me, you saved them. Thank you." Her smile was unsteady. She had to enjoy their time together with no regrets. "You're a fantastic man, Luke Grayson. I'm glad I met you." No matter what happened, she'd never be sorry for loving him.

"You want to go back to the hotel and find your department chair or do you want to go home?"

"Home."

THEY NEVER MADE IT. SHE MIGHT NOT HAVE WANTED TO see her department chair, but Dr. Thomas Watts very much wanted to see her. So did several of her other

colleagues. Obviously pleased and touched by their seeking her out to show their outrage and support, Catherine
sent Luke an apologetic glance and asked Brandon if a
table was available.

"Number seven," Luke said.

Catherine didn't realize number seven was the family
table until Brandon removed the RESERVED sign. The smile
she bestowed on Luke was tremulous. "Thank you," she
said, sitting down.

He nodded, then noted with rising irritation that Lee
Perkins sat next to Catherine. The man didn't miss a
trick. But Luke had a few of his own.

In a very short time, Lee had to leave to answer the
phone. On returning, his annoyance was obvious—there
was no one on the phone and his seat was taken. Grumbling, he took one of the chairs drawn up to the booth.

Crossing his arms, Luke leaned against the wall. He
planned to stay close in case Catherine needed him.

The hairs on the back of his neck prickled. Instinctively he knew whom he'd see before he lifted his head.
Ruth Grayson, a strange expression on her face, stared
back at him.

Straightened, he frowned. He started toward her, but
she shook her head, then smiled unsteadily at him. Turning, she and Amanda followed the waitresses to a table on
the patio.

Hands on his hips, Luke tried to figure out what had
put that strange look on her face and came up blank. He
loved her despite her driving him crazy with all the irritating women she had thrown at him.

Laughter erupted from the group Catherine was with.
He glanced around and looked straight into her eyes. He
felt the jolt all the way to his toes. Dr. Watts said something to her and she turned to answer him.

Luke felt her reluctance as surely as he felt his own.

He quickly amended his earlier thought. Catherine might be headstrong, but never irritating. Her propensity toward being strong-willed came from her family background, her independence, her tender heart. He admired her as much as he found himself worrying about her.

"Excuse me, Luke," Nacona said, a tray of drinks in her hands.

Luke glanced around to see Nacona staring at him, laughter dancing in her black eyes. "Sorry."

"No more than some of my friends will be." Stepping past him, she began serving the drinks.

Luke went to find his mother. So it would be all over the restaurant in less than thirty minutes that he was staring at Catherine like a love-struck kid. So what? He could handle it.

Five minutes later, Luke wasn't sure how any sane, honest man said he understood women. He'd come out on the patio to see his mother laughing and chattering with Amanda and two other women they'd joined. Whatever had been bothering his mother was obviously short-lived. Wanting to be certain he had asked to speak to her in private.

She'd come, then after he'd asked her why she had looked so sad, she had almost teared up, told him it was because she loved him, kissed him on the cheek, and went back to her friends.

Since his mother could evade a question with the best of them, but had never lied to him, he believed her. *Women.*

Leaving the patio, he went back inside intending to get one particular woman and go home. Seeing the threesome that entered the restaurant, he resigned himself to disappointment.

"Hello, Richard, Naomi, Kayla. Having a late lunch?" Luke asked.

"Hello, Mr. Grayson, but you forgot Teddy," Kayla told him, holding up her teddy bear.

Luke smiled down at the pretty child. She was a cute little thing. "My apologies to both of you. Hello, Teddy."

"Hi, Luke," Richard said, one hand clasping Naomi's elbow, the other Kayla's free hand. "We saw your truck outside. Naomi wanted to talk to Catherine."

"Hello," Naomi said, scanning the restaurant. "Is she here with you?"

"Yes, she's in the back with some of her colleagues," Luke answered, steering them out of the entryway to a wooden bench on the side wall away from the crowd.

Naomi's gaze came back to Luke. "Do you think I could see her for a minute or call her later if she's busy?"

It was the first time Luke remembered Naomi looking him directly in the eye or her asking for anything. "It might be hard for her to break away, but she'll be at the cabin later on. Richard has the number."

Naomi nodded. Her grip on the canvas bag tightened, then she faced Richard. "Could you please take Kayla and wait for me in the Jeep?"

Richard regarded Luke with a frown. "Are you sure?"

"Yes. I need to talk with Luke alone," she said, momentarily gazing down at her wide-eyed daughter. "I wouldn't ask you if it wasn't important. Kayla will be safe with you."

The uncertainty left Richard's strong features. "By the time you join us, we'll have decided what to eat for lunch." Catching Kayla's hand, he stood.

"Thank you." She didn't take her eyes off them until the double wooden doors closed behind them.

"That wasn't easy, was it?" Luke asked.

She stared at him as if she hadn't expected him to understand, then said, "I wanted to dislike you."

"Does that mean you don't?"

"You're the reason my ex-husband found me this morning and tried to force me to go back to him," she said, amazed that the words came out so calmly.

Luke tensed. His gaze going beyond her. "Where is he now?"

"Richard and the police sent him on his way," she told him. "My ex-husband said someone ran the registration of my car. That had to be you. You never trusted me, did you?"

Now that she was looking at him, Luke felt uncomfortable. "Not at first."

"Yet you helped me?"

"Because of Catherine at first, then because of your little girl, then because you weren't standing there with your hand open," Luke told her honestly. "I'm sorry about your ex finding you, but it was important that I check you out."

She bit her lip. "So you know Jones isn't my last name."

"From the start. It took another day to get your real name."

"Then you learned about Gordon?" she asked in a whisper, experiencing shame all over again that she had let him dupe her.

"Yes."

"You didn't tell Catherine?"

He leaned back against the bench. "She worries too much as it is."

A man being protective of a woman had been an oddity until she came to Santa Fe. "Catherine said you were working on something for her and that's the reason you looked so serious all the time. She said you were a good man." Naomi glanced down, then up again. "I want you to know I don't blame you. You were only trying to help Catherine. I hope you can."

Remnants of rage flashed briefly across his dark face.

"That matter was cleared up this morning. That's the reason she's with her colleagues, they're celebrating."

"Then you were able to help both of us." Naomi stood. "I realize you did what you felt you had to, but I don't like the idea of personal information on me in your possession."

"Already shredded," Luke said. "I don't know what went down with your ex, but another protective order might be advisable. Neither you nor Kayla need to live in fear."

She patted her canvas bag. "We just came from court, where I obtained a temporary protective order. Because Catherine and Richard care about you, and because you helped me regardless of the reason, I'll always be thankful. Goodbye, Luke."

"Goodbye, Naomi. Stay at the hotel as long as you like."

Her shoulders straightened, a smile touched her thin face. "Thank you. I'll pay you back. It shouldn't be too much longer. Richard is helping me look for a place."

"Richard is a good man."

Her face brightened. "I know. Kayla adores him."

Luke lifted an eyebrow. It seemed Kayla wasn't the only one who adored Richard. He stuck his hand out. "Friends?"

"Friends."

"I'll tell Catherine to expect your call."

Smiling, she left. Luke gazed out the window to see Richard get out of the back seat of the Jeep and open the front passenger door for her. Besides Catherine, Naomi had Richard in her corner. A good man to have.

CATHERINE TOOK GREAT PRIDE AND A LOT OF PLEASURE in finally being alone with Luke. She was sorry she had missed Naomi and Kayla, and was more than ready to leave the Red Cactus when everyone finally departed. "Did we bore you again?" she asked as they crossed the parking lot to Luke's truck.

"Looking at you is never boring."

She stopped and stared up at him, touched, very pleased. "Luke."

His hand palmed her cheek. "Don't look at me like that. We still have twenty minutes before we reach the cabin."

She shivered in anticipation. "Is your house closer?"

Luke's black eyes narrowed. "Yes, but so are prying eyes and wagging tongues."

"Then why are we standing here?" Pulling his hand, she ran toward the truck.

THE TWENTY-MINUTE DRIVE SEEMED MORE LIKE TWENTY hours. Luke had already dismissed the guard he had watching the house. The truck had barely braked, the motor cut before he was reaching for her hand. Unmindful of closing the truck's door, they ran up the steps. With a jab of the key and a twist of his wrist, they were inside. Greedily he pulled her to him. She went.

The taste led to another and another. Clothes were quickly discarded. On the couch with the sun pouring over them, his mouth trailed kisses over her heated body, pleasing her where he touched, teasing her where he did not.

She twisted beneath him. "Luke, I can't wait."

His head lifted, his hair flowing down his shoulders. "Neither can I." His mouth came down on hers, the same instant he slid into her velvet heat. The twin pleasures had her hips urging up, a moan slipping past her lips. His thrusts were deep, and fast and sure.

She wrapped her legs and arms around him, loving him, glorying in his strength, his power. He was all that mattered to her—and soon she'd have to leave him. Her heart cried out in protest, her arms tightened, she moaned his name.

As always, he heard. His hands locked beneath her hips, joining them closer, taking him deeper.

Pleasure whipped through her. She forgot to think, to worry, only feel. Stroke for incredible stroke, she matched his driving need until her body tightened. His name was a hoarse cry. Again he answered. They went over together.

She came back to herself to feel Luke nuzzling her neck. One more night was all she had. "I still want you."

His head lifted, coal black eyes stared down into hers. "Then take me."

With a supple twist of his body, Catherine found herself on top, her hands pressed against his muscular chest. "I can't decide what I want to do first."

"Take your time, I'm enjoying the view." His strong, callused hands stroked from the curve of her shoulders, down her arms, crossed to her stomach, then swept up to her breasts gleaming in the light.

"Beautiful." His hands closed over their soft weight, gently caressing her. "Taste like cinnamon mixed with brown sugar." His lips fastened on her nipple, gently drawing it into his mouth, his tongue circling the taut pebble.

Suddenly, amid the growing pleasure and heat, she knew what she wanted. With hands that trembled, she drew his head away. "Do you know how incredible you make me feel?" She continued before he had a chance to answer. "Let me show you."

Pressing her hands firmly against his wide chest for him to lie back down, she bent over him then kissed his thickly lashed eyelids, rubbed her cheek against his strong jaw, nipped his tempting lower lip. "I love the way you're built. Powerful and perfect," she murmured in appreciation. "The first time I saw you with your shirt partially unbuttoned in the woods, I wanted to touch you, like this."

"I wanted to touch you, too," he said, his voice rough, his hands clamped around her waist.

She smiled, a soft, slow, secret smile. Lowering her head, she flicked her tongue over his nipple, then blew her warm breath across it. Luke groaned. Her head lifted only enough to meet his hot, piercing gaze. "Did you also want to do that?"

"Yes."

The smile came again. "Let's see what else we can agree upon."

By the time Catherine finished their "comparative analysis," Luke was sweating and rock hard. Her soft, sweet, mouth and quick little tongue had teased them both unmercifully. When he had finally ended their torture, and slid into her hot, moist sheath, their lovemaking was as frenzied as their first time that evening.

Spent, and too tired to move to the bedroom, he settled her in the curve of his arm. "You cold?"

"Never with you," she murmured drowsily.

Drawing her closer, Luke stared out the window to the forest and mountains beyond. In the past they had given him peace, renewed his spirit, left him content. He glanced down at the woman sleeping trustingly in his arms. Before he realized it, his lips brushed against her hair. At times strong and vulnerable, at times fierce and tender, she had invaded his solitude, his life. If he wasn't careful, when she left, she'd take his peace with her.

LUKE AWOKE TO THE RINGING OF THE TELEPHONE. Catherine, her naked warmth wrapped around him, stirred. He pulled the comforter up around her neck. About an hour ago, he'd awakened to find her chilled and had taken her to his bed. His tough hide might be used to the drop in temperature in the mountains, but hers wasn't.

The phone rang again.

"We're not in," she mumbled, her eyes still closed.

He kissed the top of her head. "It's probably for you."

"I don't care."

"I'd agree with you if your friends and family were the patient, trusting type. One of us better answer the phone."

Her tousled head lifted. She peered at him through half-closed eyes, then regarded the ringing phone on the night table. "I talked with Mother yesterday and Helena this morning. Dianne is in Bermuda."

"Answer the phone before the state police show up again."

"Bossy," Catherine said, then grinned and slowly eased her body enticingly across his to the other side of the bed to the phone.

Luke's black eyes narrowed. "You'll pay for that."

"Promises. Promises." Grinning, still on her stomach, she picked up the phone. "Hello. Hi, Naomi." Sitting up in bed, she pulled the cover over her breasts and watched his gloriously naked body stroll into the bathroom to take a shower. Her breath fluttered out. "Oh, my."

Catherine grinned. "No, no, I'm fine. I just saw the most magnificent animal. All that exotic grace and leashed power just took my breath away."

Luke stopped and gazed back at her, heavy eyebrows lifted.

Blowing him a kiss, she waved him on into the bathroom. "Luke said you wanted to talk with me, how can I help?"

As Naomi talked, Catherine's smile faded. The story was an old one, nothing new, but that didn't make it any less important to the woman and child involved. They had lived the nightmare and were just beginning to awaken. The healing would take time.

"You call me anytime you want to talk. I think you've made the right decision to remain in Santa Fe. There are good people here. I want to see you, Kayla, and Richard at the Red Cactus for my signing in the morning and I won't take no for an answer. I have some books for Kayla. Great. See you then. Good night."

Hanging up the phone, Catherine tossed back the cover and went to take a shower. Luke had left while she was talking to Naomi. Naomi had found the courage to face her worst nightmare and start to live without fear. Richard had helped. All Catherine could hope was that if there was an attraction, that Richard would be patient. Naomi wasn't likely to want anything heavy, but she could use someone she could count on. Stepping under the spray of the shower, Catherine's thoughts turned to Luke. Before she left, she was getting him in the shower.

CATHERINE CAME OUT OF THE CABIN'S FRONT DOOR to see Luke sitting on the porch. Hero was by his side. The animal jumped up and went to her, his tail wagging.

"Hello, Hero." Leaning down to pet the hybrid, she regarded Luke with a smile. "I think he's growing on you."

"I owe him."

"How?" she asked, sitting down beside Luke.

Quietly he told her about the intruder. "If not for your pet I might have missed the real culprit." Luke regarded the animal. "I owe him, but I'm not quite sure what to do with him. He can't take a plug out of every stranger that comes up here."

"You can teach him not to," Catherine said.

"Catherine, I don't know . . ."

"Please try. I know you can do it."

"And how do you know that?"

"Because failure isn't a word you accept for yourself or others. Because you'd never turn your back on someone who helped you. You'll teach him. You have too much honor not to."

His arm went around her neck. "Catherine, you're quite a woman."

Your woman she wanted to say, but couldn't. She pushed the sadness away and lifted her mouth to his. There'd be time enough for sorrow after she left.

CATHERINE WAS THE CENTER OF ATTENTION.

Every now and then Luke caught a glimpse of her smiling face through the crush of people crowded around to talk to her or to get a book or books autographed. Many of the people from the workshop had taken the opportunity to bring their children, increasing the numbers. To provide more space, most of the tables in the Red Cactus had been removed. Even so, you couldn't walk two feet without bumping into another person. From the smiling faces of people clutching books, they didn't mind.

His mother and Amanda Poole were all smiles themselves. Why shouldn't they be? The book sales were steadily climbing and people happily paid full price. The Women's League and the bookstore were going to come out sitting pretty.

Speaking of . . . Luke made his way through the crowd to where Catherine was sitting. Pretty wasn't close to describing how beautiful, how vibrant she looked in the lemon double-breasted jacket. Knowing only three gold buttons on her vest of the same color separated him from the satin softness of her skin was as much torture as it was pleasure.

He recalled comparing her to the yellow flower of the prickly pear cactus when they first met. As he had thought, there was a way to pluck the bloom without being pricked by the hundreds of tiny thorns, if one knew how. She caught him looking at her, flushed, and accepted the book from the next person in the long line.

Luke's lips curved into a smile, certain her thoughts had paralleled his. He'd never enjoyed a shower more, never was more grateful for the strength of his body . . . and its endurance. Deep inside Catherine, her arms and legs wrapped around him, hearing her cries of pleasure as the water beat down upon them was like nothing he had ever experienced. Catherine made a man want to give and give, then turn around and give some more.

Brandon walked up beside him and noted Luke's expression. "I suppose it's too late to watch your back."

Luke glanced sideways at his youngest brother. "This is different."

A long sigh escaped Brandon. "That's what I'm afraid of. I can't decide if I'm pleased for you or should lock you in a closet until you come to your senses. If you go down, Mama won't rest until we're all married."

Luke went still. Slowly his gaze centered on Brandon. "What makes you say something like that?"

"Because you've changed." Brandon shook his dark head. "You can take or leave women. Mostly you leave them. Not this time. Where Catherine goes, you go."

"I was working on a case for her," he defended.

"And holding her hand and touching her every chance you got." Brandon shoved his hand in Luke's direction. "Look at you. Wearing a sports coat and a tie for the past two hours and you've yet to complain. You hate crowds, yet, just now when I walked up, you were smiling like a kid on Christmas morning."

The truth of Brandon's words hit Luke full force. "Catherine's been through a lot. I'm just happy things worked out for her."

"We're all thankful you caught the creep, but we aren't looking at her as if she's the cherry on the top of an ice cream sundae," Brandon accused.

"I'm not either," Luke flared.

"Luke," Brandon said, clearly unconvinced.

"I care about her, but it's not any different than with any other woman I've been out with," he said.

"Then you won't care that a guy over there is hitting on her."

His face hard, fury whipping through him, Luke whirled. All he saw was Catherine talking to a woman and her two children. He turned back to Brandon. "That was dirty."

"But necessary. You've never been the jealous type before either." Brandon's hand rested on Luke's tense shoulder. "Big brother, I think you better decide if you want to get the hell of out Santa Fe or make Mama's prophecy come true. Whatever, I'm with you."

Luke didn't see Brandon walk away. He was too busy trying to look inward.

He cared for Catherine. Hurt for her when she was hurt. Thought her too soft-hearted for her own good and worried about her, but that was as far as it went. Sure, he didn't want her to leave, didn't like to think about it, but that was just because they were great in bed.

Positive of what he was feeling, he turned. A group of children were clustered around Catherine, their young faces bright with wonder, their eyes glued to Catherine as she read from one of her books. Kayla sat in her lap holding Teddy. She held the little girl lovingly, but was careful to make eye contact with each of the other children listening.

Gradually the hum of conversation and the tinkling of glasses ceased. One by one, people turned, and strained to hear what she read. Luke found himself just as caught up in the soft, lilting voice.

"Love is magic and Keisha knew if she kept the magic to herself it would wither away, but if she gave the magic, it would grow strong. She gave the magic to her new baby brother who took so much of their mother's time, and watched him wave his tiny arms and smile at her.

"Love is magic that can touch the coldest, hardest heart. But it has to be given freely, without regret, without expecting anything in return. For only in loving unconditionally can the magic be released. The end."

There was a full five seconds of silence, then the room erupted into applause. This time Luke didn't join in. Before the enthusiastic crowd blocked his view of Catherine, he saw her pull Kayla closer to her, lean her head against the child's, her smile tender and sad.

Then, she glanced up and their eyes met. He felt the pull of her eyes from twenty feet away. Denial was impossible any longer. The truth stared back at him. Now he just had to decide what he wanted to do about it.

CATHERINE'S BOOK SIGNING AT THE SANTA FE CONNECtion that afternoon was equally successful. A line stretched from her table down the aisle and out the door.

Luke watched with open delight as she warmly greeted enthusiastic parents and coaxed shy children to tell her their names. She was marvelous with people. Her genuine sincerity was evident in the patience and attention she gave to those around her.

Finished, he thought she'd be tired after signing autographs for hours, but she insisted on spending her last day in Santa Fe enjoying the sights. Her reminder that she was leaving made his chest feel odd. He didn't have time to dwell on it because when they walked outside the book store, Richard, Naomi, and Kayla were walking toward them.

Luke wasn't surprised to see them. Catherine hadn't had much of an opportunity to speak with Naomi earlier. Before Catherine left, she'd want to make sure the other

woman was doing well. Catherine's capacity for love as-
tounded him.

"Thank you again for all the books, Miss Catherine,"
Kayla said with a wide grin. "Teddy thanks you, too."

"You're both welcome," Catherine said, smiling down
at the child.

Luke's chest felt funny again.

"Catherine, you sure you want us to go?" Naomi
glanced at Luke.

"Positive," Catherine returned and tucked her arm into
the crook of Luke's.

Whatever Catherine wanted, Luke wanted her to have.
"I thought you and I were going to be friends?"

"That's the reason I said what I did," she told him, smiling one of her rare smiles. "You don't need us tagging
along."

"Yes, they do, Mama. Miss Catherine said we could go
to a museum that's just for children," Kayla reminded her
mother.

The adults laughed. "Smart girl," Richard said.

Catherine looked up at Luke. "Where to first?"

"I guess the Palace of the Governors." He had taken
the other women out to dinner and driven them around,
but he hadn't been their walking tour guide. "It's the oldest public building in the United States," he heard himself
say.

"Fantastic," Catherine said, leaning closer. "Lead on."

LUKE WASN'T MUCH FOR SIGHT-SEEING, DIDN'T LIKE
crowds, but as the day progressed he found himself enjoying the afternoon. The familiar and unnoticed became
new and exciting with Catherine by his side.

More than once, he caught himself admiring paintings
or statues of a mother and her child or family gatherings.
One in particular, of a Native American storyteller with a

group of children around her held him captive for long moments.

"She's beautiful," Catherine said from beside him.

"She reminds me of you." Luke tenderly gazed down into Catherine's face. "A strong woman who gives to others."

Catherine's smile was sad. "Thank you."

He frowned. "What's the matter?"

"Nothing." She pulled away and walked over to Kayla, whose interest in the gallery had waned. "Kayla, why don't we go outside and I'll finish telling you about the rest of the butterfly's adventures?"

"Goody," Kayla said, happily going with her.

Naomi turned from viewing a pictographic diary documenting the battle of Little Big Horn.

"She'll be all right," Richard said, his hand light on her shoulder.

"I know." She turned and looked at him. "We both will."

Luke walked outside and stood listening as Catherine wove her tale. She looked beautiful and natural holding Kayla. She deserved children of her own. The thought caught him off guard, then the certainty and the rightness grew. The pressure eased in his chest.

She deserved children of her own. His children.

CHAPTER SEVENTEEN

BONELESSLY MELLOW, CATHERINE CURLED AGAINST Luke. The day had been wonderful and showed every indication of continuing to be. There had been a few bad moments when she had looked into Luke's eyes and was confronted again with her inability to have children. But she had refused to give in to self-pity, and enjoyed the dwindling time they had left together.

She and Luke were now in what was becoming their favorite spot, on the couch in front of the immense window in the great room. She couldn't imagine anything more perfect than lying in his arms, watching the fire he'd built, listening to the rhythmic beat of his heart.

"When I saw you this morning with Kayla and the other children today, it hit me," he said softly.

Something inside her went still and quiet. She couldn't breathe. *Please don't say it, Luke. Please.*

"I imagined you holding our child."

"Luke, no." She came upright in a frantic rush to her feet. Keeping her back to him, one hand clutched the back of a chair.

Her reaction stunned Luke. "I'm not very good with words, because I've never had practice saying them to other women. I love you, Catherine. With every beat of my heart and every breath I take, my love for you grows stronger. Will you marry me?"

Each word was like a dagger to her heart. Luke's love was something she hadn't let herself believe she could ever possess.

"Catherine, what's the matter?"

Say something witty and sophisticated, her brain screamed, but nothing came. The pain and hurt were too deep.

"Catherine?"

In her mind's eye, she saw him reaching for her. She made herself move. If he touched her, she'd crumble. "I-I can't marry you."

"Why?" The question twisted the knife deeper.

"I don't want to discuss it." She started toward her room.

"The hell we won't." Catching her arms, he turned her. Seeing the anguish in her face, his anger vanished, his voice softened. "Talk to me. Whatever it is, we can work it out."

"Please, just let it go," she begged, her voice as unsteady as her legs.

"Not until I understand why you're tossing my proposal back in my face."

"This wasn't supposed to happen," she whispered, trying and failing to free herself.

"You can't dictate to your heart, Catherine." He reached toward her face and she flinched. "What is it?"

"Just don't touch me," she cried.

His head jerked back. A muscle leaped in his jaw. "I didn't know my touch offended you all of a sudden. I won't bother you again."

His proud shoulders stiff, he headed for the front door. In her heart, she knew that would be the last time she ever saw him. Hurt, defeated, rejected. No matter the price she had to pay, she couldn't do that to him.

"I can't have children."

Luke halted abruptly, then turned. Catherine's expression was as tormented as her words had been. He felt her misery, her agony. He closed the distance between them in three long strides. Despite Catherine's shaking her head, holding up her hand for him to stop, he closed his arms around her, drawing her against him, his pain deep as he remembered his words earlier of her with their children. He shut his eyes and willed the lump in his throat to disappear; there was nothing he could do about the tears on his lashes.

"As long as I have you, nothing else matters," he told her. "I love you, Catherine. Nothing will ever change that."

Shaking her head she forced herself out of his arms. "You're not thinking clearly, Luke. You're trying to be noble. The doctors were very specific."

"When was that?"

She didn't want to talk about it, but if he understood there was no chance of her having children, he'd accept her decision. Pinning her gaze in the middle of his chest, she told him about the tumors, the surgery, and the doctor's prognosis.

"Have you seen a specialist since?"

Her startled gaze flew up to meet his. "Why should I? The scarring isn't going away."

"Then you aren't certain? May—"

"No," she cut him and his hope off. "I can't have children, Luke. Accept it and get on with your life with another woman."

"Is that what Roderick, your fiancé, did?" he asked with growing certainty.

"Yes. His mother told me I was no longer acceptable."

"What did he say?"

"I never saw or heard from him again after I told him."

"So you think I'm as selfish and heartless as that bastard, that I'd turn my back on you after you told me?" he said harshly. "You have that little faith in me?"

"I have that much. You'd stay no matter what, and I couldn't live with knowing you were trapped in a marriage by honor instead of love." Her voice trembled. "Neither of us would be able to forget your mother wants grandchildren."

"This is between us. My mother's wishes don't enter into it. It's what we feel for each other that counts." He stared intently at her. "You once told me that no one can predict the future. Looks like you're trying to, and depicting me as the one to want out. You could just as well get tired of me first."

Not loving Luke was impossible. "Then it seems to me that I'm saving us both a lot of trouble."

"Then you're not as brave as I thought."

"I guess not." Her arms wrapped around her waist. "I better finish packing."

"Did you lie, Catherine?" he asked softly.

"Luke, please let it go."

He was so close, she felt the heat of his body. "Did your face, your eyes, your touch lie to me today when they all said you loved me?"

"The answer won't change anything." She wanted to run, but her feet wouldn't cooperate.

"Yes it will. All you have to do is tell me you don't love me, and I'm out of your life forever." He moved until their bodies touched heart to heart. "Four words—I don't love you—and it's over."

More than the heat and hardness, she felt his enduring strength and power and yes, love. Tears streamed unchecked down her cheeks. "I can't."

"Thank goodness." His head rested against hers, his hands closing with inexorable gentleness around her upper forearm. "Thank goodness."

Catherine accepted her weakness. "Just because I love you doesn't change anything, Luke. It makes me more determined that we don't see each other again. This afternoon every picture you stopped to admire, every statue you touched had children in it."

"We can adopt," he said.

"Tell me you wouldn't want your own children?" she asked, already knowing the answer.

His gaze didn't waver. "The children I wanted were because of you. I love you."

She shook her head. "It's over."

Black eyes blazed. "You're trembling in my arms and you expect me to let you walk out on me. All I have to do is touch you and we both want."

With her body craving his, there was no denying that what he said was true. "That's why it should end here and now. You want more than sex, and that's all I can give you."

His hands tightened. "Bull."

"I was selfish in seducing you, thinking only of what I wanted."

"Don't you get it, Catherine? I love you. Don't be afraid to trust me. I'd never leave you. I'd always be there."

Sorrow and tears sparkled in her eyes. "That's what I'm afraid of. You said marriage and children go together. With me, you'd have none."

"We'd have each other, Cath," he said. "Give our love a chance."

"Forgive me. Goodbye."

This time when she turned away, Luke let her go. Her mind was made up. Stubborn and loving, she'd put his welfare ahead of her own. He'd said she wasn't as brave as he thought. He was wrong, she was braver. He stared out the large window. He couldn't see the woods or the mountain peaks beyond, but he knew they were there.

The inner peace the knowledge had always given him wouldn't come. He wasn't surprised. When Catherine left, she'd not only take his peace, she'd take his shattered heart.

CATHERINE COULDN'T SEE WHAT SHE WAS THROWING in her suitcase, her vision was too blurred. With each article of clothing, the tears flowed faster and faster. It hurt. Like someone wrenching her insides out. Of all the things that had happened in her life, loving and losing Luke had been the worst and the best. She could only imagine carrying, then holding a child conceived out of love. With Luke, she had experienced the shimmering ecstasy of love and the shattering heartache of loss.

Slamming the suitcase lid down, she picked it and her purse up. So what if she didn't have all her clothes? She had to get out of there before she broke down completely.

Yanking open the door, she left her room. She kept her gaze fixed on the front door.

"Going someplace?"

Her throat and mind were too full to think of a plausible lie to tell him. Ten feet and she'd be out the door.

She never heard him come up behind her. But suddenly he was there, blocking the door. "It's dark outside."

Although she knew it was fruitless, she tried to go around him. In one seamless motion he sidestepped in front of her. She could feel the trembling in her body increasing, the knot in her throat thickening. "Please."

"I'll always be there and answer when you call me, Catherine." His arms closed around her.

The luggage dropped from her hand. Her arms went around his neck with a desperation she was unaware of. The tears started in earnest and there was no way she could stop them.

"Don't cry, Cath. I'm here." Picking her up, Luke took

her to his room and closed the door. Sitting her on the bed he slipped the dangling purse from the crook of her arm, pulled off her jacket and shoes, then picked her up and got under the covers with her. "I'm here. I'm here."

"Make me forget, Luke."

"Catherine, we need to tal—"

Her mouth found his, the urgency and need as bold as her hands on the zipper on his pants. "Please, Luke." Her hand closed around his masculinity.

His breath shuddered out over gritted teeth. "Cath—"

"Please."

With a hoarse groan of defeat, his mouth fastened on hers. The kiss wasn't gentle. She hadn't expected or wanted it to be. Too many chaotic emotions were raging through them. Fear. Regret. Pain. Anger. But the emotion that emerged with each heated kiss, each feverish touch, each ragged sigh was love.

There was as much desperation as passion when he buried himself deep in her liquid heat. They clung to each other fiercely, caught up in the fiery rapture. Stroke for incredible stroke, she matched him. Higher and higher they climbed together, unwilling for the end to come, but unable to stop its approach.

Then it happened. Her body tensed beneath him, his above. Their cries mingled as they found completion together.

For a long time afterward, Luke held Catherine, feeling the aftershocks sweeping through her. And in spite of the sexual gratification of his body, there was a need for something deeper. "Catherine."

No sound came but her uneven breathing. She wasn't asleep.

He rolled to his back, taking her with him. "Have it your way. I'll talk, you just listen. I love you. I've never said those words to another woman, nor will I."

Beads of moisture dropped on his chest. Tears. His hold tightened. "You're the only woman for me, Catherine. My love won't fade, it will only grow stronger." He kissed the top of her bowed head. "If you don't want to get married, we won't. Just don't shut me out. Give us a chance."

Luke stared up at the ceiling and prayed to his gods that she'd listen. Yet something warned him that, like the night he and his brothers and sister had prayed for their father's safe return and their prayers had gone unanswered, this prayer would also.

CATHERINE AWOKE WITH A SPLITTING HEADACHE. TENsion and tears were a bad combination. Cautiously, she lifted her head and stared straight into Luke's coal black eyes. Sitting in a chair on the other side of the room, he looked as tired as she felt. She had caused that. Her eyes shut tightly.

"Catherine?"

The touch of his hand, the concern in his voice opened her eyes. "I—"

"I brought your suitcase in here. Take a shower and get dressed. I'll start breakfast." Then he was gone.

Catherine lay back in bed fighting the stinging moisture in her eyes. Neither one of them could get through a rehash of last night. She could think of only one solution, and Luke would hate her forever.

Throwing back the covers, she got out of bed. Not giving herself time to change her mind, she retrieved a card from her purse, then picked up the phone on the night stand and dialed.

CATHERINE DRAGGED OUT THE SHOWER FOR AS LONG as she could manage. Twice Luke had come to check on her. Her makeup and dressing ate up another twenty minutes. She checked the small platinum watch on her arm. *Please hurry.*

The thought was barely out of her mouth before she heard the door bell chimes. Picking up her luggage, she slung her purse over her shoulder, and left the bedroom. She halted abruptly as the small group of people in the foyer turned to her. She had expected only one. Tightening her grip on the suitcase, she continued.

Luke crossed the room to her. "Why did you call her?"

Ruth Grayson, her face pinched with worry, was right behind him. "Yes, Catherine, why? You said Luke needed me. He seems fine."

"My mistake. If you'll excuse me."

"You're not going anyplace until this is settled between us."

She glanced anxiously at his mother. She'd miscalculated again. Luke loved and respected his mother, but he wasn't afraid to speak his mind in front of her. "Let it go."

"Everybody leave," Luke told them, his gaze locked on Catherine.

"No." She shook her head, refusing to look at him. "Don't you understand I can't go through it again? It's over—accept it."

"No." This time it was Luke who voiced the refusal.

Her hands clenched, her head fell. "Luke, I can't be what you want."

He grabbed her shoulders and dragged her to him. His mother's startled gasp, and the forward surge of his brothers and sister, did nothing to deter him. Turbulent emotions swirled in his black eyes. "You're what I want. Can't you understand that?"

"Luke, let her go," his mother said, her voice trembling. "Luke."

Morgan's large hand settled on his brother's rigid shoulder. "This is no way to handle this."

"Stay out of this," Luke said tightly.

Sierra, Pierce, and Brandon traded worried glances. Luke had always been the leader, the one everyone deferred to. If he wouldn't listen to Morgan or their mother, they weren't sure what to do. Help came from the least-expected source.

"Don't make me despise myself any more than I already do." Catherine's trembling hand rested lightly on his chest. "You love your family. I don't want anything to jeopardize that. I seem to keep getting it wrong." She visibly swallowed. "I only meant to love you."

"God, Catherine." He crushed her to him, felt her scalding tears against his skin. He could hold her body, but not her heart, her mind. Abruptly, he set her away. "Go. Run. But you'll never be able to run away from our love. The Muscogee language had no word for goodbye. No matter how far you go, you won't be able to run far enough, fast enough." Releasing her, he turned and stalked out of the house.

Unknowingly, Catherine took a halting step after him. A strong hand on her arms stopped her. She looked up into eyes as black as midnight, and as turbulent as a summer storm.

"Morgan, let her go," urged his mother.

"I can't do that, Mama," Morgan told her, his gaze never leaving Catherine's. "Unless you're planning on staying, I can't let you go after him."

Catherine's head fell. "Someone should be with him."

"You just ripped him to shreds, what do you care?" a feminine voice lashed out.

"Sierra, be quiet. You haven't seen them together," Brandon admonished. "Can't you see she's as torn up as Luke is?"

"He's hurting," Sierra defended, her small body quivering with fury.

"So is she. But until we have all the facts, Luke might not take it kindly if you bash his lady," commented another brother.

"Pierce is right, Sierra," Morgan said. "Sometimes things aren't what they seem."

Sierra separated herself from her brothers. She studied Catherine's face, ravaged by tears and pain. "If you need a place to stay until you work things out with Luke, I have an extra bedroom."

Catherine was totally caught off guard by the invitation. So were the other Graysons. Sierra wasn't fond of overnight guests.

"Thank you, but I have a plane to catch." Catherine reached for her luggage.

Sierra's small hand closed around the handle first. "I'll take you. You're in no shape to drive."

"Thanks, but—"

"Luke isn't known for his patience," Morgan interrupted. "If he comes back, all hell is going to break loose."

"And you can bet you won't be leaving anytime soon, if at all," Sierra added.

Catherine palmed her forehead. Things were going too fast. "I have a rental."

"I can drive it, you can go with Mama." Sierra gave the suitcase to Morgan, stuck out her hand to Catherine for the key. "If we're going, we better get started."

Digging in her purse, Catherine handed her the key. They all swept out of the cabin and she was left to follow.

Five vehicles were parked behind Luke's truck. Ruth had apparently called her other children when she thought Luke was in trouble. A close family where children would be loved and spoiled. There was no place for her.

She gazed into the woods. Luke would be there alone. "He shouldn't be by himself."

"He won't be." Morgan led her to his mother's 4×4 and opened the door. "I don't usually interfere in other people's personal lives, but Luke is special. He deserves the best."

"I know. That's why I'm leaving." Getting in, she shut the door on Morgan's puzzled face.

By the time Ruth had turned around, Morgan, Brandon, and Pierce were nearing the woods. Catherine abruptly sat forward in her seat. "The wolf hybrid. I forgot. He bit the man who tried to break into the cabin."

Ruth kept going. "They'll be fine."

Catherine wanted to ask if they could communicate with animals, also, but didn't. She wanted to do nothing that might precipitate a dialogue. Sitting stiffly in her seat, she stared straight ahead. In an hour, she'd be at the Albuquerque International Airport, and then she'd be by herself.

THE GRAYSON MEN HADN'T GONE TEN FEET INTO THE woods before meeting Luke and Hero. The warning growl came from deep within the animal's chest. Fangs bared, his gray hair bristled on his back. One by one the brothers stared at the animal until he sat back on his haunches, his fur smooth, his fangs hidden.

"Nice pet," Morgan said, his hands on his hips.

"Belongs to Catherine," Luke said, his attention on the two cars leaving. "I'm glad she let Mama drive her to the airport."

The men chuckled. Pierce spoke to the frowning Luke. "I'm not sure she had a choice. Since you weren't there, the Little General took over." He shook his dark head. "Sierra does like taking charge."

"This time I agree with her." Luke started toward the

cabin. "Come on. I need to call Sierra and ask her and Mama to stay with Catherine until her plane departs, then find Daniel."

RUTH MADE IT TO THE AIRPORT IN JUST SHY OF AN hour. After checking in the rental, she and Sierra insisted on seeing Catherine to her gate. Too drained to argue, Catherine agreed, thinking they would leave afterward. An hour lengthened into two and the Grayson women remained.

Very clearly Catherine recalled how Ruth had stayed with her at the Red Cactus when she had been frantic with worry. Whatever Catherine had done wrong, she hadn't turned Ruth completely against her. She tried to take small comfort in that, but it was impossible. The pain inside her went too deep.

Finally the call came for her to board. Strangely, she wasn't as anxious to leave the women's company as she had thought. "Goodbye, Ruth, and thanks for everything."

Ignoring the unsteady hand extended toward her, Ruth hugged Catherine. "Is there any hope that you might come back?"

"No." She faced Sierra. "Thanks and goodbye."

"I'm not as polite as my mother. Why are you walking out on my brother?" Sierra asked, curiosity more than censure in her voice.

Ruth didn't chastise her youngest child. Her attention centered on Catherine.

"Because I love him."

Turning, she entered the boarding terminal and took her seat in first class. She stared out the window at the tarmac until the gray surface blurred. Finding her shades in her purse, she put them on.

Hang on for just a few more hours, she told herself.

She repeated the litany over and over during the course of the flight. She was the third person off the plane. Obtaining her luggage, she went outside. She had just hailed a cab when she heard the familiar sound of her name.

"Catherine."

Catherine glanced around to see her mother rushing down the sidewalk toward her. Tall and regal in an Anne Klein antique-white pantsuit, Elizabeth Stewart enveloped her daughter in a hug. Catherine's throat grew tight; the tears she had been holding at bay spilled down her cheeks.

Elizabeth took one look at her daughter's face and steered her toward the waiting cab. "We'll talk inside."

After they were seated, Elizabeth gave the driver Catherine's address, then sat back with Catherine's hand in hers. "It appears I was right to take Luke Grayson's call."

"Luke?" Catherine's head came up.

"Yes. Daniel tracked me down for him, then Luke called and demanded to speak to me." Elizabeth wiped the tears from her daughter's face. "You look terrible. What happened?"

"Your foolish daughter fell in love." Catherine closed her eyes and leaned her head back against the seat. "I promised myself I'd never regret loving Luke, but it hurts, Mother. It hurts so bad."

"Oh, baby." Elizabeth squeezed her daughter's hand, feeling helpless and not liking it. "All men aren't selfish like Roderick."

Catherine spoke without opening her eyes. "I'd be the selfish one if I married him, Mother. Luke deserves a whole woman."

"Do you think another woman could love him more?"

Her eyes snapped open. "No."

"Then you are being selfish. You're condemning Luke to either second best or loneliness." Elizabeth sat back in her seat. "Love is hard enough to find. No one should toss it away."

THE CALL CAME CLOSE TO THREE FIFTEEN THAT AFTER-noon. Luke was waiting. The conversation was brief.

"Did her mother get there on time?" Ruth asked.

"Yes," he answered, hanging up the phone and observing the attentive expressions of his siblings. "Now you can all go home. I'm fine."

Morgan, his long, jean-clad legs stretched out before him, crossed his highly polished booted feet. "You're always trying to get us up here, and now you want to throw us out."

"I've got Pierce on the run," Sierra said, moving her knight.

"That'll be the day," Piece returned, studying the chess-board.

"I didn't marinate those steaks for nothing," Brandon said, getting up to go to the kitchen.

Ruth's fingers expertly danced across the keys of the baby grand. "Playing is the only way to keep it tuned properly."

All excuses, because they loved him and worried. For Catherine's sake, they needed certain information. "Brandon, get back in here."

He waited until his younger brother came running back. "I need to tell you something that I don't want going past this room. The only reason I'm telling you is because if I'm lucky enough to convince Catherine to marry me, I don't want her hurt unintentionally." He took a deep breath and told them everything. "Mama, if you have grandchildren, they won't be coming from me."

Getting up from the piano bench, she went to her eldest and took his hands. "Catherine is a wonderful, caring woman. Your happiness is enough. I'd be honored to have her in the family."

Different words with the same support came from each of his siblings with accompanying suggestion as how to get her back. Sierra opted for a tried and proven method. "You could always kidnap her the way Uncle John Henry did Aunt Felicia."

Luke nodded, considering, then smiled for the first time all day. "I just might do that."

CHAPTER EIGHTEEN

SUMMER WAS BEAUTIFUL IN LOS ANGELES. THE SKY WAS blue and clear; the air filled with the lush scents of flowers in bloom. People were happy everywhere Catherine went. She had every reason to revel in the season herself, she thought, as she prepared herself a glass of iced tea.

Her publisher had been ecstatic over her latest book, *Graywolf the Guardian,* the story of a spirit wolf who kept watch over a little girl while she was lost in the forest, then led her to safety. Her department chair had assured her she was now in the top two for department head of Developmental Psychology at her university. Her reputation was intact. Rena Bailey was in jail and no longer a threat to Catherine or her own children. More good news had arrived in a letter from Naomi just that morning.

Naomi had written to say that she and Kayla were doing well in their own apartment, which Sierra and Richard had helped them find. Naomi had gone for her second interview with the Santa Fe School District and was hired for the fall term. Richard was taking her out to celebrate, just the two of them. It wasn't a date or anything, Naomi wrote, but the excitement and nervousness and admiration for Richard came through clearly. Ruth had volunteered to keep Kayla.

Catherine had felt an odd shift in her heart when she had read that sentence, but she had refused to indulge in

Until There Was You 283

self-pity. It was about time Naomi and Kayla learned to live without fear. Still, she set the glass on the countertop without drinking.

Included in Naomi's letter was a message from Richard that Hero was all right, and that the two teenagers involved in his shooting had been found. Ironically, they had been worried about the animal they'd shot and had finally worked up enough courage to go back and look for him. Luke had been in the woods with Hero and found them instead. Luke had told Richard the scare Hero had given the young boys was worth a hundred gun safety classes.

From Luke there was nothing.

In the bright yellow kitchen of her condo Catherine gazed out the kitchen window to the small back yard. Yellow jasmine climbed profusely over her wooden fence to offer an arresting backdrop for the stone bench where on rare occasions she could relax with a book.

Catherine's hands gripped the edge of the countertop. She hadn't been able to relax since she'd left Santa Fe. Her home that she had meticulously created no longer brought her peace. The spaciousness, the plants, the many windows all reminded her of another home high in the Sangre de Cristo Mountains. A home where she could never belong.

She dreaded nightfall when she climbed into her lonely bed. There was no strum of a guitar to lull her to sleep, no strong arms of the man she loved to hold her. She missed Luke. The three weeks apart had increased the ache, not diminished it. She couldn't recall the last time she had done more than pick at her food.

Missing Luke was like missing a part of herself. And she hadn't heard a single word from him.

For a man who said he loved her, he certainly wasn't beating down her door to get her back. Stop it, she ordered herself, or this time she really would go crazy. Pushing away from the counter, she picked up the glass of tea, dumped it into the sink, and rinsed the glass.

"This is what I wanted."

Then why do you hurt and hunger for him?

Leaving the kitchen, she went to her office and cut on her computer. She was days behind on the computations for her research paper. If she wasn't careful, for the first time in her teaching career, she'd miss publishing a yearly paper. At least Jackie had resigned, and she had a new assistant for the coming term.

Catherine's fingers hovered over the keys while she reread her notes. Moments later she flipped the computer off and stood.

In her unsettled frame of mind, she wasn't in the mood to delve into "The Lasting Effect of Dysfunctional and Fractured Families on School Age Children." Her hand tunneled through her hair. She had to snap out of her melancholy. Maybe a walk would help.

Grabbing her house keys from her purse, she left the house. She was stepping off the stone porch when a black Lincoln Continental pulled up to the curb. Her steps faltered, her hand gripped one of the curved black railings framing the five steps. Her heart rate going crazy, she stared as Luke emerged from the driver's side.

The unexpected sight of him took her breath away. He looked magnificent. His wide shoulders filled out his tan sports jacket to perfection. His long legs were encased in dress slacks. She couldn't help but remember when her hands had greedily clutched his muscular body to hers, her fingers had locked themselves in his straight black hair to bring his sensuous mouth closer. Her mouth dried, desire swept through her.

"Hello, Catherine." Closing the car door, he crossed the sidewalk and stood looking up at her as if it had been three minutes instead of three weeks since he had last seen her. "Seems like I caught you just in time."

The greeting was polite and impersonal, and took her completely by surprise. She blinked, quickly recovered, and pushed away the mild annoyance and, yes, hurt. She'd always had little patience with indecisive adults. It was disconcerting to find she was among their number. "Good evening, Luke."

He came up another step, then another, until they were eye to eye. "I know it's short notice, but I thought you were the best person to handle the job for my clients."

"Clients?"

"Yes." Luke looked over his shoulder at the couple who had emerged from the car. "Dominique and Trent."

Trent and Dominique Masters stood on the sidewalk, their arms around each other, their expressions troubled. Dominique had been wearing white the last time Catherine has seen her, but unlike now, her stunning face had been radiant. Trent's broad shoulders were braced, his handsome face lined with worry.

At their wedding less than six months ago, the good-looking couple had been immensely happy. Bothered by the drastic change, Catherine rushed down the steps and embraced Dominique. "It's good to see you." She shook Trent's hand. "Hello, Trent."

"Hello, Catherine." Dominique moved back into her husband's arms as if she was his anchor.

"Hello, Catherine," Trent greeted, his voice uncertain. "I'd really like to speak with you. Would it be possible to call me when you return? We have a hotel room in town."

Catherine didn't have to think about her answer. "I was just going for a walk. Come on. We can talk now." Bounding back up the steps, very much aware of Luke, she opened the door to her condo. "Can I get you anything to drink?"

They all declined. She motioned them to seats in the living room. Bright light streamed in through the arch of windows. Sitting on the deep-cushioned burgundy leather sofa, Catherine tried not to recall when the sun had poured over her and Luke in an intimate embrace, when neither would have tolerated the distance separating them. "What can I do for you?"

"Help Trent find his mother," Dominique answered as soon as they sat. Luke remained standing.

Catherine frowned. She had read in one of the numerous news articles covering their engagement that Trent had been raised in foster care. "You want me to help you gain permission to open your files?"

"Thanks to Luke, that won't be necessary." Trent leaned forward, excitement creeping into his deep voice. "He's found a woman in Atlanta he thinks is my mother."

Reluctantly Catherine's attention went to Luke. "How? It's been over thirty years."

"A lot of painstaking hard work and luck. Trent was with someone until he was approximately seven days old, he was in good general health, and he had been circumcised. The last bit of information told us he had been born in a hospital. So somewhere there was a record of his birth." Arms folded, Luke leaned against the side of a Queen Ann chair. "We inputted a two-week time span with infants' birth dates and mothers' names into the computer to locate both and find any infants who were unaccounted for."

Catherine's eyes widened. "That must have taken months. Not to mention the cost."

"Money's not important," Dominique and Trent said almost in unison, then glanced at each other with unquestionable devotion.

Trent Masters was well-off and owned his own trucking firm, but he was nowhere near the league of Dominique or her mega-rich brother, Daniel. But that wouldn't matter, Catherine realized studying the couple. Whatever resources Dominique had were Trent's and vice versa.

Impatiently, Dominique pushed her thick, waist-length braid over her shoulder. "What we need is you."

Catherine's frown returned. "I don't understand."

Luke straightened. "We need an unbiased, experienced observer that can tell us if the woman we believe to be Trent's mother is being truthful when we question her."

"You can do that," Catherine told him.

"Yes, but it might get sticky," Luke said. "Joann Albright is the wife of a very influential businessman who has political aspirations. They have two adult children, and to all outward appearances are the picture-book family. In fact, they were once voted family of the year. Everything tells me this is going to be rough. You have a way of soothing people, making them feel comfortable. If we blow this meeting with her, we may never get another one."

He was right, of course. Only a very small percentage of the mothers who abandoned their children were remorseful or wanted to see them again. "What led you to her?"

"She and her six-day-old son were involved in a one-car accident. The car ran off the road on a clear day and ended up in a lake. They managed to get Mrs. Albright out, but they never found the child."

Luke regarded Trent, his head bowed, his hands clasped in Dominique's before he continued. "According to the report, she kept repeating the child's name over and over, and demanding the rescuers let her go. She had to be forcibly restrained. When Mr. Albright was contacted, he thought there had been a mix-up. She had had a Cesarean section and was supposed to be in bed. The house staff told the investigator that Mrs. Albright advised them she'd take care of the baby and she should not be disturbed. She arrived at the hospital in shock, and hysterical. The reason for her being in the car was moot after the devastating loss of their first child. From Atlanta to Columbia, South Carolina, where Trent was found, is almost a straight shot. It was months before she was seen in public after the accident, and when she was, she was pregnant."

"Luke, it's not unusual for parents to have another child after such a tragedy," Catherine said. "They see it as a way to ease the pain and heal, but . . ." her eyes saddened. "No child can replace another one."

Trent's dark head came up. "The note my mother left with me in the hospital bathroom said, 'Keep him safe. I can't. Tell him I loved him. I did, but he won't remember.' If she was in an abusive situation like the authorities thought, why would she give me up, then have another child that she kept?"

The hurt confusion in his voice and face were readily discernible. "I can't answer that, Trent, until we learn more. I do know the reason women stay is complicated. It has to do with a myriad of things, their need for love, the way they were raised, or simply survival."

"But she was out," Trent reminded her.

"Leaving, to you or me, may seem as simple as walking out the door, but as I said, it goes much deeper than that. A woman might be dependent upon the man for financial support or might think that something she had done or didn't do deserved such treatment. She may feel something is lacking in her."

"And blame herself," Dominique said, her body rigid, her beautiful face tight with emotion.

"Exactly, but they shouldn't," Catherine said, her expression turning thoughtful. No one was sure why Dominique and her first husband, a very wealthy man, had suddenly divorced, but Catherine suddenly got a strong vibe that Dominique might be talking from experience. "It takes a very strong woman to walk."

Trent squeezed Dominique's hand. "And a stronger one to keep walking."

"I couldn't agree with you more," Catherine said, thinking about Naomi and other women she had worked with. "Is there any indication that Mrs. Albright had been abused or battered?"

"A broken arm from a fall down the stairs when her second child, Zachary, was nine months old," Luke related. "No other hospitalizations, but their doctor is an old family friend and one of the rare breed that continues to make house calls."

"How do you know that?" Catherine asked.

"She's had numerous prescriptions for sleeping pills, antidepressants, and pain pills filled at the neighborhood pharmacy over the years. Not enough to indicate addiction, but according to the doctor's computer records, she's only been to his office three times in the past five years."

Catherine held up her hand. "Forget I asked. I don't want to hear anything about information obtained from confidential medical records."

Luke grinned. "If you say so."

Catherine caught herself before she grinned back.

"So is tomorrow convenient to fly to Atlanta?" Dominique asked. "Daniel sent his private jet to take us."

Catherine's heart rate sped up with dread and anticipation. A sure sign it was too soon to spend any length of time with Luke. "I have a meeting in the morning."

"Can't you cancel it?" Dominique asked.

"I'm afraid not," Catherine said, unable to meet any of their eyes. "I can recommend someone to take my place," she offered.

"That won't do," Luke said. "Besides your credentials

and expertise, we need a person we can trust. The tabloids would have a field day with this information."

Hands clasped, Catherine leaned back in her seat. "Dr. Franklin has an excellent reputation. She and I have worked closely several times in the past."

"She isn't you," Luke said, his voice deep and almost caressing.

Catherine's body stirred with remembered passion when his voice had been a heartbeat away. "I'm sorry."

Dominique sat forward, her brow furrowed. "Surely whatever this meeting is isn't as important as helping Trent verify if this woman is his mother?"

"I'd help if I could." Catherine's voice shook.

Trent opened the attaché case by his feet. He removed a pale blue baby blanket. Standing, he walked to Catherine, the blanket clutched in his fist. "For thirty-four years I've wondered and worried about my mother. Did she abandon me out of love or selfishness? Is she safe? Happy? Does she ever think of me?" His large hands shook. "Now I have a chance to find out. I can't rest thinking she made sure I was safe, then went back to being abused. Please help me."

Dominique was up in an instant, going to Trent, but her angry gaze was on Catherine. "Help Trent or I—"

"Dominique," Luke said, cutting her off. "Catherine will make the right decision. Here's the name of the hotel where we'll be staying tonight." He handed her a business card with the information written on the back, his gaze piercing. "I'd take myself off the case, but for reasons I can't divulge, that's not an option. Trent and I need you."

The words went through her. She had never turned away from a child in need no matter how painful the encounter. No matter his age, Trent was still a child waiting and wondering about his mother. If he were willing to face what might be a devastating encounter, she had to be strong enough and brave enough to help him.

Catherine stood, her attention on Trent. "I'll help you in any way I can."

"Thank you, Catherine." Relief swept across his handsome face.

"I'm sorry," Dominique said sheepishly. "I should have known you'd help."

"Don't be. You love Trent and you'd fight the devil to keep him happy." Catherine's hands fisted. "Don't ever be sorry you love."

"Thank you." Dominique smiled and leaned against Trent.

"We'll wait in the car." His arm securely around his wife's waist, they left.

Unmoved, Luke stood a few feet from Catherine. "Good advice."

"If you want my help, we have to set some ground rules." Unclenching her hands, she shoved them into her pockets to keep from touching him. "Strictly business."

Black eyes studied her for a long time. "You're not sleeping."

"Luke, please."

His eyes narrowed.

She vividly recalled what had happened the last time she had said that to him. She wanted to step back, but her feet refused to cooperate. Her mind wanted to move, but her body craved his touch.

"We were going to eat after we checked in to the hotel. Want to come with us?"

Surely that wasn't disappointment she felt because he hadn't touched her. "No, I have to work on my research paper."

"Whatever you say. We'll pick you up at eight in the morning. Our appointment is scheduled for three so she'll be alone. We'll add you to the crew. Dress casually." He walked to the door. "See you in the morning, Catherine."

"Goodbye."

Catherine stared at the closed door Luke had walked through without a backward glance or one touch. She had what she thought she had wished for, for Luke to accept her decision, and all she could think of was that nobility hurt like hell.

LUKE HADN'T SLEPT ANY BETTER AFTER SEEING CATHE-rine than he had the previous three weeks when he had tossed and turned in his lonely bed in Santa Fe. All during the night in his hotel room he kept remembering his first sight of her. He hadn't liked what he had seen.

She had lost weight and had dark smudges beneath her eyes. Seeing her hands stuffed in the pockets of her slacks, her face shadowed, he had wanted to take her into his arms and never let go. From the sudden light in her eyes, she had wanted the same thing. Then the longing was gone, replaced by wariness.

It had taken considerable willpower to hold back then, and even more when he had picked her up that morning from her condo. She looked as if she hadn't slept any better than he had.

Thankfully during the drive to the airport and then on the flight to Atlanta, Dominique, in trying to ease Trent's trepidations, kept the conversation going. Once there, Luke rented a van to give more credence to their cover of doing a fashion story on Mrs. Albright. Forty-five minutes later he pulled up in front of a beautiful Country French–style home on an oversize landscaped lot in an exclusive gated neighborhood.

"Dominique will do what she does best, take the photographic layout. Catherine, as we discussed, you're her assistant. I don't want to put you in any professional quandary by lying to Mrs. Albright, so Dominique will take care of the introductions. I'm the cameraman and Trent is my assistant." Luke unbuckled his seat belt. "I want her to meet Trent last. If she doesn't show any signs of recognition, we'll play it by ear. Ready?"

"For over thirty-four years," Trent said, reaching to open the door.

Dominique's hand on his arm stopped him. "If she's not the one, Trent, we'll keep looking. We won't give up."

His hand covered hers, his gaze intent. "I shouldn't be greedy. I have you."

"We have each other." She gave him a quick kiss, then reached for her camera bag and climbed out behind him.

Luke turned to Catherine, who had been watching them as well. "Regardless of what happens, their love will get them through. That's what real love is, staying together despite the curves life throws at you." Before she could answer, he rushed on to say, "Come on, or Trent won't wait for us."

Collecting their equipment, they went up the stone steps to double wooden doors framed by gleaming, three-foot torch gas lanterns. The doorbell, a series of chimes, was answered by a thin black woman in a gray maid's uniform. The front door opened to a foyer and gallery of black art. French limestone was on the floor.

Closing the door after them, the servant escorted them through the two-story entry past a wood and ornamental iron spiral staircase and an oversize Palladian window. After a brief knock, she opened the door to the library. "Mrs. Albright, the people are here from *Haute Couture* magazine."

"Thank you, Ida Mae, please bring us some lemonade," Mrs. Albright said. Shoving the book in her hand back into the floor-to-ceiling custom shelving, she smiled and started toward them, extending her hand. "Welcome to Atlanta, and to my home."

Stylishly dressed in a Dior lime green fitted suit, warmth and breeding emitted from the slender, fair-skinned woman. Faint lines radiated from her light brown eyes. Her auburn hair was short and breezy, and suited her pretty, oval-shaped face. She was fifty-six years old, but she could have easily passed for a younger woman.

"Thank you, Mrs. Albright, you're as gracious as I've been told. I'm Dominique Everette. I'd like you to meet my crew." Standing by Mrs. Albright, she made the introductions. "Catherine Stewart, Luke Grayson, and Trent Masters."

Trent, who had been holding his head down pretending to be working with a camcorder, looked up, hoping, praying, dreading. "Mrs. Albright."

Her eyes widened, her face paled. "My God, no!" The back of her hand covered her mouth. Luke and Catherine steadied the woman, then helped her into a chair by the fireplace.

"Luke, get her some water," Catherine ordered, loosening the top buttons on the woman's suit jacket.

Crossing to the well-stocked bar, Luke poured a glass of water and returned. "Here."

"Drink this." Lifting up the woman's head, Catherine aided her in taking a couple of sips.

"Are you all right?" Trent asked.

Mrs. Albright flinched at the sound of his voice. "P-please, just leave."

"Do you know who I am?"

"Yo-you have to leave. Sometimes he comes home unexpectedly."

Trent crouched down in front of her. "You don't have to be afraid of him."

Mrs. Albright's lips trembled. "You don't understand."

Catherine knelt on the other side of the distraught woman. "Mrs. Albright. Joann, we realize this is difficult for you. It's just as difficult for Trent. He's searched for answers his entire life."

"Leave me alone," she cried.

Catherine nodded toward the case.

Trent took the blanket from the case Luke handed him and held it out to her. "Did you leave this with me? Are you my mother?"

She wailed in misery, a keening cry of sorrow. Her trembling hands palmed her face.

"Mrs. Albright, we're not here to cause you any embarrassment or undue pain. But you must realize that Trent is in pain also. You're the only one who can help both of you," Catherine said.

"What the hell is going on here?" Marshall Albright stood in the doorway. His two-thousand-dollar suit fit his trim body perfectly. His salt-and-pepper hair gave him a distinguished look that made up for him not being handsome in the conventional sense.

Trent's hopeful gaze never left Mrs. Albright. "Please, I have to know."

Joann Albright bit her lip to silence her cries at the first, angry sound of her husband's voice. Over her fingertips, fearful eyes darted from her husband back to Trent. She shrank against the chair.

Albright stalked across the room. "It's a good thing I decided to come home early. What kind of staff does the magazine ha—" He faltered when his gaze touched Trent's. Rage filled his thin face. "Son of a bitch. Get the hell out of my house. Now!"

Joann whimpered. Down went her head.

Catherine murmured to her.

Dominique's hand closed around Trent's rigid arm.

"Trent, let's go," Luke said, taking his other arm.

"Not until I get some answers," he said.

"Get out," Mr. Albright roared. "Ida Mae, call the police and get Rufus."

"Father, what's going on?" asked a light-skinned woman with her mother's soft mouth and her father's gray eyes. Seeing the distraught woman, she rushed over. "Mother, what is it?"

Joann closed her eyes and shook her head.

"What have you done to my mother?" she angrily asked Catherine.

"Your mother has had a sho—"

"Shut your mouth and get out of here," Albright shouted, cutting Catherine off. "Paige, take your mother upstairs. Don't just stand there, Rufus, get them out of here."

A large black man in a chauffeur's uniform looked perplexed.

"Get them out or you're fired," Albright threatened.

"No need for that. We're going," Luke said, tugging ineffectively on Trent's arm.

"I'm not leaving until I know," Trent said emphatically.

Joann started to whimper again. Paige's arm went around her mother. "Who are you people?"

"Ask your mother," Trent said tightly.

"You bastard." Marshall Albright hurried across the room to the desk by the bay of windows.

Luke arrived at the same time. His unyielding hand grabbed Albright's arm reaching for the brass pull of a drawer. "If you're going for a gun—bad decision."

"Take your hand off me," Marshall bristled.

"As soon as they're outside," Luke said, then spoke to Trent. "Is it worth Dominique getting in the way of a bullet?"

This time it was Trent who flinched. "I don't want this

anymore." Opening his hand, he let the blanket fall to the floor. Taking Dominique's hand, he left.

Joann stared transfixed at the blue blanket.

"He's hurting." Catherine touched her hand and stood. Picking up the blanket and the case, she walked past the wide-eyed maid and chauffeur.

Luke waited until he heard the front door close, then he removed his hand from the other man's arm. "I'd give considerable thought before pulling that gun out. The woman who was talking to your wife is the daughter of a U.S. Senator. The other woman is Trent's wife. Her brother would make hell look appealing if you hurt her, that is, if Trent left enough of you for him to bother with. Then there's me. I happen to care a great deal for all of them. And as they used to say in kindergarten, mine's bigger and I guarantee I can aim straighter." He started from the room, saw the distraught Joann and walked back to Albright.

Luke's eyes were hard. "For as long as it takes, someone will be keeping an eye on Mrs. Albright. If she has an 'accident,' you better find a hole and crawl into it, because I'm coming back and you'll know what fear is."

"Get out," Albright said, his face red with rage.

"Remember." Leaving the house, Luke got in the car.

"Let's get back to the airport," Trent said. "I have the answer to my question."

"I love you, Trent," Dominique said, her voice thick with misery and unshed tears.

His arm closed tightly around her, turning his lips to her hair and away from the imposing facade of the house. "You're my salvation."

Luke fastened his seat belt and started the motor. "You can go, but I'm staying. She's afraid."

Trent reached for the door handle. Luke hit the automatic lock and pulled away. "I took care of it. She's safe."

"But for how long?" Trent stared at the house through the back window.

"For as long as it takes." Luke stopped at the entrance of the gated community behind two other cars. "Somehow, I'll get a chance to talk to her again and get the answers we need."

"That may come sooner than you think," Catherine told them. "While her husband's attention was on you, I slipped her one of my cards and told her we were staying at the Four Seasons downtown," Catherine explained.

"I knew we were right to bring you. Now all we have to do is wait," Luke said and drove through the gate onto the street.

CHAPTER NINETEEN

THE CONNECTING HOTEL SUITES WERE LAVISH. Catherine didn't comment on the accommodations when they were shown to their rooms. If all went well, Joann Albright would show up tonight and if she didn't, Catherine would deal with it later. Getting another hotel room was out of the question. If Joann did come, Catherine wanted to be there, but first there were a couple of things she had to discuss with Trent.

"Trent, there is something that I think you need to prepare yourself for."

Trent, his arm around Dominique, turned his head from staring out the window across from where they were seated on the couch. "I'm listening."

"Albright took one look at you and became enraged," Catherine said carefully. "You don't have the coloring or the build of either of the Albrights or Paige. I think you have to prepare yourself for him not being your father."

"He's not." Trent continued at her look of shock, "I didn't start this investigation. Luke came to me at the request of someone else. I'm the mirror image of a childless relative who is deceased. It was left up to me whether I wanted to see the family or not." He blew out a deep breath. "I chose not to. I didn't want to start thinking of them as family and learn it's just a case of coincidence."

"That's why we need Mrs. Albright to tell us the name of Trent's father," Dominique explained.

At the knock on the door, everyone froze, then Catherine was up and across the room. Relief and gratitude coursed through her on seeing Mrs. Albright. "Please come in."

Silently, the older woman entered, her gaze skirting the room until she located Trent standing and staring at her. She appeared to brace herself before speaking. "If I give you the answers you want, do I have your solemn word to leave and never try to contact me or my family again?"

"I've been unwanted enough in my life not to impose on people who don't want to see me," Trent said, his voice tinged with bitterness.

She flinched. "How did you find me?"

"Does it matter?"

"No, I guess not." Her grip on her purse tightened. "Do you mind if I sit down?"

"Of course not." Catherine led her to a side chair.

The self-assurance was gone from Joann's movements. She looked every one of her years, and then some. She perched on the edge of the seat and wrapped her fingers around the top of her small purse. "What is it you want to know?"

"Are you my mother?"

Her lips trembled. "Yes."

The answer came out almost inaudible, but Trent heard, and felt Dominique's hands tighten on his arm. He stared into the light brown eyes of his mother, the woman who had given him life, then abandoned him. "Why didn't you keep me?" Pain, anger, and hurt coated his words.

"I was married when I met your father. Marshall was always busy. I wanted attention and your father gave it to me. I won't go into details about the relationship, except it lasted less than a week. I kept praying through my pregnancy that you were Marshall's. Then you were born, dark-skinned, and resembling no one in the family. I knew you weren't his and I became afraid that as time passed you'd resemble your father more and more."

"Why didn't you contact my father?"

"I was afraid of the scandal." She studied the gold clasp on the purse, then glanced up. "He was an opportunist and might have tried to blackmail me."

Trent's hands flexed. "So you faked my death, then abandoned me in a bathroom with a blanket and a note."

"Selfish, but I thought necessary at the time. I was young and frightened. I've answered your questions. I hope this ends it. I don't want Paige and Zachary hurt by this."

"You protect them and toss me away without a backward glance," Trent grated.

"Yes."

With an effort, he controlled his anger. "Who's my father?"

Her hands clutched the bag. "He's dead."

"What was his name?" Trent pressed.

"Phillip Sanders." She got to her feet. "Goodbye."

Trent followed. "Wait. Do you have a picture of him?"

"No."

"Where was he from? What did he do?" Desperation was in each question.

She became agitated, her nervousness increased. "What difference does it make? I told you he's dead."

"You might not want me, but maybe my father's people will."

She paled. "The East Coast I think. He was an insurance salesman and never mentioned any other family. Is there anything else you want?"

Trent studied her a long time before he spoke. "The authorities thought you were in an abusive relationship. I used to cry myself to sleep worrying about you, wish I would have been big enough to help you, protect you. There was never a birthday on the date they gave me that I didn't think of you and wonder if maybe on that day you didn't think of me, maybe put a candle in a cupcake and wish I was there. You were always at the top of anything I wished for, the first one I prayed for. You tossed me away and never looked back." He walked to her. "Isaac was right when he said you threw me away like trash."

"Trent, she doesn't matter." Dominique reached for him, but he held up his hands and turned away. "I love you, Trent. I love you."

"I was a mistake," he said hoarsely. "A thing no one wanted."

"No. Don't say that," Dominique cried. "Isaac wanted to make himself look tough in front of his teenage gang by hurting you. Instead, you wiped that cocky smirk off his face and showed him up for the loudmouth jerk he is. Now, if you don't want me to bloody your nose the same way I did his the night he tried to kidnap me at knifepoint, you'll stop talking nonsense."

He spun around, his eyes fierce. "You should have let me handle Isaac."

Her smile wobbled, her trembling hand palmed his clenched jaw. "You know how protective I am of those I love. Guess who's at the top of my list."

"Dominique." He crushed her to him. "I love you."

"You . . . were loved. I . . . loved you."

Trent and Dominique both whirled around. The six halting words had come from Joann Albright.

"You're not trash. You were a beautiful baby and I failed you. The fault is mine, not yours. Don't you ever think differently," she told him, tears streaming down her cheeks.

She weaved on her feet, then steadied and continued.

"The only love and affection I've ever known from a man was from your father. I lied earlier. Your father was older than I was, and a fine, decent man. I met him a month before my wedding. We were instantly attracted to each other. We tried to resist the temptation, but failed. We had one beautiful night together that I'll treasure forever. He begged me not to marry Marshall, but I was afraid for him. Marshall is intensely jealous of his possessions. He almost beat a man to death he thought I was interested in. He was already becoming suspicious of us. I was truly in love for the first time and unable to hide my feelings very well. I was devastated when he left." Her face filled with sorrow. "Paige and Zachary kept me sane during these past years."

"They're adults now," Trent said, trying to understand.

"Yes, I'm fortunate that they love me and are wonderful, but if people found out about this, Marshall wouldn't rest until he had turned them against me. I betrayed him in the worst way a woman can a man." She met Trent's searching gaze. "There are reasons, but no excuses. They'd hate me. I lost one child, I couldn't go through that again."

"What's the real reason you faked my death?"

She trembled, then swallowed convulsively. "That morning I caught Marshall standing over your bed with a pillow. He said he must have automatically picked it up when he heard you crying. You weren't crying. Besides, Marshall wouldn't have cared if you were. He ignored you when people weren't around. That week there had been an article in the paper about Sudden Infant Death Syndrome, and how difficult it was to diagnose. I looked into his cold, heartless eyes and knew my worst fear had been realized. Marshall knew you weren't his. You were no longer safe." She took a breath to steady herself. "All the way back from Columbia I tried to think of a way to explain your disappearance and keep you safe. I saw the lake . . ."

"But the report said you tried to go back. You knew I wasn't in the car."

"At first it was to convince the two men who pulled me out that you were, then it was because I didn't care anymore," she told him, her voice emotionless. "I developed pneumonia and was ill for weeks. When I was finally well, I couldn't track you through the system. Afterward I didn't particularly care what happened. Staying with Marshall seemed a fitting punishment. I didn't begin to live again until I held Zachary in my arms."

"You're going back to something like that?" Trent asked, abhorrence in his voice.

"I won't fail another child, and no matter how old or self-sufficient they become, to a parent they'll always be children." She looked at Dominique. "Thank you for doing what I couldn't—loving him."

"You just showed your love in a different way," Dominique said, forgiving and not judging for Trent's sake.

"Thank you," Joann said, her voice unsteady.

"If you could obtain a divorce and keep Paige and Zachary from finding out about me, would you?"

"Crawling with only the clothes on my back," she said fiercely, then shook her head in obvious defeat. "That wouldn't happen, and I can't allow them or you to be hurt by the resulting scandal. Marshall can be vicious and cruel."

"I know," Trent said tightly. "Do you really think they'd want you to stay and risk having something else broken?"

"How did . . ." Her breath trembled out over her lips. Unsteady fingers touched her left wrist. "Zachary had a cold and I wanted to stay home with him instead of going with Marshall to a business dinner. Marshall doesn't like for anyone to defy him."

"That piece of slime," Trent hissed.

"Marshall can be ruthless, but he's never bothered the children, and since I have to be more and more in the public eye, he has left me alone. These days he's more concerned with finding out who is trying to take over his company and why some of his business dealings are going bad." She glanced at Luke. "Whatever you said scared him. I've never seen him that frightened before. After I convinced Paige that I was fine and that she should go home, instead of venting his anger on me, he stormed out of the house and was still gone when I left to come here."

"Albright may not know it yet, but he's met his match and then some." Arms folded, Luke smiled.

"I'm glad I lived to see it." Joann faced Trent. "And you. You're the image of your father."

"Phillip Sanders?"

She shook her head. "Wade Taggart."

Luke let out a yell and reached for the phone.

Neither Joann nor Trent paid any attention. "Wade Taggart," he repeated slowly.

Joann's smile was almost dreamy. "He was in town on business. We met through an associate of Marshall's. Wade was everything Marshall wasn't—kind, considerate, loving. Our love for each other went against everything we stood for, but we were powerless against it. Seeing you confirmed what Marshall probably suspected all along. Everyone wondered why Wade stayed three weeks instead of the few days he had planned."

"That means I have a family," Trent whispered in awe.

A frown returned to Joann's face. "He talked a lot about his family in Jacksonville, Texas. If you found me, you can surely find them."

"I don't have to. They've already found me," Trent

said, his voice hoarse. "Dominique's brother is married to Madelyn Taggart." He turned to Luke. "That's right, isn't it? They're the ones who hired you?"

"Welcome to the family." Luke crossed the room and slapped a dazed Trent on the back. "Come on, I think it's time I introduced you to some people who want to meet you."

"They're here?" Trent asked, astonished.

"They didn't want to wait any longer than necessary," Dominique said, smiling up at her husband.

Trent gazed down at her. "You knew."

"I knew."

He hugged her. "I'll defy anyone who says a woman can't keep a secret."

They were all laughing when Joann opened the door and stared back at Trent. "You have your family. Good-bye."

He went to her. "You're abandoning me again."

Misery and pain washed across her face. "I just thought . . ."

"Come with us. I don't want to lose you again."

Shaking her head, she clutched her purse. "This is for you and your family."

"That includes you," Trent said.

Joann's eyes misted. "Thank you."

Luke took Joann by the elbow. As soon as they stepped into the hallway they saw a slim, elderly man with snow white hair, and a robust, dark-skinned woman by his side.

"You look just like Wade," the woman said, enveloping Trent in a hug. "I'm Octavia Ralston, the housekeeper of the Circle T for over forty years."

No sooner had she turned Trent loose than the elderly man was shaking his hand. "That's soon to be Octavia Redmon. I'm Cleve Redmon. I worked for your daddy from the time we were old enough to swagger. A fine man."

"Come on, everybody is waiting." Octavia opened the door behind her.

Trent's legs wobbling, his heart trying to beat out of his chest, he walked through the door. They were seated as if for a family portrait. The men behind the four women, the children in their laps or standing beside them.

Trent just stared, drinking in the sight of his new family. There was Daniel and Madelyn Taggart Falcon with a grinning and hefty Daniel Jr., Kane and Victoria Taggart with their twins, Kane Jr. and Chandler, Matt and Shannon Taggart with their infant daughter, Tempest. The older couple Trent vaguely remembered from his wedding as Kane, Matt, and Madelyn's parents.

"My parents, the grands, Higgins, and Janice send their love. They thought it should just be your family tonight," Dominique told him.

Dominique's parents and grandparents had readily welcomed Trent into their lives and hearts. Higgins, Dominique's mother's ex-chauffeur and confidant, who reigned as second-in-command in Daniel Falcon's household as a trusted friend, had done the same. Janice was Trent's next-door neighbor and friend before he met her goddaughter, Dominique. Trent loved them all, was blessed by their friendship and love, but seeing his own blood relatives shook him to the core.

The elderly Taggart broke rank. "I'm Bill Taggart. It was just Wade and me. He was the oldest, and my best friend until the day he died. From what I hear, he'd be proud of you. This is my wife, Grace."

"Welcome to the family, Trent," she said, tears shimmering in her eyes.

"I knew I was right to help you into the family," Daniel said with a laugh.

Then, Trent was surrounded with hugs and laughter and slaps on the back. But that wasn't all. "We missed your birthday, and Thanksgiving and Christmas are always special family days for us. We all agreed it is time to catch up," Madelyn said.

Trent swallowed to try to clear the knot in his throat but it just got bigger. On a serving cart was a two-tier chocolate cake with lit candles. On the festively decorated table was the biggest turkey he had ever seen. A ten-foot decorated Christmas tree with presents piled beneath was nearby.

"This was Wade's. He'd want you to have it."

Into Trent's unsteady hands, Bill Taggart placed a silver belt buckle with the initials WWT.

"It's about time you traded all those baseball caps for a Stetson." This from Kane.

Matt came next. He gave Trent a letter with the letter-head of Ferguson & Ferguson law firm. "Wade left his share, half of the Circle T ranch, to me. It should be yours."

Trent finally found his voice. "When did he die?"

"Two years ago," Matt answered.

"You've been running the ranch since then?" Trent asked.

"And before. The Circle T has thrived while others have gone bankrupt or had to sell," Matt said.

Trent understood the ownership and pride he heard in Matt's voice. He felt the same way about Masters Trucking. "I suppose running a ranch involves getting up at dawn, riding a horse, and tending cows."

"The hours are long, but it's something I love and I can't imagine raising my family anyplace else," Matt told him.

"Until Tempest was born, he'd be out of the house for good by five," Shannon said. "Now, he waits until her first feeding at six."

"She likes our bath time," Matt said unself-consciously.

Trent looked worried. "I'm improving in my riding according to Dominique, but I think we better leave things as they are. I've never been within a hundred feet of a cow."

To the Texas men who had been around livestock most or all of their lives, Trent's announcement was met with stunned silence.

Trent shifted awkwardly. "I wouldn't know the first thing about running a ranch."

"I can teach you, help you," Matt offered, then glanced at Shannon, who nodded, before he continued, "Wade left the original home site to Shannon in his will. The place means a lot to us. I'd appreciate the opportunity to buy it."

Trent frowned. "But you weren't married then."

Matt's arm curved around his wife's waist. "Wade was doing a little matchmaking. He was a good man."

"I wish I could have known him," Trent said softly, then handed Matt back the envelope. "Wade Taggart gave me a family. That's enough. I know about working to build something to call your own. Keep the Circle T with my blessings. Do you want to handle transferring the title back or should I contact my lawyers?"

A strange smile on his face, Matt accepted the envelope. "I'll take care of it. My lawyer has had more experience." He spoke to Dominique. "You called it."

Dominique nodded emphatically, then looked up at her puzzled husband. "I told them all you wanted was your family. I knew you'd understand how much the Circle T meant to Matt and his family. Daniel told them, too."

"What if Dominique and Daniel had been wrong?" Trent asked out of curiosity.

"It was a chance we had to take," Bill Taggart answered. "Wade would have wanted us to reach out to you. If you had taken the ranch, it was your right."

"Like Madelyn said, family means everything to us," Grace Taggart said simply. "And that means you."

"Besides," Kane said, his craggy face curving into a smile. "Matt is so bossy you would have left in two days. Ask Shannon. I'll always wonder how she worked on the ranch with him. He even tried to boss her obstetrician in the delivery room."

"There's no need to go into that." Matt flushed and pinned a laughing Daniel with a superior look. "At least he didn't threaten to call security."

The grin slid from Daniel's face. "Dr. Scalar only did that to aggravate me."

Most of the people in the room laughed at Daniel's affronted expression. Luke wasn't one of them. Stepping forward he closed his hand around Catherine's cold one. Her hand flexed, but she didn't attempt to pull away.

Trent finished the introductions. "I'd like you to meet Dr. Catherine Stewart, who helped to make this possible, and Joann Albright, my mother."

Joann began softly crying. Trent curved his arm around her. "If you cry, you won't be able to see me blow out the candles of my first birthday cake."

It was a child who asked the question all the astonished adults were too polite to ask. "You never had a birthday cake, Cousin Trent?" Kane Jr. asked, his four-year-old face suitably appalled.

Cousin Trent. The lump tried to come back, but this was too important. "Not by myself. We always had group birthdays for that month," Trent answered.

"I wouldn't like that," Chandler said, her small hands on her waist. "K.J. and I have our own cakes."

Trent hunkered down to them. "Then, I say you and your brother are very lucky to have such loving parents."

"You want us to help you blow out the candles?" Kane Jr. asked. "There's an awful lot of them."

Chandler regarded him solemnly. "You must really be old."

The adults chuckled.

"Sorry, Trent," Victoria said, smiling, shaking her head at her son and daughter. "They're as outspoken as their father. We usually just have the numeric candles."

"That's all right." Standing, Trent reached for their hands. "Let's go blow out those candles."

"Don't you dare until I get back with my camera," Dominique admonished and dashed out the door. By the time she returned, Trent, Kane Jr., and Chandler had practiced for their big moment. The twins would take the bottom layer; Trent the top.

They did it. No one seemed bothered that they ate the cake before the dinner. The Taggart twins let Trent know that they were great at opening presents also. He enlisted their aid. The gifts ranged from poignant, a photo album of Wade from infancy to adulthood, to practical, or so Cleve had thought when he'd hand-braided Trent one of his prized ropes. Amid the laughter of Trent trying to rope a chair, Bill drew Joann to one side.

"I hope he won't be harsh with her," Catherine said, slipping her hand free.

"He won't," Luke answered. "Wade never married. From what Bill told me, Wade talked about a woman he had met in Atlanta, but said it hadn't worked out. That information helped narrow the search. Wade came to Atlanta to settle his great aunt's estate. The woman he met must have been Joann."

"He loved her all those years," Catherine said sadly.

"He died not knowing if she loved him back, but he never passed up an opportunity to help a woman through hard times, never became involved with anyone else. Never became bitter. Kane, Matt, and Madelyn became his children."

Catherine's chest felt tight. They were speaking about Wade, but it could just as well have been Luke they were discussing. "She did what she felt was best for him."

"And condemned him to a life without her." Luke stared at Catherine. "Which one do you think he would have wanted?"

"She wanted him to marry," Catherine cried, talking about her own wish for Luke. "She wanted him to be happy."

"How could he be without her? For some men there is only one woman," Luke said, his love unhidden in his face. "Joann learned too late. I pray you don't." He strode away.

Catherine was left alone to watch the close-knit family and special friends celebrate finding Trent. She felt like an outsider and realized she was. Each adult person there had someone they were committed to. Except herself and Joann. Catherine gazed at the other woman, who stood, as Catherine did, apart from the gathering. Her eyes were sad and filled with regret. When she left, she'd go home to a man who had abused her.

What will you go home to, Catherine?

The answer came quickly. Nothing and no one.

WITH EVERYONE HELPING, THEY MANAGED TO TAKE ALL of Trent's gifts to his suite in one trip. Plans were made to meet for breakfast. The women left to put the children to bed. The men decided they weren't finished talking and went downstairs to the bar. They'd see Joann to her car. She was going to spend the night with her daughter. Trent had convinced her to wait until morning to return home. Luke handed Catherine the key to her suite and went with them. He was next door in number 728.

Saying good night to Dominique, Catherine went to her

room and crawled into the king-size bed. Rolling over on her back she stared up at the ceiling. Was it a lack of trust that kept her from committing to Luke or lack of love? Or both? Selfishness? Whatever, the end results were the same, lonely years ahead of her with nothing and no one because Luke was the only man she'd ever love.

Her eyes shut tightly as she tried to figure out the right thing to do. What would be best for Luke? He'd never get razzed about inappropriate behavior in the delivery room with her. With her, he'd never hold a cherubic child of his own like Daniel Jr., or bathe his own little angel like Tempest, or get help to blow out his birthday candles from his outspoken children like K.J. or Chandler. With her, he'd never have any of that. All he'd ever have was her and her love.

The last thought replayed over and over in Catherine's mind, and with it came a calming certainty of what she had to do. Opening her eyes, she sat up on the side of the bed and picked up the phone for the first of two calls she needed to make. "This is Dr. Stewart. I'm checking out."

MARSHALL ALBRIGHT AND HIS MISTRESS WERE SO involved neither heard the four men enter the bedroom of the high-rise apartment Marshall listed as a business expenditure. The light clicked on. A camera flashed.

Cursing, Marshall tried to get out of bed, cover himself, and hide his face from the flashing camera at the same time. He managed to get out of bed, but the sheet he grabbed happened to be the same one his twenty-two-year-old mistress/receptionist clutched, leaving Marshall to have a full frontal picture taken.

"You bastards," he shouted, diving for the sheet and getting back under the covers. "I'll ruin you. I'll make you wish you were really left in that lake. I'll make all of you wish that." None of the four men seemed bothered by the threat.

Luke lowered the camera. "Get dressed, Miss Hopkins, and go home."

She didn't waste time or bother with modesty. She jumped out of bed and grabbed her clothes.

"Come back here," Marshall shouted. When she kept going, he snarled, "You're fired."

Kane closed the bedroom door. Matt stood easily by his side, their eyes as hard as ice.

"I don't think you have the authority to do that," Trent said with disgust.

"What the hell are you talking about?" Marshall asked.

"As of five this afternoon, I own sixty-nine percent of your business assets, and by five o'clock tomorrow, I would have called a special board meeting and ousted you as president."

Outrage reddened Albright's face as he stared up at the broad-shouldered man with long salt-and-pepper hair tied at the base of his neck. "Who the hell are you?"

"Trent's brother-in-law. Daniel Falcon."

Marshall gasped and shrank against the headboard.

"I told you," Luke said. "You messed with the wrong family."

"But . . . but surely you're a sophisticated man of the world, and understand this," Marshall said, licking his lips nervously. "You probably have someone on the side, too."

"You're a fool, Albright. Every time you open your mouth you just confirm it more and more," Daniel said with distaste. "What you see as sophistication, I see as deceit. Now you're going to listen to me and do as I say or you'll end up someplace selling pencils on a street corner."

"You can't—"

"Yes, I can," Daniel interrupted, his voice cloaked in steel. "If not for your family, I wouldn't care what happened to you. Now shut up and listen."

Marshall Albright shut up and listened.

LUKE WAS KNOWN AS A LONER, ENJOYED HIS solitude, but when he stepped onto the hotel elevator with Daniel, Kane, Matt, Trent, Bill, and Cleve, he never felt his loneliness more keenly. The elderly Bill and Cleve were once again regaling Trent about old times with Wade. Both had their hands on Trent's shoulders. He was a part of them now.

Earlier it had taken considerable persuasion on Kane's part to make the two remain at the hotel. They all knew what might be waiting for them at Albright's apartment, what Daniel planned, and none of them wanted the two involved. The elderly twosome had only relented after Kane expressed his concern that if they all left and the women or children needed them, none of them would be thère. Bill and Cleve hadn't augured further. Family was all to the Taggarts (which included Cleve and Octavia), just as it was to the Graysons and Falcons, and now that included the Masterses.

Luke glanced at Trent, grinning and nodding his head over a story of cocky Wade trying to ride his first wild bronc. Happiness looked good on him. All the problems with his mother weren't worked out, but at least he now had a chance to develop a relationship with her. Perhaps in the future, he'd be able to meet his half-brother and half-sister. Especially since Mrs. Albright was going to be a safe, free, and wealthy woman. Daniel and Trent had made sure of that.

The elevator door slid open and Luke stepped off. He had his own reason to be happy. Catherine was in for a surprise when she boarded the jet tomorrow. Instead of going to Los Angeles, they were going to a private isla—

His thoughts reeled to a halt. For a long time he could do nothing but stare, then he was running. Pushing the cleaning cart to one side, he rushed into Catherine's suite. "Catherine. Catherine."

An elderly woman slowly emerged from the bathroom. Her gloved hands were clamped around a sponge.

"Where's the woman who was in this room?"

"Come on, Luke." Concerned, Daniel laid his hand on Luke's tense shoulder.

"Where is she?" he repeated, his voice sharp and demanding.

"She checked out."

Luke swung around to see Dominique standing in the connecting doorway. He rushed to her. "You let her go? You didn't try to stop her?"

"I agreed with her decision."

Anger swept across Luke's face.

Trent started toward them. Daniel stopped him with a shake of his hand.

Instead of retreating, Dominique moved closer. "If I didn't love you so much and you hadn't helped Trent, I might consider not telling you."

"You know where she is?" he asked, hope and desperation mixed in his voice.

Amusement danced in Dominique's black eyes. "She said to tell you twenty-eight is your lucky number."

He left running. It took two tries to insert the plastic key correctly. His heart pounding, he pushed open the door to his room, number 728.

Catherine in the blouse and slacks she had been wearing earlier, stood in the middle of the room, her hand clamped around a rolled sheet of paper.

Hope and love swept through him. Luke started toward Catherine, then stopped. The need to hold her almost overwhelmed him, but they had an important issue to discuss.

The hesitant smile faded from her face. More than his next breath he wanted to see her smile, wanted to hold her in his arms, but first she needed to know he had changed his mind about an important aspect of their relationship. However, there was one certainty that would never change.

"You know I love you."

"I do."

At the slow blossoming of her smile, some of his uneasiness faded. "And you know I'd never do anything to hurt you."

"I do."

The love and trust in her big brown eyes made his chest tight. But if she couldn't accept his decision . . .

"It's because of how much I love you that I have to go back on my word." He jammed his hand into his pocket. He was a coward to drag this out, but he had faced the pain of losing her once, he wasn't sure he could do it a second time. "I want us to belong to each other, totally, irrevocably committed to each other."

Her head lowered.

Fear coursed through him and took him closer. "You understand, don't you?"

"I do."

No longer able to keep from touching her, his fingers gently circled her forearm. "Cath, I don't want an affair. Trust me and my love enough to marry me."

Her head lifted. Love shimmered in her eyes and glowed in her face. "I do."

It hit him all at once what she had been repeating. He swallowed and tried to calm his racing heart. "You mean the 'I do' as in, you'll take me for your lawfully wedded husband?"

"I do." On tip toes, she brushed her lips across his again and again. "Yes. Yes. A thousand times yes."

His mouth came down on hers. The kiss was one of passion and tender restraint and love. "I'll always be there for you."

Her free hand palmed his face. "I finally got past my own fears to realize that. I saw the regret in Joann's face and saw myself in the years to come."

He kissed her palm. "I love you."

"I love you." Her face saddened for a moment. "I regret not being able to have children, but I'd regret not loving you more. If I'm enough for you, I have to have faith that I'm going to go on being enough for you. Until there was you, I didn't think that was possible. In your arms, nothing is impossible."

He kissed her again. Lifting his head he picked her up. "How long do you think it will take to plan a wedding?"

"Give me three months," she told him as he placed her on the bed. "Mother will scream it's not nearly enough time to plan a formal wedding though."

"Three months is about my limit." Impatient fingers began unbuttoning her blouse. "I'll rack up a lot of miles between Santa Fe and L.A."

"Not for long."

He stopped and stared down at her. She lifted the paper in her hand. "My resignation."

He was stunned. "But you love teaching. You were up for the head of a department."

"Nothing can compare to being in your arms, loving you." Tossing the paper aside, she went to work on unfastening his pants. "I always figured number twenty-eight was going to be your lucky number."

"Mama will be on cloud nine."

Catherine's hand never paused. "She sure sounded happy when I called her tonight."

"You called Mama?"

"I wanted her to know that I could do something no other woman could do."

Luke's breath quickened as her hand closed around the hard, heavy length of him. "You certainly can."

Catherine chuckled, then sobered. "No other woman can love you the way I can."

"About time you realized that." Off came her slacks.

"I'm slow, but not stupid." His shirt followed.

"I'll love you forever," Luke pledged.

"And I'm going to love you right back. Starting now."

EPILOGUE

SUNLIGHT STREAMED THROUGH THE BEAUTIFUL stained glass windows of the packed church. The myriad of hues turned the yellow and white flowers decorating the sanctuary and altar into a wash of colors, giving the feel and impression that those gathered were sitting in a field of wild flowers.

Ruth Grayson sniffed quietly as she sat in the front pew and listened to Luke's sure, strong voice repeat his marriage vows. Catherine's rang just as clear and true. They were so much in love. Ruth didn't doubt for a second that their marriage would endure a lifetime. If a higher power had decided there were to be no children, they would all have to accept it and move on.

With the linen handkerchief Felicia had given her, Ruth dabbed her eyes. During the exchange of rings she wondered if there would ever be a time to tell them that Catherine had been her choice from the first. The other women had been given a fair chance, but Ruth had known Catherine was the only woman to make her eldest happy. Oh, well, perhaps not. It wasn't important now.

Her gaze went to Morgan standing proudly by his brother's side as his best man. He didn't know it, but he had already met his future wife.

A mother's work was never done.

Morgan would be next.

Dear Readers,

I'm delighted that St. Martin's Press reissued *Until There Was You*, the first book in the Graysons of New Mexico series. As a gift to my supportive readers, I've included a story of Luke and Catherine's first Christmas, called "Christmas and You."

Enjoy.

Happy Holidays,

Francis

CHAPTER ONE

ON THIS FIRST DAY OF DECEMBER, CATHERINE GRAYSON couldn't imagine a more incredible time to be in love than the Christmas season. Valentine's Day was all right, but this morning she sensed something magical in the air. Or perhaps she was thinking that way because of the gorgeous man in bed with her.

Lying next to the sexy, muscular body of her husband, Luke, Catherine felt safe and cherished. Luke was honest, intelligent, dependable, compassionate—and all hers.

Her protector.

Studying the impossibly long black lashes, the high cheekbones, the proud nose, the sensual curve of his lower lip, framed by lustrous straight black hair that fell to below his broad shoulders when standing, she resisted the tempting urge to kiss him awake as he'd done to her countless times. This moment was too precious.

It wasn't often that anyone caught Luke Grayson unaware. She could hardly believe she'd awakened first.

She grinned impishly; perhaps she had worn him out last night. She pressed her fingertips to her lips to stifle the laughter threatening to bubble forth. No one at the faculty of UCLA or here at St. John's University, where she was a visiting professor, or anyone at her publishing house would ever think that cool child psychologist and children's author, Dr. Catherine Stewart Grayson, was a little—all right, a lot—wicked when it came to loving her husband.

There was good reason. Not a day went by that Luke didn't show her that he loved her and only her. Accepting the invitation the past summer to speak in Santa Fe was the best decision she'd ever made—even if a deranged parent had tried to discredit her. Luke had uncovered the plot and saved her sanity and her career. And even knowing his mother had set them up, they'd fallen in love.

Ruth Grayson was a remarkable woman and a determined match-maker. So far she'd proven she knew how to pick 'em. Luke's brother, Morgan, had fallen in love with a wonderful, talented sculptress, Phoenix Bannister, and married shortly after Luke and Catherine were wed.

Brandon, Pierce, and Sierra had better look out, Catherine thought. But she didn't have a doubt that Ruth would find the perfect soul mate for them—just as she had done for them. Each day Catherine counted her blessings in being married to such an incredible, protective man.

Luke considered her feelings in all things. Their first Thanksgiving together had been her first away from her parents. She'd tried not to show how much she missed them and her older brother, Alex, but you can't hide much from an ex–FBI agent. She should have remembered the lesson she'd learned that first night they'd met. But she hadn't wanted to dampen his enjoyment of Thanksgiving with his family, so she'd tried not to think about her parents and brother.

She and Luke had gone to his mother's house shortly after a late breakfast on Thanksgiving to help set the table and get everything ready for the "feast," as Brandon called it. All of Luke's siblings were there and crowded in the kitchen. By the time they'd arrived, the dining table was beautifully set with sparkling crystal and ornate flatware, the nearby sideboard loaded with dishes Ruth and Brandon had prepared.

"Catherine and Phoenix, after dinner we're overloading on football games, then we'll decorate the tree," Brandon said, placing parsley around a spiral ham.

Catherine had seen the beautiful ten-foot spruce in the living room when they'd arrived. For just a moment her smile had wavered. Her family had followed the same tradition. Trying to hide her sadness, she had glanced around and seen Phoenix and Morgan at the end of the kitchen counter. Phoenix had her head on Morgan's shoulder.

Although Phoenix was estranged from her father, her face glowed with love, happiness, and contentment. Morgan's family was now hers, and he was hers. Catherine's smile brightened and she shook away the momentary sadness. They were blessed women to have found men who would love them always.

"Not this year, Brandon," Sierra told him with a mischievous grin, and then bit into a golden-brown tea cake. "It's my turn to watch what I want."

Pierce and Brandon had looked stunned. Morgan and Luke smiled.

Sierra's grin widened, then she explained. "Mama only had one television when we were growing up so we always took turns watching programs. It carried through as adults when we get together for holidays. Brandon had his turn on Labor Day because he traded with Pierce on the Fourth of July for a cooking special on PBS."

Brandon groaned. "Please tell me we aren't going to have to watch a chick flick or a fashion show."

"You have to think of our new sisters-in-law," Pierce said.

"I wonder if you had control of the TV, would you have that same thought?" Sierra asked sweetly.

Pierce, always charming and honest, had the grace to flush, then smile. "Eventually."

Laughter rang in the kitchen filled with mouth-watering aromas and love. Luke curved his arm around Catherine's waist. "Are you all right, Cath?"

"With you, always."

Before he could comment, the doorbell rang. "Catherine, please get that," Mrs. Grayson had asked as she sliced a delicious-looking three-layer hummingbird cake.

"Sure." Catherine had gone to the front door, expecting to see whoever the guests were for the three extra place settings in the dining room. Her parents and brother stood on the porch.

She'd been overcome with emotions. She'd laughed, cried, hugged them. Then she hugged Luke, who had set up the surprise visit. "I never want you to have a moment's regret for marrying me," he said.

"That could never happen," she'd told him, and meant it. Luke made each day brighter and happier, just as he did now, simply by being there.

She couldn't wait to give him his present on Christmas Eve. It had taken a lot to pull it off, but she was determined that their first Christmas would be one he'd always remember.

"You're happy."

She jumped, then laughed. Luke stared back at her with the most beautiful black eyes she'd ever seen. "You were faking."

His arms curved around her, drawing her naked length to his. "Admiring my beautiful wife."

Her finger traced his lower lip. "And I was admiring my gorgeous husband."

Luke snorted. "I keep telling you we need to get your eyes checked."

Add not being conceited to the long list of his sterling

qualities. "I have twenty-twenty vision." Removing her finger, she nipped his lower lip.

"That bite is going to get you into trouble."

"Promise?" she teased.

His hold tightened, his eyes darkened. "Don't you have an early morning appointment?"

Her eyes widened. The meeting was part of Luke's surprise. She couldn't be late. She tried to scramble out of bed, but found herself held against a hard chest. "Luke, I don't want to be late."

"Then we'd better get to it." He took her mouth in a kiss that swept through her like wildfire, while his hand moved over her, leaving her craving more. Sliding his hands beneath her hips, he brought them together.

She arched into him, locked her legs around his waist and her arms around his neck. Her last coherent thought as he loved her was that besides being shameless, she was very, very lucky.

AS SOON AS CATHERINE PULLED OFF, LUKE PICKED UP the cordless phone in the kitchen and called Morgan. "You all set?"

"Yep. How about you?" Morgan asked.

"The same. Everything is in the back of my closet," Luke told him, wandering to the coffee maker. Good thing it was on a timer. He and Cath stayed in bed as long as possible in the mornings. "Does Phoenix suspect anything?"

Morgan chuckled. "Not a thing. It helps that she's occupied working on a new sculpture."

"Cath is finishing up a lecture series at the college and working with Mama and the Women's League to collect food baskets and clothes for families in need for the holidays, so she doesn't have a clue either." Picking up the carafe, he filled a mug. "I think this is one of the best ideas we've ever come up with together."

"This definitely won't get us into trouble like when we were growing up."

"I— Hold on. Hero's back." Luke opened the back door to see the wolf hybrid looking up at him. After a heartbeat, he trotted inside.

"Thought you might show up." Opening the refrigerator door, Luke pulled out a roasted chicken and removed the plastic top. "I still say Cath is spoiling you, but since you only show up a couple of times a week, it means you still hunt for your food and won't become domesticated." Luke pitched the chicken.

Hero's strong jaws clamped on the meat. Luke wiped his hand on a paper towel, then went to open the back door.

Hero trotted out again. "See you in a couple of days." He watched until Hero disappeared into the woods, then he closed the door. "I'm back," Luke told Morgan.

"He stick around this time?"

"Nope, I think he's afraid Cat might try to give him another bath. He waited until she'd gone, but when she comes home and sees he's been here, she's going to go in search of him and he'll let her find him."

"Another male who can't resist the right woman," Morgan said.

"Isn't that the truth," Luke agreed, his laughter joining in with his brother's.

"I WANT EVERYTHING TO BE PERFECT," CATHERINE SAID from her seat beside Brandon at the family table in the Red Cactus.

"It will be. Otherwise I wouldn't have gotten up at this crazy hour," Brandon said, then yawned.

"I appreciate it, Brandon," Catherine said, meaning it. "But to tell you the truth, I wasn't sure how you'd feel if I didn't consult with you to help with planning the get-together on Christmas Eve and then the dinner on Christmas."

"Huffy," Sierra said across from him. She smiled into his narrowed gaze and took another bite of eggs rancheros.

"I want Luke's favorite dishes, the dishes you grew up with," Catherine told Brandon, used to the good-natured teasing between the siblings. "I want to start our own Christmas tradition as a married couple."

"Tradition and family are important to Luke," Pierce said from beside Sierra.

"To all of us," Brandon added.

"I know, but I want you to enjoy yourself, and not have to worry about cooking or serving," Catherine said.

"He'll have to be unconscious for that to happen." Sierra sipped her orange juice. "We've found it easier to stand back and let him be in charge."

"And because none of you, besides Mama, can or will cook," Brandon told her.

"There is that." Sierra placed her empty glass on the table and folded her arms. "So what's on the menu?"

"Hors d'oeuvres for starters. We'll have crab cakes, savory cheese puffs, lobster, and smoked salmon to keep the crowd from becoming restless on Christmas Eve before we have the enchilada dinner and tamales. Then on Christmas we'll have herb-roasted turkey, Luke's favorite, applewood-smoked ham, stuffed chateaubriand, and several side dishes and desserts," Brandon finished.

"It sounds absolutely fabulous," Catherine said.

"It will taste the same way," Brandon said.

"That's our Brandon, not a modest bone in his body." Pierce finished off his breakfast burrito.

Sierra laughed. "Since he can back it up, I suppose he has the right."

"Just teasing," Pierce said, placing his napkin on the table beside his empty plate.

"Trying to backtrack," Brandon commented, "I suppose I'll see both of you for lunch and dinner today."

"It's so nice when you're so well understood," Sierra quipped.

"My thoughts exactly." Pierce lifted his hand and high-fived Sierra.

"This is going to be wonderful," Catherine commented, as she placed a small spiral tablet back into the attaché case beside her. "Christmas is such a glorious season."

"And don't forget the side benefit," Brandon said, then continued at Catherine's puzzled look. "Mama is taking a break from trying to marry us off—so I can relax and enjoy the holidays."

"I'm glad I'm not next in line." Pierce grinned. "I have plans for the holidays."

Sierra wrinkled her nose. "We know, making memories in case Brandon fails."

"Which I won't do," Brandon said adamantly.

Catherine glanced at the determined faces of her in-laws. "I don't want to run the risk of being stoned, but I'm glad your mother decided to help Luke find a wife. I've never been happier. I can't imagine my life with anyone else."

Sierra picked up her glass of water. "Just because Mama got it right with you, there is no reason to believe she'll be on target for the rest of us. I enjoy being single."

"That goes double for me," Brandon said. "One of the perks of the restaurant business is enjoying the women who come here."

"Yeah," Pierce agreed. "It would be like placing a starving man before a banquet and asking him to choose only one item. Cruel."

"Yeah, cruel," Brandon repeated.

Sierra shook her head. "I pity the woman who gets either of you."

"Because that means you'll be next." Pierce grinned at her.

She scowled at him, then Brandon. "You two better stand strong if you know what's good for you."

Pierce picked up his nearly empty glass of orange juice. "You needn't worry. I'm enjoying the banquet too much."

"I couldn't have phrased it better," Brandon said, lifting his glass of apple juice.

Sierra held up her glass. "To the last three Graysons standing. May we reign forever."

Their glasses clinked against the others, then they drained the contents.

Catherine looked at the three and knew it wouldn't do any good to tell them that marriage was wonderful. They'd just have to wait and see. "Thank you for helping me with Luke's surprise. I want our first Christmas together to be memorable."

"As long as he has you, it will be," Sierra said.

Touched, Catherine felt her throat sting. "I love all of you."

"Don't get misty," Sierra teased. "Or Brandon will cry."

They all laughed. "Can't have that. You know that you can each invite guests," Catherine told them.

All three adamantly shook their heads. "Women get the wrong idea if you take them to meet your mother. Take them to a holiday affair and you're asking for trouble," Pierce said.

"He's right," Brandon quickly agreed.

"I'll have to agree with them," Sierra said. "Our friends drop by but no one we've gone out with—much to Mama's disappointment."

"Then invite anyone you wish. Thanks to Brandon, there'll be plenty of food. I plan to make a roasted vegetable tart, baked sweet-potatoes casserole, a stuffed pork crown roast, and a pineapple-coconut cake. Phoenix is bringing pecan praline candy," Catherine said. "She said she has to hide it from Morgan or he'll eat the batch in one sitting."

Sierra sat up straighter. "Luke is almost as bad when it comes to your pineapple-coconut cake. I'm hitting the kitchen first thing to make sure I put aside some cake and praline for me."

"Save some for me," Pierce requested.

"Pierce, if I were you, I'd get my own," Brandon advised him. "Sierra had two slices of Catherine's cake the last time she invited us over and then took the last slice home. She mows through Phoenix's pecan pralines the same way."

Pierce studied his baby sister, who smiled sweetly back at him. "I'll grab my own."

Catherine's lips twitched. "Since this will also be Phoenix and Morgan's first Christmas together, she's having brunch for everyone at their house the Sunday after Christmas. She's planning on surprising Morgan as well."

"I'm meeting with her at lunch to go over her menu," Brandon said.

"Another tradition and more food." Sierra rubbed her hands together in glee.

Catherine smiled. "Thanks again. I don't want to keep you any longer. I have one more stop before I have my first lecture."

"We have to make a run ourselves. We need to finalize what we're getting Mama for Christmas." Sierra stared at Brandon. "Someone has been dragging their feet."

"I just happen to think a new oven would serve her better," Brandon commented.

"So will the Dior and Chanel suits," Pierce said.

"With bag, shoes, and jewelry to complement both, she'll be stunning." Sierra nodded her head emphatically.

Brandon massaged his temple. "Please don't talk clothes. Besides, I still want to get her the new oven, the side-by-side refrigerator with a TV in the door panel, and the automatic dishwasher."

Catherine laughed as Sierra gave her brother an incredulous look. "Tonight Luke and I are going to look for a tree and decorations for the house and the tree."

Brandon shuddered. "If there was ever any doubt—which there wasn't—Luke has it bad, this puts it to rest. He hates shopping just as much as I do."

Catherine nodded. "He suggested it. Your brother is simply—the best."

Sierra grinned. "He thinks you're pretty terrific, you know."

"I know." Catherine picked up her attaché case. "Goodbye and thanks again for the help."

"You're welcome," they chorused.

Catherine waved Brandon and Pierce back to their seats as they started to stand. Midway to the front door she heard laughter and turned to look. Brandon, Pierce, and Sierra were part of a close-knit, loving family that now included her.

For a moment, just a moment, Catherine thought of her infertility. She and Luke would never have children, watch them grow up, watch them marry and have children of their own. Yet, they were blessed in so many other ways. What was one regret compared to so much happiness? She had Luke and, for that, she counted herself the luckiest woman in the world.

FIFTEEN MINUTES LATER, CATHERINE KNOCKED ON Naomi Reese's apartment door. Her friends had come so far, and she had a long ways to go, but thanks to the owner of the truck in the parking lot, she was steadily getting there.

Knowing Naomi would look through the peephole before unlocking the door, Catherine waited patiently for the double locks to disengage.

"Catherine, good morning," Naomi greeted warmly.

"Morning, Catherine." Dr. Richard Youngblood stood a few steps behind her.

"Good morning, Naomi and Richard. I just wanted to make sure you both were coming over Christmas Eve around eight to help with Luke's surprise," Catherine told them.

For a moment, Naomi's gaze lowered. "You're having family. May—"

"And good friends," Catherine interrupted. "I want you both to come."

"We'll be there," Richard said. "This morning I stopped by so we could take Kayla to pick out a tree once she wakes up."

Naomi smiled, the uncertainty leaving her pretty face. "She's so excited. I could hardly get her to go to sleep. This is going to be her first Christmas where she doesn't have to be—" Naomi abruptly stopped, bit her lower lip.

Catherine started to reach out her hand to comfort Naomi, but Richard had already stepped beside her, his hand lightly touching her arm before falling away. Naomi, like Catherine, might have chosen the wrong man the first time, but they'd gotten it right the second time. Neither Naomi nor Kayla had to be afraid again.

Naomi's shoulders straightened, her chin lifted, the barest hint of a smile played around her mouth. "Should I bring anything?"

"She makes an apple pie that will make you slap your mama," Richard said with a chuckle.

Naomi blushed, then laughed. "Richard."

Catherine thought laughter looked good on Naomi. "The apple pie sounds wonderful." They had enough food, but Naomi needed to know that she was appreciated and valued. "I'd better go, and remember, it's a surprise. Goodbye."

"Goodbye. We will," Richard and Naomi told her.

Catherine started back to her car. This was really shaping up beautifully. Luke was going to have the surprise of his life as they began a new family tradition. And if there came a light snow on Christmas Eve for them to wake up to a white Christmas, it would be absolutely wonderful.

CHAPTER TWO

LUKE HAD TO WORK IN A HURRY. EVERYTHING HAD TO be finished before he left to meet Catherine. "I think we're almost finished." He anchored the last lengths of Christmas lights that outlined the eaves of the log cabin.

"Come on down, and we'll see if we did as good a job on your house as we did on mine," Morgan called from the ground.

Luke climbed down the ladder and pulled the remote control out of his pocket. "With all the hammering at your house, it was a good thing Phoenix was busy working in the studio you built for her in back of your house."

"When she's working, she tunes everything out except me,"

Luke laughed. "We're two lucky men."

"Amen to that." Morgan nodded toward the control in Luke's hand. "You're going to test it?"

"Nope. Like you, we're going to turn it on together. We're creating traditions here."

Morgan nodded in understanding. "Phoenix hasn't had a real Christmas since her mother died. This year has got to be special."

Luke clapped his brother on the back. "It already is. She has you."

"As you said, I'm a lucky man."

"You both are." Luke glanced at his watch. "I'm meeting Cath in twenty at the tree lot."

"We're having ours delivered," Morgan said, heading for his BMW Roadster.

"That's what you get for being partial to driving a baby car instead of your truck," Luke told him.

Morgan patted the fender of the sports car. "Ignore him. Everyone doesn't want to drive a behemoth."

Luke chuckled and opened the door to his Dodge Ram truck. Morgan mostly used his truck to haul his horse trailer with his and Phoenix's horses. "Hug Phoenix for me."

"Do the same with Catherine." Waving, Morgan climbed into his car and pulled off.

Luke took one last look at the lights on the cabin before getting into the truck. "I can't wait to see Cath's expression."

"WHY ARE WE STOPPING? DO YOU THINK THERE'S A problem with the tree?"

"The tree is fine," Luke reassured her as he'd done every couple of miles since they'd left her car at his house in the city. They still spent most of their time at the cabin, the place where they'd met, fallen in love, and first made love. "I just want to show you something." Luke opened his door and got out. Catherine scooted out behind him.

As soon as her feet touched the ground, he curved his arm around her small waist. "You never cease to amaze me. If it wasn't for the headlights, it would be pitch dark. Any other woman would be asking questions, instead of getting out of the truck twenty yards from the house."

"I trust you. Besides, you didn't once complain while I

was trying to decide on the right tree and the theme." She looked up at him. "I want everything to be perfect."

He dropped a kiss on her lips. "With you it always will be. Now." He turned her toward the cabin and stepped behind her. "I have a surprise for you." He pulled the remote control out of his pocket and handed it to her. "Push the button."

She looked at him a moment, then did as he'd requested. Her breath caught. The house was outlined in a thousand twinkling white lights. "Oh! It's beautiful."

Luke placed his chin on her head. "I heard your mother mention that you had traditions of your own that you'd miss this year. One of them was outside lights."

Catherine turned in his arms. "You also heard her say that she's never seen me happier, and that she couldn't have wished for a better son-in-law. We'll start our own traditions."

He grinned, hot and sexy, and full of promise. "I know one."

She grinned back. "Let's get home and start working on it."

Laughing, he tugged her to the truck. She eagerly followed.

THE DAYS WERE GOING TOO FAST, CATHERINE thought as she stepped out of the bath tub. Only seven days remained before Christmas, and she had so many things to do, but at least everything was ready for Luke's surprise, and the house was decorated. The gold and silver theme had worked beautifully. Garland and white satin ribbon graced the stairwell. At the foot of the stairs were Mr. and Mrs. Santa Claus in silver-and-white fur robes.

In front of the immense picture window was a twelve-foot Douglas fir decked with beautiful gold and silver balls, and white doves. Luke had placed the angel, dressed in pure white, on top. Afterwards, they'd made love in front of the tree.

Catherine paused to reminisce about that magical moment. Each day kept getting better and better.

There was a brief knock on the door before it opened and Luke stuck his head inside. His hot gaze slid over her body. "A moment too late, I see."

She sighed in regret. "If I didn't have an appointment with your mother and members of the Women's League, I'd lose the towel."

"Maybe my timing will be better in the morning. In the meantime . . ." He stepped inside. "I wanted to give you this."

Catherine stared at the beautifully wrapped box in heavy gold paper with a white satin bow. "You want me to open it now?"

"Yes." He held the gift out to her. "This is the first Christmas of many we'll share together. Since I can't imagine a more complete life, and since seven is special to the family and is supposed to be the perfect number, I wanted to give you a gift each day for the seven days leading up to Christmas to say thank you for being my wife, my love."

"Luke." His name trembled from her lips. "I love you so much."

His thumb brushed away the tears on her lashes. "Open it."

Swallowing the lump in her throat, Catherine untied the bow and lifted the lid. The sides collapsed to reveal a snow globe with a cabin surrounded by snow. Her heart thumped. Her gaze sought his. "It's this cabin."

He smiled, pleased, and pointed to a side switch. "Push it, and then look closely."

Catherine did as requested. Lights illuminated the inside of the cabin, and when she looked closer, she saw a man and a woman inside kissing.

"It's musical."

Catherine wound up the spring, then upended the globe. As "Silent Night" played, a soft blanket of snow fell on the cabin with the lovers inside. She was touched beyond words. "Luke, thank you."

He brushed his lips across hers. "Thank you for loving me, for trusting me with your love."

She batted away another tear. "I'm going to give Ruth an extra hug when I see her."

"Can I have one now?" he asked.

Setting the globe on the marble vanity, she went into his arms, kissing him, caressing him. This was going to be the best Christmas imaginable.

THAT SAME MORNING, PROPPED IN BED ON HIS ELBOW, Morgan stared down at a sleeping Phoenix. It was a sight he'd never tire of. First the soft smile would touch her tempting mouth, then the smile would gradually spread over her beautiful face. Her eyes would slowly open. And in their haunting depths, he'd see a love worth dying for.

And as now, as she began to rouse, he'd feel an overwhelming love for this woman that made his heart pound and his body want. He knew he always would.

She was the one and only. No other woman would ever capture his heart.

"Good morning," Phoenix said, awakening fully and twining her arms around his neck.

"Good morning," he said, brushing his lips across hers, a part of him wishing they could linger in bed. He rolled away before temptation got the better of him. Having his jeans on helped. "Get dressed. I want to show you something. I have your clothes ready."

She watched him grab his shirt before she reached for the thick red sweater on the bed. She threw him a teasing look. "No undergarments."

He grinned down at her. "This won't take long."

She grinned back. "Then by all means let's go and hurry back."

PHOENIX'S CURIOSITY WAS PIQUED EVEN HIGHER AS Morgan bundled her into his car and pulled out of the garage. It went off the chart when, fifteen minutes later, he turned into a winding driveway that led to a large ranch house. Instead of stopping, he drove around back and braked in front of three greenhouses.

"We're here."

"And here is . . . ?"

Picking up her hand, he kissed it. "You'll see."

Opening his door, he came around and opened hers. She didn't need to wait on him, but he liked doing small things for her, and since she was crazy in love with him, anything that made him happy was all right by her.

With his arm curved around her waist, he went to the first greenhouse and opened the door. The pungent smell of rich soil and fertilizer tickled her nose. Flowers in bloom with rich red, yellow, blue, and purple blossoms spread out before her. "It's beautiful."

She loved flowers, but because she became so caught up in her sculptures, they didn't fare very well with her.

"I thought you'd like it, but I have something else to show you." He tugged off her gloves. "It might be in the low forties outside, but it's easily in the seventies in here."

Smiling, she allowed him to lead her further into the enclosure. If anyone would have told her that an incredible, thoughtful man like Morgan would love her, she would have called them crazy. He was everything she had ever dreamed of and so afraid she'd never have.

He stopped and stepped in front of her, his face serious. "I love you, Phoenix. You give so much in your work, and to all those around you with the joy of your smile, the honesty of your loving touch. I wanted to give you something that mirrored what you so effortlessly give with your quiet strength, your incredible sculptures that speak to everyone who sees them. This is my gift of love."

He stepped aside to reveal a lush crimson rose tipped with the red-orange of fire. "The Phoenix Rose."

Her gaze snapped from the beautiful flower in full bloom to his. Stunned, she couldn't speak.

"A client lives here. His hobby is growing roses and creating hybrid strains," Morgan told her. "When he mentioned a new rose and described it, I knew your name would be perfect. After he saw your work, he agreed."

Tears sparkled in her eyes. "Morgan."

"You and the Phoenix Rose both toil long hours before showing the world your breath-taking creations, both of your work requires heat—yours the furnace, the rose the sun—to reach full potential, both you and the rose had to go through years of trials before you were ready to emerge."

She hugged him, her arms tight, her body trembling with emotions. "I love you. I love you," she repeated, the only words that she could get out, but also the most important ones.

"I know. Let's go home." Picking her up, he headed for his car.

LUKE AND MORGAN WERE ON A ROLL. THEIR WIVES loved their second-day gifts of a black cashmere travel blanket and the travel pillow case, the case a perfect fit for airline pillows. On Day Three, Catherine woke up to a charm bracelet with wolf and heart charms on her wrist.

Phoenix's platinum charm bracelet held a rearing horse charm and a snowflake charm.

On Day Four, both women had to wait until they emerged from their baths that night for their gifts. Both had incorrectly assumed their breakfast in bed with heart-shaped pancakes and freshly sliced strawberries were their gifts for that day. They were both wrong.

Luke took great pleasure and time in giving Catherine a full body massage. Afterwards, he slipped on her aroused body a seafoam silk halter gown, matching robe, and slippers, and then promptly tossed aside them aside and took her to bed.

Phoenix's negligee was a blush-pink, two-piece silk set with a matching robe and slippers. Morgan tossed in the bonus of the massage to the sensual delight of them both.

Luke and Morgan went to sleep with smiles and thoughts of tomorrow, and the women sleeping peacefully in their arms. They might be giving the gifts, but they were getting pleasure from it in more ways than one. They didn't have to wait for Christmas; they already had the perfect gift.

RUTH GRAYSON NEVER STOPPED THANKING GOD AND the Master of Breath for aiding her in bringing her two eldest sons together with two women of quiet strength, intelligence, and artistic talent. Their family was blessed by their presence.

"Who would have thought Luke and Morgan would be so romantic?" Sierra quipped as she sat in one of the four lounge chairs in La Valva, a boutique in downtown Santa Fe that specialized in couture evening wear. "Seven days of Christmas with a corresponding number of gifts for each day is pretty awesome." She chuckled. "Even Pierce is impressed."

"It only takes the right woman." Ruth looked at her youngest and most headstrong child. "Or the right man."

"I did not hear that." Sierra eyed the artful display of petits fours, truffles, and chocolate-dipped strawberries on polished silver trays, the bottle of sparkling cider chilling in the silver wine cooler, a stiff-backed waiter standing nearby. "Besides, I'm way down on the list."

"But you *are* on the list," her mother reminded her.

Before Sierra could comment, voices could be heard coming from the front of the store, which was just as well, Ruth thought. Sierra believed she was invincible, but her time would come. Ruth came to her feet as did Sierra while her sons and their wives, accompanied by the store owner, approached.

The surprise on Catherine and Phoenix's faces was as priceless as it was heartwarming to Ruth. After they'd all had dinner together, the women were told their help was needed to pick out a gift. They didn't know the gift was for them. The store was closed to provide Catherine and Phoenix with a private showing of evening gowns.

This was Day Five so they would get five items: an evening gown and accessories, a trip to New York for New Year's Eve, tickets to the theater, an invitation to the after-party, and a stay at the Plaza Hotel.

It did Ruth's heart good that her sons had included her in the surprise, and that they planned to match the amount their wives spent with a donation to the Women's League. She had done well in choosing. She would do so again.

CATHERINE WAS IN A HURRY. CHRISTMAS WAS TOMORrow. She had so much to do and the clock was going at warp speed. Shrugging on her short wool coat, she pulled a knit cap over her head, grabbed her gloves, and started from the bedroom just as her cell phone rang. Retracing her steps, she dumped the contents of her purse, grabbed the cell phone, and continued out of the room. "Hello."

"Hello, yourself," her mother greeted. "I thought I'd call since we're all packed to fly out in the morning. You sound rushed."

"A bit." Catherine picked up a large shopping bag in the kitchen and let herself out of the back door. She shivered, then smiled as a cold blast of air hit her. The temperature was dropping, and if the weather man was right, she'd get her snow tonight. "I've decided to use live greenery for the table tomorrow, so I'm going to look for some."

"I suppose ordering is out this late."

"Exactly." Catherine stuck the phone between her shoulder and ear, pulled on her gloves, and continued into the forest that surrounded the cabin. "I'll use whatever I find that strikes my interest. Luke helped me set the table before he left to meet a client, but he'll be back by six. He thinks some of the faculty is coming tomorrow."

"He'll be surprised when he sees your guests, just as he's surprised you for the past six days. I wonder what he'll give you today," her mother mused. "I think it's giving your father ideas." She laughed. "You'll love the five days you'll spend at the Cloister resort on Georgia's Black Banks River."

Catherine stopped to consider an odd shaped piece of wood and a small vine. "We plan to fly out when Morgan and Phoenix can get away. It's going to be a wonderful trip."

"Just like your marriage."

Catherine paused to look at another vine with red berries, then continued. "I'm the luckiest woman. Although I'm not having much luck finding what I'm looking for. I thought I might find something by the small hidden lake Luke loves, but there is nothing here."

"There's enough ivy on the house for me to bring you bags," her mother commented.

"No, thank you, I want—" Catherine paused as she heard something in the bushes.

"What is it?"

Catherine's hand gripped the phone, then the noise became louder. Out stepped Hero. Relief rushed through her. "You scared me. Mother, it's Hero." Smiling, she reached out her hand. "Hello. I didn't forget you for tomorrow."

"Catherine, I'm still uneasy about you and that wolf hybrid," her mother warned.

"Hero wouldn't hurt me," she said, stepping nearer to the animal.

The hybrid's teeth bared. He growled low in his throat. More hurt than afraid, Catherine slowly drew her hand back.

"What's that sound? What's going on?" her mother asked, fear in her voice.

"Something is wrong with Hero. Perhaps he's hurt again. I don't under—" A scream locked in her throat as he lunged at her, then tore free.

"Catherine! Catherine! What is it! Answer me," her mother demanded, but there was no answer, only silence.

LUKE AND MORGAN WERE IN THE PARKING LOT OF THEIR office building, headed toward their vehicles, when a chill chased down Luke's spine. He stopped in mid-stride. "Cath?"

Morgan frowned at his brother. "What is it?"

Shaking his head, Luke reached for his cellphone just as it rang. He intended to get rid of whoever was on the line so he could call Cath. He'd been taught by his maternal grandparents to trust his instincts. Something wasn't right. "Hello. Can I—"

"Luke, something happened to Catherine," her mother

blurted, her usual calm voice near hysteria. "I was talking to her as she looked for table decorations in the woods. The hybrid showed up. I heard him growling, then . . . then she screamed. The line went dead."

Luke's gut clenched, his heart thudded, then he was running to his truck with Morgan on his heels. "Hero wouldn't hurt Catherine," he told her. What he couldn't bring himself to say was that another wild animal might have. "Do you have any idea where she was?"

"She mentioned she was at the small lake you like."

"Hold." He turned to Morgan. "Cath might be in trouble at the lake. Call Dakota and have him clear the way with a squad car, but either way I'm not slowing down until I'm at the cabin." Knowing Morgan would carry out his orders, Luke jumped into his truck and sped off. "Don't worry, Mrs. Stewart. I'll be at the cabin in twelve minutes."

"Hurry, please, just hurry."

LUKE WAS NEVER SO GRATEFUL TO SEE FLASHING police lights. He fell in behind the patrol car at the second traffic light, unsurprised to see Morgan on his bumper. If Luke didn't miss his guess, his entire family was on their way. His hands flexed on the steering wheel as he fought to keep the fear at bay. "Cath, please be all right. Please."

He prayed all the way to the cabin. He braked sharply behind the patrol car, then slammed out of the truck, racing for the woods. "Cath! Cath!" He fought panic, tree limbs, and underbrush until he came to the clearing near the lake and almost went to his knees. He rushed toward Catherine's prone figure.

"Cath," her name was the barest whisper of sound.

Her head lifted. She glanced over her shoulder. "Luke." That was all she was able to get out before he had her on her feet and in his arms, crushing her to him, then she was at arms' length as his gaze ran the length of her.

"Are you all right? Your mother called me."

"Just shaken up," she said, then hastened to explain as his grip on her arms tightened. "Hero saved me from a wolf. I screamed when I thought he was attacking me, but he knocked me out of the way, then stood over me, challenging the wolf until it left. I can't find my phone. I think it fell in the lake. I've been trying to coax Hero to come out of the underbrush ever since. I was going to try for another couple of minutes, then go home to call Mother, but I knew she'd call you, and you'd reassure her that I was all right and then you'd come find me."

"Cath." She knew him so well. He hugged her to him and reached for his cell. "We'll call her now."

"Already done," Morgan said. "I also called Mama."

Luke turned to his brother to thank him. Instead, Luke's gaze widened in surprise. He'd expected his brothers and sister, but standing with them were Daniel Falcon and his wife, Madelyn, her two brothers Kane and Matt with their wives Victoria and Shannon, Daniel's sister Dominique, and her husband, Trent. "What are you all doing here?"

Catherine placed her head on Luke's shoulder. "They're one of your Christmas presents. I wanted to start a family tradition with family and good friends on Christmas Eve. All the parents and grandparents are coming in the morning so we can open all the presents. I guess I spoiled the surprise."

"You did not. It's a wonderful surprise." Luke tenderly took her face in his hands. "You're safe, and that's all that matters."

"Luke's right, Catherine," Sierra said. "What do you think if we start the party a little early? Mama is at the cabin with Daniel Jr., Tempest, and the twins, Kane Jr. and

Chandler. I'm sure Brandon already has the food ready. The restaurant closed ten minutes ago."

Her brother shook his head and curved his arm around her shoulders. "You're right, and since you're hungry as usual, you won't mind coming back to the restaurant so I can load up your SUV."

"Not in the least." Sierra turned to Morgan. "I'll pick up Phoenix on the way back."

"The pecan praline she's bringing wouldn't have any bearing on that decision, would it?" he asked.

"It might."

"Thank you, Sierra. That's a wonderful idea," Catherine said.

"I'll also let Naomi and Richard know to come early. Mama won't mind watching Kayla. Naomi, I hear, bakes a mean apple pie." Laughing, Sierra left with Brandon.

Catherine smiled at her sister-in-law, then turned to her guests. "I'm so glad you all could come, this is going to be wonderful. We can leave as soon as I get Hero." Catherine started to drop to her knees, but Luke held her upright. "I can't leave him here after he helped me."

"I never thought you would." Luke faced his family and extended family. "I guess you know how it is to love someone unconditionally. Their happiness is yours." There were nods and knowing smiles. "Thought so. Morgan, Pierce, please see everyone back to the cabin. Cath and I will follow."

"Thank you for not sending me away," Catherine said as they were left alone.

"Purely selfish reasons." Luke kissed her. "I'm not ready to let you out of my sight." Dropping to his knees, he peered into the brush. In seconds, Hero crawled out and eyed both of them.

Catherine hunkered down beside Luke and Hero.

"Thank you, and for helping me, there'll be no more baths for a month." Hero barked and they laughed.

Catching her hand, Luke came to his feet and picked up the shopping bag. "Let's go home. I haven't given you your present for today."

"I'm sure I'm going to love it as much as the others, but you're the true gift."

Stopping, he stared down at her. "I love you so much."

"I know, and that's what makes loving you such a pleasure." She kissed him on the lips, then started toward the cabin with Hero beside her. "We'd better hurry. We have to start the tradition right."

A few feet farther, snow began to fall. Smiling, Catherine leaned her head against Luke's shoulder, her arm curving around his waist. "Christmas and you, I have my perfect Christmas."

Luke hugged her closer. "And I have mine."

LAUGHTER AND GOOD CHEER FILLED THE CABIN. Mounds of gifts surrounded the tree. No one seemed to mind eating on paper plates and leaving the formal table setting in the dining room for tomorrow. The children were asleep and the adults were enjoying each other.

Luke and Morgan had presented their gifts for Day Seven to their wives—no cooking on weekends for the next seven months—much to the good-natured groans of the other males and cheers of the females. From the stairs, Ruth smiled down at them. Love, when it was right and shared, was priceless.

She couldn't wait for the rest of her children to know such happiness. Smiling, Ruth went inside the bedroom where the children were sleeping and closed the door. Someday, the grandchildren she would watch over would be her own.

Brandon, the nurturer, was next.

Read on for a sneak peek at Francis Ray's next
Grayson Friends novel

NOBODY BUT YOU

Coming Winter 2009
from St. Martin's Paperbacks

CAMERON PRAYED FOR THE RIGHT WORDS. HOW DID HE explain to a four-and-a-half-year-old that his father had "found" him? At least Caitlin hadn't claimed he was dead. "Your mother and I wanted to talk to you about something very important."

Joshua looked from one to the other. "I won't play in the fountain or go down to the lake unless an adult is with me. I remember."

"I know you won't," Caitlin said. "This is about—" She paused, bit her lip.

"Your father," Cameron finished for her. Dragging it out certainly wasn't helping anyone.

"You know my daddy?" Joshua asked, his small voice filled with wonder.

"Yes," Cameron answered.

Joshua, his eyes round with excitement, jumped up from his chair and went to stand in front of Cameron. "Where is he? Can you take me to him?"

Things were moving too fast for Caitlin. "You remember I said that your father loved you, but we decided we didn't love each other and we went to live separate lives, that we didn't know how to find each other?"

"Did he find us?" he asked his mother. Her mouth trembled, but she didn't say a word.

"I'm your father, Joshua," Cameron answered quietly, his voice unsteady.

Joshua looked at him as if he couldn't quiet comprehend what he'd just been told.

Caitlin knew it was time. "He's your father, Joshua. He's found you."

"You're my father?" Joshua asked, his voice as unsteady as his father's had been earlier.

Cameron swallowed, and swallowed again. "Yes, son. I'm sorry it took me so long to find you, but I'm here now and I plan to stay."

"Daddy!" The boy launched himself at Cameron, his arms wrapped tightly around his neck. "I knew you'd come! I knew it! I told Mommie you'd find us one day, and you did."

Over Joshua's head, Cameron caught Caitlin's strained features. If he didn't miss his guess, she was just beginning to realize how much she'd deprived Joshua. Knowing Caitlin's tender heart, it wouldn't be easy for her to accept.

Hefting Joshua up with one arm, Cameron stood and asked, "You about ready to see my race car?"

"Wow."

Cameron smiled. He was fast learning that "Wow" was Joshua's favorite word when he was excited. "Caitlin, do you need to get anything before we leave?"

"Maybe he should go another day." She stood as well, her hands curled into tight fists.

Cameron thought he knew why she was apprehensive. "I've already alerted the crew we're coming. No practice race is scheduled for today. We'll have lunch afterwards."

She was living her greatest fear. How could she save her baby? "He's probably tired from the trip. Maybe tomorrow."

Cameron set Joshua on his feet. "I left my cap on the dresser in my room. Could you please go get it for me?"

"I'll get it, Daddy." Joshua took off running.

Cameron had to swallow. *Daddy*. He'd never in his wildest imagination thought Caitlin might be carrying their child. They'd always used protection. As soon as Cameron heard his son's pounding footsteps on the stairs, he stepped closer to Caitlin. "Today, Caitlin. Putting it off won't change anything. I want to show Joshua the stock car, introduce him to my crew."

"I—"

"I'm leaving in ten minutes, and when I do, Joshua is going to be with me."

"I don't want that life for him," she said, her voice trembling.

"That's not for you to decide."

Joshua came running back into the room with the cap. "Here it is, Daddy."

Daddy. Emotions clogged his throat again, then laughter escaped. Cameron scooped Joshua up in his arms, took the cap, and put it on his son's head. "That way I won't lose it again."

"You coming?" Cameron asked.

"I need to work on the script." She tried to smile and failed miserably.

"Thank you." He knew what it cost her to let her son go without her. She'd walk through hell for Joshua. He didn't agree with her decision to keep Joshua's birth a secret, but he knew she had done it out of fear, not malice.

To let him go without her, to a place she feared, said a great deal about her love for Joshua. She was putting his needs above her own. She wanted them to have this time together.

"We'll be back for lunch and go out to dinner," Cameron

promised. Walking over to Caitlin, he leaned Joshua toward her. "Kiss your mother goodbye, and tell her you love her so we can go."

Joshua dutifully leaned over, put his arms around his mother's neck, and kissed her on the cheek. "Goodbye, Mommie. I love you."

Her arms clung to Joshua for a moment before she stepped back. "You mind Ca—your father."

"Yes, ma'am."

Cameron wished he could get his own hug. Heck, he wanted the kiss as well. "He's safe with me. He'll never be out of my sight."

"I know," she said. Her voice trembled, she blinked rapidly.

He started from the room, then pivoted and came back to her. He didn't ask, didn't pause. He simply curved his hand around her neck and brought her lips to his. She gasped in shock, allowing his tongue to thrust inside, swirl, taste the heady sweetness that was uniquely hers, and maple syrup.

Joshua's giggles brought him back to his senses. The kiss had been an impulse but no less enjoyable. From the flare of desire in her dark eyes, she had enjoyed it as much as he had.

"You looked as if you needed that." His gaze narrowed on her moist lips again. "I'd forgotten how—"

He abruptly stopped. Caitlin's wide eyes were now fastened on Joshua, who was studying his parents with interest. "We'll be back by lunch." This time when he started from the room, he never paused.